PRAISE FOR

DUET
FOR
THREE

"POIGNANT AND GRATIFYING"
Publishers Weekly

"IMMENSELY TOUCHING AND ACUTE"
Kirkus

"A LOVELY, RARE NOVEL"
Library Journal

"CAPTIVATING . . .
A BOOK OF UNCOMMON DEPTH"
Booklist

"UNSPARING, PAINFUL, WITTY,
AND SURPRISING . . .
REMARKABLY POWERFUL"
Alice Munro

"INSIGHTFUL AND UNFLINCHING"
St. Louis Post-Dispatch

DUET FOR THREE

Joan Barfoot

AVON
PUBLISHERS OF BARD, CAMELOT, DISCUS AND FLARE BOOKS

No character in this book is intended to represent any actual person; all the incidents of the story are entirely fictional in nature.

AVON BOOKS
A division of
The Hearst Corporation
105 Madison Avenue
New York, New York 10016

Copyright © 1985 by Joan Barfoot
Published by arrangement with Beaufort Books
Library of Congress Catalog Card Number: 86-22249
ISBN: 0-380-70375-0

The Beaufort Books edition contains the following Library of Congress Cataloging in Publication Data:

Barfoot, Joan.
  Duet for three.

  I. Title.
PR9199.3B3715D8   1985b   813'.54   86-22249

First Avon Printing: December 1987

part

ONE

1

When Aggie wakens, it's to an impression that something has happened to alter the ordinary sensations of coming alert for the day, something not nice. They are irritating, these moments of being not quite sure what is going on, being lost for the right word, rooting around for the proper explanation. That can happen to anyone, of course; even Frances says, "Oh gosh, Grandma, there are lots of times I can't remember somebody's name or where I've met them." But Frances is young. Aggie is eighty, and knows that memory has dimensions Frances has no reason to imagine.

But this, this morning, is less to do with memory than with identification: what exactly is different, and wrong?

Smell. This old pink room where she has laid down her aging, now old, pink body for the past sixty years is as familiar to her as the freckles on the backs of her hands. It looks as it always does when the sun is just up, light in streaks across the hardwood floor. She is always grateful for the light.

But it smells unpleasant. Usually it would smell of dusting powder, and floor wax, and years of accumulated this and that. This, she sniffs, is acrid, piercing, sharp in the nose, and nasty.

There is further unpleasantness involving her skin. Half of her is warm, as it should be, but the rest is chilly and uncomfortable. The flannel nightie is rumpled around her hips, as it usually is in the morning, but cold. Wet.

Oh Jesus, hell and damn, can she have peed the bed?

It's one thing to be old, and to weigh two hundred and seventy-odd pounds, and so to be more or less helpless—well, not helpless,

3

but needing help for certain things, like getting out of bed. Or even to be dying, which of course at eighty one is, and is aware of, if not reconciled to.

But to pee the bed! There are unconsidered horrors in that. If that's happened, she has crossed some boundary she hasn't taken into account; no minor lapse, like forgetting how much sugar should be combined with rhubarb for a pie.

How could she have done such a thing?

This is appalling, disgusting. If she is appalled and disgusted, what will June be? What in the name of God will June have to say? She will have something to say in the name of God, June who so often speaks in His name, as if He were not very adept at the language, a foreigner for whom she takes it upon herself to translate.

It's not as if this can be transformed with a joke. Sometimes it's possible to fool people that way, make them think something is less serious than it is, but there is nothing amusing about lying here with clammy hips.

Maybe she could get up? If she set her body rolling, like a child pumping a swing higher and higher, if she could get it going back and forth hard enough and fast enough, she might shoot right off the bed.

But would she land upright, on her feet, on her toes? More likely she would simply roll off the edge, and then she would be lying on the floor, in much the same position she's in now except that it would be hard instead of soft. Although, to be sure, dry instead of wet.

The mistake must have been the cup of tea too soon before going to bed, leading to this other grosser, more dangerous error. The chill is spreading upward, and she is shivering.

Awake now, she has a clearer recollection of the middle of the night. She remembers thinking, ''I'd better call June and get up.'' She remembers thinking how much effort was involved, for such a small result.

She would have to call out several times to waken June, who would finally come in, tying her old striped terrycloth robe around her bones, slip-slopping in her furry pink slippers, grumbling. Aggie would reach up, June would reach down, and they would push and haul until Aggie was on her feet, June side-stepping as Aggie swung upright.

"Go back to bed now, before you really wake up," Aggie would say. "I can manage."

But June would sigh and say, "It's too late, I *am* awake." She wouldn't be lying, either, because she never lies, and would force herself to stay awake to prove the point. At breakfast, she would yawn heavily.

Aggie would take the six steps from her bedside to the doorway. The hall light would be on. She would turn left and take another eight steps to the bathroom door, reach in and turn on the light. Inside, she would close the door behind her. June might or might not be standing in the hall waiting, her arms folded across her skimpy chest. What a meagre bosom she has, compared with what in Aggie was once rather pert, then briefly became voluptuous, and now is heavy and inert.

Then there would be the relatively simple job of turning, hoisting her nightgown, and, leaning forward slightly, settling herself carefully on the seat. Letting go.

Finished, she would set one hand carefully on the edge of the sink beside her, the other beneath one buttock, and push herself upright. Retrace her steps, and apologize to June.

So much effort, so many details, such dislocation, all for a cup of tea too many. She remembers thinking, "Oh, to hell with it."

Less sensible is a recollection of warmth, release, relief, a brief steamy kind of comfort, a pungent but not unpleasant smell, lulling her back to sleep. It seemed simple at the time, pleasing to have solved a difficulty, without effort, in the dark.

Quite a different matter now, however.

June is up; can be heard walking past Aggie's door to the bathroom. Water running, sound of flushing, then that irritating gargling. The steps returning and halting, the knob turning on Aggie's bedroom door, the door swinging inward. She must say something, must think of mitigating words.

But here is June, her expression altering as she stands there, and Aggie feels her own features must be changed, thinks all her dismay and shame and fear must be right there on her face, and when she says, "Oh, June, I think I wet the bed," it sounds just awful.

2

Well, it's perfectly obvious that's what she's done. The smell. Oh God (a prayer, not a blasphemy), what next? This is too much. This is out of the question, beyond everything.

Really, is it not enough to have to haul Aggie out of bed, and help her get dressed, averting eyes from an appalling amount of old flesh, to get her settled downstairs in her creaky spring-broken chair in the living room, with a plate of something to nibble at and a pile of books beside her? To race around making breakfast for the two of them? To make sure before she leaves for school that Aggie is settled, has what she needs to get her through the day? And then to spend another, probably difficult day in the classroom, edging her way to retirement, which is still five years away?

Isn't it enough to come home and make supper for the two of them and spend part of the evening baking, if Aggie hasn't managed a turn in the kitchen during the day, which sometimes she still can. Baking so that Aggie will have more fattening fuel to get her through tomorrow, which will be much the same for both of them as today? And marking tests and setting lessons and going to bed exhausted and bone-weary and discouraged. Praying for forgiveness and hope? Forgiveness for small sins that have slipped out, not even, compared with what other people do, very serious ones. And hope, which is undefined. June cannot be sure what she might hope for, but hoping is certainly a Christian duty.

But this is too much. Now what is she supposed to do? Duty is one thing; facing this quite another.

"Oh, Mother," she says, beyond anger at the moment, although she may be angry later, thinking about it. "How could you?"

"I don't know. It just happened. Help me up."

This is different: no defiance or sarcasm or blasphemy this morning.

Wanting him to talk firmly to Aggie, June has complained to their doctor, George Bannon, about her mother's language. She thinks he should have some authority that she lacks. Unfortunately George, who is only in his thirties, seems more amused than upset. It seems to June that he treats her own concerns too lightly.

He told her, "Well, you know, age comes differently to different people. You should try not to let it bother you. I'm sure she doesn't mean anything in particular by it, and it may do her good, let things out. Be grateful she's alert enough to swear. It could be worse."

"But it's unsuitable," June argued. She is aware that despite the care she gives her mother, which should count for something, George doesn't like her much. He's delicate, a little refined, remote, with her, whereas with Aggie he's likely to be laughing, slapping her on the shoulder. "It's wrong, much less for a woman of eighty. It's embarrassing."

He sighed. "Well, look at it this way: some old people become physically incontinent. In your mother's case, it may be other things that are loosening. Her tongue may be a bit incontinent, in a manner of speaking, and after all, of the two, which is worse?"

But both? What will he have to say now that this has happened? Surely this is corruption even he will be able to grasp.

Aggie's nightgown is cold and damp and clings to her hips. "We'd better get you out of that. Do you want a bath or just a wash?"

"A wash will be fine." How meek Aggie sounds. How odd it is, to hear her meek. June wonders how far she might go with a chastened mother, but the thought, of course, is unworthy.

Aggie lifts her arms and June, bending to reach the hem, pulls the blue flowered flannel nightgown, now stained, over her head and hands her a robe. The covers of the bed have been pushed aside in their mutual efforts to get Aggie on her feet. Standing, they both regard the broad yellow stain on white sheets. "Excuse me," says Aggie, leaving on the journey to the bathroom she should have made several hours ago.

June rips off the sheets and stares at the mattress, which is also marked. What does one do about such a thing? For once, it would be nice to have a man around. A man could do something with this, lifting the mattress, making it disappear, hairy muscled arms just—dealing with it.

She'll be late for school if she doesn't hurry. "I'll have to leave it until tonight," she tells Aggie, who has reappeared in the doorway looking a little less meek. "I haven't time now."

Carefully, trying not to touch the damp parts, she gathers up the sheets and takes them downstairs to the laundry. Then she washes and washes her hands.

She finds Aggie making breakfast, which is unusual. Ordinarily Aggie says she finds breakfast too boring to bother cooking, although she will eat it, of course. "I only like making interesting food," she has explained. "Surely that's all right, after all these years." But today, maybe to disprove what she has done, to demonstrate that she is capable and useful, she is making breakfast. It is too bad, though, that she has fried the eggs sunny side up. They look, lying one on each plate, like yellow stains on white sheets.

"Sorry"—June pushes her plate away—"I'm not very hungry. Do you want to go to the bathroom before I leave?"

There are words that won't sound the same any more. Simple sentences will reverberate, hanging in the air with new significance.

Walking to school and walking home are June's own times. Frequently she speaks with God, although not in some people's chatty way. Some people talk to Him as if He's their best friend, offering bits of information and making requests, trivial and informal. June examines her soul and prays. God is not her friend; He is the architect of her life, and sees the little sparrow fall. She seeks His help in getting through the day, but offers the day to Him. "Thy will be done," she says in her prayers, somewhat nervously.

Today, however, there is this new development to contemplate. She can see that it is quite sad, in a way: that a woman like Aggie, so filled with pride, should come to this. There has to be pity for a humiliation like that. Aggie would hate being pitied. There is some satisfaction in feeling sorry for her. Anyway, pride is a terrible sin. Humiliation may offer a degree of redemption.

"To be in control, that's freedom," Aggie has told her. June, disagreeing, argues that control, resting as it does in the hands of God, is an illusion. She supposes she still believes that, even this morning, but the illusion is exhilarating in a way. This is something new, a pleasant self-indulgence.

But June knows that freedom, whatever Aggie says, is something that can only be read about, not actually experienced. It's like the universe, or a television program about people starving far away. One supposes these things exist, all the distant stars and all the bloated bellies; but they can't be known, not really. That's what freedom is like: a concept only.

In the classroom she wields her pointer, instructing in the arithmetic of addition and subtraction and the parts of sentences. Her mind is elsewhere: on what to do with the mattress, and on what she might do with freedom, if there were such a thing. It's like looking into the sun: brilliant but painful, and possibly in the long run damaging.

This situation, that's something she cannot be expected to deal with. Not Aggie, nor George Bannon, nor June herself can reasonably demand that. Surely she has done enough.

There are places for people who have accidents in their beds. And then what? Then she would have the house to herself. And then what? Anything. Everything would be altered, from the moment of getting up to the thoughts in her head.

She must see George. He will be the first to realize, whatever his sympathies, that she cannot be expected to bear this, too.

At the end of the school day she stands and sighs. At the sound of the bell, the children have raced away. Their laughter and shouting fill the halls, and then the yard and then the street—released, they seem to expand in volume, increase in power like splitting atoms. It is discouraging to have spent so many years offering lessons, and then to see that the children's greatest desire is escape.

This, too, she will be free of, although not for five years.

"You see," she tells George in his office, looking for the proper words, "when I went in to get her up this morning, I found she'd had an accident in the night. You know?" He does.

"I don't see how I can manage. I don't think I can keep going. Something's going to have to be done."

"Yes," he agrees, "I can see how hard it must be."

"Besides, I'm out all day. It isn't safe. Anything could happen."

And it is true that sometimes when she is coming home from school, going up the stone walk to the front door, she has a vision of her mother sprawled dead on the floor inside, probably the kitchen floor, having tried to do something a little too strenuous, or to get something just out of reach, probably a piece of food. Her dress will be up around her hips, her underwear will be showing, and there may be a little blood on her head if she's hit a corner of the table or a cupboard on the way down.

"It's just getting too dangerous, leaving her alone all day." June spreads her hands helplessly.

He is regarding her gravely; she wonders whether he sees truth or lies, and how he assesses motives. "I'll drop around and see her in a day or so. We may have to do some tests. We'll see if we can't think of something."

"George Bannon's going to drop around in the next couple of days," she tells Aggie later. It is a little terrible to watch her understand that someone knows besides the two of them. June can at least let her absorb that by herself; and anyway there are things that need doing. The mattress, for one thing, but that turns out not to be so hard. The stain, touched tentatively, is almost dry, and turning the mattress is a manageable effort. Being thin doesn't mean she isn't strong, in a wiry way.

There is supper to get and schoolwork to do and Aggie to bathe and put to bed. Unspoken weapons hang in the air. They are both uneasy. Doing the dishes, June whistles hymns angrily. When June was little, Aggie whistled in anger. June whistles "Shall We Gather at the River," and slams dishes in time. She wonders why she is upset; maybe because while something has changed, nothing has happened yet. Or because her motives are not pure. Or because, given the glimpse of freedom, possibilities, she is caught short, without plans.

She prays on her knees beside her bed. She remembers to say Thy will be done, but, as always, suspects the words lack absolute sincerity. She also prays for perfect faith, although that is taking a terrible risk, since it is quite possible that perfect faith is only achieved in perfect pain.

When she sleeps, she dreams about putting up new curtains in the living room. In the dream, the curtains match the room's newly painted walls, all a dark blue, so that sitting down in the centre of it when the job is done is like sitting on the bottom of the ocean.

3

Aggie has been listening to her heartbeat. Sometimes she has to be careful about that, sometimes it takes off like a lumbering old workhorse, heavy and graceless, thundering too fast for its weight. It's usually when she reaches for something just a little too far away that this happens, or when she tries to climb the stairs without resting at every other step.

Looking down, puzzled, at her body, she wonders just where in there her heart is hidden, how far inside it is, beating out against the flesh. Once it was right up near the surface, but that was when she was young and slim. Memory is a damned irritating thing. She knows she was that girl who had that agile body, but now there's so much knowledge and experience wedged under her belt along with all the cakes and cookies that it can't be interpreted with innocence, which is the quality she feels it must have had at the time.

Either innocence or ignorance. Maybe both.

It is stupid for a woman her age to be homesick. What kind of eighty-year-old woman thinks of home as a place where she hasn't lived for sixty years?

She would not, after all, go back; did not, when that was a choice. It must be the girl she misses, not the place.

Foolishness. Dangerous foolishness, too. It doesn't do, to go wandering off on tangents. Some people get off the track and can't get back. Old people can make it a habit. At her age, sharpness is all.

There are goose bumps on her arms. She ought to be in the kitchen, where it's warm, instead of in the chilly front room. She might bake something to keep warm. Life and heat are always contained in kitchens; more so, however, in the days of woodstoves. That was real fire, up close, not like an electric stove, which merely glows. Back then, people faced up to flames, aware of the fires of damnation.

Those men and women, those Scottish Presbyterians, among them her grandparents who died before she knew them: they came to this new country, and maybe it was what they were looking for, or maybe they were just tired of the travelling (although they abhorred laziness), but they settled down on rocky land. Pretty enough, acres of bush and little unexpected streams, small hidden lakes, but the rocks! Maybe they sought out stones, though, in search of the harshness that toughens the soul.

In any case they cleared the bush and picked the stones and loaded the rocks and, waste not want not, built them into fences. Fences around little farms, maybe a hundred acres or so. They had no grand schemes, no ideas for staking out huge properties. Content and, she thinks, likely gratified to struggle.

Hardship and struggle were their morality, their grey road to heaven. Evangelists in their dour way for the ease of an afterlife that had to be earned. The greater the suffering, the labor, the duty performed, the greater the reward: making their trades with God.

But she was only a child there. Maybe her memories are too much about their rules, not who they may have been. She has wondered since what their views were, for instance, when they went upstairs at night, wives and husbands, to their small, dark, musty bedrooms. Did passion and tenderness flow out of them then? Did the women wrap arms around the men's shoulders, and stroke their hair in the night? Did they whisper tender or erotic words to one another? Aggie cannot, still, imagine any of this happening with those prune-moralled men, but who can tell? She knows it is not unusual for people to take odd twists in the dark.

Certainly something happened up there. Did the women lie still and grimly accepting, alert to their duty to produce farm labor in the form of strong sons and daughters, in much the way that downstairs it was their duty to produce quantities of jams and pickles? Did the men, shutting their eyes against sins of the flesh, simply thrust children into the bodies of their wives?

Surely not. There was tenderness and fondness: the way her father would come in from the cold after doing the chores and touch frigid fingers to the back of her mother's neck while she sat darn-ing socks, making her shriek. Her mother would laugh and slap at him with the socks. Aggie knows quite well that children cannot tell what goes on between their parents. They see, as June so often proves to her, only what suits them, and only from their own perspective.

Children, even daughters who are almost sixty years old themselves, are selfish creatures where their parents are concerned.

In daylight, the men were big and had rough hands and red skin, with veins purpling in their cheeks. (Not, of course, from drink, but from hard work done outdoors.) Looking at the fathers, one saw the sons. The progression of aging, like the rules, was built in, so that whatever age they were, they appeared the age they would become.

And by God there were rules to cover every possibility. Playing cards was not permitted. The men could smoke pipes but not cigarettes. No one drank or swore. Gluttony was frowned on, but a hearty eater praised. Then there were particular standards for the women and the girls.

Sundays were days of profoundly boring rest. Dressed in their best clothes, families drove to church by horse and buggy. Home again, they were to sit quietly contemplating the glories of a creator who specified a day of rest in an endless round of labor. In church and at home they thanked God for His blessings, that He gave them what they had, endlessly, to work with. Aggie viewed God at the time as another Presbyterian Scot, bearded, frowning, judging and stern. Most of the men looked like that, for that matter. The only difference with God was that He was much older, more like a grandfather.

Ruggedness, since it was what there was, became a kind of beauty. A great rock in the middle of a field might mean heavy labor for men and horses struggling to remove it, but it was also grand. It was like the word of God, firm, weighing people into the earth. There was no romanticism about this, the way Frances sometimes speaks of buying a hundred acres or so up north as a kind of retreat. It was survival, and so both desperate and reassuring.

Aggie had an older brother, an older sister, a younger sister, and two younger brothers. They are all dead now. They were all sturdy and young, and now they are all dead. This still astonishes her, when she thinks about it.

The boys worked in the fields and the barn; the girls worked out
there too when they were needed, but mainly in the kitchen, where
they prepared to feed the boys, fed the boys, and cleaned up after
feeding the boys.

Oh, the meals! Mounds of potatoes, thick fatty slices of beef,
homemade bread with homemade butter, jugs and jugs of milk,
huge serving bowls of carrots and peas, wide wedges of fruit pies,
apple and rhubarb and raisin. In the house where Aggie grew up,
the kitchen windows were always steamed, the table was either
being set or being cleared, and even in summer the woodstove
blasted heat for all the cooking and the baking. The boys sweated
over cows and crops, and the girls sweated over the stove. But they
all sweated.

For a time, they went to school, learning enough to read, add,
subtract, and write simple sentences. The rest was foolishness.
Also, they were needed at home. Aggie raced her brothers home
from school until it was time not to go any more, falling breathless
and dusty into the kitchen. Her older sister, Sylvia, told her it
wasn't nice, a girl running like that. Her little sister, Edith, three
years younger, was pretty and pudgy and couldn't keep up with
either Aggie or the boys. Both Sylvia and Edith were plumper than
she. No one would have dreamed she would die looking the way
she does.

Out of school, they ran through the fields, their legs scratched
by whipping weeds and coarse grass and sharp grains. The one who
was caught was thrown down and tickled. Aggie was the one
who would not beg the others to stop.

The work in the kitchen was hardest at threshing times, when
there might be twelve or fifteen men to feed, great lashings of food
required. But even so she could creep away for a while, slip out
behind the barn and watch the horse-drawn wagons pulling up, piled
with hay, dust motes flying in the sun as the crop was pitched into
the great mows in the barn. It was the smells that drew her: the
fresh horse droppings baking in the sun, the sweat on the skins of
the men and the horses, and the sweetness of the hay. Then back
in the kitchen would be the steam.

"Oh Aggie," her mother said, shaking her head, "where have
you been?" And sometimes, "I don't know what'll become of
you." Still, she praised her stubbornness, and her wits. "Nobody'll get the best of you, my girl" was her praise, and "Don't
you get thinking you're too smart" was her warning.

Who could know that elsewhere, in cities maybe, there were people dancing and drinking champagne? Who, if they had known, would have failed to call it sin?

On alternate Saturdays the horses were hitched for a trip to town. Here, there seemed to be elements not necessarily accounted for in the rules.

There was a spastic youth who wandered up one side of the street and down the other, arms jerking and twitching, sometimes chased by children throwing small stones or calling names. People avoided looking at him, as if what he had could be caught with a glance.

Or there was big, shabby, heavily pockmarked, dirty man, leaning against a store swaying a little, eyes closed, or standing at the side of the road shouting crazy things at people going by. "Oh, for goodness' sake," Aggie's mother would murmur, tugging at her children, directing their attention away.

And there was a woman who might be glimpsed on the street. It was a wonder to catch sight of her, like a flashing good-luck pebble in her tight, bright dress, make-up, and shoes with too-high heels. Oh, here was sin in the flesh, although Aggie couldn't have put a name then to the sin. But something exotic and unmentionable that made her mother reach forward and tap her husband on the shoulder and say, "For heaven's sake, won't this horse go any faster?"

There was something bad about these people. Even the spastic boy must have done something, since God had marked him down for such special punishment. "Never mind," said her mother. "Pay no attention."

Not that Aggie wanted to have limbs that twitched, or to be drunk and crazy, or to wear too-bright, too-tight dresses on the street. She did wonder, though, how these people got that way, what they'd done to get there. But righteousness was on the side of blindness. Like June, who shrugs and says, "God's will." June says, "You ask too many questions, Mother. Things aren't so complicated if you look at them the right way." Aggie's mother said, "Hush now, you don't need to know such things."

Otherwise, her mother and her daughter aren't much alike. Aggie suspects June's faith of being a crutch and a judgment. She suspects June of depending on God to carry out her dirty work.

Her mother's belief, on the other hand, given the harshness of its rules, was reasonably kind.

Aggie was only a child in the First World War, when her older brother, who was named for their father, went away. She remembers him proud, strutting in his uniform, before he left. And she remembers her parents sitting alone in the front room for a while one evening, and then her father coming into the kitchen and telling them, "Young Will's been killed."

He went upstairs alone to bed, his footsteps sounding strange and slow and heavy. Their mother sat alone behind the closed door to the front room. They finally put themselves to bed, lying whispering in their rooms upstairs. As far as they could tell, their mother stayed silent and alone in the room below.

But she had breakfast on the table for them the next morning, and if her skin seemed stretched and tight, her eyes were dry. She kept going. That is what Aggie remembers mainly about her mother: she kept going, always, until she abruptly had a stroke and died on the kitchen floor when she was sixty-eight.

Aggie's own grief at her brother's death was a child's. The war was so far away, it was a kind of romantic myth, and death and injury were heroic and grand. She understood, from the way he'd worn his uniform, that he would have been brave. What struck her was that people could simply vanish.

It was so strange and remote a death that it must have been hard, for its very mysteriousness and distance, on her mother; not anything like falling out of a hay mow or drowning in a pond, which was the sort of death that could at least be grasped.

But she continued to say, "God's will be done," or "God knows what's for the best," and seemed to believe it. She was not angry at God for the death of her son, or for the unrelenting hard work, or for the fact that all her hard work never was rewarded with prosperity.

Did she accept events so quietly because she anticipated a reward in heaven, or did she put a distance between herself and misfortune by placing God in the middle, fielding pain through Him? Whatever, her faith seemed comforting, which is a good deal different from June's, as far as Aggie can tell.

Oh, she is old, she is old, and her mind trails off here and there. People say, "Those were the good old days, when right was right and wrong was wrong, and people took pride in what they did," and there's a softness in their voices, a nostalgic drifting in the eyes. That sort of thing annoys Aggie, who knows perfectly well the good old days were hard work and narrow rules and necessity.

So many changes, although no doubt this is the boring litany of the old.

Still, it is extraordinary to have gone from outhouses to lavish bathrooms, two and three to a house. From pumping water from wells to flicking taps. From woodstoves to gas ranges, and from root cellars and dark cool basements and ice boxes to freezers and refrigerators. From horses to cars, and then to airplanes and jets and rockets. From the punishing day-long labor of cooking and cleaning and laundering to a few moments of pushing buttons.

It's a wonderful thing to sit on a toilet in a warm room instead of hurrying through darkness to a smelly outhouse. Of course this is something she should have thought about the other night, not now, when it's too late.

She's never been free to travel, but she imagines how astonishing it must be to move among continents in a matter of hours, not weeks.

But the real change is choice. In her day, Aggie could not have seen a way to break the pattern, to say no, and Frances can. That seems a greater leap than a mere journey from, say, the earth to the moon. Travelling between continents and planets, that's just a matter of technology, wires in the right places and certain calculations. But being able to say no as well as yes, that is progress, that is revolution.

She's of two minds, however. All this change has also brought a loss of sorts. There is something to be seen in old photographs: a quality in even the oldest of them that she doesn't see in pictures now, despite improvements in cameras and film. What it may be is that, as the clarity of sharp, distinguished color and form has grown, the clarity of character has diminished. The old photos may have turned brown, the faces faded, the tinted cheeks may no longer be so rosy and the poses may be stiff and formal, but there is something riveting about them: in the squarer jaws, the sterner faces, the stonier eyes. Those pictures do not show people who think anything is easy.

They have simplicity, perhaps, but never ease.

Aggie herself is in some of these photographs, a child, a girl, almost a woman. She would have trouble interpreting now the small, sharp brown face of her childhood or her youth. A picture of her now would be blurred, lacking edges.

There is one that marks the dividing line between her childhood and adulthood. She was eighteen. Sylvia was married by then to a young farmer from down the road. Her mother said, "Will, we should get everyone together for a photograph. They'll soon be all grown up."

So everyone dressed in Sunday clothes, the horses were hitched, and they went to town, to the photographer's, nervous, giggling, conscious of appearance. This was unusual, since spending time before a mirror signified vanity, but for this one event, pride in appearance became a virtue. Aggie blushed when the photographer said, "Fine-looking family you've got here," and thought he was looking particularly at her.

That photograph that marks the final moment of her being young shows a girl who is slender, high-cheekboned, rosy-tinted, looking solemnly at the camera, sitting beside Edith, with the others—the two remaining brothers, Sylvia and her husband, and their parents—grouped around. Her face contains some delicacy, fragility, and hope. It's not exactly a joyous face, but there is strength and sturdiness in it, and in the straightness of the spine.

That slim girl's heart is the same heart that now pounds so hard against layers of flesh. Where is the connection? She might be inside Aggie now, buried away in there, struck still by time, protected in the past. Rather the way it was when she was expecting June, keeping someone fragile and not ready for life yet safe inside.

The girl in that picture had three wishes: to marry, to be a mother, and to be free in her own grown-up life. And how many people have made three wishes and had them all come true? Is she not extraordinarily fortunate, to have made three wishes and had them granted?

All very well in a fairy tale, of course; something else in life.

Or, as Frances would say, "Oh Grandma, what a fuck-up."

4

June works in the evenings, as her father used to, at the dining-room table. A brass floor lamp behind her chair casts light over
her left shoulder, the way it should to avoid eye-strain. She has to
be increasingly careful about such things; all sorts of bad things
may happen, not least of them failure of the eyes. Blind, she could
not teach, would have no job, would be poor and would starve.
The smallest things, like a poorly placed light, can have cata-
strophic results.

It may all be the will of God (and He has a way of testing with
disaster), but she foresees possibilities, accidents. She might be
walking home from school and a car loaded with the sort of young
louts that hang around on street corners, the kind she crosses the
road to avoid, might career around a corner, missing the turn, and
roll up onto the sidewalk right where she is, crushing her. She can
hear her own bones cracking. "You're all skin and bones, June,"
Aggie has always said, making it sound as if June is too insubstantial to survive, and there are circumstances, such as that speed-
ing car, in which that would be the case.

But taking one of the rickety old buses the town runs also has
its hazards. Sometimes, if she is loaded down with packages or
groceries, she does take one the few blocks home from downtown.
She feels fairly well protected in a bus, since it would take quite
a crash to do much damage. But how careful are the mechanics
hired to maintain them? The brakes or steering might fail at any
instant. Who knows the intricacies, the potentials for failure, in a
piece of machinery like a bus? June might be killed. Worse, she

might be crippled in some painful way. And who would look after her then? Not Frances, for sure. Frances is not the sacrificing kind. She will not do for June what June has done for Aggie.

Even sitting indoors is unsafe. Even a sturdy old brick house doesn't offer much protection against someone who decides she and Aggie are vulnerable. June keeps the drapes closed at night and makes sure the doors are locked. Still, anyone could get in, smashing a window or doing some clever criminal thing with the locks. There may be rumors that the two of them keep cash in the house, it's the sort of story that goes around about women on their own. And aside from that, there is random violence. It may be pretty well unknown around here, but she reads about it in the newspapers and sees it on TV. Aggie would be no help. And terrible things could happen to June. She may be aging, but she is not yet old, and men are animals.

She prays to God for protection. But faith is a two-edged sword, inviting His testing. There are times when she feels like a regular Job, and while God may move in mysterious ways, the results can sometimes appear, even to a faithful human eye, peculiar as well as wondrous.

Pending terrible events, however, she has to get through each day. Tonight she has marked the arithmetic test she gave today. Three children have failed. It is depressing and irritating, when she has explained a thing so clearly, how often they don't hear, or can't be made to understand. Some classes, of course, are better than others, and some years are better than others. But there's always at least one small, impenetrable mind.

Can she really have spent almost forty years at this?

Finished, she puts the tests and tomorrow's lessons in the big leather briefcase that belonged to her father. He used it for the same purpose, and the wide strap over the top is worn thin, the holes for the brass buckle have grown large with age and use, and the buckle itself is scratched and worn, not shiny the way it was when he used it. Still, it's remarkable how it's held up, how well things used to be made.

Aggie has been very quiet tonight. A while ago, June heard her shifting in the front room, but there's been silence for a while. George will likely come tomorrow, and Aggie may be thinking about that. It's too bad, but what can she expect? Although this morning the sheets were dry.

Standing in the doorway between the dining room and the front room, June sees only the back of her mother's head; the rest of her is encased in the old easy chair. June would have liked to throw it out years ago, it got so shabby, and of course had no springs left at all, from years of taking Aggie's weight, but Aggie refused. "It fits me," she said, and by then it did, like a dress, her body filled it up so thoroughly. "We'll just have it refinished." Which would have hidden its shabbiness, if not its shape, but then Aggie spoiled it, insisting on a light yellow pattern with tiny flowers, which looks ridiculous. It's as absurd as decking Aggie out in lace and feathers.

She must have dozed off. June can see her head nodding, and there are periodic snorts as it jerks and she almost wakens. As a moment between them, it's almost peaceful; but only because Aggie is asleep.

Aggie's hair is white. She used to wear it wrapped in tidy braids around her head. At night before she went to bed she brushed it out, and when it was down she looked like an entirely different person, someone soft. June rarely saw her that way, but when she did, was startled at the way Aggie would be regarding herself in the mirror: as if she were seeing someone else.

Since Aggie has gotten old, however, and since the hair has turned white, and since weight combined with age has left her unable to deal with all the brushing and twisting and pinning up involved in braiding, and because June certainly doesn't have time for that sort of nonsense, her hair has been cut short. It seemed, when it was done, with the lengths of soft white hair spread across her lap, amputated from its roots, that Aggie might weep. But now she has a permanent every six months to keep it waved and curled, and it's quite easy to deal with.

Coming up behind, June sees that Aggie's hair has become not only white and short and waved, but thin. There are small pink patches where the scalp is showing through. It's odd, skin where there should not be skin. June has an impulse to place her hands over those naked places on her mother's head.

But Aggie is abruptly awake, turning to see what's behind her, alerted either by her own breathing or by a sense of her daughter coming up on her. From the front, June sees what she usually does: a fat, old, greedy woman.

"George may come tomorrow, so you should probably have a bath tonight. You'll want to be clean."

Breasts flap and belly droops, thighs roll and calves quiver, as
Aggie ripples into the tub and out. Once in, June only has to wash
her back, and her legs from the knees down. Aggie can manage
the rest herself, might almost manage the whole thing herself, except that it is just that shade too risky. Bending to put the plug in
the drain, she might topple. It's difficult for her to undress herself.
And in that one teetering moment of stepping in, her balance could
be just slightly off, and for someone Aggie's size, being only
slightly off balance could be something like a tree blowing down.

So June's arm must be there to support the weight if it's needed;
and what would she do if Aggie really did crash? Be crushed beneath, no doubt. Also, there is something backward and unnatural
about a daughter caring for a mother. It ought to be the other way
around; but then Aggie has always been contrary.

And maybe, after all, this is only how things round out: someone who fed and diapered and bathed comes, at the other end, to
being fed and diapered and bathed. It hasn't come quite to that yet.
The last thing to go will be Aggie's ability to feed herself. When
she can't reach for food, she'll really be on her last legs.

Going to bed and waking up the next morning, June feels a sub-
terranean excitement, a sort of thrumming, like Christmas when she
was a little girl, when her father was alive.

That was a childish pleasure, of course. She would go downstairs when he called to her on Christmas morning and find gifts
that were concrete, specific, and desired: a doll, a game, a dress.
On this day, when George may come, there should also be a gift,
but a grown-up kind: an event, or a movement toward an event.
That is more subtle and not something that can be touched, but far
greater than a doll. Harder to grasp, as well.

Today she can manage anything; which is as well, since it's
happened again.

"Oh, Mother."

Poor, miserable Aggie. She looks smaller in defeat. June has
sometimes wondered why her mother can't be like other old people, who get quiet and shrink and seem to curdle a little inside their
bodies, whereas Aggie has only increased, in size and volume.

Now George can hardly say, "Aside from her weight, she's
healthy as a horse, for somebody her age." And Aggie cannot tell
her favorite death-defying joke. "Isn't it wonderful," she likes to
say, "that I'm dying in perfect health?"

Now her sins accumulate, and she surely has to shrivel.

"Never mind, Mother. Come on, let's get you up."

There is more kindness than unkindness in her this morning. But
would there be if she did not detect freedom in these sheets?

Aggie is bewildered. "I don't understand." She looks so helpless.

"It's all right, it's probably something simple and George'll be
able to fix you right up. Now let's get you cleaned up and
dressed."

It's quite a thing, not loving. Once, Aggie accused June of being
un-Christian.

"Whatever do you mean? Of course I'm a Christian."

"No, June, you're pure Old Testament, all judgment and revenge. What about charity?" Charity, Aggie said, was love.

But love, which is supposed to conquer all, could hardly manage
the Everest of Aggie. Of course, there are different sorts of love,
but all that means is that there are also different sorts of failures to
love.

The love of a daughter for a mother, that's one. But how is it
possible with a force like Aggie, who has dipped into June's life,
rummaging around, taking out anything she wanted? Like Frances.
And what has she given? She may claim that when June was a
baby, her hands not only fed and diapered, but also held and comforted. She says that when June cried, she danced and sang with
her. June would not say her mother is a liar, but she has no sense
that those gestures ever occurred. At best it is true that Aggie rarely
struck her.

What has Aggie's charity been? She has had only power and
pride, and now, standing mute and humiliated while June strips off
her nightgown, no longer those.

Then there is Christian love. But Aggie has always been too
massive, too present, to love in that general way that seems, in
practice, to be mainly a sort of intense goodwill.

The best that can be done in the same house with Aggie is survive. It's like one of those slow tortures practised in wars, or in
one of those dirty little countries to which the missions send used
clothes: someone with a knife, just breaking the skin of a victim
here, now there, all over but just a little, so that there are only
small oozings of blood and the trick is to see how long it takes to
bleed to death.

Well, June has no intention of bleeding to death.

"We'll put something especially nice on you today, shall we, Mother? Because George may be coming?"

She doesn't really mean to frighten Aggie, but it is intriguing, this little power of words. Once again the sheets go downstairs to the washer, and later the mattress will be turned again. She must stop somewhere today and buy a plastic sheet. Nothing will happen overnight to move her toward freedom. Well, nothing new will happen overnight. But she can see the end, if not quite the form getting there will take.

She leaves a subdued Aggie sitting in the front room, a plate of date squares and a book beside her. It's odd, but interesting, how she is.

But interesting is Aggie's sort of word, her kind of cruelty, surely, not June's. It's the word Aggie uses when something, usually unpleasant, has happened and she has thought about it and decided how it felt and what she learned: and then pronounced it interesting. When her own husband, June's father, died, Aggie would have been sitting downstairs after the funeral thinking the whole thing had been quite interesting. June doesn't actually remember that, since she was upstairs mourning in her own room at the time, but she is quite sure that's what would have happened.

As far as June can tell, interesting is good enough for Aggie, all that can be asked.

Maybe when June is free, she will be able to concentrate on her own hope, which is for salvation. She may spend her freedom in contemplation, rather than in good works. They are equal in the sight of God, she understands. After all this, she would be able to stand quite a few years of silence and peace. Meanwhile, there are moves to be made. June's step, heading to school, is light and brisk, and her thoughts are turned more to plans than prayers.

With Aggie gone, she will redecorate. She will change all the walls, all the sprightly wallpaper and light colors. She will search down beyond varnish and paint to the rich, dark wood of the banisters and baseboards.

She will also put extra locks on the doors, although what difference the absence of Aggie will make to her safety she can't tell. But she will be alone, and there is, after all, something about Aggie's bulk that seems to offer some protection.

How different it would be, having breakfast in silence; maybe having no breakfast at all, no need to bother. And to come home to quiet, no jabbings or reminders or responsibilities.

From almost a block away, she can hear the uproar of the schoolyard. In a few moments she will have to be a teacher, her daily transformation that requires a straightening of the spine and a tightening of the face, achieving the sternness that protects.

There are thirty small faces to be met each day. The faces change every year, but they're all the same to her. Sometimes a middle-aged man or woman will stop her in the street and say, "Hello, Mrs. Benson (or Miss Hendricks, depending on who she had been at the time), do you remember me? I was in your class twenty years ago" (or thirty, forty). June hardly ever remembers, but will say politely, "Oh yes, and what are you doing now?" as if she did.

She would just as soon keep her distance from the children, even the ones who have grown up to look not too menacing. Children are scary little things, close to the ground, as if they keep their ears to it, picking up vibrations from the earth. They are passionate in their little feuds and friendships, but the causes of their passion are puzzling and unpredictable. A mood can change in an instant. Like animals, they sniff out vulnerability. They are cruel, children are, and primitive.

Like a trapeze artist or a lion-tamer, she has been dangling herself in front of them daily for forty years. She certainly never expected it to be for so long. If she'd known, she might have chosen something else; although in those days there wasn't much else a woman could do. Be a nurse, perhaps, but that would have been even worse. At least here the only blood she has to deal with is from a scraped elbow or knee, or maybe a nosebleed in the classroom. Life and death would be terrible things to be responsible for, and so much unpleasantness besides, with bedpans, and tubes going here and there in people's bodies.

It's not only the children: the teaching itself has become bewildering and far more difficult. It used to be that there were particular methods and particular lessons. Children memorized poems and multiplication tables, lists of prepositions and names of continents and countries. They might be mischievous, or disobedient, and even bad, some of them, but they could be punished. There used to be a chair in the hall outside her door, and a misbehaving child could be sent out there for a scolding or the strap. She intercepted notes when they tried to pass them, and read them aloud, which soon put a stop to that. Whisperers were told to speak aloud and tell the whole class what they had to say.

Now even the little ones sometimes grin openly at her, and she hears them giggling and whispering. She may no longer punish as she sees fit. She is told to be "creative" in her teaching, whatever that may mean. If they are interested, the principal has suggested, they will learn. He is much younger than she. Authority, she notices, has skipped past her: policemen she sees on the streets are just peach-cheeked babies, and the doctor, George Bannon, is only Frances's age. Even the other teachers are young, arriving eager and staying a while and moving on, like the children passing out of her classes. She is the only one who seems to be permanent.

Those other teachers behave like children, too, playing in the schoolyard, throwing baseballs around, running and shouting. There seems hardly any distance at all between them and the pupils. How do they keep order? Well, the answer of course is that they don't. Standing in the hall, she can hear shouts and laughter from other classrooms.

In the staff-room they talk about young things: buying clothes and houses and having babies. They lean toward each other over tables. She suspects that, when she comes in, they glance at her and feel sorry for her. Either that or they don't notice her at all.

June knows she is not one of the popular teachers. She knows quite well that, behind her back, pupils call her "old beaky-brain", although it makes no sense to her and she has no idea what they mean by it. It's another example of their incomprehensibility: sounds, she supposes, that appeal to them, but meaningless, nonsense sounds, intending but not specifying insult.

It doesn't matter what they call her, if she does her job and they learn what she has to teach. She supposes some of them will remember her, for her thoroughness if nothing else. Beyond that, it should be of no concern.

There was a teacher, older than June, who was adored. She taught Grade 1, and little girls clung to her, competing for her attention and affection. They walked her home from school jostling each other to be beside her, holding her hands. At recess, they showed off. "Look Miss Pearson, I can turn a somersault," that sort of thing. When she retired, parents she had taught came with children she had taught to an enormous reception for her. The adults jostled each other to get close. And all Mabel Pearson ever did, as far as June could tell, was wear pretty dresses and smile a great deal, speak gently to her pupils, and allow her hands to be held by sweaty, sticky little palms.

What will be done when June retires? Nothing like that outpouring of affection for Mabel Pearson, who, even now, at seventy, can walk beaming down the street being stopped by forty- and fifty-year-olds still keen for her approval.

June can see herself at that stage, sailing along being greeted, if at all, with deference and perhaps a touch of fear. No one will clutch at her arm, which is just as well. She has often thought how unpleasant it must be for Mabel Pearson, being clutched at all the time.

Respect, that's something she learned from her father: the respect a teacher warrants. Certainly in his day that was recognized by other men, who, she saw, greeted him in the street with deference; even people like the banker tipped his hat to her father.

The inexplicable thing is how her honorable, upright father could have brought himself to marry Aggie, even granting that she may have been attractive at the time. It seems to have been his only lapse in judgment. June does not believe at all the things her mother says about him. And even if they were true, she knows herself—who better?—how aggravating Aggie can be.

5

Ordinarily, Aggie likes sitting at the front-room window, where she has various ways to spend the day: reading, eating, and watching. She knows a great many things about a great many people in this town. Prepared to dislike it, and finding it strange when she came, she has grown fond with sixty years of familiarity. She knows so many stories, snippets of drama, that have originated here. Many of the people involved, of course, have left or are dead. It's lonely, to have so few people left with whom to share memories—or, if not memories, at least pieces of history, certain events. How many remember the First World War, even as remotely as she does?

Oh, it is shameful, ignominious, to end up an old woman peeing the bed.

It is both more of a disaster that it has happened again, and less of one. Worse because now it is no longer a single, arguable lapse; and better because the second time it is almost familiar, not such a shock. She had no trouble identifying what was wrong, and spent no time trying to think of what to say to June, because clearly there was nothing to be said.

She is eighty years old, and of course things must be breaking down. What could she expect? She has rewarded her body with pies and cakes, and punished it with flesh. There are fires in her belly some days. There are times when it feels as if it may erupt.

If she has to die, she would prefer to explode. Mere disintegration is a horror. The best way would be to eat one cookie, one muffin, one cupcake too many and just blow up, with the taste of the last treat still on her tongue.

But she doesn't want to die.

She doesn't want to be an old woman peeing the bed, either.

And George will come, poking and probing, and Lord knows what June has in mind.

How queer and frightening, not to know what to do. There was a time when she was full of ideas. She was the one, back home, who suggested games, and found an old curtain to turn into a dress for Edith to wear to the church young people's meetings. She was the one who led the others up the rungs of the ladders into the hay mows, and leaped from away up there into the soft heaps of straw, while they hung back, peering at the distance down. She was the one who climbed high into a maple tree and hung from a limb, catcalling at her younger brothers, who could not reach so high. Later on, she may have been, for all she knew, the only one whose body sometimes burned, wanting—something or other. Even with so much work to be done, she had time and restlessness left over.

"What do you want, Aggie?" her mother demanded. "Why can't you be still?"

Well, but it got to be time for things to happen. Some secret things already had begun.

She went to church young people's meetings, and with her parents on Saturday evenings visiting neighboring families, or with her brothers and Edith on a community hay ride, and regarded the boys. They were as familiar to her as, oh, boiled potatoes, or lemon pies.

What happened was, the girls of the area married the boys of the area (who were called the boys, distinguishing them from their fathers, until they married and began to produce another set of boys) and moved onto nearby farms and began to recreate in those fields and kitchens and bedrooms what they had known in their mothers' homes.

It was a matter of waiting until the one involved made himself evident. Then there would be a period of courtship, involving a degree of chaste romance, and then the day, and freedom. She would have her own house, would make her own decisions about what to cook and bake. It would be her own floors she would be cleaning, and her own clothes, and her husband's, she would be washing. She would have her own children. Her life would be her own.

Meanwhile there was a kind of jigsaw puzzle of a man, made up of bits and pieces of familiar men, broad-shouldered and hefty, too young to have grown beefy yet, with well-muscled arms and calves (and there was no dreaming above, to thighs and hips and other mysterious parts). He had no face yet.

She talked about the wedding dress she would have, and described the rooms of her house. "It'll be bright, and I'll have all new dishes." The old dishes in their house were marked by tiny, intricate surface cracks. "I'll have everything my own way, in my own house," she boasted.

"You know, Aggie," her mother said, "sometimes I wonder if you'll be satisfied." She did not, however, explain what she meant, or what alternatives there might be.

Her mother's knack was to praise different aspects of her different children. Edith was the best cook, and Sylvia the best at sewing. One son was a hard worker, the other the most practical, and the oldest was a martyr to his country, a hero and a memory. His attributes and Aggie's were the hardest to pin down. "It's a good thing to have spunk," her mother warned, "but don't always expect things your own way." Aggie could see no reason not to. She only expected what everyone had.

Almost everyone. Because there was an alternative of sorts, although it was more something unfortunate that might happen, or fail to happen, than a choice. It was to cross that line between being an unmarried girl and spinsterhood; the difference between having a future and not. If marrying was to recreate and have purpose, spinsterhood was to be at the mercy of other people's creations and purposes. A spinster was the aunt, the dependant who would look after aging parents, or live at various times with various sisters and brothers, scrubbing floors, doing laundry, changing diapers—perhaps loving the babies but having none of her own, and knowing there was no amount of work that could pay off the debt of being unwanted, unloved, unlovable, and unattractive. A spinster thinned and dried, and her mouth grew little disapproving lines. As if marriage were a skin cream, and she aged too fast without it.

"You're getting a bit long in the tooth, my girl," Aggie's father teased, but he was a little serious. She had turned nineteen.

"Really, Aggie," her mother said impatiently, "I don't know what you want. Nobody's going to come along on a white horse and sweep you off your feet, you know."

Aggie didn't think she was waiting for any white horse. It was just that in her bed she-pictured things. There was something she wanted, if she could pin it down, and, having pinned it down, could pick it out from among the round boyish faces with their tanned, toughened skin.

In the event, it was no knight on a white horse who appeared, but certainly something different.

His name was Neil Hendricks, he was from England, and it was his first year of teaching in Canada. It was the custom for unmarried teachers in the one-room country school to board in the homes of pupils, and Aggie's smallest brother was still in public school.

Aggie's mother, who had met him at a school concert, said he seemed a nice smart young fellow, if a bit different, probably due to being English. "Oh boy, he's really strict," said her little brother. Aggie and Edith speculated about his character and appearance. He was to be with them for the winter and spring terms, arriving in the new year. They thought at least it would make a change.

He came during a storm, after dark, carrying a suitcase in each hand, cold and wet, red-faced, and bundled up in coat and scarf and hat and heavy boots. To be honest, right off the bat Aggie thought he was a pretty miserable sight, and then wondered why she was disappointed.

"You poor boy," said her mother, "you must be perished."

He wore tiny gold-rimmed glasses that steamed in the heat of the kitchen. Once the cold wore off, the flush went with it and he turned out to be pale. He sat in the kitchen hugging himself, and they thought he was still chilly.

How different he was! So thin. Aggie and Edith hovered at the edges of the kitchen as their mother made tea and served him cookies. How, Aggie wondered, would someone like this shovel snow or split wood or toss hay into a wagon? His hair was also thin, and blond, and when he dipped his head to the tea it was apparent he was balding, wisps of pale hair over pale scalp. He seemed an unlikely figure to be sitting at their kitchen table.

(Could he really have been as unattractive as she remembers? She is sometimes startled, when Frances comes to visit, that she is not as beautiful in the flesh as Aggie has envisioned in her absence.)

How thin his wrists were. How narrow his features. Such pale blue eyes, with lashes so blond they were almost invisible. He leaned toward people when they spoke as if he couldn't hear properly.

There were other things, though. His voice; well, not his voice precisely, but his accent. There was a kind of foreign lilt, some parts of words more drawled and others more clipped. Also there seemed to be more grace in his slenderness than in the bulk of her father and brothers.

Too, he had to have some kind of toughness, if not the obvious sort of strength, because he had been brave enough to come here alone and begin a new life, so far from what was familiar.

"Imagine how lonely he must be," Aggie thought.

People were of two minds about a teacher. On the one hand, it seemed a failure of masculinity for a man to be concerned with book-learning, which was nothing like real work and certainly not essential. On the other hand, he would know things. He would contain a vast store of secrets, or at least things other people didn't know. It made him a little mysterious, gave him an edge. People had some respect for what they didn't know, even if they knew all they actually needed to.

Aggie, watching the blond head bobbing around their house, wondered what it contained that hers did not. She wondered if his brain looked different from hers, more stuffed and crammed. If it were split open, would little facts and thoughts fall out, rolled up neatly like bits of paper? When he looked at her family, at her, what did he see? Did he see things they didn't, because of what he knew? Could he tell secrets about them because of the way he saw?

Her mother said, "Now, Aggie, I want you to look after him especially, talk to him and make sure he's not lacking for anything and make him feel at home, because I don't have time." The hint could not have been much plainer. "But don't be forward."

She found that conversation, in the beginning, was mainly up to her. His place at the supper table was set between her and her little brother, who was too ill at ease in his teacher's presence to speak. The teacher himself seemed to have a streak of shyness, or just silence.

"You're from England, Mr. Hendricks?"

"Yes, near London."

"And do you have family there?"

"My parents. I was their only child," and he looked around the noisy table with some astonishment.

"You must miss them."

"I do, but this is where the opportunities are, or so they say back home." He dipped his head and smiled. His lips, she thought, were narrow, but not entirely unappealing.

"Is it very different here, then?"

"Well, the customs are, I suppose. The way people live. It's not quite what I expected."

"How did you think it would be?"

"Oh," and he waved a hand vaguely, a slim hand with long fingers, smooth instead of rough, pale instead of reddened, with clean fingernails and little blond hairs on his knuckles—everything about him different, down to his fingertips—"I didn't realize how cold it could get or how far apart people lived. I didn't think of education not being so important, that students just don't turn up at school if they're wanted at home."

She couldn't imagine it any other way, but nodded encouragingly.

"Some of them are quite bright, too. Still, I suppose I can try to make them want to learn. There's nothing to stop a farmer from reading, after all."

How ignorant he must find them all, how work-worn and dull, scrabbling at their rocks. For a moment she saw them from his point of view, and was ashamed.

Still, when he shrugged her attention was drawn to the spareness of his shoulders, and she had a naughty vision of her big healthy head rolling off them.

"And you?" he asked politely. "You went to school here?"

"Yes, but not very far, only to seventh grade."

"Do you like books? Do you still read?"

Of course not. There were far too many things going on to sit with your nose in a book. Reading was a school activity, and leaving school, you closed the books. "Well, we don't have many here," she hedged. "Only some school readers, and the Bible."

"But are you interested?"

"Oh, of course."

They said the way to a man's heart was through his stomach, but she thought that with this man, that was not likely the case. He was just picking at his food, but now he turned to her with interest. "I have books upstairs, you know. Would you care to borrow some?"

"Yes, I'd like that," and she lowered her eyes, well schooled
in the maidenly arts, however strong she might in fact be. Why,
she could carry pails of ice water or lemonade away out into the
fields for her father and brothers to drink; she could twist sheets
so hard all the soapy water just drained right out of them. Eyes
down and moving her hands a little helplessly, as if they'd never
done anything harder than touch a flower, she added, "Although I
wouldn't know where to begin, really."

"Perhaps I could help you."

"That would be very kind. If you're sure it wouldn't be too
much trouble."

It was not. He came down to the kitchen after supper the next
night with a book, and began to teach her. Which, as it turned out,
was what he liked to do best. Her brothers giggled, as their mother
hustled them out of the way.

Aggie and he made various kinds of progress. To her surprise,
she did rather enjoy the lessons. She could see how there might be
something to this, trying to understand, like a game or a puzzle. It
was humiliating to know so few words. "Read it to me," she asked
him, and he seemed pleased to do so. By watching closely, she
could learn.

She was released from after-supper housework. "No," her
mother said, "you spend the time at your lessons," and told the
teacher, "Aggie's so bright, it's a shame she had to leave school.
It's nice, you helping her this way."

Peeling potatoes, Aggie memorized poems. Her brothers teased
her. "Eyes on the teacher, that's what."

"Call me Neil," he told her. "This isn't a classroom, I'm not
Mr. Hendricks here." She thought that gracious and informal.

He said, "I'll pick out what you should read," and handed her
small volumes of poems, about flowers and sunsets mainly. "You
have to be careful, you know, what things are suitable." She would
have liked stories. After a while, she got a little tired of flowers
and sunsets, but he explained they must move cautiously. Some
books, some words, he said, should not be exposed to women. Or
women to them. She was never clear if his care was for the purity
of learning, or the virtue of the female. Possibly both.

She was pleased that when he read aloud, his voice deepened
with authority. He said he was pleased with her progress. It was
true that she was a keen pupil, likely the best he had, since she
was aiming for more than his other students: the man himself.

"Now," he would say, finished reading, "what do you think the poet is trying to say?" A teacher's dream, she must have been, someone bright he could train from scratch.

"It's important to speak properly," he told her, correcting mistakes in her grammar. "Language, if it's used precisely, provides precise communication. Proper use of words enables us to know exactly what another person means." Could that really be true? If so, it would certainly prevent a lot of misunderstanding.

One thing it did mean was that she now spotted mistakes of speech other members of her family made. It seemed to open a space.

Her fantasies shifted. Now she saw the two of them, in some other house. He would be reading and working at the kitchen table, and she would be sewing, cooking, and preserving. He would talk to her about a poem while upstairs, chubby, rosy, dark-haired children would be asleep. It was a warm picture, although it didn't raise much heat.

Looking at him, so different from the man she had envisioned, she began to consider bones instead of flesh.

But then there was also what she taught him. Sometimes after a lesson they went for walks out into the snowy fields where cold air bit at their throats. Out there, that was where she knew things. They went through the stable, where cows' breath made steam in the air and the bull stood stamping, held to a post by a rope through a nose ring. Above, in the barn, she showed him the hay mows and the trapdoors through which the feed was shovelled into troughs below. He walked behind her cautiously, unfamiliar with the smells and the spots where the floor might disappear beneath his feet, and the huge animals he seemed timid of, although she told him they were gentle, with the exception of the bull.

When spring came, they walked in the fields, along the lane and by the creek, watching the water flood the banks as the snow melted. "It feels dangerous to me," he confided. "There's so much space and emptiness."

She listened carefully. He didn't often speak about what he saw or how he felt, except to do with poems.

"We had such a little garden at home, compared with this."

Obviously he did not understand the rules of space, and people's own tight ways of dealing with it, the stone fences and the small farms methods of containment.

But she didn't know how to explain that sort of thing. "Yes, I
see," she said, but she didn't. She thought she must be, after all,
only an ignorant farm girl, unable to understand the menace in what
he saw, or tell him what she saw. She might know how to make
a perfect pastry, and feed a dozen hungry men at threshing time,
but she would never be able to properly express what a poet meant
to say.

She was flattered by his attention, but terrified he would discern
the scope of her ignorance.

What did he see? It was possible he only viewed her as a pupil,
a pretty dark-haired girl who would bend obligingly over his lessons, until it was time for him to leave.

Around the house, she was a little absent-minded. "Mooning
about the teacher," her brothers laughed.

"You shush," said her mother. "Leave your sister alone. It
wouldn't do you two any harm to pay more attention to what Mr.
Hendricks has to say. It's a chance to learn, having a teacher in
the house. He won't be here forever, you know."

"Boy, that's good," said her smallest brother.

"Do you like him, then?" her mother asked later. She meant a
good deal more, including, "Do you like him enough?" and "Does
he like you, and is anything going to come of this?"

"Yes, I think so, he's very nice," Aggie told her, meaning that
she liked him enough and had some hopes.

The cows were released into the fields. Aggie's father and the
boys were mucking out the stalls, and the spring air in the evenings
was cool and sharp. It smelled to Aggie of greenness and freshness, nicely spiced by manure.

But after a while the teacher would say, "Let's go back in,"
and at the door he would scrape and scrape the boots he'd borrowed from her father. Sometimes he seemed to be holding his
breath. She thought, "Well, it might not smell so good to somebody who isn't used to it."

(Frances, intrigued by differing versions, used to ask about him.
"He was a good man," June would tell her. "A gentleman, a
saint."

("Listen," Aggie said, leaning forward, "you want to know
what kind of man he was? Listen—what your grandfather was,
really, was a man who couldn't stand to have shit on his boots.")

It was May when he mentioned marriage. The day before, he'd gotten a letter from a town sixty miles away. Mail for him, for anyone for that matter, was rare.

He closed the books, ending their lesson at the kitchen table, and said, "I've been offered another job next year. In a town school. I'd just be teaching two grades, and they'd be paying me more."

What did he expect her to say? "That's wonderful. You must be pleased. Are you going to take it?"

"I think so. It seems a good move." He stacked the books and picked uncomfortably at the yellow oilcloth tacked to the table. "I've been thinking, I'm twenty-eight now, and this position will be secure. It's a nice town, well-kept and prosperous. I think you'd like it."

"Would I?" Imagine how hard, being the man and having to be the first to speak. So risky, leaving yourself open like that.

"So I wondered how you would feel about getting married this summer. I could go on ahead and get us a house, and we'd be there for the beginning of school. I'd like to settle, you see. Have a family. Could you think about it? It'll be quite a different sort of life, but you might like it."

He didn't mention love or desire, so neither did she. She ought to have asked why he was asking, though. She failed to see past her own picture, which was what she loved: the two of them, warm and companionable in the kitchen, teaching and learning, with unseen children sleeping upstairs.

She measured his mouth and his slender body. There were magical parts to marriage. He was right that it would be a different sort of life. Who knew what was out there, in other places? Potential delights were being laid out like candies at Christmas, so of course she said, "Oh, but I'd like to marry you, very much, thank you."

"Good then, I'm glad." Then he didn't quite know what to do and stood, gathering up the books, and said only, "Well then, I'll see you tomorrow."

"I'll miss you, Aggie," her mother said. "You'll be a long way off. But I'm pleased for you, really."

Aggie herself could not yet feel the distance.

Now when they went for walks they touched lips chastely at the door before going back inside. They held hands, too, although lightly, a connection of fingers, not palms. At night in her bed, she imagined him beside her, and wished for a little impropriety.

He continued his instruction with the poems at the kitchen table, but also with other information elsewhere.

"It's not a big town," he told her, "but it's prosperous, and the school is good. For one thing, children aren't expected to drop out to help at home, or at least most of them don't. It will be quite different from living here, and you'll be a long way from your family. I hope you won't be unhappy," and he looked at her anxiously.

"Then there's being a teacher's wife, you may find that an adjustment. There are certain standards for a teacher, he has a position to maintain, and his wife is the same, she has a certain position as well."

Was he worried? Did he think she would embarrass him?

"No, no, not all. It's just that you're young, and there are expectations you're not used to. Things like entertaining parents of my pupils and other people with some position. It will be a different class of people, that's all I meant."

All? She had a flash of resentment, on behalf of her parents, her sisters and brothers, the people of the area, who were not, apparently, quite good enough. Also he sounded like a teacher, not a— what? Fiancé? It was hard to find the word for him. Anyway, he was using that deeper, more assured tone of his poem-teaching.

But it was quite true that, without instruction, she might well fail to measure up. And it was also true that the big, ruddy members of her family would not fit comfortably in a banker's parlor, there was no getting around that.

"But don't worry," he assured her, "you'll do fine, I know."

He made the future sound like a foreign country. She would not be popping back and forth like Sylvia, just down the road.

He went away to find a house for them, and while he was gone the neighbors held showers and she came away with hand-embroidered pillowcases and towels with monograms. Her new initials would be AH, which looked like either an expression of delight or a sigh, stitched out like that.

"You'll be so far away," said Edith, as they lay whispering in their beds.

Aggie imagined lying in bed whispering to her husband.

Her mother came to her, sat uncomfortably on the edge of the bed. "I'm sure you know, Aggie, that there are things that will happen when you're married? That married people do?"

Well, everyone knew certain things, just from seeing the cows with the bull, and the cats in the barn with their litters of kittens. Obviously something more would be involved with people, since they were not mere animals, and her own body hinted at longings, if not at how they might be resolved.

"What you have to remember," her mother explained, "is that men are made differently. They get their pleasure with their wives, and a woman's pleasure is in her children. So you have to be patient and wait. Do you see? Whatever happens, you'll find joy in your children."

The way she put it, it seemed like a somewhat lopsided bargain. Also, Aggie was never very good at waiting, although she supposed that might be something that would come with maturity and marriage. Anyway, her mother was so clearly embarrassed that there was no way of inquiring further. There was some kind of conspiracy of silence on the matter. It might be, though, that, once married, Aggie and her teacher would find a communion of silence, instead.

There were going to be so many things to find out, she could hardly wait. On the other hand, she wanted the wedding day itself to go very slowly. She wanted attention paid to her mysterious, exotic future far away. She wanted a day of being proud, and having everybody look. Beyond that, circumstances could hardly be foreseen.

Her family and their neighbors filled up the little church. Neil looked strained and solemn and his voice quavered over the vows. Her own voice she could barely hear.

The women took cakes and special sandwiches, with the crusts cut off for the occasion, to the church basement for the reception. It was true that everyone paid attention. She hung on his arm and was proud. He spoke so seriously and properly. He made everyone else, even the women, look a little rough and shabby. Oh, they might make fun of a slender young man who spoke oddly and did not do a man's work, but they were also impressed by the unknown; and now she was part of his unknown.

She found herself a little distant with her family, although benign. They drove home from the church to get changed for the journey. It was hard to understand this really was a farewell. "I'll be back," she said, "and you must come and visit."

They weren't teasing today. They were a bit stiff, too, as if she were a different person now, unfamiliar, someone's wife and no longer their daughter or sister.

The back of the buggy was filled with her trunk and their wedding gifts. "Goodbye, then, girl," said her father, lifting her up beside the waiting teacher, who was something of a cipher in all this. In a moment of panic, she almost leaped down, an impulse to run away. But she knew what it was. "Bride's jitters," her mother had predicted, and so she took herself in hand.

She turned in her seat to look back. There was the familiar green and gold of the land; the short, plump, brown-and-grey-haired mother, in her best dress today; her stiff, bulky father; her brothers, both uncomfortable in their Sunday suits; Sylvia and her husband; and little Edith: all waving, as she waved back.

They vanished at the bend in the lane, Edith leaping up and down as if she were trying to keep them in view a little longer. And that was that.

And this was it. She smiled at him, and he smiled back.

Facing ahead, it began to seem real. The muscles of the trotting horse rippled like those on the sort of man she had once assumed she would marry. But now she and the teacher were going somewhere. There was a new, unknowable life down the road. Home and the people there were far behind.

And oh, she must be a foolish old woman, to find herself missing them now. All the noises, of people laughing and talking, and the sounds of crickets and cattle; the smells, of cooking vegetables and steaming cowshit, skunk reek in the dusk and hot pie shells and boiling dates, all the heat contained in that old house.

Also, it is no doubt ridiculous, but sometimes she longs for her mother. She would like to be rocked in her mother's lap, her head on her mother's shoulder, her knees drawn up, being comforted.

But she is not small, and cannot curl up on anyone's lap, for comfort or anything else. Her mother is dead, and she herself is old, and her own daughter has never shown a sign of desiring an embrace.

6

June's dream of heaven is rising, weightless, through clouds to a golden place. Angels, just the way they look in pictures, with their white robes and golden haloes and luxuriant feathered wings, will drift toward her. She will see, beyond them, her father glancing up. Slightly surprised, he will smile, the way he used to coming through the door at nights, and then step lightly toward her. He will take hold of her hands and because he is strong, or because she is weightless, he will swing her off her feet, around and around, hair and legs flying, hands gripped firmly in his so that she can't fall and hurt herself. They will both be laughing and dizzy. When he sets her down, he will say, "So, bunny, what have you been doing?"

Well, that's a child's sort of fancy, and she is no child. Heaven will not, of course, be so undignified. But still.

She will rise weightless through clouds to a golden place. Angels will greet her, and beyond them she will see her father looking up. He will step lightly toward her, take her hands and smile, gently and sadly, the way he did when he talked about his mother so far away. He will put his arm around her shoulder and they will walk together.

That vision lacks the joy, the leaping-up sort of feeling of the first one. On the other hand, it is more serene, and powerful enough to last eternity.

First, however, there is getting through all this to there, a matter not only of time, but of effort and faith. There are preparations to be made, a state of mind to enter. It's hard to get into the right

41

frame of mind around Aggie, who loves food and no doubt Frances, greedy for both, but is otherwise never pleased or satisfied.

And who has done the right thing here? Who has been here? Who else would clean Aggie and get her meals and help her in and out of bed, and get up in the middle of the night for her? Who else, under these conditions, would touch her stained and nasty sheets?

Still, the point is to do the right thing. Not to love, or for that matter be loved.

It's like the bright young teachers talking about the fulfilment of their pupils, or their happiness. Just what, June would like to know, do fulfilment and happiness have to do with anything? Children are there to learn, not to be happy.

But if she is here to do the right thing, what is that? It is not necessarily mere selfishness, this wish to shift her mother. Aggie truly isn't safe, left on her own all day. Not really safe, the way she would be with professionals, people who knew what they were doing, how to handle her weight and keep an eye on her movements. If she fell down, or had some kind of attack, they would be there on the spot to lift and help her, to diagnose and fix her injuries. While in June's hands she might die waiting. Safety is something. You can give up a few things to be secure. Surely at Aggie's age that's not a bad bargain.

Then, too, Aggie has too much time on her hands. It's not healthy, having nothing to do all day but read and think and sometimes bake. There is about her occasionally a distressing sort of vagueness that suggests she could do with new interests.

In the place June is thinking of, there would be crafts and visitors and other old people, things going on, although it is admittedly difficult to picture Aggie bent over a heap of small tiles, making ceramic ashtrays for Christmas gifts, or crocheting bedspreads, and it is hard to imagine her willingly listening to visiting schoolchildren singing hymns or Christmas carols. She might argue with a roommate, and June might get calls from staff complaining of her language.

Aggie's the one who talks of the excitement of change, who preaches new experiences. She ought to leap at this.

June's heart leaps as she arrives home, late because she stopped to buy a plastic sheet (embarrassing to catch the sales clerk's curious glance). George's car is outside, and, stepping somewhat breathlessly through the door, she hears voices in the front room:

his and Aggie's. How long has he been here? How much has she missed?

He stands. "June, hello, I was just waiting until you got home." He is lanky and tall, and his hands, when they're not working, always look a little incoherent, confused by lack of purpose. Now he moves one as if to shake her hand and then withdraws it, as if that would be too formal.

"Sit down, June," Aggie suggests. "Have a cup of tea with us. I made cookies, too." That must be her idea of a challenge: proving competence with food. "We were just talking about who's going to run for mayor this year. I was telling George your father once thought of running for council."

"I know. You told me." June is unhappy to hear that she sounds abrupt, almost curt. In a campaign for the doctor's vote, Aggie is offering cookies, and June clipped words.

"Apparently he almost did," Aggie tells him. "He didn't discuss it with me, of course, but I heard. Likely he'd have won, too, but for some reason he decided against it. I suppose he didn't like to take the chance of losing, he hated to lose, and then I don't imagine I'd have been the ideal candidate's wife."

"But tell me," June interrupts, addressing either or both of them, "have you figured out what's wrong?"

Aggie looks amused by the bluntness, George distressed. He smiles uncomfortably. "Not yet. And you mustn't tell anyone I've made a house call; I'd get drummed out of the medical profession.

"But seriously, we've gotten quite a few things done today—blood pressure, an internal, and I've got some blood samples. Which reminds me I can't stay much longer, I'll have to get them to the lab. Now, if things get worse, or if these tests show any abnormalities, we'll maybe have to check you into hospital for a day or so, Aggie, for X-rays and EEGs and so forth. Nothing strenuous, but I'd like to do as much as we can outside of hospital. Aggie tells me"—he smiles at June—"she'd prefer not to break her record of never being in a hospital except to visit somebody. And I'd prefer to avoid putting that sort of stress on her anyway. But we'll have to see how things go."

This, June thinks, is much too vague and unsatisfactory, hardly a step in any direction, much less the right one.

"But as far as you can tell," Aggie interjects, "I don't have some awful disease." She grins. "I'm like June, you know—I'd like to get it cleared up, although for different reasons. Mine are quite immediate. You can't imagine how rank it is, waking up in a cold, wet bed.''

Well, you have to admire her, she doesn't back off. She runs right at a problem, even a shameful one. It's like a teenager with acne going around pointing at his pimples and saying, "Look at that, boy, isn't that something awful? I can't wait till I grow out of it.''

"But what can we do in the meantime, if it keeps on happening?'' June doesn't want it forgotten, what the issue is here. "We can't just keep on this way.''

"Don't borrow trouble, June,'' Aggie says. So smug she is, so settled, in her big broken chair, with her cup of tea and her plate of cookies.

"We have trouble, Mother, there's no borrowing about it. Something has to be done.''

"Tests are something.'' George, unhappily trapped, is now flinging his hands about as if batting crisis out of the room. He may deal with physical issues of life and death with reasonable skill and equanimity, but this sort of thing is more difficult. Like a policeman called to a domestic dispute, he's in the centre of old, unknown passions, right in the middle, where it's most dangerous.

It's a bit much, the two of them looking at her with what, in Aggie's case at any rate, must be a deliberate and studied, detached and academic interest; as if it were nothing to do with her. "Go ahead, June, say what's on your mind, then.''

"Well, what about me?'' But that isn't what she meant to say, nor is it the tone she intended. The words have twisted out bitter and sad, too much a plea and too little a statement, but now she can't change or stop. "It's too hard. I can't do everything, and then something like this happens.'' She could weep, except that she never would, in front of Aggie.

In her grey skirt and yellow blouse and charcoal cardigan, in the black low-heeled shoes she wears for comfort, standing all day as she does, she takes a step toward them, threatening or appealing, and then steps back, with no threat or appeal to make.

They should never have let it come to this.

But her own skin is yellowing like old paper. It has become fine and wrinkled. There are purple veins that stand out in her legs. Even in these shoes, her feet hurt at the end of a day, and her hair has turned grey and lacks life. She is aging, she is almost old.

"Listen,'' she says, although she may mean to say "Look''.

"I can't go on teaching and looking after the house and worrying about Mother. It's awful, coming home and wondering if she's been all right. And I don't weigh half what she does, but I have to help her out of bed, and then if anything happened, I'd never be able to lift her. I'm just not young any more, and I'm not strong enough. What am I supposed to do?"

There's silence for a moment as they look at her. What do they see? Someone pitiable?

Not Aggie. "I've never known what you were supposed to do, June," she says. "You're the expert on that. You're the one who always knows what everybody's supposed to do."

George, however—maybe drawn by June's passion?—says, "I can see it must be hard for you. But there must be a solution that would suit you both."

Oh naive, hopeful, cowardly young man. "That would be a first," Aggie says.

"Well, there are homemakers who come in, or the VON. I could probably arrange for somebody, say once or twice a week, even if it's just to keep an eye."

"Look, this is my home," Aggie objects firmly. "I don't want to be knee-deep in strangers. Let's get this straight. I do understand it's hard for June, I do realize she's getting on, and I know I'm not easy to deal with. After all, I'm the one who carries this," gesturing across her body, "all the time. I know better than anyone how heavy I am. But I'm hardly helpless, and I'm not about to leave my home. You'll get it eventually, June, but I do feel you might wait."

"Now, now," George says, his hands patting the air, tamping something down that insists on bobbing up again, "there's no need, not until we know just what's wrong. And then I'm sure things can be worked out, it just takes some giving on both sides."

"That's your only advice?" June asks, the sharpness of her tone, she realizes as soon as the words are out, offsetting her advantage.

"Well, I've made a suggestion or two to Aggie. I've got to go now. You two talk things over, and if I can do anything by way of arranging a homemaker or whatever, just let me know. And I'll let you know, of course, if we need to do any more tests."

Aggie starts in as soon as he's left. "Well, June, it seems you do have things to say for yourself. I must say, you express yourself quite plainly when you put your mind to it."

"We have to do something. You must see that. And anything could happen. Anything."

"My dear girl, I've been telling you that for years. Why pick now to believe me?"

There is no nodding white-haired gentleness in Aggie now, with her little pig-eyes snapping out from the pouches of flesh. The bigger she gets, the smaller her features seem. Now she looks like one of those gingerbread cookies she used to make, just raisins set in for eyes.

"Look, June, it's my risk after all. It's my death you seem to be worrying about. And as I said before, it's my house. You may stay or go as you please, but I stay."

But this house is in June's blood. This is the one place in the world she belongs. Here is where her father came through the door at night, and where he told her stories and read to her. Here is where she later felt his spirit hovering. She still has some idea of at least a part of him here, watching out for her. The one time she did leave, she found herself exposed, unsafe. She distinctly remembers her mother saying, years ago, "I hate this goddamned house." That was when June's father was alive, so maybe she wasn't talking exactly about the house. But June loves this place, the home of her earliest, best self.

"So, June, what's it to you if I'm willing to take the chance that if I stand up, I might fall down, or if I try to move too fast my heart will stop? I don't see you'd have to actually *do* very much if you came home and found me dead on the floor. Make a couple of phone calls, maybe. But then you could step right over me and make yourself a cup of tea and be out of the room in no time, and by the time you looked again I'd be gone. One minute I'd be there, dead as a doornail, and the next minute you'd be free to do whatever it is you think you want to do. Think of it as a kind of climax: not a moment you'd want to miss, surely."

How can she make jokes about death, or even speak of it so lightly?

"Be serious, Mother. We have to do something. I think," and here is inspiration, "even Frances would agree with me there."

It seems to work. For once, Aggie is short of words, a little shrunken. Had she not thought of that, of Frances finding out? Had she not considered her admiring granddaughter knowing she has accidents in her bed at night?

"That's good, June," she nods finally. "That wasn't nice, but you're definitely improving."

"Well, you know, at least we should go look at the place."

June's error; Aggie is alert and upright again. "What place?"

"You know."

"But say the words. How do you think you can get me there, if you can't even say the words?"

It is extraordinarily, surprisingly difficult. Even in her own mind, June's hardly used them. She can see the place, so why say it? How difficult do things have to be? "I think, Mother," she says carefully, "that we ought to both go and have a look at the nursing home." There.

"I see." Aggie pauses. "Well, you may. It might be good for you to see what you're talking about, but I never like going into places I might not get out of. Who knows, you might not bring me home. They might not let me out. Anyway, I don't have time to waste."

"An hour, Mother. What's an hour?"

"At my age, maybe all the time there is."

Well, why doesn't she have the grace to die, then? Soon June herself will be old, and when exactly is she supposed to have a life? Time never seemed so precious until the last few days, when she could begin to see it as her own. And it's slipping away, just— slipping. Her whole life seems to have seeped away, without her noticing particularly.

"You do realize," Aggie says, "that if I weren't here, you'd miss me." What on earth is she talking about? Miss all this? Miss a whole lifetime of memories, the past that Aggie is, just sitting there? It's like being a perpetual child, living with your mother, it's like always being dragged back, a quicksand of the past. Where's the future in it?

This greedy old woman eats up a life the same way she consumes a pie.

"What would you do with all those hours you spend just being mad at me, if I weren't around?" Aggie asks.

"Oh, I'd find something." Intending to sound airy, June hears that the words have come out grim. In the first year or so of Aggie's absence, she might just sleep. She might wake up to find, like Sleeping Beauty, that everything was changed.

They sit in silence for a few moments. Then, "Tell me," Aggie says in the bland voice that warns of a trick question, "what do you think death is, anyway? Do you ever wonder what it's like?"

Well, that's one of the benefits of faith: that one knows. Death is a passing, painful or peaceful, to a different world, where one is either punished or rewarded, with eternal pain or eternal bliss. That's what one knows, with faith, although what either eternal pain or eternal bliss may feel like remains a divine mystery.

"I think," Aggie continues, "that you just die. Then eventually you turn back into soil. Remember when Frances came home from summer camp, that song she'd picked up? 'The worms crawl in, the worms crawl out, the worms play pinochle on your snout,' remember that? Maybe after all the most important thing is eating right, so you turn into good soil. Do you think?"

"I think you shouldn't make jokes. Also, it would be a lot easier if you had faith."

"But of course it would be easier. Doesn't that make you suspicious? It's like following a recipe: a cup of sugar and three tablespoons of old clothes for the Salvation Army, a quarter-pound of butter and a cup of prayer.

"You know, June, when I was little, learning to cook, I had to follow recipes exactly to get anything to turn out, and I used to watch my mother slap pies together any old way and they'd be so much better than mine. Because the ingredients came so naturally to her she didn't really have to pay attention—a lump of this and a dash of that, while I had to measure so carefully. But finally it got to seem natural to me, too, and I didn't have to measure either.

"But you, you have all those rules like a recipe, and you never get comfortable enough to forget about them. You always have to keep checking. I'd never have been any kind of cook if I'd needed to look up how much sugar a banana cake needs every time I went to make one. I just *knew*. Why don't your rules come naturally to you like that, after all these years?"

"Oh, Mother, leave me alone. Why do you have to think about food all the time?"

But of course faith *is* a recipe. It's not a bit like cooking, though. Even June can make a cake or a pie fairly well by eye, but if there's a little too much flour or sugar, or not enough, it's not particularly important. There's a range of acceptable taste. Faith is different. It's one thing or the other, good or bad, enough or not enough. If a cake turns out badly, you can throw it out, but no one takes such a risk with eternal life.

June does have the feeling, though, that her faith these days is falling short. There are flaws in her motives: a lack of generosity, a shortage of will to cast away her own life, in the manner of martyrs.

The good thing, the best thing, is not to pray for herself, but for Aggie, for a revelation, a redeeming moment for her. No doubt it is wicked to resent any intrusion by Aggie into her prayers. Also to resent the possibility that He might in fact hear her, and provide Aggie with salvation. What would have been the point then of all June's efforts, her scrutiny of the rules, if an old sinner like Aggie could win grace at a snap of divine fingers?

Anyway, at the moment there are chores to be done. She leaves Aggie sitting downstairs while she tackles the plastic sheet. It crackles as she fixes it around Aggie's mattress. She supposes it will soften, get broken in one way or another, but meanwhile Aggie is going to find it irritating.

Later, over supper, she looks across the table, watching Aggie's head bent over her plate, cleaning up the first course quickly, eager for dessert. If she could have chosen, who would she have picked as a mother? Not too many people spring to mind as possibilities.

Not her aunts. The members of Aggie's family always struck June as loud and alien. Aggie's favorite, on the rare occasions when they visited that farm, seemed to be her younger sister, Edith, but June could never see anything special about her. To her they were all, men and women, too brawny for comfort, although in time her own mother became easily the brawniest of them all, and even that farm family seemed a bit taken aback by what she turned into.

The men, Aggie's brothers, were big and rough, and in the evenings leaned back on their wooden kitchen chairs, tilting them onto two legs, and laughed and sometimes sang old Scottish songs, bellowing out the words, or crooning them. Occasionally a work-roughened hand would ruffle June's fine blonde hair, but she was timid and didn't interest them much. Sometimes when they sang the Scottish tunes, she saw tears in their eyes. "Road to the Isles", she remembers. She didn't see why they would feel sad, especially when none of them had ever been to Scotland.

The women would cook and serve and eat, and after June had gone to bed in the small dark room that had once belonged to the sisters, she'd hear them talking below in the kitchen. There was a stovepipe hole in the floor of the bedroom, and up through it floated odd words, and occasionally laughter.

There was always far too much food there, heavy and bloating. During the day, June's cousins would race through the fields. They dared her to leap the creek, but she shied like a horse at the idea of landing in the cold rushing water with the nasty sharp pebbles beneath. She couldn't possibly climb those ladders into the hay mows, going straight up and so high, with round wooden rungs that a foot could so easily slip on. Nor did she like rolling in the straw; bits of it got into her hair and down her neck, and she'd be forever picking it out, while it scratched. She always went home injured in some small way.

On the other side, on the other hand, was a family she never met, but with whom she feels perfectly familiar. Her father's parents, about whom he told stories and of whom he showed pictures, lived in England, just outside London, and there he had left them to come here to a hard, raw country, where somehow he found her hard, raw mother. Then there was neither time nor money to go back even for a visit, and he never saw them again, and June never saw them at all.

But there is something peaceful just about the idea of them. Partly it's England, old and experienced, with a certain overview, a perspective of centuries of making and observing history, so that June feels the country itself must move more slowly and gracefully.

Also, there's a picture of his mother that June's father kept on his bedside table, and that is now on June's own bureau. It shows her standing in the rose trellis of a garden, with her hand resting lightly on a bloom. It's just the way she would have touched June, if that had been possible: lightly and with affection. And that's how her voice would have sounded, too, speaking to her only grandchild.

What her father described of the three of them remains June's picture of the ideal English life: a little cottage, with a little green property, and roses, dozens of roses. His mother won prizes with them. He recommended her to June as an example she might follow. "She's a lady," he always said, "a real lady." Dainty, and wearing white gloves, June imagined.

June pictured her father: a sweet little boy in the gardens, his mother near by, squatting, working in the earth around the roses, clipping, weeding. They would talk gaily back and forth, quietly, no irritation in their voices. He'd be wearing short pants and a white blouse, maybe knee socks, and his fine blond hair would be a little long, with a wavy bit slipping over his forehead. His mother would be wearing a long white dress with a matching broad-brimmed hat, a picture hat. This is the picture June has in her head, although she knows, of course, that no one tends roses in a long white dress.

Of her grandfather, the picture is less clear. He was a haber-dasher's clerk who went off each morning to work and returned home at night, as fathers do. "She's the one who sacrificed so that I could get an education," June's father said. "She scrimped and saved and did without things, clothes and travel, she always said she'd like to see the continent, but it all went for me and my ed-ucation." They must have loved each other very much, to have given up such a lot.

"She was also the one who said I should leave, start over in a new country and make something of myself," he told her. "It was hard." Well, June could hear how hard it must have been. Why was it for her he saved his stories and not for her mother, who was, after all, a grown-up and his wife?

But he was teaching June what is important: duty and a sense of sacrifice. He was passing on a legacy of courage, the way other families pass on silver spoons and cake plates.

Every month her grandmother wrote, her letters in neat round handwriting on fragile lilac paper. They spoke of weather, and the deaths, births, and marriages of people entirely unknown to June. It was puzzling, how a letter might complain of rain while here the snow was deep, and so her father taught her about climates and how different they were in different parts of the world. It made them seem even farther away, not even sky a common factor.

What would he have written about in his letters home? Probably his work, the weather, and June. She can't imagine what he might have told them about her mother.

He sent them photographs of June, and her grandmother wrote back saying what a lovely little girl she was, and how they longed to see her. She longed to see them, too. She imagined herself there, in an entirely different life. There would be tea in the afternoons and quiet times in the garden, and voices would be soft and fond.

Instead, they were all separated and sad. She pictured that cou-ple, her grandparents, in their garden in the evenings, greying and alone, speaking of their much-loved son so far away. "Oh, they must miss you," she said, and cried a little, and her father hugged her. "You have a tender heart, you're like your grandmother that way. She could never stand things to be hurt. She'd never kill anything, except for bugs, and getting rid of moles in the garden."

Even a child could tell that her own mother lacked certain of these qualities: that she was not a person with a tender heart, and had no real gift for sadness, regret, or sacrifice.

June would still like to go and see where her father grew up, visit his school and the house where the three of them lived together, walk through the tended gardens, touching the roses her grandmother grew with such care. That might be something she could do with freedom.

But they've been dead for so long, and by now everything must be changed and gone. It will all be in different hands.

And right now there are dishes to be done, and another evening just the same. She sighs, and stands, and says to Aggie, "I bought a plastic sheet today. I've put it on your bed." She would have liked to be the kind of person her grandmother was, but circumstances have not, after all, permitted her to be gentle and tend roses.

7

Aggie wasn't entirely teasing when she told June she doesn't have hours to spare. So it is frustrating and infuriating to have gone through an entire day of wretchedness. Beginning with damp sheets, proceeding through maundering memories of a wedding and high hopes, then George's visit and the unpleasantness with June—she does not have time to waste this way. She would like to be achieving grace, but finds herself stuck dealing instead with mere discomfort.

Fed up with the past and anticipating George, she at least hauled herself to the kitchen to bake. Still, she let George know when he turned up that he should have called first. It's the sort of thing you have to put a stop to right away, this insulting business of being bypassed, ignored; something that can happen too easily if a person's old or infirm in some way. People start talking over your head, making arrangements, not consulting or asking, as if you're a thing to be shifted about, organized behind your back. You have to put your foot down firmly.

"I'm sorry, Aggie, you're right." She likes someone who can admit he's wrong.

"Never mind. Just don't do it again."

"Fresh cookies! Can I have one? Then I guess we should have a little chat."

A chat is one way of putting it. Settled in the front room, he begins an interrogation of sorts. At least it's George, and not a stranger. She remembers the first time she went to him, after her old doctor, the one who delivered June and later Frances, died. "I guess your husband's been gone quite a while, hasn't he?'' he'd asked, and she'd laughed.

"Gone? My husband was gone when he was alive. If you mean dead, yes, he's been dead for years." As she was leaving that first time, George told her, "You're an interesting woman, you know. My most interesting patient, I think."

She was pleased, proud to be interesting. It made her trust him more, and assume his support and possibly even his affection. So now it's odd to be wondering what side he may come down on.

"This business, these accidents," he begins, "how often have they happened?"

"Just twice." Once was huge and appalling; twice is terrible, but perhaps can be made to sound trivial.

"Do you remember anything about it? Did it happen in your sleep, or were you aware at all?"

Oh dear. She takes a deep breath. "The first time, I remembered the next day that I'd had this thought that I was saving June and me both a lot of trouble. Not waking her, you see, to get me up. I can't explain that at all. It was just being stupid in the middle of the night, you know how fuzzy things are then. I remember when I was little, dreaming I was falling and then waking with a thump because I'd rolled out of bed. I think it must have been something like that."

"Is that what happened the second time, too?"

"No." This is more difficult. "No, I don't remember a thing."

"Mmhmm," and he frowns. It's the sort of "mmhmm" she sometimes used with the teacher when he was explaining something about an event they had to go to, or people they had to entertain; or when June was telling her some event from school. That vague, busy-with-my-own-thoughts mmhmm.

"Do you have any ideas, George?"

"Not yet, but I'd like to check you out as thoroughly as I can today. The usual sorts of things, blood pressure and so forth, and some samples as well."

It turns out he means both urine and blood samples. The first requires her to pee into a little jar he pulls from his bag. How awkward it is, in the bathroom, squatting over the thing, unable to see where she's holding it, doing it all by touch and missing quite a bit, and keeping her balance, too.

"What next?" she asks brightly, handing it over.

"Do you have something else you could slip into that would make things easier? Or a sheet, could you wrap yourself in a sheet?"

"What on earth are you planning to do?"

"For one thing, an internal. It's the same as in my office, except it saves you the trouble of coming in."

It's quite a struggle, getting out of her dress on her own. At one point she traps herself inside it, stuck with her arms up, pulling, with it wrapped around her head. A bit terrifying, until she gets free.

The moment of panic over, she wedges her arms under the straps of her brassiere, pulling the hooks around to the front to get it undone. She has to sit on the side of her bed to roll off her panties and stockings.

She pulls a spare white sheet around herself, although it seems to gape somewhat at the back. She can feel, sitting on the edge of the bed, air on the flesh there. It makes her uneasy, as if she's open for anything: a knife coming up behind.

Funny, that. When did she go off nakedness? There was a time when she felt most invulnerable in her own skin, and now it doesn't seem enough.

George, with his stethoscope, is leaning over her, listening, prodding, not speaking. She looks at her thighs spreading the sheet wide, and wiggles her toes, all gnarled—how did her toes get so old, without her noticing?

Oh, it's a disgusting old body, sure enough. June keeps saying, "For heaven's sake, Mother, have you no pride? Don't you care?"

She might have once, but that was a good long time ago. Regarding her body as flesh, she can certainly see it is unattractive; quite gross, in fact. But looking at it from the inside, as its inhabitant, she finds it pleasing and comforting, cosy, like a warm house. There is a sharp Aggie like a needle safely embedded inside this rippling pincushion, and there is an imposing Aggie whose bulk is perfectly expressive.

And isn't that thought pretty fancy for somebody who, when it comes down to it, just eats too much and weighs too much? She starts to laugh, and George straightens, removes the stethoscope. "Am I tickling?"

"No, just a private joke."

Is that a doubtful or suspicious glance? Does he find it very odd, a patient laughing at her own thoughts?

Examining her body, does George agree with June that, after all, it is too much to manage? He may also find it repulsive, but then, he's seen it before, and anyway, what need does she have to impress a young man with her eighty-year-old flesh?

"Your body is a temple," June likes to say, and so it is in a way, but more of a monument, really.

His hands on her body are impersonal, as undesiring as the teacher's ever were. But more intent. Also, he has more flesh to probe than the teacher did.

The internal is an interesting procedure. Not arousing, naturally, but speculative: how might this sort of thing have felt, in other circumstances?

"Am I hurting you?"

"No." Her eyes are closed; more interesting to feel than to see.

A nudge in one direction, a shifting in another. What does George feel? Mere hidden bits of body, she supposes, a case in which hands do the work of the eyes. What he touches must mean something to him, but to her it's vague and far away.

Surely she had more feeling down there once? Lucky Frances, who says, "I'm sorry, Grandma, I don't really know how to describe it. It's kind of a heat that all gets concentrated in one place and everything's just there. And then it fades."

And Frances makes her living with words? Still, Aggie remembers dreams of young men coming to her bed.

"I can't find," George says, pulling away, "anything wrong there." He strips off the glove and puts it in a plastic bag, which he tosses into his medical bag. She pushes the sheet back down over her thighs. Oh, those thighs! Tree stumps her father might have needed a team of horses for, to haul out of the earth. And her poor white wrinkled overburdened feet sticking out, all flat and for some reason sad.

"Now, I think, some blood samples." She does not look away as the syringe draws her blood into a tube.

"You seem to have brought the full kit with you, George."

"Well"—he smiles briefly, glancing up—"I thought it would save you some trouble."

"More?"

"Just a couple. Temperature and reflexes." He begins tapping at her knees.

"You'll have to hammer harder than that for me to feel very much."

Finished, he stands and packs his bag. "Can you get yourself dressed? I'll wait downstairs, if you can manage."

What is going to come of this? She is not used to being frightened. To lose control, to no longer be able to say, Now I shall stand, I want to go here, or there, eat this or that, watch such and such a program, or turn the TV off and read this book—to face losing that is a fear. Age and bulk, those are restricting enough. She can no longer say, "I'd like to run down the road," or even "I feel like getting out of bed," and then do it. But still, she has her preferences and routines.

And what would she do for food, living elsewhere? Who would offer plates of cookies and slices of cake throughout the day? She might go mad with the lust for sugar. Forbidden fruit, or, in her case, forbidden tarts and muffins and cakes. If there were a reward for getting old, it ought to be to have no cravings. Surely that's not much: to have small desires filled.

Well, it's all fear. And the fear, finally, is of dying, loss of control carried to the extreme, in an unchosen, inadvertent, unwilling moment of a whole life whirling away. So that what may happen is a startled, stubborn expression some undertaker has to work at, to mold into something more peaceful and accepting.

Should she bother putting her stockings back on? No point, really, for George. Except to prove she can. Sighing, she sits on the bed and begins to pull them up. So difficult, trying to reach her feet.

Speaking of undertakers, she ought to write down and make clear to June just what she has in mind, so there's no misunderstanding. She has no wish to have people staring. She's had quite enough of that, just walking down the street. A closed coffin and incineration will be fine. She would give away her organs to the needy, but they'd hardly be worth salvaging. Also, she doesn't want some minister, particularly of June's choice, speaking sanctimonious, irrelevant words over her. It would be nice if a few people wept. Probably she can count on Frances for that. June may shed some tears, but for more equivocal reasons.

Well, it's human enough to want to be remembered, isn't it? But she won't be, not past June and Frances. So, then, something eye-catching in the way of a headstone, to make people think, "I wonder who she was, then?" Something arresting and succinct, with a little punch to it?

Something like,

IN THE WRONG PLACE
AT THE WRONG TIME
WITH THE WRONG PEOPLE

Of course, not everyone would see that as her final joke, her last laugh.

She is chuckling as she edges down the stairs, holding the banister firmly. Too late, she sees George below, watching her. He must think she spends all her time alone heaving with lunatic amusement.

"I was just making up tombstones," she explains. "I always think the ones with just names and dates are so dull, don't you?"

This does not seem to unwrinkle his little frown. Really, she must pull herself together. There are more ways than peeing the bed to dig a hole for yourself, it seems.

"So then," she begins firmly in the front room, when they've gotten their tea and more cookies, "what do you think?"

"Your blood pressure's a bit high, not bad considering your weight, but we'll give you something for it. I'll get the samples to the lab, and we should have the results in a few days, if there isn't too much of a backlog. If something does show up, we may want to do more, because we do want to be sure about things, don't we?"

"Speaking for myself," she says drily, "certainly *I* do." George, it occurs to her, may be losing his appeal. Speaking to her as we, as if she were some other, more malleable and meek old person. She bets a nursing home would be just like that, all the we's and dear's, condescension from the mouths of babes.

"At this point," he goes on, not noticing, "I only have a couple of suggestions. The practical one is, don't have anything to eat or drink after, say, eight o'clock at night. That ought to help. Can you manage that?"

"I expect so. Although, you know, I'm not used to being hungry."

He smiles. "No, I don't imagine you are." It is disquieting to expect a comradely grin and get a professional smile.

"The other suggestion is a bit more vague, and I don't know if it'll help. But, you know, it's an interesting thing about the mind, the way it sets up patterns. Usually that's good, it's how we learn things like typing or playing the piano, or a lot of surgery for that matter: doing the same movements over and over until the brain snaps into place and follows the right routes without your having to think. Unfortunately, it works the other way, too, I guess what we call bad habits. You do something—unfortunate—and that sets you up for a pattern, so it happens more easily a second time."

"Well, that's cheerful. What do I do, stay awake all night?"

"No, of course not, but maybe if you concentrate when you're awake on not having it happen when you're asleep, it'll help. Somebody like you, with a sharp mind, it might work. Anyway, something may show up in the tests that's perfectly simple to fix and we'll have you right back as if none of this had happened."

He credits her, and also June, it seems, with the quality of forgetting.

And now June pops glinting through the door, all hope and excitement. How depressing, that giving life is not just a matter of giving birth. Later comes this liveliness of June's, emerging from Aggie's decay.

But Aggie is no saint, to die on behalf of someone else. She tells June later, when George is gone, "You'll have to save yourself, you know."

June looks at her blankly. "What?"

"Never mind." Stupid, speaking thoughts randomly like that. Maybe she really is losing her marbles. To redeem herself, she launches an argument about nursing homes, throwing in death as a bonus, and feels she acquits herself reasonably well.

"Concentrate," George said, and so tonight in bed she tries. But her body, her comfort and her friend, has turned treacherous and mysterious, rebellious and strange. She saw her own blood today. If more tests are needed, she will go to hospital, where her insides will show up in pictures. She is used to thinking of her body from the outside. Inside, the parts are just supposed to work; or, if they're not working, to make themselves known with pains or little aches. Muscles tighten and weaken with age, and bones become brittle, but what happens to organs? She pictures them losing their healthy pinkness, turning grey like liver left out in the sun. Or a brown heart, like the ones she used to stuff with breadcrumbs and onions and spices for supper.

Events are turned inside out. Her body is not quite listening to her any more. Even June may not be listening to her any more. It would be nice to still have the gift of crying. She hasn't cried for years: the day Frances left for university, and she had to turn back inside alone. And before that, when? Funerals of family, the grief of missing particular people. Now, when she should cry for herself, she lacks the required tenderness.

Self-pity, she thinks impatiently. Nothing is more irritating than self-pity. Irritation, although lacking the high healthy calibre of anger, is something. Some passion, keeping the heart beating.

And, after all, isn't it amusing that she, the advocate of change, is now suffering from an overdose? Not just the accidents, bad enough; but also the alteration in the power balance here. And heaven knows it's dangerous. Someone like June, unused to power, is likely to mishandle it. Dictatorships result. Well, you see it all the time on the news, in countries where revolutions occur. New leaders may come to power with the purest motives, the greatest will for the greatest good, and turn into murderers and torturers. The cruelty of the righteous is quite a thing. At least Aggie recognizes her own corruptions: greed, pride, and maybe, at one time, lust; she feels she understands them reasonably well. And she enjoys her greed, is proud of her pride, and can still be furious that her desire was dismissed. But June—June fails to see the dangers of her righteousness. In the classroom, Aggie has heard, she can be arbitrary, harsh. That's unfortunate enough for the children, but now Aggie also seems to be in the position of a pupil, in danger of being sent to the principal's office to be punished for a transgression.

There was a time when Aggie had in mind a daughter with gumption. Should she be pleased that June is showing some, although perhaps in a somewhat sly and underhanded form?

Maybe, like a disgruntled old sow, Aggie should have rolled over on her unsatisfactory offspring at birth.

Frances had an abortion six years ago, telling Aggie about it, although not, of course, June. "There's no way I could raise a baby on my own," she said. "Maybe some day, but not now. And it isn't as if I'd marry the guy the way people used to. He's nice enough, I like him all right, but we'd have been terrible, married."

She said it was a hard decision and no doubt it was, but Aggie is sometimes amazed at Frances's confidence in her choices. But it is also her willingness to experience, and her confidence, that Aggie is so proud of.

Frances felt stupid, she said, for having gotten caught, especially at her age. Stupid! In Aggie's day, girls were banished, they did not get off just being stupid.

"If only" is a foolish game, and regrets are obviously futile. But Aggie caught herself wondering at the time: if she'd known, would she have had June?

What if she hadn't?

What a monstrous confession of failure that must be, to wonder what other life there might have been without her.

But of course she would have had her. Even after all these decades of disunity, it appears they still have continuing desires for transformations. Also it is always interesting, if puzzling, trying to track June's emotions, which jerk about like wound-up toy soldiers, little stick figures making their abrupt and rigid turns.

If it is true that June would miss her, Aggie must admit that the reverse is also the case. Who else, when it comes down to it, is there to care about, if not care for?

Frances, of course, but she's three hundred miles away, writing for a magazine, travelling here and there, and doesn't often get home. Only June is actually on hand.

And surely if Aggie can say it was her own time and place that withheld possibilities, the same can be said for June? She may only have been too close to Aggie's time, the twenty-one years between them not long enough. Although it also seems that in any time, June would close choices around her; that it would make no difference when she had been born: she would be determined to make her world small.

The kind of daughter Aggie had in mind would not be sneaking around making doctor's appointments and buying plastic sheets. She certainly wouldn't have been the sort of daughter to try to pray away her rage. The kind of daughter Aggie had in mind would have turned on her long ago, hands on sturdy hips, and said, "Oh, for God's sake, Mother, pull yourself together." She would have said, "Look, I'm grateful to you for raising me but I'm on my own now, and so are you." She would have said, "Oh, go to hell with your complaints and your greed and your dying."

Aggie has to laugh: such a strange wish for a mother to have, a daughter who could say, "Oh, go to hell." Other dying mothers must wish to hear quite different words from sad-eyed daughters.

Her failures seem to have been the crucial domestic ones. It's with those closest that there has been this distance. Not just June, but the teacher, too.

Not her fault with either of them. But maybe after all this time she could say not his either. And certainly not June's, locked between them. How was he, after all, to know that Aggie had looked curiously at his shoulders and his lips, and that at night before they married, she pictured him coming to her bed? That she might have been capable of lust, that old-fashioned word, forbidden wantonness?

Just as she had no way to know that when he asked her to be his wife, his vision was not of companionable evenings in the kitchen and rosy children sleeping upstairs and poems shared and learned and embraces of some tenderness. What he must have had in mind was someone tractable and pretty, who could be taught to speak correctly and pour tea and smile at people graciously. He wanted a wife for the teacher, not necessarily for himself. He talked about rules of behavior, but in connection with appearances in public. He never told her the rules he thought should apply between the two of them.

It's not such a tragedy, as tragedies go. To spend unhappily a decade of what has turned out to be quite a long life is nothing compared with starvation and war, or having a child grow up to be a murderer, a thief, a rapist. Her heart has never actually been broken, even if such a thing is possible.

The pictures he brought with him showed a chubby little boy. There was something else, maybe nothing to do with her, that caused him to dry and shrivel.

Although he loved June, there's no denying that. There's no telling, Aggie supposes, where love may pop out unexpectedly, like a random tulip from a misplaced bulb.

It seemed to her that something peculiar began to come over him as soon as they were married. That being married was something like a suit he put on, with a certain attention to cut and appearance, but without thought to how it fit. He knew how he wanted them to look together, but had no knack for being with her with no one watching.

They spent their wedding night at an inn along the road to their new home. She has been pleased to see, travelling back in later years, that it has been demolished for a road-widening project, and their room has made way for the gravelled east-bound shoulder. They lay for a few minutes in darkness and silence. She heard him sigh, once quietly, a second time with something like determination, and then he was fumbling about, doing things with his body and with hers, and instead of the warmth she might have expected there was, first, a quite sharp pain, and then a surprising sense of foolishness. In the darkness, he felt like a silly stranger awkwardly doing a peculiar thing. His breathing changed, and there seemed to be a frog in his throat, and drops of his sweat fell onto her body. She felt him tense and shudder, and that was that.

"There," he said, as if he'd finished marking a set of examinations. And, "Are you all right then?"

Was that what the fuss was all about, what her mother had tried to tell her? "Is that it?" she asked, which of course was a mistake, but she said it without thinking.

He was, naturally enough, offended. "What did you expect?"

"I don't know. It's just, it doesn't take very long, does it?"

"You'd hardly expect it to, would you?"

So much for a communion of silence. "I don't know. I don't know anything about it."

"I know." He patted her hand. "You're a good girl." The idea seemed to please him. He turned away and a few minutes later his breathing was deepening into a snore.

She, however, lay feeling the drops of his perspiration drying on her body, confused and a little offended herself. Heat was one thing, but warmth might have been nice. And of course she was good—how could she have been otherwise?—but what did he think that meant? That she was just another mattress lying there?

But no doubt she had it all wrong. Probably also she was over-tired and tense, and that always made her cranky. She only needed a good night's sleep. And perhaps a child. Had her mother not promised her happiness in a child? But how did something so significant result from a small, quick, and inexplicable event in the darkness? Surely there ought to be more, something flashing in the night.

She could feel dampness seeping out onto the sheets. Would this be blood, or what? It was unfair to be annoyed that he slept so easily. Naturally he would be worn out after such a long day and then all that up and down, not easy for a man who wasn't strong. Compared with him, she hadn't been expected to do much today, really, except be in certain places at certain times.

When she woke in the morning he was already out of bed and dressed. In the light, he was a familiar figure once more, although the circumstances were awkwardly intimate and she was at somewhat of a disadvantage, still lying there in bed. Maybe next time, she thought, they could leave a light on, so that it wouldn't feel like a stranger.

"I'll go down and get the horse hitched," he said. It seemed tactful of him to let her get up in private. "You should hurry, we have a long way to go today."

They planned to be in their new home by nightfall. Here was the first day of being married, and the sun was shining and who knew what would happen? Here was her new life. Last night was dim, although she was a little sore down there.

There was evidence on the sheet: a little blood, and something else as well, dried and stiff. Embarrassing, that someone cleaning up after them would know. But he was in a hurry, waiting, and she had to wash and dress and get a move on, although there was a kind of gumminess about her body that she wanted to clean away. The best she could do was pull the top sheet and a blanket over the marks. Whoever cleaned the room would trace them to her, but she would be long gone by then.

At breakfast when he spoke, he didn't seem exactly to be look-ing at her—more at her shoulder, or her chin, or off to one side. Also, his face had taken on an unusual redness. Did last night have some significance for him that she had missed, an exposure that in daylight embarrassed him? In that case, he wouldn't be wanting lights left on.

"Are you ready?" he asked, standing. "Be sure and wear a hat, we'll be out in the sun all day. I'll get the cases loaded."

It was a scorcher, heavy with humidity, not even a breeze, and the sun beating down. The horse could not be hurried on a day like this. Having to just sit, nowhere to move, felt odd and inactive.

His knuckles, as he held the reins, seemed particularly tight, and he didn't speak. But maybe he was only worried about the horse, not that it was spirited at the best of times. She, more accustomed to animals, might have been better to do the driving.

"Is something the matter?" she asked finally, timidly, after nothing had been said for really an uncomfortable length of time.

"No, of course not." He glanced sideways at her. "Only we have to get so far today."

There were birds, occasionally dogs barking, and the sounds of the horse's hooves on the dry dirt road. She grew more restless. If words used precisely meant precise understanding, what did silence signify? Precise disinterest? Nothing to say? But they had years to-gether.

What had they talked about before, in the kitchen and on their walks? Poems, and what they saw. For the moment, she couldn't think of a single poem she had learned, and probably none of them would have been appropriate to the moment anyway. That only left what there was to be seen, which wasn't much and certainly nothing extraordinary. Still, she began to point things out: a farmer up on the roof of his barn, making repairs; horses that whinnied at theirs and approached the fence by the road; a cluster of cattle lying under the shade of the single maple tree in a field. "I always think," she said, "that they'd surely be cooler under the sun than all jammed together like that."

"You know," she said a while later, getting concerned, "we really ought to stop and water the horse and let him rest." Did he think an animal was a machine that could just keep going? Really, he didn't know much; about some things, anyway.

When they stopped, she jumped down. She was hot, but also bored. While he watered the horse, she stretched her arms and paced a few steps. That became a little hop and a skip, a bouncing up the road a little, just to get some feeling back.

"Aggie!" What a strange, sharp tone, and how red his face was when she turned, almost as flushed as the night he arrived on their doorstep in the storm—almost steaming. "What on earth do you think you're doing?"

She turned back, walking now. "Just getting some exercise. I'm not used to sitting." Closer, he looked actually angry. Whatever could he be angry about?

"Get back in this buggy." And heavens, didn't he sound like a teacher reprimanding an unruly pupil, though? "You're a married woman, not a child, you know. What do you think that looked like, a grown woman skipping up the road?"

"Who was looking?"

"I was, if that counts. But anyone could have, coming along."

"What's the matter with you?" Really, she was getting annoyed. "What difference does it make?"

"It makes a great deal of difference if people see the wife of a teacher romping in the street."

"Well, I'm hardly likely to romp in the street, am I?" Maybe it was because he was speaking to her as if she were a child that made her want to behave like one. She felt like sulking, or sticking out her tongue at him. And this was the first day of their marriage?

"I won't have you," he continued, "making a display of yourself."

Whatever happened to the timid young man who walked in her tracks because he was unsure of where the trapdoors were? Apparently they had moved from her territory to his.

"Why are you angry? I didn't do anything."

"I'm not angry. I'm just telling you."

Probably he expected her to say, "I'm sorry, you're right, I'd forgotten, I won't do it again." Something like that. She'd never said such words in her life, and didn't much feel like it now. However, there didn't seem to be anything else to say, so she sat back rigid against the seat, arms crossed against her chest. And on they went, except that she no longer troubled to point things out.

"Things may be difficult sometimes, dear," her mother had suggested. "Especially at the start, it may take a while to sort things out and get used to the way each other does things. It's hard work sometimes." That had sounded at the time like a warning, but now seemed encouraging: as if this small unpleasantness was something simple and trivial, a mere sorting out of customs. That would be all right, then. Just now, though, she didn't feel like talking.

There were subtle changes in the countryside: fewer stone fences and more split rail ones, weaving toward the road and back, all interlaced and, to her eye, a little flimsy. Here, the big problems must have been bush instead of rock. Still the same hard work, though. Some of the farmhouses were made of wood instead of stone. They too seemed less solid, less safe and warm.

The men in the fields looked the same, though: burly and hot. Sometimes they waved, strange passersby catching their attention. She waved back, ignoring his frown.

"It must be about time for lunch," he said, glancing upward, as if, she thought scornfully, he could tell time from the sun. "Where is it?"

"Where's what?"

"Lunch."

"What are you talking about?" Did he think she carried sandwiches in her suitcase? She was sitting right here beside him, where did he think she would have come by food?

"Didn't you ask at the inn for them to fix us something? What did you think we were going to do for food all day?"

"I don't know. I guess I thought we'd stop somewhere."

"But you knew we don't have time to spare; it'll be nearly dark by the time we get there anyway. Do I have to think of everything?"

"If you did think of it, you should have mentioned it. Or told them yourself. I didn't even know they'd make us a lunch."

"But that's what they do. We ate there this morning, what did you think?"

Oh, this was ridiculous. Hot and snappish and stupid. Who was the child here now? Who was petulant and sour? "We'll just have to go hungry then," he went on, and frowned.

What did he care? He never had much of an appetite.

There would be thousands of meals in the future, and she quite understood they would be her job. But not yet. "I guess we will, you're right," she agreed. At home they would be sitting down right about now to eat. There would be slabs of meat, a heap of mashed potatoes, and carrots or peas in bowls. And one of her mother's pies, waiting to be cut.

She was the one who was hungry, so why was he the one who was angry? A teacher of many parts, it seemed, busy unveiling his various characters.

Poor Aggie, poor teacher, poor horse, she thought. This was no way for married life to start, whatever her mother had said. Certainly her own feelings were not those of a new bride, adoring her new husband. A real bride would want to reach out and maybe just touch his arm. She would be talking with excitement about their future, as they travelled to the new home in which they expected to spend the rest of their lives.

The sun was so hot, it might be boiling her brains. It did almost feel as if her hair beneath the hat was sizzling. Glancing at him, she saw his jaw working. When he stopped again to let the horse drink and graze and rest, he sighed. She didn't bother getting out this time, just closed her eyes. She understood from his sigh that she was supposed to make the next sound, which was supposed to be an apology. Well, it would be a cold day in hell before she said she was sorry for anything.

Where had she learned that expression? And was it swearing? She didn't care. She wasn't exactly angry; maybe what her mother would call "in a rage". Whatever it was called for either strong words and violence, or silence and the best stillness she could manage.

The motion of the buggy as they started off again was gentle and, with her eyes closed, soothing. After a while she wasn't even very hungry any more. With her eyes closed, she wasn't really there at all.

She fell asleep with a little smile. It was an awful thing, she knew, but she was smiling because she knew that when he noticed, it would make him furious.

8

What a mean piece of mischief, that epitaph Aggie sprang on her at breakfast. What an insult, for one thing; for another, what a wound.

IN THE WRONG PLACE
AT THE WRONG TIME
WITH THE WRONG PEOPLE

"That should catch people's attention, don't you think?" Aggie laughed.

"If that's what you want, I'm sure it will."

It's certainly clear enough, even as a joke, which of course it must be; even Aggie wouldn't really want that carved in granite. Just blatantly saying, "You're not the daughter I wanted, you're not what I had in mind at all." Not that she hasn't always picked away at the various ways in which June fails to measure up: her standards, her body, her clothes, her views. Her very staying here caring for Aggie is, in her mother's eyes, a sign of failure. But to put it into words, as tersely as this joke epitaph, that's really cruel.

So today June will go to see the nursing home and seeing it, she will be able to picture Aggie here and there in it. It's Aggie's own fault, since she's the one who insisted June face the words. Now the words bring it closer. Of all people, Aggie ought to realize the power and authority of giving names to things.

God has tested her with Aggie, but it is not His fault. It wasn't her father's fault, either. Aggie can say all she wants, "For heaven's sake, June, you were just a child," but a child knows. Those children at school, they sniff out things that are perfectly true. That's why you have to be so careful with them.

What June remembers of Aggie from when she was a child is her footsteps: clicking swiftly around the house, often almost breaking into a run. Always busy, except when she sat down abruptly to read. Racing, racing, no time to spare, and what did she do that required such fine scheduling? Washing, ironing, mending, sewing, cooking, cleaning—unskilled work that anyone could do, not like real work, not like being a teacher. Wasting energy on things that would only be dirty and crumpled and torn and eaten by tomorrow.

And then later Aggie made a living making things to be consumed. For years, the lines in her hands were white with flour, and she smelled like perspiration and raisins. Everything she did contained its own destruction. Maybe that's why she has no faith in a permanent grace.

In the hall mirror June checks her hair, seams, and hem. It's not only a matter of dressing properly, but of self-respect. Standards. This is something she never managed to get through Frances's head: that keeping up appearances and standards is important. Never in all her life would June consider having breakfast in her housecoat, or checking the mailbox on the porch without combing her hair, or lounging in a chair with her feet up.

"For goodness' sake, Frances," she has said, seeing her daughter, in jeans and an old T-shirt, slouching on the couch, an ankle resting on a knee, like a man. Or with her legs sprawled, arms waving, a cigarette like an extra finger.

"Jesus, Mother, who cares how your legs are crossed as long as you're comfortable? Leave me alone."

Apart from self-respect, there is the matter of other people. Frances has been known to wear her bathing suit out in the front yard, and shorts downtown, shrugging, seeing nothing wrong with that. "I dress up when I work, Mother. Surely I don't have to bother here. Why can't I just be comfortable?"

What kind of person is comfortable looking like a tramp, June would like to ask, but never has. There are some things about Frances that it's better not to know. The word tramp is no longer in vogue; that Frances might be one is unthinkable, although sometimes June has wondered, watching her, what or who may have touched her. She does not give an impression of innocence. She says things like, "Never mind, Mother, I'd rather be a woman than a lady anyway."

Aggie's fault. Aggie who taught Frances she could do anything, had her climbing trees when she was a child, and itching to leave home when she grew up. "Get out and do things," Aggie advised, and never mind what June thought.

Did Aggie set out to achieve a granddaughter who thinks only of her own convenience, who refuses difficulties and makes frivolous choices? Probably. But some day Frances will crash, and what will her grandmother have to say to her then? Events even out. Or so June hopes.

Frances talks about freedom, but means only selfishness. Where would she have been, if June had aimed for freedom? They would have starved, the two of them. They would have been homeless. It's all very well for Frances, with her education and her work, her tearing around the country wearing jeans, but she judges from that perspective. She does not understand what was impossible for June. She may be in her thirties now, but she is still harsh and young that way.

June wonders what another life might have been like. There are religions, heathen ones, that offer the possibility of returning after death in other forms. Then a person could come back and try it differently, take another run at it, see it from a different point of view. Have a different mother, take a different husband, maybe bear a different daughter. One might come back unaware of consequences and lacking a sense of goodness, which in many ways might be a relief. On the other hand, there would be the terrible tedium of repetition. Imagine going through all the years of a life, and then having to do it all again.

Also, as June understands it, there is no guarantee in those faiths of a return in human form. Wouldn't it be just her luck to come back as an insect, living in a crack, waiting to be stepped on; or as a stray kitten, wet and cold and feeding out of garbage in the middle of the night? She might return as a baby bird, the weakest one, nudged out by bigger brothers and sisters, falling to earth and lying there helpless until the hungry stray kitten she might also be came along and made a meal.

Striding along the sidewalk, June suddenly sees herself from God's perspective, far away and looking down. To Him her life must be only a moment. He may see the little sparrow fall, but all her tribulations are fleeting, part of His purpose and His pattern, but done quite soon. She may be only briefly filling in some space for Him that has needed filling for some reason. It's all very well for Him to be patient, but He is eternal and gets things His way. What about her? She only has a little time, and has never gotten what she might have wanted.

"Oh my God," she prays. He might strike her down on the spot for her ingratitude. "I didn't mean it."

What will the nursing home be like? An institution, at any rate, along the lines of a school or a hospital. Well, it might not do Aggie any harm to live in an alien environment. Let her give up a few things, live under someone else's rules; Aggie, who accuses June of taking pleasure from sacrifice. "Why can't you admit you're pleased to give things up?" she's asked. "I see it in your face, you know. If you looked at yourself, you'd see pride and satisfaction written all over you."

One of them has to sacrifice in this situation, and surely it's Aggie's turn; Aggie, who has always managed to turn events to her own advantage. Surely God does not want June martyred to other people's selfishness. That isn't fair.

Oh God, she's done it again: accused Him of unfairness. "Help me," she prays. "Help me to know Thy will."

"Be careful what you pray for," Aggie warned once, laughing. "You never know how you'll get what you ask for."

On her lunch break, June phones the nursing home and speaks with the administrator. A man named Atkinson, with a low and careful voice. There are no beds at the moment, he says, and there is a waiting list, but he would be happy to show her around.

Then she calls Aggie. "I'll be late home. I'm going over to take a look at the nursing home. Unless you want to change your mind and come with me?"

"Oh no, thank you."

"You know, Mother, what you imagine may be much worse than what is."

"You may find that. What I generally find is the reverse."

Everyone knows the nursing home from the outside. It's big and modern and low-slung, like an extended ranch-style house, and has little patches of concrete and bits of lawn where, in warm weather, some people sit outside. People were unsure of their views toward the place when it was built a few years ago, June remembers. Certainly it would be clean and efficient, and possibly even kind, they said; but not like home. Some of the private homes that had been taking in the old may have been darker and perhaps more cavalier in their care, and even in some cases unkind, but they were regular houses, not too swift and brisk. It seemed, too, an uneasy way to make money, this shiny new building that was part of a chain, processing the old instead of hamburgers, caring for those who did not have their own homes or people to look after them.

Aggie has her own home, and her own people. Or person, rather. She has a house and June. Nevertheless.

It's five blocks from school to the home. June wonders what it would feel like, making this journey instead of going straight home. One thing: there'd be no guilt here. She'd see Aggie regularly, taking her whatever treats she wanted, and magazines and books. She will pay for the best possible care, just the way that, when the time comes, she will provide the best funeral she can afford, none of this cheap casket and cremation nonsense, but a proper minister and a nice plot and a headstone with some dignity. She will not be caught stinting.

She supposes regular visits would impose a certain burden. She doubts there's any way to clear Aggie out of her mind, no matter what, so already there is a blemish on the purity of being left alone. But things are owed. They are not only owed, but are seen to be owed. She will not have people saying she has treated her mother shabbily.

In her eagerness, she is slightly early for the appointment.

The red-brick building is L-shaped, with the main entrance at the join of the L. A heavy set of glass doors leads to a second set; all the weight and effort involved must keep the old people pretty securely indoors, she supposes. She is blasted, stepping through the second doors, by heat. What on earth temperature do they keep the place at? What will Aggie, accustomed to drafts and windows on which frost forms on the inside in winter, think of this? But of course the body adjusts, to temperatures and other things.

Despite the heat, there are people sitting in a small lounge wearing sweaters, or blankets bundled around their knees. So thin they are; just bones, really. This is how June will look in ten, fifteen years: whatever spare flesh there may be hanging as loosely as an old dress or a baggy suit. She feels the kind of shiver up her spine that Aggie used to say was somebody walking over her grave.

Here are old people shrivelling. And for all that Aggie's bulk is awful, and for all that June has wished her to age appropriately, through shrinkage, when confronted with real examples she is a bit appalled. Imagine Aggie so frail, so chilly. Imagine her not laughing and patting herself and saying, "Never mind insulation, June, I carry my own."

Aggie won't suit this place at all. She will be too big and boisterous, too demanding and noisy. Like putting hot mustard on porridge, moving Aggie in here. Oh but really, she's getting just like Aggie, transforming everything into food.

"Mrs. Benson?"

She turns to see a man much younger than she would have thought, from his voice or his position. "I'm Jim Atkinson." Another one in his thirties, ordinary—but can he be ordinary? A strange choice of career, surely, being in charge of old bodies. Hair neatly clipped and a brown suit, tan shirt, brown tie and shoes, and no doubt brown socks. "I believe you said you're here on behalf of your mother?"

"Yes, well, I wanted to take a look, so that we could discuss it properly. If you don't mind."

"Not at all, it's a pleasure." A pleasure? "I think I mentioned that there's a waiting list, although it's not terribly long and spaces, as you understand, can come up quite suddenly. Why don't you come into my office and tell me a little about your mother? Is this a decision you've made or something you're still considering?"

"I suppose we're still only thinking about it, but I expect it's pretty well inevitable." She'd noticed, out in the lounge, that the furniture was plastic-covered, presumably so that accidents could easily be wiped away. But it's plastic in here, too, in his office, and why ever would that be? "I'm a teacher and out all day, and I worry about her home alone so much. And she's difficult for me to care for now."

He frowns slightly at that, but aren't the people here supposed to be difficult to care for? Isn't that the point?

"What sort of problems does she have?"

"Mainly it's that she's quite heavy, and it makes it hard. I'm not that strong, you see, or young." It is not yet the moment to mention accidents.

"Is she alert?"

"Oh, heavens, yes. Smart as a whip."

This, she realizes, must be something like parents trying to get a badly behaved youngster into a private school: touching up sins to look like virtues. A destructive child who smashes things might be described as active. Wait till he finds out what she means by smart as a whip.

"This weight problem, how serious is it?"

"Well, it keeps her from doing some things by herself. I mean, I have to help her dress and get out of bed and have a bath, that sort of thing. It's not that she's immobilized, just too much for me to handle on my own."

"And how does she feel about coming here?"

"I don't think we've really come to grips with it. Neither of us having seen it. We can't make a decision until we see."

"Well then," and he stands, not a very tall man really, a couple of inches more, maybe, than her five foot six, "why don't we take the tour? What about her? Will she be coming for a look?"

"I hope so. She didn't want to today, though."

"When she does, just let me know. Perhaps I'll be able to re-assure her if she's uneasy. Most people are. It's quite an up-heaval."

This man will be breakfast for Aggie. He'll find it quite a challenge being reassuring.

"I'll tell her, thank you."

"Now out here," gesturing past his doorway, "is one of the lounges. We have several, of different sizes, for the residents and for when they have visitors. Of course, there's visiting in the rooms, but unless a resident is bed-ridden, most people find that a little awkward. The rooms are quite large, as you'll see, but they're not really meant for groups of people.

"I should explain how we've divided the place. Down there," gesturing left, "is pretty well set aside for people confined to their beds, or the senile. It doesn't sound as if that would apply to your mother, so we might as well go the other direction, and actually, the rooms are all the same anyway."

They turn right, where there is, first, a large, bright office with a board of red lights and clipboards on a counter and several young women in white.

"We have a large nursing office, and, as you see, it's simple for a resident to get help. They each have a buzzer beside their bed that sounds in here, and the red light goes on. And aside from that, staff are in and out of rooms, so supervision is pretty well constant. I gather your main concern is that your mother might injure herself while you're out?"

"That, and if she did, I might not be able to help her even if I were there."

"It's quite a burden, the worry, isn't it?" Maybe he really is sympathetic. Has she not wished for sympathy? He sounds, however, more sanctimonious than anything else. If Aggie were here she'd put him in his place.

"I know," he continues, "it's really quite a heart-breaking dilemma, and a big step for everyone concerned. But we know that, and we're here to help."

Shut up, she would like to say; but of course one doesn't do that.

There are two women sitting in wheelchairs in the corridor. Another, gripping a handrail, is taking a very slow walk. "We try to encourage people to exercise as much as they can." Creeping along a wall doesn't look like exercise, and June, who does so much brisk walking, tries to imagine the state of body that would require such slow, concentrated, and painful effort. Harder to imagine is the determination the woman must have to set out on this journey, eyes down, watching her feet, willing them steady.

As June and the administrator reach her she stops, looks up. "Supper will be on soon and you'd better get the table set. The men will be in shortly, you know." Her sharp eyes are commanding.

June looks, bewildered, at the administrator: "She thinks you're her daughter, I expect. Older folk sometimes get confused about time and people. Never mind."

But the old woman is watching, waiting. "I will," June tells her, nodding. "I'll do it right away."

"That's fine then, dear." The eyes return to the feet, and the walk continues.

"I thought you said the people with serious problems were at the other end?"

"Oh, well yes, but you see there's a difference between senility and confusion. I often think it's comforting for them, slipping into the old days occasionally. Like that old girl, sometimes she just takes a little trip into the past, that's all. Especially when they don't have visitors very often, sometimes they mistake other people for their family."

Aggie would love being called an old girl.

"It's a kindness, really, just going along with them."

Maybe so, but what does he know? He's not old. When she is old, June doesn't want to be humored by strangers.

Although that's what she just did, herself.

What would it be like if Aggie caught this disease, this confusion? What if she went off to live in some other time, maybe back to childhood, with her mother and her sisters, whom she has spoken of so fondly? What if she failed to recognize June, and mistook another woman for her daughter?

Wicked thought. But it would be something to see Aggie lose something, like her mind. If it just happened; not something wished for.

"Down here is the dining room for the people at this end, and over there's the big television lounge." Here is more plastic-covered furniture, including two couches and a variety of wheelchairs. Ten or eleven people are in here looking at a game show turned up too loud, although whether they are watching it is another matter. All the colors in the place, June notices, are vivid: oranges and yellows and greens. She supposes it's intended to be cheerful, but it feels false, lacking dignity, considering this is a place for people who are, when it comes down to it, likely to die pretty soon.

But what's the matter with her? If it were dark she would criticize that, too.

A couple of people seem to be nodding off; two or three others are knitting or crocheting. There are only two men. "It's mostly women," she remarks. "Are the men somewhere else?"

"Oh no, it's mixed. But you know," and he grins, "you women outlive us men. There simply are more old women than old men." He speaks as if this a point for women. How could it be, if this is what more years come to?

But it's clean and bright. No doubt the care is excellent. Aggie would be fine here. Look at all the people—and she must get lonesome, after so many years of women popping in and out of the bakery.

The dining room is filled with long tables, with straight-backed chairs with seats covered, inevitably, in plastic.

"What about meals? What sort of food do they get?"

"The best. They're designed by dietitians in our head office; they do complete monthly menu plans particularly designed for the elderly, and we stick right to them. You'd probably also like to know that besides government inspectors, the company sends around its own, so even if we wanted to, which of course we don't, there's no shirking in the care."

"But visitors can bring food in too, can't they? My mother has quite an appetite, quite a sweet tooth."

He frowns dubiously. "As long as she can manage it on her own, I don't expect that's a problem. But it isn't necessary, you know. As I said, we provide adequate, healthy meals, and snacks, too, in the evenings—cookies and fruit juice. Now," he moves on, "there's also a general-purpose and meeting room. Ministers and priests come in and hold services, and sometimes there are concerts. School children and so on. And once a week we have a crafts instructor. We do encourage people to be active and take part in things."

Just about what she'd expected; but even seeing the place, it's hard to picture Aggie squeezed into the television lounge, overcrowding it all by herself, or bent over some creation in yarn or clay. "Mostly my mother likes to read."

"Well, that's fine. Active minds are just as important as active bodies." He'll get no argument there from Aggie.

"Now you'll want to see the rooms." Actually, she pretty well has seen them. All along the hall, not one door was closed. She has seen something like a dead man, lying fully dressed on a bed, eyes closed and hands folded across his chest. Also a woman curled up in a ball, her dress hiked around her hips, thighs showing. June is permitted to stare as if they were paintings, or sculptures.

"Why are all the doors open?"

"Mainly for supervision, so staff can keep a quick eye that nothing's gone wrong. It's a safety thing."

"Don't they mind?"

"Who? The residents? Oh, I don't think so. I expect they know it's for their own good."

"My mother is quite a private person."

"Well, you know, for private things, like a doctor's visit, the door's closed, of course." But surely privacy is more than that.

"Now, as you see, we have several types of rooms. There's the single for just one person, fairly expensive though. Then a semi for two, that's the most common, and what we call a ward, for four."

Each room has a large window and a narrow bed, or two, or four, with metal sides that can be drawn up, like cribs. Each bed has a white curtain that can be drawn around for privacy of sight, if not of sound. The walls are light yellow. There is a small closet for each person, and a plastic-covered chair beside each bed. There are bedside tables, and bureaus, and people's faces staring out from photographs on walls and tables. These must be reminders of those who have been loved, out in the world. Does it help to have those faces handy, or would it hurt?

"It can't be quite like home, of course, but we've tried to make it cheerful and bright, and, as you see, residents are welcome to bring small things with them. Photographs or knick-knacks, nothing big, naturally, but those small things can be so important."

What would Aggie bring? A picture of Frances. Books. A small refrigerator full of food. An oven, perhaps. Her own bulk would fill a room.

"There are a couple of things to consider when you're deciding what type of room your mother might prefer. The costs, of course, and I'll give you a brochure when we get back to my office about all that, and also some photographs, so you can show your mother. And then what kind of person she is. If she's someone who likes to be alone and you can afford it, a private is something to think about. On the other hand, if she's gregarious she might prefer a ward. Mind you, it's possible to change if one arrangement doesn't work; there are also internal waiting lists. It may be that when a bed does come up it'll be in a ward, and if that isn't what she prefers she'll be able to move as soon as another type of room is available. You see?"

"Yes." But what's best for someone both private and inquisitive? "I would guess a semi-private," June says, but realizing it is only an unhappy compromise. Aggie will not fit so neatly. Bathrooms are shared. Aggie, who likes to read on the toilet, would find this yet another irritation.

It's a funny thing about revenge: here are all sorts of possibilities, and here she is, horrified. Maybe it's the thought of outsiders that offends. It has always been the two of them, and something is broken when others come into it.

"Now let's go back to my office and I'll give you those brochures, and you can ask any questions you may have."

Heavens, it's expensive. "The government pays a share," he explains. "And there'll be her pension. Still, that will leave a certain amount for you to pick up, depending on the type of room."

"It's a lot for a bit of a bed and meals."

"Oh, but it's much more than that, after all. I always think it's worth a great deal to know that the people you love are getting the best possible care and that they're safe and well supervised. And, too, it's not all expenditure, if you think solely of costs. You'll have fewer expenses at home, and when you add in the value of having the total burden of care taken off your shoulders, well, that's just incalculable.''

True enough. Priceless, really.

"Now," he says, closing files, "have you decided if you'd like to put her name on our waiting list? I should warn you, there's a steady demand. It's best to move quickly, although I wouldn't want to rush you or your mother into anything. It's just that even with her name down, it could be several months. Or it could be only days or weeks. You understand, these things are somewhat unpredictable.''

So this is it. How stupid, to hesitate. After all, she can put down Aggie's name and it doesn't mean much, until the time actually comes. She tries to recall the anticipation of freedom. It only needs a signature to step toward it.

She thinks, walking home, they will both adjust. It's only that she would have expected to feel lighter, not this weight.

Oh, but she would hate living in that place herself. Being called dear, and wheeled around willy-nilly, handed a book, or not, at the whim of someone busy with other things. Maybe being fed unnecessary pills, and sleeping too much. Aggie would get hungry just knowing there was a limit to her food. It would make her crazy, not to be able to go into the kitchen to whip up muffins or a pie. She would flail and curse; maybe they would tie her down and muffle her.

June shivers. What if this is also her own future? What if she falls and breaks a brittle bone, or the car she imagines comes swerving around a corner now? To be crippled, or hurt, and suddenly old. But that doesn't bear thinking about. Everyone adjusts. Either you die or you get old, and the latter requires certain adjustments, and that's all there is to it.

She can just hear Frances. "It's awful, Mother," she will say. "It's a terrible thing to do to her. She'll hate it." She will be perfectly sincere, of course, reflecting on its awfulness, but she will not say, "I'm strong, you've done your part, I'll come back and take care of her." Sacrifice, even for someone she no doubt loves, is not one of Frances's gifts.

Certainly she won't lift a finger for June herself, if that time comes. Frances will be ruthless. She will point out what her grand-

mother has taught her: that she has her own life, and must get on
with it. Uncomfortably, June can also hear her saying, "After all,
Mother, I know it isn't perfect, but you'll get used to it, you'll
adjust."

"You're late," says Aggie, who has, for once, made supper.

"I told you I was going to see the nursing home."

"So you did. I'd forgotten."

Liar. Eyes don't lie. Aggie's features may be set in nonchalance,
but June detects fear somewhere in the eyes.

She sets her own face to oblivious cheer. "You really should go.
I was impressed. It's clean, and you'd like how bright it is, and
there are no end of things to do. You can tell they take good care
of people, too, and the administrator is really very nice."

"Do you remember, June, in India years ago, and then in the
States, when protesters would just go limp and police would have
to carry away dead weights? Totally peaceful, but so effective."

June had decided not to tell anyone about putting Aggie's name
on the waiting list. She needs time, but she's sure that once she's
accustomed to the idea herself, she will find it a precious and powerful secret, something like a pearl in her dealings with her mother.

"And that's what I'll do," Aggie is saying. "I'll just lie down
on the floor and you'll need a crane to move me."

It's hard to keep a secret, though. It's such a big thing, this impending freedom, and confusing too. So many things are unspoken;
and might they not become more real and less disputable if they
were said? There ought to be somebody she could talk to, she
should have someone to whom she can tell secrets.

Aggie, across the supper table, is looking at her defiantly. Apparently she has made some point which June has missed.

"Anyway, Mother," she says, "I wasn't going to mention it yet,
but I put your name on the waiting list while I was there. You
have to do that because there are people lined up waiting. We can
still talk about it, but I had to put your name down."

Later they go upstairs together to get Aggie ready for bed. June,
walking slightly behind, her hand on her mother's elbow, steadying
her in the cautious ascent, is surprised at how bent Aggie has become. Maybe she doesn't usually look too closely.

But tonight she sees the dimples of fat beneath the material of
Aggie's dress. This newly noticed slumping of her mother's shoulders may be partly because of weight and age, but may also come
from years spent leaning over things: June, the bread that had to

be kneaded, the batter in bowls that had to be mixed, the tubs of washing that had to be scrubbed, and all the lines of print she has pursued. As well as Frances. All that has combined to bend her somewhat.

When June was in her gawky adolescence, Aggie used to say, "Stand up straight, for heaven's sake. Walk tall." June would like to say now, "Straighten up, Mother." Because this is no time to look at her and see frailty, or any sort of caving in.

It occurs to June that weakness could, in some instances, be a more powerful tactic than strength.

In her bath, when Aggie is in bed, she considers her own body. She dislikes waste, including flesh, and there is no waste on her, but something must be shrinking, because her skin seems to be coming loose in places. On her breasts and her stomach and her thighs, and on the undersides of her arms, there are little pluckings of skin that don't appear to be attached to anything. Aggie may bend, but it is June who is shrivelling, like those old people in the nursing home.

9

Waiting list, shit. Lying in bed, Aggie once more listens from a distance to the too-quick thumping of her heart. One fast way for it to end, a pounding and, presumably, a stab of pain, and then—what? A dead weight, as threatened, for June to deal with.

It's a good thing only the aging, the old, know they may die at any moment. If the young knew, they would spend their lives in terror, paralysed. Like Frances, who hasn't learned yet that any step, one wrong move, may be fatal, so she can still dance off in all directions, trying variations. This is something Aggie taught her. She takes credit for her daring. When Frances was just a baby, Aggie would lean over her as she tried to lift her head, or roll over, or crawl, and then walk, and say, "Come on, you can do it, keep trying," and eventually Frances would. And when she was learning to talk and count and read, Aggie would tell her, "Come on, you can say it, you can figure it out," and now Frances can, and does, say anything. Now the situation is a little reversed, and she teachers Aggie words.

June nags Aggie about her food, and Frances about her smoking. Frances says, "Oh, Mother, leave me alone. We're all entitled to some sins, you know," and grins. Aggie says, "Good God, June, a diet would kill me. I'd go into shock," and laughs.

Maybe June likes telling people that they're going to die, and that somehow they will deserve it, having brought it on themselves. How did she learn to be so cautious and afraid? Surely, Aggie tries to recall, she must have told June the same things she told Frances: you can do it, try again. Certainly she told June no end of things when she still had her inside her body.

Too bad it isn't still possible to pray. But she realized years ago that prayers have a nasty way of being granted in ways that aren't at all what a person had in mind. She decided, when she gave them up, that whatever God there might be must have a devious and peculiar sense of humor.

However, the alternatives, wishing and hoping, appear in these circumstances to be flimsy tools.

Somewhere out there tonight is her name on a waiting list. Just that, her name written down, is a theft of sorts. Bits and pieces of her seem to be escaping.

She cannot, looking down her body, see beyond her chest, home of her heart; great lolloping bosoms, as they used to be called, drooping, a little painfully, one to each side. Beyond, further down, must be the tricky unpredictable part that is no longer holding its own.

Once, she looked down her body with pride. Well, she's still proud, but of different things. Then, it was round breasts that would fit nicely into a cupped hand, if there had been a hand willing to cup them, and a trim brown torso, a gentle little belly and such strong thighs—not long legs, but sturdy, compact ones.

But if the teacher was, for one thing, a man who didn't like shit on his boots, he was also a man who preferred darkness to light, and whose desire was for order. He was a teacher, but only in the classroom, no longer in a kitchen.

("He was," she said another time when Frances asked, "a man who arranged all his books in alphabetical order. By author."

("Yeah," Frances nodded, "I see."

("What's that supposed to mean?" asked June. "What's wrong with that?")

Who, Aggie wondered, among the people she later came to meet, was out watching in the dusk the evening they arrived, weary in the cool air, after a long, peculiar day, the first one of their marriage? Sullen and hungry they drove along the dusty streets, passing red-brick houses with their broad verandahs, where people were sitting out watching the sun go down, drinking lemonade or tea and chatting. Did they know it was the new teacher and his new wife passing by? Did they think, "What a nice-looking young couple," or "My goodness, there's a pair of thunderclouds"?

Aggie sat up straighter in the buggy. Odd, to live in a place
where houses were separated only by strips of lawn, not acres. Odd,
too, that when they stopped, it was in front of a house not distinguishable from the rest: another two-storey red-brick with broad
white-painted verandah, stone walk, and small front yard. Except
that it was empty, a little overgrown out front, and curtainless. She
pictured wandering into the wrong house by mistake, coming home
from shopping.

While he unhitched the horse and handled the bags, she stood in
the front hallway alone.

The place had a dry and dusty, closed-up smell, and yet it wasn't
dusty; someone, it seemed, had come in and swept. A mystery intruder had also, she discovered in the kitchen, left eggs, milk,
cheese and fruit in the ice-box, which held a fresh block of ice,
and bread and cake in a cupboard. The banister going upstairs felt
smooth and solid. The whole place seemed smooth and solid.
Someone had also made up the bed in the largest of the three bedrooms. All this was very kind, and it occurred to her that she would
have really been in trouble if there'd been no food tonight. And it
would have been an effort, in her present mood, to do the little
chores, like making up the bed.

She made sandwiches and sliced the cake and wiped the fruit.

Back of the kitchen, a trapdoor led to the cellar. She tugged it
up and here, where no one had looked, balls of dust went rolling.
Peering down the steps, she glimpsed cobwebbed shelves that
would eventually be lined, she supposed, with her preserves. At
the moment, it was musty and damp. She wondered if many houses
here, well-kept and prim on the outside, were like this in the hidden, indoor places.

Tomorrow she would give it a good going-over. She might not
feel at home yet, but that would come. Things bubbling in the
kitchen would help, smells she knew, and daylight.

There was a small barn at the back for the horse, and an outhouse. Also, there were two large maple trees hanging heavily over
the house, and she wondered how much light the kitchen would
get. She could see the teacher out at back, unhitching the horse,
pumping water for it. More slowly, she went through the place
again. Even lighting oil lamps, she wondered at its darkness.

The trouble was the colors. The walls were painted heavy greens
and blues and browns; the linoleum was a brown-and-yellow pattern, dulled and old; the furniture was brown, too, and the base-

boards, stairs, banisters, and doors were all dark wood. The place seemed muffled by darkness. It might be better once it was thoroughly cleaned, not merely wiped. She, no doubt, would be better with a meal and a good night's sleep. What was dark, she could brighten.

"Where'd the food come from?" he asked.

"It was here. Someone must have brought it in."

"Good thing they did."

After the meal, when she'd washed up, she paused in the doorway to the front room. He was kneeling, boxes of books around him, putting volumes on the shelves. These must be books he'd had in storage and had delivered here. Like the furniture: just here when she arrived.

"I think I'll go up now," she said shyly.

"That's fine," he said, not looking up.

She might not have known much, but she knew this was not how bridegrooms behaved. Respect for a new wife and her sensibilities might be one thing; lack of interest quite another. There was an impasse of some kind here. Maybe she only had to apologize, although hard to say for what. She was still awake, wondering, when he appeared.

Frances jokes about "getting laid"—that's one expression for it these days—but perfectly descriptive, Aggie thinks, of his technique, laying her like a plank, hammering her efficiently into place, flattening her down properly.

Then, "Is the bed made up in the other room?"

"No, why?"

"Because I thought I'd sleep there. I have to get a good rest, and I'm used to being on my own. Besides, you know, you snore." She would have laughed, except it didn't sound as if he meant it to be funny. "I'm sure we'll both sleep better that way."

She wasn't the only one who snored; she could hear him through the walls. The house, for all its solid appearance, was deceptive that way.

She might be puzzled and unhappy and a little angry, but she got out of bed the next morning and faced the day with a sense of purpose, rolling up the sleeves of her house-dress.

Even in daylight, the place was depressing. "Did the furniture come with the house, then?" she asked him at breakfast. He looked surprised, and once more offended.

"Of course not. Why on earth would you think that?"

She shrugged. "I guess because it doesn't look like my idea of new furniture. I'd thought maybe something bright. The place is like a dungeon."

"It just needs a good cleaning. That's what you'll be doing to-day, I suppose?"

"Well, that's the first thing."

From room to room she moved, scrubbing and polishing and waxing and dusting. The place got cleaner, if no lighter, as she got dirtier.

Something was odd about the shelves in the front room. So many books: had he read them all? If so, what did he know? Her fault, perhaps, was contained in one of them. She might be guilty of something she was too ignorant to understand. Little packages of knowledge—like buying a bag of sugar or a pound of shortening, each one containing a certain amount of nutrition or taste or learn-ing. Hungry, she made herself a sandwich in the kitchen and won-dered what had struck her as odd. "Oh, for heaven's sake," she thought, and went to check. Something had been strange, all right: all in alphabetical order.

("He'd get so angry if I put one back in the wrong place," she told Frances.)

The downstairs, at least, was clean when he got home. Her hair, however, was hanging in strings, her dress had ripped beneath one arm, and she had lost track of time, so that she was just bringing in a pail of water to wash herself when he arrived. He didn't say anything, although his nose wrinkled. He might at least have men-tioned all her work.

("Your grandfather," June told Frances, "was a fastidious man.")

("Fastidious nothing," Aggie snorted. "He was antiseptic.")

He didn't appear in her room that night, but went right by to his. She thought of this one now as her room, and that one as his. She was a little surprised how easily and quickly a person could get used to things. Still. Here she was, in her house, her territory, and her new life. She could hear her mother: "You make your bed and you lie in it."

"It's still very dark, don't you think?" she suggested in the morning, tentatively. "It might be brightened up a little."

"Do you think so? I think it's fine." Head down, staring into his tea as if that were the end of it.

Well, she certainly wasn't going to spend another day sweating away at the place when she would only be shining up the gloom.

It was only a few blocks to the main street. Closer to downtown, if that's what they called it, more houses were frame than brick or stone, and they were smaller and closer together. But there were huge maples lining the streets, and a little cool breeze, and quite a lot of people compared with what she was accustomed to. She couldn't distinguish faces properly, with no names for any of them. She could see, however, that they dressed for shopping, and that she might have worn a hat, at least; it seemed to be the custom.

The grocery store was small and jammed with goods. "Ames Groceteria" said the sign. The plump little woman behind the counter watched as Aggie regarded the shelves. "Is there something I can get you today?"

"Yes, but I'll have to think a minute. Almost everything, I expect. Do you deliver?"

"Certainly. We'll have it to you this afternoon. I don't believe we've met. I'm Mrs. Ames."

"I'm Mrs. Hendricks." That sounded ridiculous, someone else entirely. "Aggie," she amended firmly.

"Of course, you'll be the new teacher's wife."

"That's right." Was that what she was to be here? She felt the weight of it. How odd, to have position but not a name; anonymous. Still, she could see what he meant when he'd warned her she'd have a position to maintain here. Different from merely being old Will MacDonald's middle daughter, which she was used to being. And after all, that was just as anonymous.

"So you'll have moved into the old Campbell place," this Mrs. Ames was saying. She did not offer her own first name, and Aggie wondered if there was a time and place, a length of acquaintance-ship, required before real names were given. If so, she had already blundered, giving hers. She could see a day of errors as she fumbled her way into place in this town.

"Is that what it's called?" Would it be the Hendricks place at some point, and how long would it take to make it that?

"Well, they built it, the old folks. They lost a son in the war, and their daughter moved away and now they've gone to live with her and her family and had to sell it up. But, of course, now," and the woman smiled, "it'll be your place."

"Yes, it will, won't it?" and Aggie smiled back. It was friendly enough here, or could be; she'd just been frightened for a moment.

"Mind you," Aggie went on, "there's a few things to be done."

"Yes, I imagine it would have got a bit run-down. Ab Campbell's been sick the last few years and Beatrice pretty much spent her time looking after him."

"Oh, it's not bad. Mostly just a matter of paint and wallpaper. Can you tell me where's the best place to look?"

Mrs. Ames laughed, all white teeth and dark curly hair. "The best place, I don't know. The only place is Sinclair Hardware down on the next block. He'll have what you need, and if he doesn't you're out of luck." The bell over the door tinkled, and another customer came in. "You look around and see what you need," and she moved away saying, "Good morning Mrs. Johnson, and what can we get for you today?" For an instant Aggie was lonely; as if she'd lost a friend.

Starting from scratch to stock a house was quite a chore. They needed everything. It wasn't like home, where you just went to the basement or the root cellar for whatever was required, or made it. She didn't even have ingredients for baking.

Mrs. Ames returned. "My gracious, it'll take a while to fill all this."

"But you can send it this afternoon?"

"Oh yes. I'll just start an account for you, shall I? We do up the bills every two weeks."

"That's fine. Thank you."

"Good luck at Sinclair's. I hope you find what you want."

Oh, after all it was an ordinary town, nothing so frightening. A friendly voice, a pleasant beginning. The little stores, all built together, followed each other plunkety-plunk along the street—a pharmacy, a milliner's, a women's dress shop, a tailor's and a barber's, a bank, a restaurant, and across the street, for heaven's sake, a tavern of all things, right out in the open. The sun was warm. She suspected her walk had a jauntiness to it, and wondered if the teacher would find it lacking dignity. The idea made her smile.

Still. She paused outside the hardware. She could not pretend he wasn't going to be awfully upset. Certainly he'd made his meaning clear: he liked the rooms the way they were.

On the other hand, he wasn't there all day. His territory was the school, whatever went on when he went out the door. And had she not talked, for some years, about the home she would have? Much of this venture might not be working out precisely as foreseen, but surely this could.

Had he not blamed her for the lack of food on their trip? Had he not considered it her responsibility? And if she was responsible for such homely things, surely she must be responsible for the walls and floors as well?

The store smelled dry, with a touch of sharpness—sawdust, maybe, and bags and packages of powdered plaster, and liquids like shellac and paint. She might not necessarily buy anything today, but there was nothing wrong with looking.

Except that almost right away she found the perfect paper: pale blue with small cream flowers in the pattern. She saw it immediately on three walls of the front room, with the fourth wall painted cream. The difference that would make! Perfect in another way, too; both light, for her taste, and surely also dignified, for his. "You've decided then?" asked a man who might be Mr. Sinclair or not, but who did not introduce himself.

"Yes please. I should have measured; I'm not sure how much I'll need. At least a dozen rolls, I expect."

"Well, there's always more. That's not one of our more popular ones. Not," he added quickly, "that there's anything wrong with it, I like it myself. Just, people seem to be going more for bigger patterns these days."

"I'll want paint to match, enough for a wall. But then, it'll take several coats I expect," she added doubtfully, recalling the nasty dark green.

"No trouble. Do you want it delivered this afternoon?"

What a luxury, these unexpected pleasures of living in a town: that one could walk down a street, go into stores and point at this or that, and go away and have things magically appear later on one's doorstep.

Not today, though. She had to do a little thinking about the teacher and how to approach this.

"Tomorrow morning? Early?"

"First thing, if you want. Eight-thirty, nine?"

"Nine would be best." Just to be sure he was gone. Just in case she didn't mention it tonight.

Back in the house she stood in the front room imagining it tomorrow. A day from now it would be entirely altered. Oh, but she would have to work fast to get so much done that it could not be undone. So, she realized, she wasn't going to tell him. Never mind. She'd already seen him angry. There were no surprises in that direction.

Still, she took special care with supper and was quietly polite and didn't mind too much when he made another swift appearance in her room and vanished. "Well," she thought, "if that's all he wants." It wasn't much, and it also seemed not to have much to do with her. On the other hand, a day ahead spent accomplishing something was exciting. She pictured other things she might do, plans for other rooms.

She began as soon as he was out of the house in the morning: moving furniture aways from the walls, covering it with sheets, wrapping a scarf around her hair. When all the paint and wallpaper arrived, she had it piled in the front hall. There was so much. Where should she begin, to get the most accomplished? Paint the wall—easier than dealing with the paper, and faster, and by the end of the day it might be dry enough for a second coat. It took an hour, and while it now looked only peculiar, the green showing through like damp spots, the room had begun to grow and brighten.

The wallpaper, through, was a chore; all the matching of delicate flowers really was a trick, and she wouldn't have quite enough to finish. But to alter the spirit of the place in such a broad fashion, to stand back and see that she had made this change, that was really something. She didn't even stop for lunch.

It was almost done. She would do the last part, which would involve moving his precious books so that she could get behind the shelves, tomorrow. It would be nice to get the second coat of paint on, though; would give a much better idea of how the room would be.

"Whatever," she heard his astonished voice from the doorway, "do you think you're doing?" For a man who put stock in words, and who had told her they should be used precisely and not wasted, that seemed a fairly unnecessary question. Any fool could see not only what she thought she was doing, but what she had in fact done.

She stepped back from her work, turned and smiled brightly. There were steaks of paint across her forehead and one cheek, and her hands were sticky, and wallpaper paste had worked into her knuckles and beneath her fingernails. "It's nice, isn't it? Much more cheerful. Of course, it's not quite finished."

"But I didn't say you could do this." Blank astonishment, followed by outrage. "This is *my* house. Who said you could change it?" His house, as if she had painted something that was really his, like decorating his body with stripes, or drawing daisies on his chest.

"I live here too."

"I want it the way it was."

"Too late, I'm afraid." How airily, how daringly she spoke. "Anyway, wait till you see it finished, you'll see how much better it looks. It's just a bit funny now with the green showing through on this wall. The paper's nice, isn't it? Pretty, but dignified."

"But how could you do this without my permission?" He still couldn't seem to believe this.

"Why would I need your permission?"

"Because you're my wife. You don't just go ahead and do things without asking me."

So she was owned, like a house and some furniture and a bunch of books? "Oh, don't be so silly," she said, impatient now, stalking past him. "Watch out for wet paint. I'm going to get cleaned up for supper. Only soup and sandwiches, I'm afraid."

She could feel rage thundering into all the nooks and crannies of her body, making her tremble so that it was hard to do up the buttons of the dress she was changing into. She was no servant here. Who did he think he was?

"And how," he resumed over the soup, "were you going to pay for all this?"

"I had Sinclair's—that's the hardware store—put it on a bill for you. We have an account there now and at the grocery."

"So I'm to pay for it. I don't have a say in what my house looks like but I have to pay for whatever you choose to do to it?"

She shrugged. It was a matter of tactics: what would irritate him most? As when she fell asleep smiling in the buggy, she chose to be calm. "It's up to you, I suppose, whether you pay or not. But you probably should. I don't expect it's a good thing for a teacher to have bad debts."

So here were the newlyweds, together in their kitchen. Not quite as she had pictured it.

("It was like knitting a sweater," she told Frances, "and having it get out of control, so you wind up with two necks and six arms and all the patterns muddled with flowers and stripes and diamonds—you could knit and knit and never make sense of it. But of course you couldn't stop knitting, that wasn't done, so you just had this—mess—you had to keep working at as best you could.'')

There was no question of going back home. They would still love her in their way, as she loved them in her way; but she was supposed to be gone, taken care of. They were even proud of how she'd been taken care of, moving off to a new, foreign sort of life. It would hurt them, and certainly dismay them, if she returned. And she would be something even worse than a spinster: a no longer chaste woman without a husband. Unheard of; or, if heard of, a disgrace.

She could see surviving here by caving in. She supposed that was an alternative. Or she could *not* give in, in which case either he would have to, or this house would be a battlefield. Well, it was early days. She smoothed her dress over her hips as if she were patting armor into place.

"You'll stop right where you are," he commanded, regarding her sternly over his sandwich. "Whatever you'd planned, just don't bother."

"I can hardly leave the front room the way it is, unless you like it streaked. That would really impress people, wouldn't it?" Was she so daring? That's what she remembers saying, anyway.

She went upstairs as soon as she had done the dishes, while he did his schoolwork at the table in the dining room. She could feel the muscles in her arms, shoulders, back, and legs tightening. By morning they would be cramped. Tomorrow she would finish off the front room.

Then what? Now that he had ordered her to stop, she could not. He would think, if she did, that she had learned obedience. Compromise, then. She could let him have the dining room, where he did his work, and his bedroom.

"Don't touch anything else," he warned at breakfast. "Don't you dare do anything else." She sipped her tea, said nothing. "Did you hear me? Finish the front room, since you have to, but no more."

"Of course I heard you."

Animals marked their territory by peeing around the edges. She was marking hers with the smell of paint.

She did her room a dusty pink, and liked it so well she did the third, still-unused bedroom with what was left. He could keep his military blue, if that was what he wanted. He came home sniffing the fumes, but did not comment. Maybe he thought she had only finished the front room. He might never notice the change in hers, since he only saw it in the dark.

That left the kitchen, now grey with brown trim (what sort of people were those Campbells to have lived like this?). Especially now, with the rest lightened, it was heart-sinking to go into it. And, after all, the kitchen was clearly hers. He had no interest in it, did not have to spend hours in it every day. Not that that would make a difference. There was no getting around it; this would be mutiny.

Should there not be a middle ground here between his way and hers? There must be techniques, or how did people live together? One needed patience, discretion and time, she supposed. It must be like dealing with stubborn children: one humored them, or tricked them. But there were no children here; only two grown-ups, both wilful and stubborn and possibly spoiled.

The kitchen must be yellow, she decided, to make it seem like sunshine despite the shading trees out back.

She worked nervously and swiftly. She needed, again, to have a great deal done by the time he got home. She wouldn't say she was frightened—never frightened—but she was tense, anticipating battle. "It will not be all his fault," she thought. She was definitely goading him.

It was a matter of power, that's what it came down to. Marriage, surely, should not be reduced to that? His power was that she would dress up for teas with the parents of his pupils, and would smile graciously and probably make cupcakes and those fancy sandwiches with the crusts cut off. She would do his washing and his ironing, and prepare his meals and keep the house tidy and clean, and allow his thin body with its peculiar spasms to enter her room and her body at night. Her power was that none of this would touch her, if she didn't want it to.

She was raised, after all, to be a wife, and knew the job down pat. Also, she had a certain pride, that she could darn the heel of a sock so that it wasn't lumpy, or make the perfect banana bread. She had skills that were called for here and a job to perform. But that was only part of the bargain, in exchange for which she received a roof and a name. Naturally, beyond that there ought to be love, at least fondness, perhaps passion, and maybe joy, but none of that, she supposed, was essential to the bargain. At least defiance was passion of sorts, and whatever his response was, it would likely be passionate also.

The kitchen was difficult to paint—all edges and interruptions, a stove and an ice-box to work around and shift, and doorways and a window. She was far from finished when she heard him come through the door into the hallway. She heard the clump of his briefcase being set down, and the rustling as he took off his suit jacket, the clinking of a hanger. She was proud to see that her hand did not waver as she crouched, meticulously edging along a baseboard.

She heard a sniff, and steps, and an indrawn breath, but after all, what could he do?

Brown shoes appeared, a hand flashing to her wrist, grabbing so that the paintbrush, spraying yellow splashes, flew across the floor. He hauled at her arm until she was facing him, and there they were, face to face, toe to toe. What did they recognize in that moment? Nothing they'd known before about each other.

His free hand twisted back, whipped forward, snapped into her face open-handed, knocking her sideways so that she might have fallen if he hadn't been holding her wrist so tightly.

No time at all, it seemed, went by, and certainly no thought, but her own free hand hauled back and cracked across his face, sending him stumbling a step sideways so that he did let go. She watched with a vague sort of interest as the marks of her fingers rose on his cheek, and he watched as, presumably, the same happened on her face. They were frozen, a pair of crystal figures, quite still and clear. It was nice, she thought, being so clear.

Finally, however, he dropped his eyes. His body sagged, and his shoulders slumped. He regained ordinary proportions. Now, maybe, he was ashamed that, underneath the teacher, the Englishman, or even just the man, under the thin layer of learning and the habits of civility, there was this savage. He was also perhaps ashamed that for an instant they had been entirely intimate. If they had shared loving bodies they would not have known so much.

He turned and went upstairs. She turned and saw splashes of yellow paint here and there, where they did not belong. They came off easily with a rag and turpentine. She watched her steady hand as she finished the delicate job of painting along the baseboard. She found she was quite hungry, and made a heap of ham and tomato sandwiches. The food tasted a little of paint. Still hungry, she baked bran muffins and ate three.

Later she washed herself. Standing naked in her room, she regarded herself in the wavering glass of the mirror and was surprised to find that really her body was quite appealing. In that moment in the kitchen, she had felt enormous, huge and powerful. What she had in fact was a compact and sturdy body, with marks of fingers still standing out red on her face, and a bruise forming on her wrist. That might fade, but she would not.

Sixty years later, she has a body to match that moment in the kitchen. And now June wants to move her, has put her name on a waiting list?

Oh, the investment she has in this house—how could she leave it? Her blood is in its walls, her victories in its air, her pain and bruises in its floors. Her innocence is curled up, maybe in the basement. Also, her freedom and experience are here, likely downstairs in the kitchen.

Some of the blood that is in these walls was even spilled for June. Because after quite a long period of chilly, distant days, and nights separated by the wall between their rooms, he resumed his periodic swift appearances, which led finally to some result.

"I hear you're expecting," women said, meeting her in stores and later dropping in for tea and trading stories. Oh yes, indeed she was expecting.

Love, she was expecting love again, although of a different sort. She was expecting someone to whom she could give love, and who would return it. A tiny body at her breasts, and then small arms around her neck. A little voice. Thumps and falls and footsteps, scabs on little knees.

"Are you hoping for a boy or a girl?" the women asked. It didn't matter. Just someone whole. She was expecting someone of her own.

It was not as if he expressed much interest. She saw him staring at her sometimes, or at her growing belly rather, and occasionally he asked, "How are you feeling?" but the question did not seem more intimate than his "Good morning". Once more he stopped coming to her room at night.

She, now, talked throughout the day. Hearing her own voice was strange at first. She hadn't realized how mute she had become. Now she carried a companion with her at every moment, and wasn't a bit lonely any more. A perfect intimacy, two people in this one body, and now that she'd discovered the secret, she might do this again and again, for years and years, filling up all the spaces with plump and dark-haired babies.

"Hello, honey," she'd say first thing in the morning, surveying her body, wondering at what it contained. "Let's see now," pulling back the curtains and looking out the window, "it's sunny today. After he leaves we'll make a cake and then maybe go out and do some gardening." She did not think of identifying him as Neil, or the teacher, or your father; didn't mention him at all except to point out his schedule and what they, she and the child, might accomplish in his absence.

Oh, she told the child everything: about her family and the farm, the work there and how loud and warm it had been, the people here in town and what they would do together, once the child was born. "I'll read you stories, and we'll sing and tell riddles and jokes." She spoke of the preparations she was making. "I'm knitting you a yellow hat. It'll have a little white puff on the top, I think." Or hemming diapers, sewing little outfits. She offered as commentary on all the day's activities. "I'm measuring bran for muffins now, and then I'll chop the dates."

In the absence of the child itself, she regarded her body, containing it, with love. She stroked her palms across her belly. She was proud of what felt like her own accomplishment, and would have enjoyed pointing out the changes in her shape and size to people on the street. But "I think," he told her, "you should start staying in from now on. It's not exactly proper, how you look. Anything that's needed, surely you can order in?" Yes, she supposed she could. And learned that when it reached a certain obviousness, pregnancy was like madness: something to be locked away, like a crazy aunt in the attic, out of embarrassment, for fear of causing offence.

Actually, she was relieved to be spared the chore of shopping, and no longer went to church. Also, since she was unable to go out, women came to her, bringing small baby gifts, tales of birth, advice. Together in their privacy, they let their hair down, with an unpinning and falling of words. "The pain!" they told her. "But when it's over you forget it." Although, she thought, obviously they had not.

All this seemed like an initiation into a secret society, her badge of membership in her distended belly.

She could see how it would continue afterward. "This is my daughter," she would say to people, these women, or "This is my son." The child would be laughing, pink and healthy. People would stop on the street and smile. It would break things and spat-ter food, cry and giggle and get its clothes dirty, climb trees, skip rope or stones, and throw rubber balls at the side of the house and catch them. They would go for walks together, she and the child, and she would point things out and give them names. They would bake cookies, and sit down together to eat them. In the middle of the night, she would leap out of bed at a cry and offer comfort. Or would go silently into the sleeping child's room, just to look.

When it leaped and kicked inside her, she held her hands over it, to feel. "You're blooming," the women told her. "Some people don't take to expecting, but you certainly have." She looked in the mirror and approved. Her checks were rosy, just like the old days. She must have gotten pale as well as mute during the unexpectant months of marriage.

She grew impatient for the event, developed a longing to touch and be touched by what she had already created. She walked upstairs at night imagining small arms around her neck, a soft and sleepy head resting on her shoulder. It was like a Christmas card, the picture: all tenderness and sentiment.

She ate and ate; eating, as the women said, for two. She imagined how healthy this child would be, already so well fed.

Her pictures were only of the two of them. Where would he be? Around, of course. Here and there. Off in a corner, likely, working away at the dining-room table, wafting quietly about his chores, insignificant.

She would eat and grow and he would hover about, shrinking. She would be so large he wouldn't be able to reach her at all. If he tried to climb her body, he would slip off.

The women were right that there was a lot of pain, and it went on for quite a while. They were also right that afterward she could not precisely recreate it in her memory.

"It's a girl," the doctor said, leaning over her at last. "You have a healthy little daughter."

He went away for a few minutes, and when he returned, he was carrying a flannelette-wrapped bundle, and Aggie watched him float across the floor as if in slow motion, and say, drawing back the blanket, "Well, here she is, all cleaned up. Her father thinks she's wonderful."

Tiny, tiny little thing. All bandy-legged and everything closed, her fists and curled feet, pursed mouth, and wrinkled eyelids. Her hair was blonde. Aggie's brother, the one who died in the war, was born blond. Her mother said his hair was almost white then, and stayed fair until he was five or six years old, when it abruptly began to darken.

"Early to tell," said the doctor, "but I'd say she's the spitting image of her father. Same bone structure, you can see that." He was smiling down at the two of them; a sentimental man, entranced by mother and child and the miracle of his work.

She was a little puzzled that this small creature didn't much resemble the child in whom she'd been confiding. She'd thought of someone larger, darker, more fully formed. More complete somehow, although there was nothing actually missing from this baby that she could see, all its fingers and toes accounted for. And, after all, it was ridiculous that a newborn would open her eyes and her mouth and say, "I haven't been able to tell you till now, but I want to thank you for all your attention. Telling me so much. I feel we're very close." Or anything like that. Really, she had to laugh at herself, although laughter hurt.

"Now," the doctor was saying, "you have plenty of milk, and all you have to do is put her here, like this," and he shifted the baby to Aggie's breast, "and she'll do the rest. It's quite wonderful, you know, that they know right away what to do." And it *was* wonderful that the little lips immediately closed around her nipple, earnest intention pulsing away behind the tiny closed eyes.

"And don't worry, all new mothers are a bit nervous at first, but you'll find it comes as naturally to you as it does to her. Mother's instinct, I've never seen it fail."

Was it odd to have become so heavy and cumbersome, and then to have produced such a light result? Certainly it was peculiar to feel that the real child was still to come. Not that this baby was not hers, or that she wasn't pleased, or that there was anything wrong or unpleasant about her, or unlovable; of course Aggie loved her. But where was the other one?

She fell asleep, and was only vaguely aware of someone taking the child away.

When she wakened, the baby was sleeping in the cradle beside her bed, and Neil was standing in the doorway. She felt much better now. Really, the child was a lovely little thing, and anyway, transformations were always possible.

But considering transformations: look at him. His eyes, fixed on the sleeping child, were wet. Aggie, astonished, saw a tear break out and roll down his face. Why would that be? He was—entranced, that's what. She had never dreamed that while she was expecting, he also might have been. The expression was so naked she could see that he'd had no adjustment to make here, that there was no discrepancy between whatever he'd expected and what was.

How had he been looking at her, then, these past months? As a vessel, she supposed; a mere container.

Later, when the baby cried, he came and held her tenderly for a moment before passing her to Aggie. He watched briefly, but if he was looking at her breasts at all, it was with an eye for their capacity, not their beauty.

The next morning he said, "I've sent off the birth certificate. I thought we'd call her June Frances, if you have no objections."

She certainly did have objections, although not especially to the names. "You don't mean to say you've mailed it without consulting me?"

"I didn't think you'd care. You never mentioned you had any names in mind."

"You didn't either. Why ever June Frances?"

He was, after all, a little sheepish. "I thought June for the month and Frances for my mother. It's a name that goes back in my family. I thought she ought to have it too."

"And if I had other ideas?"

"I suppose we could change the June part, but it'd be an awful rigmarole, now that it's been mailed."

She'd thought maybe Anne, for her mother, or Edith for her sister, or Edith Anne.

On the other hand, this baby with, as the doctor said, his bones might be more a June Frances. And her Edith Anne would be someone else, some other time. Anyway, she didn't care enough at the moment, except about the principle, not being asked.

What was important, and astonishing, was that he had some capacity for love. A bit of a blow, really, that the child was the end of his desires.

Now a bit of a blow that the end of Aggie's desires is in the hands of that child, grown up. Somehow, right from the start, Aggie's love must have fallen short, or been disregarded, and this is what it's come to.

10

Love, Aggie wanted to discuss? "It wasn't just your father, you know," she said at breakfast with something, a certain wistfulness, in her voice. Or maybe only doubt. Maybe even she did not believe what she was saying. It's odd, though, what is remembered and how much must have been forgotten. And the older June gets, the less, it seems, she remembers. As if it were other Junes entirely who lived different parts of her life.

She recalls moments here and there: running to meet him at the door when he came home from school; how he picked her up and threw her into the air and caught her, until she got too big, and then he'd take her hands and whirl her around, feet off the floor, until they both were dizzy. "So what did my bunny do today?" he'd ask.

He took her to church on Sundays. Aggie wouldn't go. "You should, you know," he said, but she refused. "I've gone enough in my time. I have other things to do." What did she do?

Most often June went downstairs to the Sunday school in the basement, but sometimes he let her stay with him, in the high-ceilinged, dark-pewed cool and quiet church part. She loved the hymns, and their own two reedy voices singing. It was hard to sit still during the sermons, though.

When he left for school in the mornings, until she was old enough to go with him, she stood at the door waving goodbye. Sometimes she cried, and her mother held her back, shaking her, saying crossly, "For goodness' sake, he'll be back, he always comes back." Aggie so often sounded angry. That and her rushing around: that's what June remembers. And being slapped once (although only once) when she got in the way as Aggie carried a load of wash out to the clothesline. Aggie tripped and the clean clothes spilled and got dirty and had to be washed again, and June got slapped.

Also, it's confusing, but she has an impression of her mother tightening over time, a drawing in of her lips, a thin tension, and that's funny because in fact she was getting bigger and bigger.

He told June his stories, from books and about his home. Aggie claims to have hugged June and read to her and sung songs, also, but June has no recollection of that. If her mother did those things, surely June would have some memory? Or if she did, maybe her heart wasn't in it, so it made no impression.

But June's eighth birthday party is something different. Half a century ago and there it is, real as yesterday; more real in a way, since it made things clear, whereas yesterday did not.

"You're getting all grown up, aren't you?" her father said one evening. "Pretty soon you'll be eight years old," and he looked almost sad. She nearly said, "No, I won't grow up for a long time," so that he wouldn't sound sad; the same way she never told him she didn't believe in Santa Claus any more, because it seemed it would hurt him. Her mother might say, "Eat up, June, we have to get some meat on your bones," but her own desire was to stay small.

He smiled. "How would you like a birthday party? You could have, say, eight friends, one for each year, and whatever food you want, and games and paper hats."

That was one of the things she loved about him: that he opened up such visions, possibilities.

"I could have anything?"

"Whatever you want. Just this once."

She wanted hot dogs and soda pop, chocolate cake, and ice cream.

This was during the depression. She didn't understand at the time all that meant, but she did know that even though her father had a proper job, extra care was being taken. When she went shopping with Aggie on Saturdays, she saw her studying the meat longer than usual, and buying cheaper cuts. Sometimes fruit was passed over, and when her mother baked, she used less sugar. The garden was expanded. Among June's friends, even those who had been prosperous, clothes lasted longer, there were more hand-me-downs, and lunches were more often tomato sandwiches than meat. There were rumors, whispered talk, of some families in trouble. A birthday party was a luxury.

Aggie was quick, of course, to point that out. She said a party would be frivolous, unnecessary. Her father, though, said, "Every child should have one, and this is as good a time as any." He and June designed the paper hats she wanted. Her mother would buy the tissue and make them. June's would be tall and blue, with a glued-on golden star.

He went out and bought material for a birthday dress. Pink taffeta. Taffeta! June touched it with wonder. It was slithery and crackly, glamorous and grown-up. "I thought you'd like it," he said.

"Taffeta!" Aggie cried. "For God's sake, do you have any idea how hard that stuff is to sew?" But while she threw up her hands and rolled her eyes and sighed and complained, he just stood quietly looking at her, holding out the material.

For what felt like hours, June stood rigid on a chair while her mother knelt, pins clutched in her teeth, adjusting seams and putting up the hem. Aggie bent over the sewing, the material slipping beneath her fingers, whispering small curses. "Damn," June heard. "Oh, damn."

Still, with whatever resentment the dress was made, every stitch ended up in place and each fold fell perfectly. June twirled in front of the mirror in her room, a vision of stiff pink, the tight bodice flaring into skirt, the matching bow splendid at the waist. When she wore it downstairs to show her father, he said, "Oh, that's nice, bunny. Say thank you to your mother."

At school there was a certain competition for her invitations, whispers of who would be going and who would not. Because she was liked, or because she was the teacher's daughter, or because, in such hard times, a party was so rare? The reason didn't matter. What mattered was to be the centre of attention.

She saw herself at the party, perfect in pink taffeta, graciously accepting gifts, nodding at her guests, distributing hot dogs and cake. "Would you care for more?" she would ask politely. "Oh, thank you, do you like my dress?" and "What a lovely gift, how kind." She rehearsed in her bedroom at night. "So glad you could come," she said, nodding to invisible guests. "How nice."

Aggie made the crinkly paper hats and bought the food. The day before the party, she set up games in the front room. On a piece of cardboard, she sketched a crude, cartoon sort of donkey and cut it out, and from a piece of cardboard she fashioned a long, full, drooping tail. She colored it purple with one of June's crayons. June worried about it a little: that her friends would laugh at it for the wrong reasons. Also, that they might laugh at Aggie herself, already overweight and somewhat sloppy.

But at the party there was Aggie, patting one girl on the head, putting an arm around another, distributing affection easily, even taking part in the games, letting herself be blindfolded and turned by the small hands of June's friends and laughing when she saw she'd pinned the donkey's tail to its ear. "Your mother's fun," whispered a little girl. She *was* fun, too; just not anyone June recognized.

Her father, on the other hand, stayed mainly in the background. He smiled and spoke kindly but didn't join in, did not appear as the joyful man she knew. Of course, though, he was the teacher and these friends of hers were his pupils. A certain distance had to be maintained.

The house grew warm, the taffeta got a little limp, and she forgot to be quite as gracious all the time as she'd intended. The gifts, beyond the glittering paper, were something of a disappointment after all—a handkerchief here, a little cloth doll there. It was difficult to be enthusiastic.

Still, the party itself was a success. She imagined her friends talking about it the next day at school, laughing about how good the games were, how lavish the food had been, boasting about it loudly, in front of those who had not been asked. Aggie, with her own taste for sweets, had made a luxurious cake: dark chocolate layers separated by date filling and slathered with chocolate icing. Inside were little prizes, charms and coins—a special, extra touch. Ice cream was also to be served.

Eight candles were burning when Aggie carried the cake in from the kitchen. "Make a wish," her father said.

(What did she wish for then? Probably something silly, like good marks. What she would wish for now would be colossal. She might wish to be loved. But now she's too old to believe in wishes. Now she prays, and the only love to be prayed for is God's.)

Aggie, at her end of the table, began to cut the cake, topping each slice with ice cream, and passing it around. The girls' high spirits bubbled over into hysteria. Hot and over-excited, they began

giggling, snorting and poking at each other; June, too. This was
the best part. No one would forget this pure shared joy.

Disasters always seem to happen in slow motion. There was
June, bent over laughing as a plate arrived in her hands at the same
moment the girl beside her nudged her. The plate slipped, the cake
swept into the air, separating from the ice cream, and went plung-
ing into her lap while the ice cream slapped across her chest.

She watched it all happening, amazed.

Chocolate stains slithered down her body, and there was a little
plopping sound as the ice cream hit the floor. Suddenly no one was
laughing. There were little gasps and sucked-in breaths. June stared
at the disaster of pink taffeta, so carefully and unwillingly stitched
over so many hours. She could not believe this. In a moment it
would go away, she was sure; it was something like a nightmare,
but she'd wake up.

"Jesus Christ!" she heard. It was very loud and made her look
up. Aggie was standing at the far end of the table, her hands
planted on it in fists. "How could you be so clumsy? You've
ruined your goddamned dress!"

Had she never shouted before? Of course, but not like this, not
in front of people, and not swearing. June could feel her father
standing, moving in behind her, putting his hands on her shoulders,
looking over her head at her mother. June stared too.

Does Aggie think something like that could be forgotten? That
was no mere expression of anger. It was rage and fury, and something that looked like hatred. And it wasn't for a single incident,
either. It was for everything. It was not something June interpreted,
but something she knew, right into her bones.

"It's all right, bunny," her father was saying quietly, bending
over her. His voice was a little shaky, a bit high; he must have
seen, too. "Here, I'll just wipe off the worst of it." He looked up.
"Everybody carry on, eat up before your ice cream melts. It's
nothing serious." He knelt beside her, sponging at her dress, while
the others, very quietly now, began to eat again. His kindness un-
did her. "Come on, bunny, don't cry, it's just a dress, it's not important. It could happen to anybody, it's all right."

It was nice of him to pretend she was crying for the dress.

"Oh, for God's sake, quit bawling." Through tears, Aggie was
just a huge, dark, powerful form standing at the far end of the table.

"Stop it," he said quietly. To Aggie, not to her. But what exactly was he telling her to stop? Hurting June? Hating them? June

thinks now that he meant it absolutely. He wanted her mother to stop being, to vanish.

Quickly and uncomfortably her friends finished eating and left, sliding as unobtrusively as possible out the door.

What a mess June was: drenched in chocolate and tears, her party ringlets limp and dangling, even her white stockings wrinkled around her ankles. All that awful brown smeared across her dress. Her mother began to clear the table silently, stacking the dishes, picking crumbs from the floor, her mouth set in that bitter way she had perfected. Her father was saying over and over helplessly, "It's all right, don't cry. It's all right."

"It's damn well not all right," Aggie snapped finally. "Take her upstairs and wash her. There's water in the basin in my room, and a clean cloth. Get that dress off and get her into a nightgown. And throw out the dress, it can't be cleaned. Jesus."

"There's no need to swear."

"Go to blazes."

He smiled at June a little shakily, and took her hand. His hand was so dry! Hers was wet. When she thinks of it, it seems his hands were always papery-dry, like an old man's.

They were both uneasy in Aggie's room; it was so clearly hers, more or less forbidden to them both in normal times.

He'd never undressed June before, and was clumsy and ill at ease about it. The heap of pink taffeta lay spoiled on the floor. "I know it's early," he said, "but maybe you should stay up here in your room, and I'll come and tell you a story." He told her the one about Goldilocks and the three bears. Had he forgotten she was growing up? Did he think her safer as a baby? Did he like her better as a baby?

Too old for the story, she heard it in an older way. The danger of what Goldilocks had done struck her: how dangerous it was to be where you didn't belong, how risky to fall asleep when it would be wise to stay awake. How foolish, taking safety for granted.

What she could not make out was what she'd done that was so bad. Certainly she'd been clumsy, but that didn't warrant a look like that. It must have been something from long before a ruined dress. What did her mother blame her for?

Later, she heard them shouting, which was rare, and she cried again because it was her fault somehow, and downstairs, her father was suffering for some flaw in her that her mother could not bear.

11

"Oh, for God's sake, June," Aggie snaps, "I don't remember your damned birthday party. Why on earth would I? How can you still be harping about something fifty years ago?"

"How could you have forgotten?"

Actually, Aggie does have some recollection of making a taffeta dress, but not the occasion. In the depression, she made almost everything she and June wore, and some of the teacher's clothes as well. But June expects her to remember something about spilled cake and ice cream? Really, she's going to be a very silly old woman if she keeps this up; if she doesn't learn the importance of proper memory.

"It was the expression on your face."

"What?"

"Hate." Said flatly. "It looked like hate."

"How ridiculous. You mean, as if I hated *you*?"

"Me. Everything."

"Oh, June, how could you have imagined a thing like that? Of course I didn't hate you. Haven't I been trying to tell you how much I wanted you, it wasn't only your father who did?"

But did she love June? An obedient child, yes. When they went out together, people said, "She's so like your husband, isn't she? And such a good little girl." Not at all what Aggie had had in mind, not a daughter who resembled him, or one who was good. This quiet obedience merely showed a lack of imagination, as far as Aggie could see.

"I know what I saw." June pauses. "If it wasn't that, what was it?"

"Honestly, I can't remember. I simply don't remember anything about it. But I suppose I might have been angry. I might just have been fed up. I was so fed up, June, you can't imagine. It was nothing to do with you, though. I'm sure if I was angry, it was him, not you."

Part lie, part truth. True that she couldn't have hated the child. Disapproved of her sometimes, or was disappointed. But not true that it had nothing to do with her. It made everything worse, how much he loved his daughter. She felt her own child had been stolen. And he never once returned to her room after June was born.

"I think," she says, daring a great confession, "I might have been angry that you got along so well. Sometimes I didn't think either of you even noticed I was there, as long as the house was taken care of and your meals were on the table." She might be drunk, dizzy with admission.

At least June's face has softened. At least she looks more curious now than resentful and accusing.

"But if you liked me, you didn't show it."

"I did, you know. You just don't remember."

Well, she did like the baby: danced with her when she cried, and sang to her and really did make an effort to alter images. It was something like what she had done before she married him: changing the vision to fit reality.

She, too, told June stories, reading little books to her and talking about the farm, her family. Her stories didn't seem to grip the child, though, not like his. Perhaps, unlike Aggie's family, who could be visited, his people were more alluring, being so far away.

Their voices, their speech, were so similar, his and June's. When they spoke, the sound went through her head like a drill. It was irritating to have to hold onto June when he was leaving for school and feel her excitement when the time was coming for him to be home. She was like a little animal, sensing his approach.

Aggie remembers a decade of being married, a muddy-colored recollection involving a sense of trudging. Determined, hard-working days, and a child who was turning out as unexpectedly as her marriage. Their failure, his and Aggie's, remained inexplicable; how they managed to disintegrate so forcibly and irrevocably and so swiftly. Maybe it was a fault in her mind then that she couldn't work it out, or, having worked it out, resolve it. That's a theory. What she *felt* was that he was entirely wrong-headed, a disputatious bully, a frantic, feeble dictator who had mistaken her for someone else.

Looking at him sitting across from her at the supper table, she could think, "Well, to hell with you." But there he was, not just in the flesh, in his brown suit and white shirt, but a presence in her life, like a headache. Even when she was angry, she was angry with him, so that in a way it was his anger. What would have happened if she'd said, "Listen, sit down, let's talk about what's wrong and what we can do to fix it"? That's the sort of thing Frances would do; Frances, who sometimes lapses unfortunately into the words of silly magazines, advocating "openness" and "honesty".

Well, what would have happened? Probably, like the gingham dog and the calico cat, they'd have eaten each other up.

As it was, they only gnawed at each other's edges. He left her money for household spending under the sugar bowl on the kitchen table every Friday. She might say, "Well, we can't eat your position, can we?" Or she could regard his Sunday suit doubtfully as he was going out the door to church and say, "It's too bad, you know, it's gotten shiny at the back like that, when you can't afford a new one."

They weren't poor, just had to be careful. But it was a way of digging at something important to him: his ability to make a living and his status. Not much, after all, compared with the wounds he could inflict: that he did not find her tempting or appealing.

Either to try to find the key to all this, or to escape, she can't recall which, she began to read. She does remember thinking that she was damned if he'd have any advantage, including whatever he knew from those little packages of information on the front-room shelves. And that sometimes it was nice to hide in other lives. But damned if she could tell, wading through his books, just where he thought his advantage lay. These were for children, small moral tales. They were not power, and certainly not wisdom. They did help her learn words and gain confidence. She found it increasingly easy to hear words flowing into sentences, and sentences into paragraphs, and paragraphs into stories. It was like doing exercises, building strength. But to what point? To learn that it was bad to lie and steal, and manly to be brave? These were things you could learn by listening to sermons.

"Have you been dusting my books?" he asked irritably. "Some of them are out of order. I wish you'd put them back where you found them when you're cleaning."

It occurred to her that she did not see him reading, except when he was preparing lessons. She'd had an impression of a learned man, but he seemed to have stopped at some point. What kind of teacher must he have been? Likely the sort of husband he was. Except that she thought he was a little afraid of her, whereas naturally he would not be afraid of his pupils. Perhaps he was also afraid of that glimpse of himself in the blow he had struck once, the marks of his fingers on her cheek. He probably hadn't known he could do a thing like that.

The blow she struck, answering him, was instant and instinctive, not a defence but a response. If he were ashamed of his moment of weakness, she was proud that, without thinking, she'd taken care of herself. That did not seem to her to be violence; more an assertion, a proper positioning of the two of them. A wordless setting out of the rules: do that and this will immediately occur.

Just standing up against him gave her an advantage, since he had not expected it. Like a fighter going into the ring assuming an opponent with shorter arms, he was bewildered to find himself facing someone of precisely the same reach. The one more surprised, dismayed, and affronted is the one who loses.

She discovered an atlas on the shelves of books. It contained not only maps of the earth, but sketches of the solar system. From Neptune, Mars, or Mercury, all the upheaval in this house was insignificant: rather like God's perspective, peering down from heaven. From high in one of the trees at the farm, her brothers had looked small, gaping up at her. You could cause quite a lot of unintended pain, throwing something from a height. She'd tossed an apple at her smallest brother once, and hit him in the chest and knocked him down. Maybe God didn't quite realize the effects down here on earth, in her front room, of the smallest of his finger flicks.

So many countries there were, and continents, signifying so many people of so many colors and customs. So many possibilities there must be, then. Finding out one thing led to another. There was, she found, an expanding progression in all this. She got quite frantic about it for a time; trembled in the desire for a further fact, the definition of an unknown word, some magic piece of knowledge that surely must be out there, if only she knew just where to look. She carted the dictionary with her through the day, replacing it on the proper shelf shortly before he was due home. She discovered the town library and hid books beneath her bed.

It was hard, choosing between fact and fiction. Both were vital, after all. Simple information: what crop is grown where, the location of deserts, the periods of kings and queens and the names of plants—all of it counted, all of it was useful. Just knowing was an edge, a gain. Oh, she cared for June as well, scrubbed the floors and cleaned out the ashes of the woodstove, continued to mend and darn. Most of all, cooked and baked and ate, her hand reaching out absently for another cookie as she read another chapter in another book, ending a day flushed with facts and food. Perhaps it was just as well, from that point of view, that June was such a good child.

Whatever hurt, like the sound of his pen scratching on paper in the dining room in the evenings, or his snores in the middle of the night, or June's periodic cries, or the sound of his briefcase being set down in the hall, the tap-tapping of his papers being knocked into line on the table, or his knees cracking when he bent to pick up an eraser he'd dropped—all that could be soothed, in the day, with food, and reduced by knowledge. How could a woman who knew the capital of Peru and the names of the explorers of America be hurt? What could damage a person who could recite the names of all the planets, and all the continents of the earth, and all the oceans? She was making herself a fortress of facts.

Novels had an interest of another sort. They told of men moving, leaping around the world from event to event, with great occurrences of significance and heroism, passion of various kinds. Revenge and honor and blood. Nothing to do with washing dishes and making meals and patching sheets and scrubbing floors and getting to the end of the day. It seemed reasonable to conclude that the lives of men offered the chance to shift scenery and conditions.

There were no changes in her life. There was instead his voice droning on in the front room, telling Jane his endless tales of England; and his whoops of joy when he came through the door and lifted up his eager daughter. There were his little lectures, his instructions and rebukes, about the condition of his books and her behavior in the presence of company. His punctuality: meals to be served at six-fifteen; his footsteps going past her door at ten-thirty at night; his feet hitting the floor promptly at seven in the morning.

The rhythm of relief when he left the house, and the weight of knowing he would be back. The drudgery of all the small jobs involved in running the house, and having them all to do again the next day. Dishes washed were dirtied again, sheets laundered had to be washed again, shined floors got scuffed, and dust resettled on windowsills and furniture. June bathed had to be bathed again the next night; June weeping had to be comforted again and again. There did not seem to be an end. It seemed, most days, a matter of surviving from one moment to the next, of drawing the next breath and taking the next step. Of keeping running and keeping reading.

Keeping eating, too: the banana cakes, blueberry muffins, date squares, and oatmeal cookies. They soothed pains and avenged her. As if the food were flesh, she devoured it. Her slim belly became plump, then rolling. Her thighs began to ripple, her chin sagged and doubled. Her features, and her feet and hands, came to look tiny against the bulk of the rest of her. She became imposing. If he glanced in her direction, she must fill up his view. It wouldn't be so easy for him to pretend she wasn't there.

He grew small and insignificant beside her. When they had to go out, usually to school functions, she thought they must look fairly odd. Certainly she was no longer what he must have had in mind, as the appropriate wife of a teacher.

It is ridiculous, of course, and wicked, too, to compare her life then with the lives of prisoners, of people who are scooped off streets by secret police, taken to dark cellars, and tortured. Of course there were no electrodes attached to her body, and the soles of her feet were not beaten by switches. Her pain, unlike that of tortured prisoners, was dull, not sharp. But it was constant, lodged somewhere below the heart, just above the waist, and was accompanied by a tiny perpetual headache. She could no longer remember how it felt to be without those pains. Words and food soothed, but did not cure.

She prayed for freedom, although without a clear idea of exactly what God could do for her. She only asked for some miracle and meanwhile she ate and worked and read. By the time she was thirty-one, she was fat, literate, furious, and disappointed.

(But every disappointment toughens. Frances once said to her, "Grandma, you're a tough old bird," meaning it affectionately, as a compliment. But there are different kinds of toughness. Aggie's, she fears, has added scales. She is afraid she is dying with a crusted soul.)

How sad, how unfortunate, that he wound up with a fat woman out of whom he tried, once, to beat wilfulness. Naturally he would have preferred some slim meek woman who would deliver his small pale child without fuss. Just as she would have preferred a robust man whose chidren were adventurous. She might have felt pity for him.

This is the importance of proper memory; not birthday parties.

That winter when she was thirty-one set records. There was more snow than anyone in town could recall, and between snowfalls the temperatures dropped bitterly. "This is one for the books, all right," people said.

Aggie rather liked it. Apart from the kitchen, the house was hard to keep warm, and hanging out the wash with mittened hands fumbling with clothespegs was difficult. Bringing it in again, stiff and frozen, was also tricky; sheets could shatter like glass. But her own padded body was a kind of protection. She did not need to go around bundled up like the teacher and June. At night she lay listening to winds roar and whistle around the house and found the sound more stirring than menacing. For once, the weather was as violent as the little seed of fury she contained, and she lay with fists clenched, limbs rigid, skin flushed, hearing the destruction.

There was no such pleasure for people who had to go out. Neil and June struggled to school together, hand in hand, ploughing their way out every morning and home at night. They came in wet and cold, steam forming instantly on his glasses in the warm kitchen. June's pale-blue eyes rimmed with red and her nose running. They clapped their hands and hugged themselves and wore layers of sweaters. Aggie warmed June's nightgown in the oven before sending her to bed.

June came down sick, and then he did, although he kept going to school for a few days until he lost his voice and had to give in. Aggie had a lot of extra work then, with two patients, a lot of running up and down stairs with juices and soups and hot-water bottles. She made them hot lemonade and wrapped their throats in warm greasy rags and rubbed their chests with liniment. It was odd, touching him: hairless and smooth, and so narrow she could feel the breastbone and ribs beneath the skin. Too much pressure sent him off into a spasm of coughing; otherwise she might have been tempted to dig her fingers right in, through the flesh.

Sometimes he was sleeping when she went into his room. It was interesting, watching him without his knowing. How vulnerable he was, lying there. A stranger. What did she have to do with this man? She could not make out what could have induced her to alter visions. He was thirty-nine, and just like a child sleeping. She thought there must be a way to get free of such a person, it ought to be easy; but apparently not. Weak people, she saw, had the force of a multitude of the strong.

Without his voice, he had to point at what he wanted, or write it down. He couldn't call out to her, so he clapped his hands when he wanted her attention. His room was close and dark. There was too much human flesh in it for such a small room; their flesh in it together made it smell somewhat peculiar.

And then there was June, tossing and feverish and demanding. Poor little girl. Aggie sat on the edge of her bed and stroked her forehead and read stories to her. Really, it was all a great deal of work, and there was no time to spare for books or baking.

She was amazed she wasn't sick herself, spending so much time with them. She was proud of her body standing her in such good stead.

The weather improved and so did June. In a couple of days she'd be ready to go back to school, and he would follow shortly. Aggie could see an end, to this at least.

Throughout it all, and it went on for more than a week, it did not occur to her to call a doctor. Doctors, in her experience, were for things like chicken-pox or scarlet fever or whooping cough, certainly not for colds.

The morning she went into his room and didn't immediately hear the rasping of his breath, she abandoned prayers. At first she thought he was better, and sleeping. She stood in the doorway, looking at the heap of blankets. Closer, however, the view was different.

He was on his side, his right hand clutching the pillow as if he'd needed something from it—perhaps a breath. His eyes, unfortunately, were open, and so was his mouth. She thought later it might not have been so terrible if his eyes, at least, had been shut. He must have put up quite a fight for the last tiny trail of oxygen.

(Once, back home, she'd been exploring up in the barn and come across one of the barn cats, its limbs stretched rigid, eyes blank and open, the same peculiar combination of absence and tension about its body. "Distemper," shrugged her father, who took it off on a shovel to bury it.)

He looked so plain. Just a small, plain man. This wasn't what she'd meant at all. God could surely not have heard a request for death in her prayers for freedom. "Oh, God," she whispered, backing away. This time it was a protest.

"Mother," June was calling. "I'm awake, can I get up? I'm thirsty, can I get a drink?"

There were all those moments when she'd looked at him and thought of getting free. God must have misinterpreted, or taken her too literally. Brutal. And could He plan, with one of those grand sweeps of His that massacre whole peoples for small errors, to free her entirely?

Panicked, she bolted to June's room. But June was sitting up looking peevish, her eyes clearer and her fever down. "You can get a drink of water," Aggie told her, "but then come right back to bed and stay quiet. Daddy isn't well, and I have to go out for a few minutes."

However could she tell June? What she wanted was to crawl under the sheets, huddle beneath the blankets, and be comforted. Also to protect June against any further whims God might have in mind.

Outdoors, it was white and silent. Standing on the porch she looked around, wondering just where she had thought she would go, and what she'd intended to do.

Down the block and around the corner was the minister's house. To deal with this error of God's, it seemed reasonable to go to His interpreter. She began to run through the heavy snow, clumsy in the rubber boots she'd pulled on.

"Good gracious," said the minister's wife. Aggie supposed she must have pounded on the door, and heaven knew what she looked like. "Whatever's the matter? Come in, you'll catch your death out there."

She was led to the kitchen. A cup of tea appeared. There was an arm around her shoulder, and a calm voice in her ear. "Now you just come with me," leading her upstairs, directing her to a bed, helping her lie down, "and I'll send my daughter right over to June. You just try to be calm, my husband will take care of things. I'll be back in a minute."

It was not calm that came, although it was reassuring that unpleasant details were being taken care of, but anger: how dared God misinterpret like this when He was supposed to understand perfectly? This must be a punishment, then. But of whom? Of her, for lacking love and grace? Or for something petty, like not going to church? A petulant God, that would make Him. Or was it aimed at Neil, whatever sins he might have committed; or at June, who had done nothing at all?

She wanted an explanation here, someone to account for God's perversity, this way He had, apparently, of caricaturing longings. She could ask the minister's wife, but when the woman returned, Aggie had no words.

"My dear, everything's being done. My daughter's gone to June and my husband has sent for the doctor. And, well, you know, he'll make the arrangements, too. So you can just stay here and rest as long as you like and not worry."

But obviously in a world of mad events, one would be best up on one's feet, alert and if possible fighting back. "No, thank you, you've been very kind, but I think I should go home to June."

June, who had now been told, looked up at her with enormous eyes. She was just a little girl, not accountable in the way adults were, or God should be, but she was furious and frightened, and she did say, "You killed him." And repeated, "You killed him. You let him die."

That was a possibility, and Aggie considered it. She could see that it might be the case. Not through any action, of course, but perhaps through lack of it.

"Now, now," said the doctor, "your daddy was very sick." He turned to Aggie. "It just turned into pneumonia, I think. There wasn't anything you could have done, you know, you mustn't blame yourself. And he wouldn't have suffered for long, not really."

But what if she had called the doctor days ago? Was he telling her comforting lies? There must be cures.

"You know, June," said the minister, "your daddy's happy now because he's with God. God needed him because he was such a good man." June turned away and faced the wall.

Surely there were such things as oxygen tents, or drugs, something that a doctor could have done. Still, it came back to God. No one told her a doctor might be needed.

Confused, Aggie watched as people flickered through the house on unknown errands. They murmured regrets, which meant at least that they did not discern guilt in her, or responsibility. But then, the idea would never occur to them.

"Such a fine man," they said. "Such a fine teacher. He will be missed." Really? If she'd been the one who died, what would they have known to say?

They brought food, and hovered. They seemed to be waiting for some action on her part. She understood finally that they must be waiting for tears. She had none, however. It wasn't exactly grief that she was feeling: just that something important that she couldn't identify was missing.

He was laid out in the front room, and people filed in, filed past, filed out. There seemed to be so many of them. Had they all respected him, or liked him? Was it for Neil or for the teacher? And who was there for her, the teacher's widow?

That night before the funeral, when everyone had left, she pulled up a chair beside him. He was lying on some kind of white satiny pillowy material, inside the shiny wooden box. He wore his best black suit, and his hands were folded neatly on his white shirtfront. Expressionless, of course.

The room she had made so light was now too light, the cream color inappropriate. At the moment, she could see how he might have felt about the dark.

He looked smaller, more fragile and also more firm. There was so little to him. The undertaker's pots and brushes had given a waxy gloss to his face, an artificial, fevered flush to his cheekbones. Through the still flesh of his hands, she could make out bones. How long would it take for the flesh to fall away, leaving just the white and gleaming bones beneath?

A waste. She could not see his life at all. Who was this man, her husband, this orderly heap of matter waiting to be buried? How cruel, not to be able to see.

He'd been different. There were pictures of him, a chubby little boy in short pants, blouse, blazer, cap, grinning shyly at the camera. It had amazed her that he had once been plump and smiling. She had no connection with that little boy at all.

If his bitterness had squeezed the plumpness out of him, and her bitterness had made her fat, whose was greater?

He must have been so frightened. Always, not only at the end. He'd done a few brave things: coming here alone, and then this marriage. That must have worn out his courage, and having it turn out so badly.

If she'd known before that he was just afraid, really; nothing much more than that. And now when she could have spoken, and might have tried to make it better, he was out of reach. That was what death took away: the chance for resolution.

She had an impulse to hold him, comfort him, restore the plump innocence and make it better. She felt, she thought, like a mother, not a wife. She even reached out a hand—surely she had enough life for the two of them, enough to spare that she could even restore the dead? But she flinched back from the flesh, so amazingly inert and mysteriously dead. Was this how he'd felt about her living flesh?

And, after all, what could she have said? That she was sorry. Not an apology, but certainly a regret that they'd been equally unhappy, equally adamant and stubborn. But he was the one who'd given up and died. That would never have occurred to her.

The next day at the funeral she greeted people automatically, shook their hands, heard them from a distance, listened to the minister's prayers, his eulogy, from far away. None of it seemed to apply. He said the teacher had been a wise, gentle, kind, and learned man who would be a jewel in God's heavenly crown. For Aggie and June, his family, he said, the loss of so good a man was a blow only their faith could help them endure. "Thy will be done," recited the mourners, "on earth, as it is in heaven."

June did not hear any of this. The minister's wife had said, "It would only upset her more, and really, she should remember him as he was."

Aggie had some questions and would have liked to add them to the service. She wanted to ask the minister, or anyone else who might know, if she or God were responsible. She wanted to say that she had prayed for freedom, never dreaming, and to ask what she was now supposed to do with it. What would these people have to tell her about a God who turned such a request into death?

She looked at Neil, the point of this gathering. He would be appalled if she stood, asking questions. He would say, "How could you, you ruined my funeral." She giggled aloud, and several people glanced at her, but must have mistakened the sound for a sob.

It was hard to see the men carrying the coffin, now closed, out the door; it left her almost lonely. She couldn't account for that; then she thought, "It must just be that I like him better dead than alive." Another giggle nearly escaped, and she wondered if she were hysterical in some peculiar internal way.

The women had brought sandwiches and cakes, and were making tea and coffee. People began to relax and chat. They were kind to her, and deferential toward her loss, but death itself seemed to have gone out the door with his body. In the kitchen, women exchanged recipes and discussed their children. In the front room, made spacious by the absence of the coffin, the men talked about the depression, and how long it might go on.

A lawyer said, "You come and see me when you feel up to it, and we'll go over how you stand. I have his will, you know." She hadn't known, and never thought of him making a will.

The banker said, "When you're ready, come in and we'll get the bank account switched into your name, and I'll show you how to deal with all the forms."

The doctor's wife said, "You'll be going back to your family, I suppose? This is such a big house, isn't it, for just the two of you. But you'll have no trouble selling it." Aggie nodded blankly. She had no idea, no plans.

"There's plenty of food here, dear," said the minister's wife. "You won't have to worry about cooking for a few days." Yes, there was a good deal of food. It was interesting, this instinct so much like her own: that food could heal.

Some people hugged her lightly, but there were no real embraces. Perhaps she did not seem embraceable. Back in their own homes, she thought, they would be making tea and sitting in their warm kitchens, discussing the funeral and news they'd heard, and talking, too, about the teacher and Aggie herself. They might say, "She kept a good grip on herself." Or, "She took it pretty calmly, I must say." They would speculate on what she would do now.

She had no idea what to do, but June was upstairs. Poor little girl; although not so little any more, ten and at a gangling, awkward sort of stage. How would Aggie have felt if her father had died when she was ten? What would she have understood? She couldn't, at this point, imagine. And then June had been so close to him, and her grief would be special, however incomprehensible.

"Go away," she told Aggie in that high, harsh voice that was so much like his when he was angry. She stared at Aggie with those pale-blue eyes, also so much like his, and so hard to see into.

"It'll be just like him watching me," Aggie thought. Her first view, really, of the future since the event.

How strange it was, the silence of the house without him, considering he had never made much noise. No footsteps on the stairs, no creakings from the next room or snores filtering through the walls. Instead of lying awake irritated by his little rustlings, his presence, she was aware of absence. The sound of him brushing his shoes, the slap of the polishing cloth, the tapping of his pencil against his teeth when he was thinking, the little groan of relief he always made as he lowered himself finally into his bed, had been enraging. Silence, however, was nothing at all.

Here she was, free, but freedom seemed to be a vacancy, a lack of rules, a vacuum of passion. Still, there were edges and definitions about her now that distinguished her from the girl she had been. There were parts of her that would not be touched again, places that had been hurt now would not feel pain. This freedom, she thought, must have more to do with who she would be than with what she would do. The thought was confused. Nevertheless, if it was too early to tell, it was obviously also much too late for going back.

part
TWO

12

The night before June's wedding, Aggie came tapping on her bedroom door, holding something behind her back and looking a little shy. "Are you excited, June?"

Excited? Yes; trembling, in fact, with anticipation of change. Herb Benson. Mrs. Herb Benson. June Benson. Tomorrow she would leave this house, go down that stone walk on the arm of her husband. For years she had seen herself doing this, and turning at the end, waving a dignified, adult farewell to her mother. Never mind that her new house was only blocks away. It would be hers.

"I was thinking downstairs about the night before my wedding." June waited, but no unpleasantness seemed to be implied. "I do hope it works out for you. I hope you'll be happy."

"I do too. I'm sure I will."

And she was sure. Herb Benson was beautiful. Of course, one did not refer to a man that way, and he wasn't really beautiful. Good-looking enough, but that wasn't what June meant. She meant that he was everything: slim and outgoing and well-turned-out. He liked everyone. Everyone liked him. It was something, just going out with him, much less marrying him. All sorts of people said hello to him on the street. True, he was just a salesman. He travelled, selling wholesale lines of furniture to stores in different towns. But he was good at it; it would be different if he were not. He was the sort, people said when she announced they were engaged, who could sell ice-boxes to Eskimos. "I know I'm only a salesman, Junie," he told her, one arm slung carelessly around her

shoulder as they walked—daringly, she felt—along the main street
after a movie, "but that's a talent too. I know it's not like being
a teacher or a lawyer or whatever, but a person should do what
he's good at, shouldn't he?"

Why, he was so good at selling (and he told her, "The first thing
about being a salesman is selling yourself. People have to like
you"), he was so good at it he even won Aggie. "Of course I like
him, June," she said. "Why wouldn't I?"

Oh, this was a man in a million: the one who really saw. Who
said, "You have gorgeous cheekbones, you know, Junie," and ran
his fingertips over them. "And a pretty good body, too," and
poked a finger at her ribs. She hadn't thought of it that way before,
had thought she was merely thin. But no: "You could be a model,
except of course you're too smart." He seemed to like it, that she
was a teacher. All in all, they found things to admire about each
other.

Tomorrow, in a mere twenty-four hours, she would be another
person. Meanwhile, on this last evening of her girlhood, here was
Aggie, looming large, spoiling the anticipation a little, but also re-
minding her how great an event this was: getting out.

"Do you remember our talk years ago about being married?"

Oh yes, indeed she did. But these were things she wasn't actually thinking about yet.

"You remember me saying it should be a pleasure for you?"
That, too.

"So I made this for you."

What Aggie pulled from behind her back and held out, an offering, was really quite extraordinary, like nothing June had ever
thought of, much less owned. A delicate pink hand-embroidered
nightgown, little vines and flowers stitched around the throat, the
sleeves, and the hem, all a filmy, gauzy, flimsy sort of material.
She was supposed to wear this? "But you can see right through
it," she said, astonished, holding it up.

"I know. Try it on. I had to guess about the size."

Well, it fit, shaping itself around June's small bosom and her
waist, falling in folds to the floor; it fit, but heavens, surely it didn't
suit. It did add something: allure, perhaps? Or glamor? It was
slinky, like a movie gown. Like something Myrna Loy might wear
for William Powell. But like a movie gown, it was not quite de-
cent, not quite her. It revealed too much, and seemed to promise
someone she was not.

Still, consider how many hours Aggie must have spent, how many books she must have put off reading, how many loaves of bread had gone unbaked, or how many hours of sleep were given up, so she could do this. What had she been thinking, sewing away in secret?

"Thank you. It's lovely." June had a momentary impulse to put her head down on her mother's shoulder, except she could not imagine what would happen then, how they would manage to end such a clumsy embrace.

"You wear it tomorrow night," said Aggie. "I hope you enjoy it." She patted June awkwardly on the shoulder and left.

This was June's last night in her old room. She looked around, trying to feel the significance of that, but tomorrow kept getting in the way. She could barely even feel her father here tonight, although for years she'd kept him hovering up in a corner of the ceiling, or just above the house. Heaven, although of course he would be there, too, seemed too far away. What would he say to her tonight? Something like "Be well, bunny, do your best." Not "Enjoy."

He would put his arms around her. She still missed that, being touched with affection. Well, Herb touched her with affection, of course, but it wasn't the same. His hands seemed aimed at something else, purposeful and therefore not quite pure.

What she liked best was being seen with him: on the street, at a movie, in a restaurant. There she was, little skinny June, or the daughter of the fat woman who ran the bakery, or Miss Hendricks the teacher—all those versions of her that people saw, out with this man. That was really something.

Especially considering his choices. This nightgown, now, put her in mind of women who were quite different.

He knew by name the cashiers and usherettes at the theatre, the waitresses in restaurants. Those women who said hello to him were like foreign objects, shiny and flashy, like the jewellery in Woolworth's. They seemed to say things with their bodies. A waitress with dyed blonde hair, dark roots showing, jogged his shoulder with her elbow and threw back her head, laughing at his jokes. "She's a bit—cheap-looking, don't you think?" June asked him later, and he laughed. "I suppose. You know, you're the expensive type. You're the kind that really costs." She had no idea what that meant, but laughed anyway, because he did.

His hands went around her, although she kept him away from certain places he would have liked to explore. "Look," he said, stepping his fingers down her spine, "I can count the bumps." She'd never really thought about her bones. Alone in her room she peered in the mirror, examining these cheekbones and collarbones he admired. Another foolish thing she did alone was pick petals off daisies, like a child.

His parents were dead, and his only sister lived out west, married to a wheat farmer. "Coming here is like having a family again," he said, "you and your mother."

And she had worried about introducing them, what he would think of Aggie, now badly overweight. "Look at the mother to see the daughter," people said, although how anyone would look at Aggie and see June was hard to imagine. She worried, though, that he would take one look and bolt.

"It's too bad you never met my father," she told him. "He was quite different. People always say I take after him."

But when she did take him home, and Aggie came to greet them in the front hall, and June said, "Herb, I'd like you to meet my mother, Aggie; Mother, this is Herb Benson," he didn't even blink. They got on, in fact, quite well. Aggie asked him about his work, his routes, the people he met, and he spoke admiringly about the courage it must have taken for her to start the bakery, making a living for herself and her child after her husband died.

"Well, I had to, you see. It was that or go back to my family, and that wouldn't have done at all."

"But why a bakery?"

She laughed and slapped at her body, setting the loose undersides of her arms flapping. "Mainly because, as you see, I'm fond of food. But also, I was never trained for anything, not like June here. All I knew was cleaning and sewing and cooking, and since I don't like cleaning particularly and I'm not that good at sewing, it only left a bakery, really."

"It must have been hard."

"You bet. Still is, for that matter, but it's mine and I like it."

That was about how she'd explained it to June, too, after a very brief period of mourning that looked more like a state of suspension than grief. "I have to do something, June; your father didn't leave us much." As if he'd been worth only money.

This was after some weeks of coming home from school to find Aggie sitting—just sitting—at the kitchen table with a cup of tea, looking out, sometimes not even any supper ready. And then one day she came home and found Aggie whipping around making lists, surveying rooms, standing around regarding various walls, her finger on her chin, looking as if she were seeing things that weren't there. It was as if she'd swept him, and his death, and a whole past life, right out of her head. Mysterious, but of course quite typical.

And suddenly there were carpenters in the kitchen, and new shelves and counters, and two new stoves, and a bigger ice-box, and the cellar was all cleaned up and cleared, and two new windows were being punched into the front-room walls—every day when June came home, changes had occurred, and it was like finding a different house. There was sawdust tracked everywhere, and now they ate in the dining room, at her father's old table, because there was no room in the kitchen any more for a table and chairs. A sign went up at the front, with an arrow: "Aggie's Bakeshop, please use rear door". Not even "Hendricks Bakery", not even that much dignity. "I want it to be my own," her mother explained. "Anyway, June, he wouldn't have liked his name used."

This was true. It was also true that it was difficult, becoming the daughter of a woman who baked for a living, instead of being the teacher's daughter. And on top of that her own grief, missing him. He'd vanished so abruptly there was no chance to say things she might have told him if she'd known; his home, her home, was utterly transformed; and her mother was a whirlwind: planning and adding rows of figures, ordering workmen about, and shouting at the manager of the bank. "It's a gamble, June," she said. "You must see, I've got to make it work. Otherwise I don't know what we'll do."

Well, what did other widows do? Surely something more decorous, more subdued.

June pretty much lived upstairs in her bedroom. She often did her homework there, and said her prayers. She held long conversations with her father, who after all must still be watching. She kept him up to date on events, although of course he would know everything anyway. His mother, her grandmother, wrote from England (sending her letters, curiously, to June and not to Aggie). "He was a lovely little boy, your father," she wrote. "I'm sure you're very much like him." June read the letters aloud, so that he could also hear, and kept them in the top drawer of her dresser, with a lilac sachet. She took from his room a few important things:

his mother's picture, and one of him as a little boy, smiling at the camera.

It was not hard to notice that her mother never cried. She avoided Aggie, but also tried to keep an eye on her. It was tricky, but there was no trusting a woman who could cause a man to vanish.

At least she was unlikely to present June with another father. Other widows might remarry, but even a child's eye could see that no man was apt to enter voluntarily into a union with such an overbearing, selfish, determined, and unsentimental woman as her mother. A man would more likely be looking for the opposite. (Although that did not explain that awful Barney, who eventually started hanging around the kitchen in the mornings. He, however, was already married, and so perhaps saw Aggie differently.)

As for June, she would be a teacher and a lady.

The second time they met, Aggie invited Herb to supper. At the table, his hand slipped into a pocket inside his vest and pulled out a silver-plated flask. "Would you have one with me, Aggie? June won't, but I thought you might not mind a drink."

"Sure, I'll try it." Aggie sipped, her face wrinkled, and they both laughed. "My, it's warm all the way down, isn't it?"

(Thank heaven she didn't take to liquor the way she did to food. "That's because I like a clear head," she has explained, "and that's not easy at the best of times. As you know so well, June." She still occasionally enjoys, however, "getting a little buzz on", which was one of Herb's expressions and one of the few things besides his wife and daughter that he left behind him here.)

"Aggie's a great old girl, isn't she?" he said to June, and she didn't trouble to correct him. It was just as well they got along, she supposed; and anyway, when they had their own place it wouldn't matter.

"It's funny," said Aggie, "he's not at all what I would have pictured for you."

"What did you expect?"

"Oh, somebody more serious, maybe from the church, or another teacher, something like that. Someone more like your father, after all."

"But you like him?"

"Well, yes, it's just—he seems so unlikely to be your type. Don't you find there's something—oh, what do I mean?—fleshy about him?"

"Not at all. He's very slim."

"No, not that. Physical. He's a bodily sort of man."

Yes, in a way. He liked to have his arm around things, or his hand resting on a shoulder, or slapping someone's back. If that's what Aggie meant. But it was nice to cross a street with his protective hand cupping her elbow, even though she'd never considered needing help to cross a street before.

Other times, however, his hands frightened her; when he got a little carried away kissing her good night and tried to reach inside her dress. Then he was strange, demanding, like a different person, and not, for the moment, gentle and respectful. She had to wonder at those times just who he thought she was.

When Aggie had told her, years ago, about what she might expect, alarming changes already were occurring. June had glanced furtively at other girls and noticed breasts developing, but could not make out if hidden, more unpleasant changes were also taking place.

She saw that the man who delivered eggs and milk and butter at the door had hair poking from his chest, the back of his neck, and heavily down his arms. Where else? It was dark and curly, whereas June's was blonde—but still. She, too, was growing odd sprouts of hair, under her arms, down her legs, and even, and this was quite horrifying, at the base of her stomach. Was she becoming a man then, getting hairier and hairier until she'd be as bushy and brawny as the man from the dairy? Well, that was one thing Aggie's little talk accomplished: reassuring her she was being transformed into a woman, not a man.

Even so, much of it struck her as mysterious and disgusting. Aggie accurately predicted hair, breasts, blood, and the possibility of cramps. Then she spoke of the real event, for which all this was only a preparation. Seeds and eggs, and parts of bodies meeting. It seemed to June, listening, that her own body was very far away and foreign, all these peculiar events going on internally, outside her grasp.

"But the important thing, June, is to be proud, becoming a grown-up woman, not a child any more. And then when you're really grown up there'll be pleasure in it for you and your husband. It's not just something you do for him, or to have children, it's for your pleasure, too. Do you see?"

No, but she wasn't about to ask. The big question might have revealed the lie behind all this. Because if what Aggie said was true, June's slim, fastidious, and gentle father must have performed

this act, and with this sloppy, ravenous woman. If they had not
even touched or spoken unless they had to, how could they have
done what Aggie described?

Still. The hair flourished, the blood flowed and even the cramps
came true. How could she tell how far the truth would go?

And how could Aggie have talked of being proud of these events,
which as it turned out were often nasty little surprises, coming at
awkward moments, like in class, resulting in stains?

As June developed small breasts and her hips broadened somewhat, the gangling angularity of her childhood grew into a sort of
grace. She was not exactly pretty, and boys didn't tease her the
way they did some of the other girls, but then, she would have
been insulted if they had. It was not crude jokes she dreamed about,
but arms. Not even hands. Just, lying in bed, she felt the lack of
a simple pair of arms. Also perhaps a shoulder.

Waiting took sturdiness of spirit. Slowly, slowly, the bakery
made money. At first Aggie told her, so many times, that they
couldn't afford things—a new dress, a trip, or anything June particularly wanted. "I'm sorry, but we just can't." That did not
mean, however, that Aggie had no money for ovens, a proper
bathroom, or new windows in the front room, all the changes she
was making. "But you see, June, I have to change the kitchen so
I can run a business here. And while the carpenters are in, I might
as well have the other work done."

Her mother seemed—unleashed, somehow. More sprawling, as if
she'd taken off a girdle, and less capable than before of order and
moderation (except in the kitchen, where she was efficient and
brisk). She sailed around the house devouring words the way she
devoured food, sometimes both at once. She left books open, face
down on the floor or across the arm of a chair, cracking their
spines. Finding them this way, June would rescue them, slipping
in bookmarks and closing them carefully, putting them neatly on a
shelf. "Where the hell did you put my book?" Aggie would demand. It was not like this elsewhere. In other houses, daughters
did not have to tidy up after their mothers. They did not have
mothers who sometimes swore, and ran their own businesses, and
made an awful racket, clattering pans and banging bowls, all the
time.

June went to church on Sundays, alone now, and found the hard
wooden pews a comfort, offering a stiffening of will. First she'd
thought God was to blame for her father's death. She'd thought He

must be cruel. But it took only a moment to realize it wasn't God but her mother's neglect. June would not have said it was deliberate, but something more typical of Aggie: plain ignorance.

And God, admiring her father's gentle spirit, had taken him. She could see why He would do that, desiring the presence of a loving soul. God's purposes, needs, and plans would be greater than her own, that was natural. And He loved her, too. It was dark and quiet in church, an hour of suspension. It was never hard to go there; the hard part was leaving to go home.

She particularly liked the song from her Sunday-school days: "God Sees the Little Sparrow Fall". It was good to know that both God and her father were keeping their eyes on her; and she was much larger than a sparrow, after all. God's voice spoke through songs and also through the new minister, who arrived in town when she was fourteen, replacing the man who had buried her father.

He was new here, but also nearly old, with white hair that shone in contrast to his black Sunday robes. Swift, powerful, and righteous, his voice, rising and falling, shouting and whispering, must be, she thought, something like what Moses heard, receiving the commandments. When he smiled, his teeth glittered, as white as his hair. Sitting in the congregation each week, she waited, tense, for the moment his eyes—extraordinary, piercing blue eyes—would seem to seize directly on hers, before moving on. Like God's eyes: stern and impersonal and harsh, and also measuring and challenging. In church, she sometimes felt things shifting inside, in the rhythms of his voice. There were moments when even the soles of her feet prickled.

Sometimes she dreamed about God. On judgment day, when she was called to the right hand of the altar, loving arms were placed around her. The heat of the embrace was a miracle, a special grace, and God wore a face she recognized, although when she woke she could never quite remember whose face it was.

Some Sundays he spoke of the joys of heaven, the reward for goodness, the pure peace of it. Other days he spoke of hell, quite graphically. "Some of you," he said, "have no doubt watched a burning barn and heard the cries of tortured animals meeting their deaths inside. Or maybe you've held your own hand too close to a stove or a flame. You *know* how much that hurts. But can you imagine pain a thousand times greater than that, and lasting for eternity? Imagine knowing that pain will never, ever end." June's arms sizzled, as if the little hairs on them were burning.

Some people disapproved of him. Not sufficiently dignified, they said; too evangelical, too emotional, not suitable. June could not find the words to defend him, to say what it meant to be told that God loved her, and found her soul beautiful. It seemed to put into perspective a number of questions, including some of those raised by Aggie. If June's soul was beautiful, what did blood matter, or flesh? Also, it was good to know there was a purpose to all this, reassuring and comforting, this sense of a sort of helpless destiny about events.

This was something June tried to keep in mind when the war came. The gleaming white-haired minister moved away then, to be a chaplain in the services, and while she struggled to maintain her faith, successfully for the most part, she did feel the loss of some of its brightness, and its sharp vividness.

Also, all the young men were being sent off to war, and dangers no one could imagine. It was important to remember that there must be a purpose to this, however hidden to the human eye, because not only might these young men die, but they were also going thousands of miles away, just when she was getting old enough for them to be of some importance to her future.

She went down to the train station after school to watch them leave. Partly she went from curiosity, to catch a glimpse of their peculiar joy in the bravery they seemed so sure of. It brought great events up close. But also she went because one of them might be hers; maybe even one of those kissing another girl goodbye with an embrace that was both sad and somehow impatient. June looked closely at eyes and mouths, lines and shapes of bones, but could not identify the one she might be losing. Whichever it was, he would no doubt be back, if that was God's will. Everyone wondered how long the war would last, but no one imagined it would be very many months.

If everyone had a purpose, then that applied as well to those who didn't go off to fight. They, too, had contributions they could make. Maybe only small things, but according to the men and women who came to town making speeches, encouraging enlistment and various other sorts of patriotism, small things could be vital, tip the balance. June went to hear the speeches partly because the meetings reminded her of church. What the speakers said was much the same as faith: that small, unseen, or apparently unimportant things could add up to something large.

There was no estimating, those speakers said, the difference between the will to fight of a lad with cold feet and that of a soldier with a good pair of heavy grey socks under his boots.

She joined a group of girls from school who were getting together two evenings a week with their mothers (except Aggie) to roll bandages and knit socks, scarves, and whatever else might be needed by those boys in the trenches so far away. The brothers and sons of some of those in the group were overseas, which gave their presence special meaning. And there was June, not only without a soldier in the family, but with an absent, selfish mother.

What Aggie said was, "Surely if you're going to knit those wretched things, you might choose different colors. Why not yellow socks, or a red scarf? Why does everything have to be grey?"

Imagine the dismay of a soldier unwrapping a red scarf. Would he not feel that the people at home found his mission frivolous? And imagine dying in yellow socks. No. Everyone said how important it was to reassure the boys, keep their spirits up. There was self-interest here, the safety of home depending, as it did, on their morale and strength. Lists were circulated of soldiers who would like letters, even from strangers. June chose three, and wrote each one weekly.

Aggie said, "No thank you, I have no interest in knitting socks or rolling bandages." She might, she thought, work up some enthusiasm for writing letters, but lost interest when June told her they'd been advised to steer clear of the subject of war, the intent being to cheer them, not remind them.

"Oh, well, then," said Aggie, and went back to her books. Apparently she'd only wanted first-hand reports, and was not interested in providing comfort.

"Do you know why there's war, June?" she asked idly.

"Of course, don't you?" Everyone knew that, and surely it should be obvious, even to Aggie. There were young brave men fighting and dying for them, and her mother sounded as if it was only a matter of academic interest.

"Well, you know," said Aggie, turning a page, reaching for another cookie, "I can't understand it at all."

"Dear Charles," June wrote her Tuesday soldier, "things are going well here. It's almost Christmas, which means examination time at school, so I'm quite busy studying as well as knitting. Perhaps you will find yourself wearing a scarf I made, although of course you wouldn't be able to tell it was one of mine." She sighed. These letters were very difficult to write. Still, perhaps the dull, daily details of life at home were helpful, a reminder of normal times.

Aggie took pictures of her so she could send them to the three soldiers. This was recommended, so that the men would have an image in mind when they wrote letters or received them. In her photographs, June was standing outside the front door wearing her best church dress: tailored dark blue with narrow white collar and matching cuffs, and her low-heeled black patent leather shoes. She thought it was a grown-up sort of outfit and was surprised, when she saw the pictures, that she looked like a dressed-up child. Also she found she had been squinting a little.

Only one of the soldiers sent a picture of himself in return: a blond, grinning young man whose features were indistinct. She stuck it in the frame of her mirror on the bedroom dresser. "When you come home," she wrote, "my mother and I would be pleased to have you visit. We have a very comfortable home, and you would be welcome." This was rash. However would she explain three soldiers turning up on the doorstep? Still, it was unlikely.

People had turned out to be wrong, expecting the war to end quickly. It went on and on. They said, "It can't go on forever," but it seemed to. And now she really was old enough for one of those boys. It was all very well to go on to the town's new teachers' college for a year, and graduate, and spend evenings still knitting and rolling bandages, and get a job at her old school, which was desperate for teachers with the men gone, and have all that part of her life going pretty much to plan. But now what?

There she was, still living with her mother, standing in a classroom in front of small children, wielding her pointer at numbers and words. She walked to school and back, and avoided Aggie as much as possible, which wasn't difficult, and waited. She read with a keen and speculative eye the lists of casualties carried in the newspaper. Wounded men were sent home, and she regarded them, too, considering. She thought she might not mind one who was on crutches, or missing some organ or limb. She could take care of him, although it would require some alteration of plans. There would be virtue in it, and purpose. It might be the sort of thing God would like. The thought of some sacrifice was warming, if only to the spirit.

Instead, she met Herb Benson one evening in a restaurant, where she had stopped with friends after one of their bandage-rolling evenings. Herb Benson, whose limbs and organs were all present and accounted for; who, after all her letters and socks and scarves sent overseas, had never been there himself. Still, she was astonished and charmed by his attention, and thought that, after all, it was more than she could have hoped for.

13

People say, "I could have died," when what they mean is, "I was surprised." But now when Aggie's heart pounds too hard, or she is made aware, maybe through pee stains on sheets, that something is going badly wrong, "I could have died" is entirely literal.

How different might Neil have been, if he had understood that he would die? Or, how different would she be, if she could get it through her head and into her bones that she is dying now? Would she be tender? More gentle? Hard to tell, when she's so busy still surviving. Events get in the way. This business with June gets in the way. It would be foolish to be gentle in the midst of battle, even if the battle is only over where she will be when she dies.

June accuses her of thinking too much. Aggie is irritated by not being able to think enough: to think things through right to the end. Instead, at a certain point she gets dizzy. She has a ridiculous urge, which she suppresses, to say, "When you're my age, June, you'll see."

Anyway, it's not as if Aggie's approach is so reasonable. Her own real death is still unreal to her; a fantasy in which everything but herself will not exist. This makes her subject to terrible fits of sentimentality, which make her cross. When June pulls off her nightgown in the morning, Aggie sometimes thinks, "I may not be putting that on again," and when she goes downstairs, she thinks, "Maybe I won't be going up again." "I may not have another meal," she tells herself at lunch, or "This may be my last muffin."

Well, it's all silly and amusing in a dreadful sort of way. Far better to be dying with flair and dash, with a flippant carelessness. She would like to picture herself dying with some wit, perhaps an epigram as her last words. Instead it's often just lonely and sloppy.

June, who asks, "How can you laugh about death?" obviously doesn't see the difference between laughing at something and making jokes about it. Joking is easy: Aggie has a line about dying in perfect health. Or she may say, "The trouble with death is there's no way of knowing. It's the uncertainty that's a killer."

All the funerals, starting with Neil's, that she's been to: her mother, her father, both her sisters and one brother. Her last brother died two years ago, but she couldn't be there.

One way and another there were distances. She'd turned into a widow, running her own business, addicted to words, and how were they supposed to know? By then, she was two Aggies away from the one they were familiar with. Then June, too, didn't fit when they visited: hung back, wouldn't join her cousins racing through fields and leaping the creek. She was afraid of the big placid animals and also, apparently, of her big rough-handed uncles, and stuck out there like a thin, pale thumb.

Nevertheless. They all came from the same place—couldn't they have shown her where they all wound up?

Again and again, she sat through funerals in that church, and went to the small cemetery where they have all been buried. So many headstones, simple and chiselled with names and dates. (So many small graves, for little dead children; life must not, then, have been as secure and hearty there as she recalls.)

All those men who held barn-raisings, the women who cooked huge threshing meals, the boys who went on hayrides, all those people with whom she might have had an entirely different life, were now marked only by stones; she continued to be astonished that they had existed and now did not.

People may talk about the miracle of life, but what about the miracle of death? Or maybe just a magician's trick: a gesture, a word, and something greater than a rabbit or a dove appears and vanishes. She might say to June's God, "What is the meaning of this, then?" in an angry tone of voice.

She has, herself, been at times a splendid Aggie, a new woman rising to each occasion—what other Aggies might there have been in other circumstances? Now, however, she's afraid that the next Aggie to appear will be the dead one.

Was that a joke?

There are moments when something—a clean laundry smell, a flash of a certain color, a word or an expression—seems to remind her of something. The sound of her mother's voice, a dress she wore to church when she was little, the pattern on one of Neil's ties—impressions flickering for an instant and then sliding away when she tries to grab hold of them. It's one thing to have gained perspective, a sense of the sweep of events, but what are these memories that are only sensations? What mitigating circumstances may be lost in them? She may be on solid ground with what she does recall, but what about the rest?

What if the catastrophe of wet sheets is just a signal of disintegration? Think of other lapses: forgetting her address, or telephone number, or what Frances does for a living, or who June is, or her own name. What if she looks at a book and can't make out the sense of it, or watches television and can't connect a plot? What if she looks at a clock and can't tell the time, or at a measuring spoon and doesn't know what it's for?

This happens, she's seen it. That little Mrs. Ames from the grocery store was one: losing her mind, not violently or loudly, but quietly, in confusion, the identities of cans of peas and packages of ground beef slipping out of her grasp. Losing her mind like setting down a purse or a pair of glasses somewhere, and not recalling quite where.

What if that happens to Aggie? This great old body wouldn't be much at all, with nothing to interpret it. She shifts uneasily in her chair.

This is the same old chair in which she spent so much time after Neil died; here and in the kitchen. She sees, from that time, pictures: still lifes and landscapes. But faded, the life burned out of them by years, like the old photographs.

All those habits that no longer applied; it took some getting used to. She would find herself listening for his step, and then recall that there was no more step to listen for. She glanced at the clock and thought, "In two hours he'll be home," before realizing that none of those old standards for judging time passing applied. At the butcher's, she might ask for three pork chops, or a roast big enough for three, and then have to revise down to just enough for two: June's small appetite and her own. Sometimes she set his place at the table and then had to clear it away quickly, before June could notice.

Poor little pale and hostile child. Aggie reached out to put an arm around her, or to touch her hair, and June glided away, out from under the embrace. There was no touching her.

So much silence. Outside because of snow, and indoors because of absence. It didn't seem to be only Neil who was gone.

In the front room, she continued to skirt the space in the centre where he had lain for the two days between his dying and the funeral. Upstairs, his room was closed and musty. Almost every day of their marriage, she had gone in and out of this room, cleaning and tidying and changing his barely rumpled sheets, and now she was looking around at its dark walls, wooden closet and cupboards, and narrow stripped bed, and wondering who the man was who had slept here. Just a wall between them, but such a wall!

"Get a grip on yourself," she told herself, but felt as if she were slipping through her own fingers. Moving around the house, she found herself resting her hand on doorways, lamps, and walls, with an idea they might hold her down. When she looked in the mirror, she saw a full-fleshed woman with eyes that surely must be strange: like peering through a hole in a fence and seeing nothing but space on the other side.

Other people, though, couldn't have noticed. When she went out to shop, people stopped to talk. "You must let me know if there's anything at all I can do," beamed the minister's wife. "Sad thing," said the chairman of the school board. "We miss him. He was a fine man, an excellent teacher. Not an easy thing to find someone of his calibre. How are you managing?" So Aggie couldn't have seemed odd or invisible to them.

In books people went on, leaving one thing for the next. In real life, it seemed one was launched willy-nilly into new circumstances without much decision or choice about it. Still, there was movement, however inadvertent. Was his death inadvertent? Or did she kill him with neglect, passivity, murder done simply by withholding something vital, like attention? Or perhaps just the force of her continuing ill-will had taken his breath away. Years ago would they have burned her as a witch?

Anyway, it was done. There was nothing she could do now about death. Also there was nothing she could do about being free.

What was she doing, sitting here? Surely she was not stupid. Where was the girl whose mother had once praised her wits, or the woman who had applied those wits to win small victories? Where was the woman who read books, and credited herself with a certain amount of information and worldliness and, as a result, some scepticism, if not yet wisdom? Apparently she did best with an opponent. He seemed to have been important to the sharpening process.

That was infuriating. She would not depend on him. Well, of course in these circumstances she could not. But she was damned if she needed him, or the memory of him, for some fired-up version of herself. He was gone, winter was going, the past was the past and nothing to be done about it. There were little rivers of melted snow rushing down the street. Sounds were no longer muffled, and smells were lighter in some way too. Things were moving on, and here she sat. It was ridiculous, and irritating to be out of step.

She could sit like a lump for the rest of her life, but what she was mourning—if it was mourning—was not the loss of him, or of love, but knowing that she had not known enough about him to miss him, and had made a mistake to begin with about love. She did not know if it made any sense at all to grieve for things that had never existed.

On the other hand, she could be pleased about certain other things that had existed and now did not. For instance, she no longer had a headache. Also, she was a little hungry. Some of the hunger might be a wish to soothe, but some of it seemed to be actually a little appetite on its own behalf.

She popped a chocolate cake in the oven and went out into the back yard. Soon, she could see, the grass would have to be mowed and the hedge trimmed. One of these weeks the garden would need to be turned over and planted. The white trim on the house was peeling and should be repainted. All these things would be up to her.

That stopped her, pinned her right to that spot on the grass where she stood: "It's up to me." The idea gathered heat and grew into "It's mine now," and "I can do anything I want." She could plant flamboyant sunflowers and poppies to replace the genteel roses and refined little lilies-of-the-valley. She could cut down a tree or two for more light, and cut windows in the walls of the house. Anything.

Well, though, beyond ripping up the garden and the house, there were thirty, forty years. Inside again, she took the cake from the oven and made the obvious choice. It was exactly right, she thought: to make a living at what she was good at and enjoyed, and to do so in her own home. Which would be truly hers, because it required fundamental changes to suit her new purposes.

But good heavens, she thought the night before the bakery opened, what if it didn't work?

Her ovens were new, and she had a cash register on one counter. The cellar contained bags of flour and sugar and bran. Everything was clean, her new stoves shone, and in the front room there was finally enough light. And she had no money in the bank, and owed a little to the carpenter.

So it had to work.

So it did work. For whatever reasons—maybe, to begin with, out of pity or admiration—she had plenty of customers, but after that first rush, they returned for quality. Pity and admiration, she understood, would only go so far.

A peculiar sort of freedom, though, and it made her laugh, such hard work for so many hours every day.

It was still and black in the mornings when she swung her feet over the side of the bed and onto the old hooked rug. Slippering down the hallway to the bathroom, and then down the stairs to the kitchen, she felt like the only person in the world. The light flashing from her kitchen window was the only break in the darkness. That ought, she supposed, to make a person feel lonely, or maybe even frightened. What she liked was the calm and the stillness.

This was so even though there was a great deal to do: bread dough to knead and batter to mix, supplies to haul up from the cellar. First the lights and then the oven and finally the sun warmed the room, heat expanding through the house.

Her shoulders and her arms grew strong: pushing at the dough, whirling the batter in bowls by hand, bending over the oven, putting things into it in one state and lifting them out a little later as something else. It was like being a magician, this skill at transformations.

True, sometimes by the end of the day the strong muscles ached, and her back gave her twinges, and her eyes were dry and scratching from all the words she consumed in spare moments. There was June, too, but really she was so quiet and removed, a person might even forget she existed; especially a person already very busy calculating demand and multiplying recipes.

In the early days, she had to tell June so often that they couldn't afford things for her. "It's still a struggle. We'll make it, but we have to be careful." So no new dresses. Also, there was a school trip somewhere, and even though it would only have cost a few dollars, Aggie had to tell her it wasn't possible. "Even if we had the money we used to, there's still a depression, you know."

"Such a good girl," said her customers. "And so smart. You must be proud of her."

Well, yes, Aggie supposed so. But surely only an idiot could have such a smooth surface, such pale eyes that said nothing; and June was no idiot. Who knew what sort of explosions might be erupting inside? And these things built up, and eventually were manifested in messy ways. When she stopped to think about it, Aggie viewed June uneasily. Or maybe she was just what she seemed, restrained. Or perhaps God took the brunt of all her passions.

In any case, Aggie was quite busy and had little time to fuss. She did, however, take the time to get books from the library on growing up, in preparation for the necessary talk with June. She tried to wing it a little on the pleasures of marriage, although June seemed neither to absorb nor to appreciate, and Aggie wasn't sure how convincing she'd sounded.

On Saturdays, she made June take over the cash register for a couple of hours while she slipped out to the library. It was good for June to face the business instead of skirting it, hiding away upstairs all the time. Well, of course it was hard on her when her friends came in. June didn't like that: exchanging Aggie's labors for money. She seemed to have some idea that the customers were buying more than bread and cakes, that parts of her were being purchased too. "I do honest work and I make honest money," Aggie told her, but it didn't seem to make a difference. "And I'm damned proud of it, and you should be too."

But June wasn't proud, although she was skilful enough at bagging bread and slapping cakes smartly into their fold-up white boxes, and ringing up sales and making proper change. Aggie tried praise, and told her, "You've caught on very quickly," but June only shrugged and returned to her room.

So what could she have done about the child? June may now complain that she suffered a lack of attention, but she seems to forget that she refused any attention that was offered.

Spending her days mainly in a world of women, Aggie heard great tales of other people's lives. What did men talk about? Sports or business. They called the talk of women gossip. She looked up gossip in the dictionary, where it was said to be "familiar or idle talk; scandal"; and one who gossiped was "a babbler". To gossip, it said, was "to tell idle tales about others, tattle; chat".

Enough to make a person suspicious of other definitions. How many words might she have learned from the wrong point of view? As far as she could see, it was sports and business that were idle chat and babbling. Even with her own business to run, she did not find finance very interesting.

The women, her customers, who came in for a loaf of bread and stayed to talk, were the ones who got down to real events. The dictionary had it backwards. It seemed to her something like the difference between the books men wrote and the lives that people really led. All that fictional roaming and leaping from adventure to adventure had very little to do with changes that were really radical.

She remembered the evening she and Neil arrived here, and driving past all those trim houses, assuming that lives were as neat as the lawns; and exploring this house, finding dustballs rolling on the trapdoor leading to the cellar and wondering if elsewhere there might be secret grimy corners also. As the teacher's wife, she'd never known. As Aggie running a bakery, she learned a great deal.

Back when Neil was alive, the man who was now mayor had been merely an alderman. His daughter was in June's class. Aggie had heard the girl boasting once, "My father is going to be in parliament some day," and June boasting back, "My father is going to be the principal." Now June's father was only a man who'd been dead a few years, and the other girl's father was mayor, but not likely for long.

"Poor Arnold," complained his wife, Emily, "he works so hard. So many meetings and long hours." The eyes of other customers met behind her back. She might know, or not, that poor Arnold, while he might well be enduring long meetings and hours, was also carrying on with his secretary. They had been seen, inevitably; his car in dark lanes and the two of them in unmistakable hideaways outside town. He would not be mayor again; the women had their votes. Emily would suffer too, a loss of pride, perhaps not altogether a bad thing. They would be kind to her afterward, although Aggie suspected that sort of pitying kindness would be the hardest to endure.

And there was Audrey Sullivan, a tiny dark-haired young woman married to a garage mechanic, and well known as a shoplifter. So well known that proprietors of stores all over town watched for her and when they caught her leaving with, perhaps, a pair of stockings tucked into her blouse or a powder compact in her purse, they called her husband, who came and apologized and restored the goods or paid for them, and fetched her home. In the bakery, her small hand stole toward a tray of cookies while Aggie bagged a loaf of bread. Well, what did it matter? Poor Audrey surely ought to be permitted one place where her efforts were successful. What, Aggie wondered, happened at home when Audrey's husband had been called? Did he try to persuade her, did he strike her or did he just sit wearily with his face in his hands? Did she weep and make promises?

What was irritating was that she was so bad at stealing, and never seemed to get better. One would have thought she'd make some efforts to improve. Also there was no discrimination about it: the woman would take anything. As far as she was concerned, apparently, a pair of stockings from the five and dime were as enticing as Aggie's oatmeal cookies.

"Maybe if they had children," the women said, diagnosing the source of Audrey Sullivan's disease. Did they consider offspring a cure? Or, like hanging, a deterrent? Perhaps only, Aggie thought, that a child imposed an order, a structure, a system, that it was very difficult to escape. Medication for wrong-headed impulses.

Unless, of course, children appeared outside the order, structure, and system. Then they were sin. Girls vanished out west for long visits with distant aunts. Their mothers were regarded uneasily; after all, whose daughter might not grow up to betray? There were so many unsavory pressures, not the least of them secret and sudden impulses toward lust. Bodies were unpredictable, capable of grave errors in moments when judgment was in short supply. Whims led to tragedies.

Aggie pictured prairies dotted with generous aunts, every home with a swelling eastern niece. Where did western daughters go? Not to eastern aunts, apparently. Much more broad-minded out there, people must be.

She smiled to herself, thinking how fortunate she might be, after all, to have a husband who was dead and a daughter who was good.

Elsewhere, she quite realized, people probably discussed her. She had a small curiosity about what they might be saying, but kept herself to herself with the women. Well, if she started, where would she stop? Would she say, "You remember my husband Neil? The teacher? We really couldn't bear each other. My daughter says it's likely my fault he died.'' They might know things anyway, just from watching. It was remarkable what they knew. Someone had the flu but would be back on her feet in a couple of days, no doubt. Someone else sprained a wrist, slipping on steps, and came in bandaged, laughing about her clumsiness, although in fact, people said, she drank. Some people got cancer. News of deaths spread like wildfire.

Between customers and in the evenings in her big chair in the front room, Aggie read novels and histories and textbooks. She read about other people's lives, how they managed and how they were seen to have managed. She read about ideas, and about systems of ideas. She decided that people in groups were different from people in ones and twos. Masses became mobs, which had their own rules. Any revolution proved that; or any social gathering. Just she and June in a room together were different, she expected, from either of them apart. Also, she thought, primitive, death-dealing passions, anarchy, always lurked beneath the surface. And even God, if He existed, seemed to act to prove His own divinity. "Listen," He said, shaking people up when their attention wandered.

She often felt herself stabbing at knowledge in the dark, and sometimes the librarian gave her odd glances, checking out her choices.

Her attention turned for a time to biology. Books on insects were particularly fascinating. Whole tiny lives going on, and whoever noticed them unless they were eating something a person particularly wanted, like the lettuce? Yet there they were, beautiful and grotesque and camouflaged, busy and full of purpose, scurrying and burrowing and chewing and spinning and flying, all, apparently, to the end of surviving. Not for the survival of a single insect, but of the group: all efforts geared to a future that would be geared to another future. Peculiar and single-minded; but it worked. Some books said it would be the insects that would survive any disaster. Where man might vanish, a bug could adapt and thrive. The books also mentioned rhythms of survival among certain animals and insects: that particular intensities of population triggered some form of mass demolition or exploration. Either they killed each other off or they split up to form new colonies.

She moved on to history, discovering it was often the study of the periodic slaughters of war, the winners and the losers, the little bits of land changing hands, whole populations shifting with new conquerors.

To see the eager young men leaving for war was like watching lemmings, or ants. This impulse to slaughter, this yearning for the scene of death, was puzzling and fascinating, and she read and read, trying to find out what the lure of it might be.

June, on the other hand, took to the war like a duck to water, and became a proper pest about it. In a peculiar way it seemed to cheer her, and certainly unleashed all her do-good instincts. "But Mother," she told Aggie impatiently, "there are men dying for us over there. Surely you could give up a little time, you could surely make some sacrifices. You might do something."

But there, Aggie thought. Was she not doing something: trying to work out what might be worth killing for?

Ideas, she gathered; systems. But how could it actually be done? Closing her eyes, she tried to place herself in battle.

Well, she could see it might be possible to drop bombs from a plane. That might not seem real. But how to lie in a hole and take shots at a person whose eyes might even be seen, the shape of a mouth, the way the hair stood up or ears stuck out?

But by then it would be too late. It would be shoot or be shot, just survival.

Surely though, those departing young men couldn't think they were merely going on an outing, like June heading eagerly for her bandage-rolling evenings? They seemed to view it as a game, with dummy bullets, guns made from twigs, like her little brothers playing kill-the-Hun around the yard, during the last war in which her older brother died.

They couldn't imagine, couldn't have understood, that they might die, these young men, fragile, mortal, and eager, marching off to embrace blood. They must have been unable to see their own blood beneath the unbroken flesh.

June, coming home in the evenings satisfied with her contribution, saw the bandages she made as white and pure and crisp. Aggie saw them bloody and pus-filled and stinking, which they would be if they were to be at all useful, and basically, she thought, that must be the difference between their points of view.

June pointed out that these men, on behalf of herself and Aggie and civilization, were lying in muddy trenches thousands of miles away, cold and wet and terrified. She seemed to find this heroic. Aggie thought it astonishing.

In books, war was one thing or another: glorious or flat. In the history books, it was flat: this treaty, that battle, these defeats, this result. In novels it was glorious: these heroes, those victories, that daring, this evil overcome. Romantic and painless. Maybe that was what misled the young men. Maybe they were under the impression that pain, after all, didn't really hurt; or if it did, they would inflict not suffer it.

The women, more intimately acquainted with blood, might have told them something about pain. Why was their pain ordinary and the young men's heroic? Maybe the men just wanted their own blood, to even things out. At least when they got where they were going, they would be occupied, quite busy dodging death, and would have to be impressed by its reality.

But here a woman wept in the bakery, broke down over a loaf of bread. New lines appeared on familiar faces.

The impulse to roll bandages and knit was understandable: they wanted some part in protection, and if they could not knit suits of armor, they would make socks. They were used to protecting their boys and providing comfort. Probably if they could have, they would have stepped in front and stopped the bullets; if for no other reason than habit.

In the books, death was numbers or nobility. In reality it seemed trivial, coming at awkward moments, catching a person in an unprepared pose. Like Neil, frozen gaping like a fish drowning in air.

And how does it come in a nursing home where it must be a daily expectation?

Maybe there she would find out what dying looks like. She has never seen it, and might like to. She would like to scrutinize the disappearance of the spirit, watch a face as that occurs. Because surely there must be something, a clue right at the moment.

It is quite possible, however, that the people there are kept anaesthetized. Maybe instead of achieving their own grace or resignation, they are merely drugged. So then, when they finally doze their way into death, the staff can tell whatever grieving relatives there may be, "Don't worry, there was no pain, she died peacefully in her sleep." They would call that a natural death. Which is what they will call hers. "She had a full life," people will say to June. "She had her time." Not considering it a waste when someone dies after eighty years, not the same thing at all as a young man dying in a war or an accident or from some disease.

Damn it, death is death, and she is no more ready for it than a young man is (but shouldn't she be?), nor is she less than he is. Only more aware, and frightened.

Oh, she would be angry to miss it, though. If she went to that place and they filled her with needles and pills, so that it slipped past. Surely there is an instant of clarity in which things are made known. It wouldn't be fair to live for eighty years and miss the moment that made sense of it all. Or for that matter miss the moment in which it was made clear that there was no sense to be made of it.

Is this an argument that would wash with June, who appears to believe that there is already perfect sense to everything? And is it obsessive or only sensible to have death so much on her mind? Like ashes to ashes and dust to dust, she circles and returns to it.

She might, she thinks, put a little more effort into her living moments. There's some sense to be made of them, too, a kind of insurance against there being no great illumination like a sunset at the end.

14

"Nice nightgown," said Herb, and they were off. It was the only time she wore it, and then only briefly. He might have admired it, but like a gift, only as wrapping for what he was really after.

"For God's sake, June," he said, "we're married." And then, "For heaven's sake, relax."

Relaxing was one thing, difficult enough. Abandonment was beyond her. What had he seen? What did he want? Did he think there was some sluttish waitress underneath her cardigans? It occurred to her that the dapper, flashing Herb, who wore trim suits and a gold signet ring on the middle finger of his right hand, may have wanted what he saw to begin with: someone respectable and proper to make a home for him. Why her, though? Why not some other teacher in some other town?

When people asked how they'd met, he liked to joke, "Oh, I picked her up." "I wish you wouldn't tell people that," she complained.

"But it's true, isn't it? And anyway, it's funny."

He was never in the war, he'd pointed out in the restaurant the night they met, because he had a bit of a heart murmur. "I always tell people because otherwise they wonder. They won't buy from somebody they think just skipped out on it." She admired his forthrightness.

It was lonely, he told her later, out on the road, driving from town to town in his beat-up blue Hudson, spending dull nights in strange hotel rooms. "You know, Junie," he said during what she

149

considered their courtship, "it's like coming home, heading here."
His smile was wide, and the skin crinkled around his eyes, laugh
lines he called them. His hair and eyes and suits were brown. His
jackets, however, concealed shiny, bright-yellow linings and a silver-plated flask in an inside pocket.

She anticipated major changes, greater than the intentions he
hinted of when he said, "Sometimes I think of settling down, having a real home, not just hotel rooms all the time." She understood, long before anything firm was said, that they would marry,
he would get a proper job in town, and she would quit hers. She
saw that he would no longer have to swear, complaining about
some customer giving him trouble over an order, because there
would be no occasion compelling bad words. Because he would be
home, they would go to church together. They would fall into the
right order of things.

And then there they were, running hand in hand down the stone
walk after the small reception in her mother's house, turning at the
end, as she had dreamed, to wave goodbye to Aggie, and climbing
into the blue Hudson to drive to their new home five blocks away.
Where Herb looked up from the bed as she entered the room and
said, "Nice nightgown. Where'd you get it?"

"My mother made it."

First Aggie with her talk of pleasure, and then Herb telling her
to relax. "Enjoy" was a word they both used. It's beyond her how
people can talk as if it's something necessary. Which it is not.
Catholics may have the wrong idea of things in general, but look
at their priests, look at their nuns.

And what sort of expectation makes chastity a virtue until suddenly a person is supposed to just throw it all away, as if the rules
no longer applied? Not that she didn't understand that chastity itself would go by the boards; it was just that no one had mentioned
relinquishing herself entirely. And here it turned out that Aggie was
right, he was a bodily creature. She felt disappointment seeping out
of him, but how dared he? She was no movie-house usherette, or
waitress, and if that was what he wanted, he should have married
one. He became a different person in this light, which wasn't fair,
since she remained unchanged.

She watched him at breakfast and thought how unpleasant it
looked, a man eating eggs and talking at the same time.

"I wish we could have had a honeymoon," he said. "I'm sorry
I have to be back on the road tomorrow. If it were summer holi-

days you could come with me. Do you want to do that this summer?''

But was he not going to quit? By summer, surely, he would have a job here and be coming home every night, although that struck her now as a not entirely pleasing prospect. "Whatever made you think that?" he asked, amazed. "I like what I do, and I'd hate being stuck in one place all the time. Besides, I'm good at selling."

"But you always complain about it. You always say it's lonely and you get tired of all the driving."

"Of course I complain, everybody does. You complain about your job too, but that doesn't mean you're going to quit."

But surely that was exactly what she was going to do: quit and stay home and have children and a normal life. Surely that was the point: to have an ordinary life after so many odd years.

"I don't see how we could afford that, Junie. Weren't you listening when we talked about buying the house? We were counting on your salary, at least for a while. I make a good living, but it's commissions, it's not regular like yours, it goes up and down. I thought we'd agreed not to change things for a while."

She could not remember any such agreement. What she recalled was some joking between Herb and Aggie about June having a steady job, and Herb saying something like how lucky her pupils were to have what he called a dish like her for a teacher. "Boy," he said, "it's sure different from when I was in school." And Aggie just kind of looking at him. June hadn't said anything, but she was sure she also hadn't agreed to anything.

She stood to clear the breakfast table. "We'd better get ready, it's after ten."

"What for?"

"Well, for church."

"Hell, you're not going this morning, are you? This is all the honeymoon we've got, just today. Come on, stay here with me. I know the first time isn't so good, but now it'll be different."

How did he know? On what experience did he base this? She regarded him coldly.

"No, I always go. You should too, people will expect you."

"Why would they? Anyway, what I expect is that the first day we're married you'll stay home."

She was furious that when she was leaving after the service, the minister shook her hand and said, smiling, "I'm surprised to see you this morning, I must say. But I see we didn't get your new husband out. We'll have to work on that.''

When she got home, he insisted they go upstairs. But he was wrong that it got better. He slipped into a nap afterward, but she got right up. She found his hair cream made the pillows smell too sweet.

She was making supper when he came downstairs, sliding an arm around her waist, nuzzling his face into the back of her neck. These gestures, which she might have enjoyed a few days ago, taking them as ends in themselves, now were a threat. The difference was being married. The difference was that before, she had a right to make things stop, and now, of course, she had no such right at all. He had all rights and there was no relaxing, the way there was with the power of God and the inevitability of His will. God wouldn't be breathing down her neck like this. God was strict and could be harsh, but at least didn't come sneaking up behind.

Still. Was he not handsome, lounging in the chair listening to a program of band music on the radio? Was she not proud to have married him?

He was up and packing early in the morning, kissed her without paying much attention, and waved goodbye from the driveway with what seemed an inappropriate light-heartedness. At school, other teachers smiled and congratulated her, and that was nice. How strange, though, to be proud with other people of being married, which meant being wanted, but when it was just the two of them, to wish not to be wanted quite so much. It all seemed to have gotten off on the wrong foot.

Funny, going home to a new and empty house: not seeing him stretched loose-limbed in the living room, and making a meal just for herself. She turned on the radio for company. It was a little scary to be alone, and she carefully locked the doors; now that she knew exactly what there was to be afraid of. She turned off the radio, in case there were noises she ought to be hearing.

Lying in bed, she discovered that the house had an entire orchestra of sounds, from stealthy steps on the stairs, to clicks of doors opening or papers downstairs being shuffled. An array of cracks and groans and heaves. "Oh really, don't be so silly," she scolded herself, and slipped out of bed to pray. "Oh God, help me." But circumstances had changed. "Oh God," she corrected, "help us."

Actually, once she got used to it, it was rather pleasant not having to make elaborate meals, going to bed early if she felt like it, or staying up late. Privacy was good, being able to kneel beside the bed and pray aloud instead of standing out in the hall whispering. On the weekend with Herb, she hadn't even attempted a bedside prayer. Well, she wouldn't have had much chance, with him grabbing, and then, too, prayers were private things, not intended to be witnessed.

She was quite accustomed to being on her own by the time he arrived home; the gravel crunching in the driveway, the car door slamming and then the trunk lid, and then there he was with a suitcase in each hand and a grin on his face. "Junie," he cried, dropping the cases, gripping his hands around her narrow waist, lifting her off the floor and giving her a little shake and a whirl that seemed playful enough, but lacking the innocence of her father's similar embraces. "Oh, Jesus, I'm glad to be home, what a trip. I missed my new bride, did you miss me?" The noise he was making! All this shouting and prancing-dancing through the house. "You don't know how much I've been looking forward to this. I've been telling everybody for two weeks about my new wife and my new house. I tell you, I'm a changed man. I want my slippers and a drink. I want a fireplace to sit in front of, isn't it too bad we don't have one? Maybe we could knock out a wall and get one put in, what do you think?"

She, however, had seen quite enough of walls being knocked out, and then there'd be all the ashes to clean up. "Oh no, fireplaces are such filthy things," she said, and knew immediately she shouldn't have.

He looked angry, then disappointed. "Oh well. What's for supper? I'm going to go change and get comfortable."

She was annoyed at herself for being hurt when later he just fell asleep. Really, she supposed, the poor man couldn't win. At least the house seemed to be keeping most of its noises to itself, now that he was home. She wasn't even sure if she'd remembered to lock the back door. Anyone might come in, but she wasn't afraid. In the quiet darkness, she even felt a little grateful to him.

"What do you say to company tonight?" he suggested in the morning. "Maybe have your mother over?"

It pleased her to have Aggie as a guest; to show her mother the proper way of things now. Also, Aggie entertained Herb, relieving June, since the day had gone in lengthy silences. It seemed they didn't have a great deal to talk about once he'd told her it had been "a hell of a two weeks on the road", and she had said that nothing much out of the ordinary had happened while he was gone. She supposed silences were all right between married people, but still, surely there ought not to be this nervous rooting around for topics to discuss. Her mind went blank wondering what they might talk about. What did they talk about before?

Obviously Aggie had the right idea. She simply asked him about people he met on the road and what they were like and if he went to their homes and how the towns looked and what he might have seen at the movies. He grew quite animated. "Mind the car springs," he laughed as he left to drive Aggie home. "I can't afford new ones." Amazing, making jokes about her weight.

"That was nice," he said later. "I like your mother."

Obviously.

"It's funny you don't take after her. I mean," he added quickly, "in looks. You'd never take you for her daughter."

"I told you, I'm like my father."

"Yeah, I guess. I've seen pictures. They must have made a pretty strange-looking couple."

"They did."

The two of them were a pretty strange couple, too, although not so dissimilar in looks. The more he reached for her, the more she moved away. Casual touches were startling, knowing now where they might lead. She grew more accustomed to his absences, and more fond of them, as well.

People she'd never before noticed particularly now stopped to speak to her on the street: his acquaintances. "How's old Herb? Back in town this weekend, is he?" Instead of being herself, out from Aggie's thumb, she found she was now his wife.

"It's my business to be friendly," he told her, and invited men over on Saturday nights when he was home to play poker, while she made sandwiches for them all.

"No sign of a little one yet?" women asked, stopping to chat on the street, nudging her.

"Not yet," smiling bravely. The question was like having these people watching when Herb came home. It was bad enough knowing God could see, and possibly even her father, although she tried to avoid the thought of that since it was paralysing, and her paralysis enraged Herb. "Oh, for God's *sake*," he muttered, and sometimes just gave up.

Oh, but she did want to be desired. She dreamed of being desired, when he was away. Just not in bed with flesh; more from a distance, maybe.

At some point he stopped calling her Junie when it was just the two of them; although when the men came to play cards he might turn and slap her lightly on the rear and say, "Hey, Junie, we got any more of those sandwiches?" As if, she thought, she were a horse he owned, thumping its rump, showing it off.

"I wish you wouldn't do that."

"Why not? It's just a tap. You've got a nice bottom."

It wasn't that they actually quarrelled, though.

Sometimes there were three weeks between his visits home. She came to think of them more or less as visits, since the house was her own so much. Sometimes, too, he left Sunday night instead of waiting for Monday morning, explaining, "I can get a head start on the week if I'm already where I'm going."

"Jesus Christ," he said, coming home and throwing open the drapes. "Why is this place so goddamned dark?"

"The furniture. It fades." Silly of her to have supposed he would have no more need to swear, once they were married.

"This stuff? How's it going to fade?"

She had chosen from his catalogue, so that they could get it wholesale through his firm, a living-room suite of dark blue, in some tough and nubbly fake material that turned out to show dirt rather badly. He was probably right, though, that it would be hard to make it fade.

"But I'm alone so much. I don't like the drapes open when I'm alone."

"Well, you're not alone now."

True.

But there were times, maybe when they were walking together over to Aggie's for an evening, when she admired him. They didn't walk holding hands any more, or with his arm slung across her shoulder, and when they crossed the street he no longer held her elbow as if she were fragile, but still, being with him on the street was pleasing.

She was, after all, old enough to be realistic about these things: give a little here and get a little there. A bargain, this for that. She was no foolish little girl with outlandish expectations, but a grown woman sensibly accepting, for the most part, what was real.

In church, the minister spoke of those who are specially tested, and she wondered if she might be one of those. It put a new light on sacrifice: crucifixions in various forms, say, for instance, nailed down on a mattress beneath her husband's body. The concept offered distance and dispassion, and that in turn made events less painful, which had, she realized, the somewhat absurd effect of making her sacrifice less potent.

She prayed, with increasing impatience, for a child. If one were to be martyred on a mattress, some resurrection of life ought to follow.

A child would make resolution possible. If she were expecting, she could no longer teach, for one thing. The money helped, of course, because Herb's cheques were variable, and whatever he said about being a good salesman, there were times that were flat and that was all there was to it. But there was no pleasure in teaching itself. She began to suspect it would have been that way for her father, too, except that he appreciated the respect it brought.

Anyway, with the war over, women were going back home to raise babies as the men returned to work, and she was out of step once more.

She longed to be one of those young mothers she saw wheeling prams along the sidewalks, leaning down to adjust blankets and fix brakes, and going into stores to shop. It looked a leisurely sort of life, luxurious, to spend days strolling with a baby.

Babies demanded order and sense, put people in their proper places. Herb would have to get a regular job, and they would be a normal family, the three, then maybe four or five, of them. She couldn't picture these imaginary children, and had no clear idea of numbers. One seemed enough for her purposes.

Then, too, his rights would be altered. With a child to protect inside her, she would be the one with rights. And, once it was born, their attention would have to be on it: he to support it, she to nourish it, and both of them to protect it. Also, she would show Aggie how a real mother behaved. She would bring her child up with care. Her child would not be reared in any slapdash, irregular way.

Eventually the doctor said, "It took long enough, but as far as I can tell everything's fine. April, I'd say, right about the middle of the month. Herb'll be pleased, won't he?"

He was. He looked, when she told him, the way she remembered him before they married: light and glittering. How much he must have changed, without her noticing. He even called her Junie again. "Oh, Junie, that's great! A baby! Jesus, my very own kid!"

Not the way she would have put it.

"You know," she said, "I'll have to quit teaching. You can't teach when you're expecting."

"Yeah, I guess. But we'll manage. It's good it didn't happen right away, so we had a chance to salt away some money. I'll just have to sell twice as hard, that's all."

"But I thought you'd want a proper job now."

"Jesus Christ," red-faced, "I wish you'd get it through your head, I have a proper job." Then, more calmly, "Anyway, where do you think I could get one here? There's nothing going now the war's over. And honest to God, June, it's nice to have a home and it'll be great to have a kid, but I couldn't stand being in one place all the time, the same old people day after day."

Her among them?

So soon the vision of her new and ordinary life was being altered. Why could she never have what she saw? Why was it always up to somebody else and what they wanted how her life was spent?

Aggie took up knitting, and brought over bootees and sweaters. "A grandchild!" she'd said when June told her. "Oh, isn't that nice. I'll like being a grandmother, grandmothers get to play with babies and spoil them." Who'd have thought she meant it literally, to spoil?

In bed, Herb said, "It's not going to hurt the kid, you know," but she said quite firmly and finally with some righteousness on her side, "No, I don't want to take a chance."

There were other things she could do, though. She could work all day wallpapering the second bedroom with dancing bears. She could hem lengths of cotton into diapers, and hook a little rug for the nursery floor, small flowers on a pale-blue backing.

Heavens it was hard, though, getting so big and unwieldy. It hurt, the weight pulling at her all the time, no getting away from it. Almost it seemed to outweigh her, carrying her wearily through the day instead of the reverse; as if she were its burden, not hers. The pasty, purple-streaked ugliness stretched out so tightly—surely she was going to burst? Her face altered, too; she could see it getting puffy, a resemblance to her mother now. Herb said, "Boy, expecting doesn't seem to agree with you, does it?" and didn't mean that it made her ill, because it didn't. Just that it made her look like someone she never would have recognized as herself. "You must keep your feet up as much as you can," the doctor warned. "Your blood pressure's a bit up, and there's too much fluid." He patted her shoulder. "Not that it's dangerous, really, but you have to be careful. You're pretty narrow, too." She supposed he tried to be delicate, but it really wasn't nice, being exposed in his examining room. Quite a trick for him to be both impersonal and kind.

They knocked her out and opened her up and left a garish scar. "It was going on too long," the doctor told her when she woke up. "But your baby's perfectly healthy. A big thumper of a girl."

Even with pain and a scar, she could see she had accomplished something here. Herb came to her hospital room with flowers, kissed her lightly on the forehead, said, "She's beautiful. Are you all right?" She was amazed herself at the feeling of a miracle—that something had been created out of nothing.

Home, he stared at his daughter with something that looked like fear. June thought it a little sweet, how worried he looked holding her, as if afraid she would break.

"You don't mind if we call her Frances, do you?" she asked. "It's a name in my father's family, and my middle name. I'd like to carry it on."

"Frances," he tried. "Fran. Frannie. Yeah, well okay. I'm not wild about it, but it's okay."

"Christ," he grumbled in the middle of the night when she woke them crying, "what's the matter with her?"

It was just that she was so hungry. She was rosy and plump and had a skitter of dark hair. Watching her voracious child, June was reminded of her mother.

There were only the two of them when Herb was on the road. Frances seemed to take his comings and goings with unconcern, not knowing, June supposed, that it might be different in other households. He arrived excited to see her, exclaiming over changes, since everything about her changed so rapidly.

June herself hadn't quite expected that someone so small could consume so much time. There was nothing she could plan that might not have to be cancelled. She could hardly go shopping with a screaming baby, but if she planned to stay home and clean, Frances might sleep on and on until June had to shake her awake. Perhaps it was an illusion that the baby did precisely what was not convenient for her, but why couldn't she sleep quietly in her buggy when June wanted to go downtown and see herself reflected in the glass windows of stores, pushing the pram and smiling gently?

Aggie made a proper fool of herself when she came to babysit, lumbering happily along the five blocks of sidewalk between their houses. She didn't exactly talk baby-talk, but her voice rose. June, watching in amazement and something else that she didn't identify but that wasn't quite nice, saw her mother actually cuddling this child.

"Never mind if she's crying," Aggie said, waving her hand as if it didn't matter. "She'll stop, you go on to church. I'll just change her and we'll sit here and rock and sing for a while."

June went, but uneasily. Who knew if something might really be wrong this time? Or, if not, who knew what Aggie was up to in her absence? She came home to find her mother cradling her laughing daughter and waltzing across the kitchen floor, looking foolish and quite unlike any Aggie she could remember.

"Come on, June, take a break, let's go to a movie," Herb suggested. "Your mother'll babysit, she likes to."

"Oh no, I don't think so. I don't like to leave Frances, she's been upset today."

"Well, then, I'm going to Larry's. There's a poker game."

He did this more and more often. It seemed she hardly saw him, but then, she hardly noticed. When he was home, she left Frances with him while she went to church. She had no idea what happened during those two hours, but, after all, he was the child's father and should be able to do that much.

"You've changed," he said sadly. "You used to like going out."

Did she? She could barely remember how things were before Frances, much less before she married. Herb was a phantom. He rarely ever reached for her in the night any more, which was fine, she supposed. Except that while she didn't like being reached for, she did not want to be unwanted.

She said, "You don't know how much work it is, you don't understand."

"One kid! How hard can it be, looking after one kid?" But when she came home from church, he handed Frances over fast enough.

When he came home, he brought Frances small gifts picked up on his travels; the way a guest would, or a Santa Claus.

It was harder when Frances began to crawl, and stand, and then walk. She had to be watched closely so she didn't hurt herself. He brought home a tricycle when she was still quite little, and June cried, "Oh, but she's too young, she'll get hurt."

"Of course she'll get hurt," he snapped, steering Frances along the walk. "Everybody does."

Did he not care about his own child's pain?

No point, speaking of pain, in even thinking about him. Insignificant, really, except for Frances, the result. And it doesn't do to dwell.

15

It may have been women who came to the bakeshop to buy and to trade tales, but it was a man who became Aggie's friend.

It was the year June was at teacher's college, and while that made no difference at all to the rhythms of Aggie's days (and not much to June's, either, as far as Aggie could see), she felt restless. Not dissatisfied, exactly, but ready to look around for more. June would, presumably, be moving on to something or other one of these days. The bakery was doing well and Aggie had even built up some savings. Reading, of course, remained fascinating. She thought the restlessness might be because things outside of books were now too comfortable, too well known.

She wondered if other people found their lives sometimes hanging a little too neatly, like a picture. There was not, she realized, anyone she could ask. Stories might be told in her bakeshop, and illnesses and tragedies and plans for weddings and holidays discussed, but not questions, not feelings. Those she had to imagine, placing herself in others' skins. She would have liked a sister handy then, to sit in her kitchen sometimes and drink tea with, chatting comfortably.

The man who had been coming to the door every morning for years and years, bringing eggs and milk and cheese from the dairy, was a burly, dark, sullen fellow who might nearly be mute for all he said to her. She told him each morning what she'd be needing that day and he would grunt and shrug and fetch it from the wagon in which he toured the streets. His horse, at least, she thought, might be grateful for her orders, since they took longer to deliver than those at other more ordinary households, and it had longer to rest, standing droop-headed and dispirited in the street. She suspected the man didn't feed it properly, and demanded too much from it. She imagined it just lying down in the street some day, giving up.

She took no particular notice when, that year June was at teacher's college, the man who delivered for the dairy was replaced. This new one was not sullen, but otherwise seemed unremarkable. She continued to give him her day's order and he, like his predecessor, carted the supplies into her kitchen. He smiled sometimes, though, and she smiled back, absent-mindedly. It occurred to her, however, meeting him at the door one day and glancing toward the street, that the horse was looking better: more fleshed and alert. "Is that the same animal?" she asked, pointing.

"Well, yes and then again no. Same horse, but he's been having a sort of change of heart." The man grinned. "That other bugger wasn't taking care of him. Poor old thing never had oats in his life. I give him a handful of oats at the start of the day and the end, so he's got something to look forward to, and I figure he'll last a few years yet. Plus, if I have to look at the back end of a horse all day, I'd just as soon it was a happy back end."

"Would you like a cup of tea? I've just made some for myself. And biscuits just out of the oven."

"My morning oats?"

They laughed, and Barney Holtom became her friend.

"You know about horses, then," she said.

"Brought up on a farm."

"Oh, so was I!"

He was a couple of years younger than Aggie, balding, with a fringe of greying hair. Also, he had a small pot-belly, although nothing like her bulk.

They traded information: that she was a widow with a daughter, and had been married to a teacher; that he was married, with three sons, and had formerly been a shoe salesman. "I spent *years* selling damn shoes, inside all the time, women coming in trying on twenty pair and buying the first. It sounds like a joke, I know, but it isn't. And smiling all the time, no matter what. People buying shoes and wearing them to whatever they bought them for, a wedding or whatever, and then trying to return them. I tell you, I damn near cracked my face smiling."

But that still seemed his most frequent expression: a smile, a grin, a laugh. She thought that this must be what beaming meant: light shining out of a good nature. She wondered how it was she hadn't particularly noticed before, and that it took the horse to draw him to her attention.

"Jesus, I better get going, I'm getting behind on my route," he exclaimed, checking his watch.

But the next morning, and the next, he paused for a cup of tea and a biscuit or a muffin. Every morning then, except for weekends—so easily it became a custom, to be depended on.

June frowned unhappily, coming down to breakfast and finding him there. Whatever did she think was going on while she was still asleep? Lusty tumbles on the kitchen floor while bread loaves rose? But what Aggie appreciated about him was not his passion, but his dispassion. The cool ear with which he listened, his remoteness from a sense of judgment, his capacity to listen seriously as well as talk, and to see the absurd and funny side of certain events.

What did they talk about? More or less everything, she thought, although she could not really tell, from his point of view, if it went that far. There was a gradual loosening in her kitchen for them both, a putting up of feet. Sometimes literally. They would sit on chairs pulled into the kitchen from the dining room, their feet hoisted with considerable difficulty onto the cash-register counter, companionable once the effort was accomplished. "Never mind, June," Aggie told her disapproving daughter, "it gets the blood moving to the brain. So we can be as clever as we think we are." She and Barney grinned at each other, and June sighed her way off to school.

Like her, Barney spent time reading, although without her keenness, more for entertainment. He liked English novels best, he said: found their quality of dry wit appealing.

"I was in awful trouble when I quit the shoe store. Boy, my wife was mad." He sounded, however, proud.

"Well, she would be, wouldn't she, with children to support. I'd have been pretty unhappy, too, if my husband came home and said he'd upped and quit teaching. What would I have done?"

"Started a bakery. Just what you did."

"Not likely. He wouldn't have allowed it. He'd have said it was demeaning or some such."

"Alice didn't think that, but she was sure as hell mad." It was obvious from the way his face softened, however, that his marriage was based on fondness. His body drew energy, it seemed, from mentioning his wife.

"The shoe store was bad enough all by itself, but it was being inside all the time, too. I missed being outdoors more. And at least this job has that, and a connection with farming, selling things that come from a farm. Anyway," he laughed, "I get to meet so many women."

"I bet." But Aggie knew that he did not stop elsewhere on his route.

She also understood that they were friends, which was a new and interesting experience, and not at all the same as a husband, even the one she might have imagined.

Barney talked about his courtship, and getting married, and it sounded much like Aggie and the teacher, except of course for the outcome. "We were both farm kids," he said. "Gosh, she was pretty. I could never think why she'd agree to marry me, but she did. And then she didn't say a word except yes when I said let's move to town. I wasn't much interested in farming, and anyway I had two older brothers and there wasn't going to be much left for me there, so I thought, okay, we'll have a whole new life, try something different. And she always went along, except for being so mad when I quit the store."

"Do you miss the farm? I do, sometimes."

"Sure, I always have. But I notice neither of us has missed it enough to go back, have we?"

She could, she thought, tell him just about anything: even the teacher, although she stumbled a little, trying to find words to describe his distaste for her body. "And you know," she said, "I didn't look like this then. There was nothing wrong with me. I think I was even attractive, maybe."

"He sounds nuts to me." Scrutinizing her features, dwarfed now by surrounding flesh, he said, "I bet you were pretty. Actually, you know, you're pretty anyway. You have a nice face. You'd be a knockout if you lost weight."

Now, why could she take that from Barney without a flicker, but lash out at June for a similar suggestion? Because, she supposed, June seemed to have a selfish stake in her appearance, while Barney's interest was detached: a mere assessment that didn't signify much, one way or another.

So she could say, without any undercurrent or hidden meaning, "I don't trust any more. Things didn't turn out to be what they seemed. So I could never have married again, even if there'd been some prospect of it, which is none too likely anyway.''

"Why isn't it likely?''

"For one thing, who'd want all this?'' patting herself. "And then, I'm a bit prickly with it. Anyway, I never meet any men.''

"Thanks very much,'' but it was a joke.

She did wonder, though, if something had been disconnected in her body by the teacher, killing desire. She could look at Barney and feel no attraction of that sort at all, no warmings or stirrings except toward his presence, his gesturing hands, and the sound of his voice.

But no, she could feel her body away inside now, still wanting, and could imagine a man who might draw her that way. It just wasn't Barney. And those small desires weren't urgent at all. She was quite used to unresolved wanting, it wasn't important any more.

She could even talk to him about that: the lack of desire for him. "I know,'' he said, "it's interesting, isn't it? I'm the same. But there's still something different about talking to you than to a fellow. It's easier with you, in a way, and we talk about more things. It's sharper, you know what I mean?''

She thought that, yes, there was more spice in this friendship with a man than there might have been with a woman. Maybe because so much was unknown. Talking with the women in the shop later in the day, there was a kind of code, an underline of shared knowledge, even if experiences might be different. There was a common language which left a great many things assumed but unsaid.

She and Barney, though, had to spell things out for each other, which required care and concentration. The detail needed, the effort at recollection, had a clarifying effect. During his morning visits, which lengthened to an hour some days, she stepped with severe attention through what she knew of her life so far. The most difficult subject was June. It was hard, admitting a failure of maternity. "She's a lot like her father,'' she said, hoping that would explain a great deal.

But it didn't, apparently. "How?'' he asked, so she showed him photographs and tried to express the character of thin dryness she felt her husband and her daughter shared.

He showed her pictures of his three big sons and of his plump and beaming wife. "That's Ben, the oldest, then John and young

Bob." The boys surrounded and towered over Barney's wife. She looked like a happy hen, protected by these unlikely large chicks she had managed to raise.

"Oh, how nice," Aggie said. "What a nice family you have," and it never occurred to her to resent this, or to be envious.

"They are nice," he agreed, "Good kids. But they're boys, you know, they're trouble all the time, one thing or another. Just scrapes, thank God, never anything serious. It's more mischief and awkwardness, not badness."

"Just be glad," Aggie grinned, "that you don't have to live with goodness."

"She does seem to be pretty straight and narrow, your girl. Sure doesn't like seeing me here, anyway."

Well, yes, no doubt; but Aggie was surprised by a twinge of irritation. One thing for her to criticize her daughter, another for him. A friend was one thing, but when it came down to it, there were only she and June, and he was an outsider in that, after all.

The day she turned forty-two, he arrived with a birthday cake. "Coals to Newcastle, I know," he said, "but I didn't want you making your own. Happy birthday." It became a custom, then, each year. For his birthdays, she baked him something special, although not necessarily a cake, since he'd have that later with his family. Sometimes a candle stuck in an oatmeal cookie or a muffin.

He always caught her at a good time of day, when she was winding up the first round of labors, the bread-kneading and batter-mixing and popping things into the oven, and not ready yet for the next round, when the shop would open. Sometimes they'd get talking and he'd say, "Damn, I hate to leave already but I have to. Remember, so we can pick it up tomorrow." But, to be honest, it was a good thing he couldn't hang around, had to leave and get on with his job. Otherwise they might have gone on too long, and he might have gotten in her way. Sometimes that happened with women who weren't in any particular hurry, and they'd stay on and on, keeping her from her work, or a book she was trying to finish.

Another good thing was that their lives, hers and Barney's, did not overlap. His wife did not shop at Aggie's bakery, and Aggie was not invited to his home. All they had was an hour every morning, like a jewel in a glass box. Within that transparent case they sustained attachment; a fondness which, she thought, was sturdier than any romance.

When Herb arrived on the scene, she discussed him with Barney, and her surprise that the eye of such a man would light on her daughter. "Do you think she's pretty? It's so hard for a mother to tell."

"I don't know about pretty, exactly, but sure, I can see she's attractive in a way. Me, I like a woman with more meat on her bones, but plenty of men wouldn't agree."

"I worry, you know. She's had no experience."

Barney only heard about Herb, never met him. Aggie tried to describe a man who told jokes he'd heard on the road, sometimes not especially nice ones, although that was neither here nor there, but followed them by slapping not only at his own thigh, but at June's, or her own. A man who liked his pleasures shared. So what did he see when he looked at June?

Aggie was afraid he saw virtue. For all that Herb was charming enough, she never thought he was particularly bright. He might well be one of those men who married virtue, whatever their own diversions. She hoped he didn't see June as someone he could mold.

"It's nice," she told Barney during the courtship, "how happy she looks sometimes. Maybe she's mellowing." Aggie thought there were possibilities in the way June leaned toward Herb when they sat together on the front-room couch, or the way her arm might touch his shoulder when she poured his tea.

Equally, however, there might be portents in her tiny frowns when he swore, or the little sighs and pursings when he made drinks for Aggie and himself. June had a habit of spreading her disapproval around, like a deodorizing household spray.

Maybe Herb didn't notice. Maybe he thought that someone wound so tightly would unwind dramatically, given the licence. Really, though, Aggie couldn't see it. "What do you think, Barney? Should I say something to her?"

"Would she listen?"

"Not likely." He spread his hands and shrugged.

Nevertheless, she baked a wedding cake and invited guests and, hoping for the best, kept her hands occupied during Barney's visits, stitching for June a nightgown that, if she were so inclined, should invite passion. Barney held up the material and whistled at the sheerness.

"I know," Aggie said, "but you won't be able to see through it really, when it's falling in folds properly."

"*I*," he laughed, "don't expect to be able to see through it under any circumstances."

Some time later, when she asked June why she married such an unlikely man, June snapped, "To get away from you." But that wasn't true, she could have left at any time. Herb might just have been the first to pay attention, and Aggie could certainly understand how that might happen.

Sometimes after the wedding, on a Saturday night when Herb was home, she was invited for supper. She could see that June no longer leaned over him to pour his tea, but not much else. She didn't feel sparks between them, but then thought that the electricity she might have recognized would be the silent, shooting type of her own time with the teacher, and she wouldn't wish that on anyone.

There was in any case little point in worrying—or time. She had her own business, her books and stories, facts and speculations, quite a few grey hairs, and, in recent years, a friend. She got bigger and bigger. She felt, sometimes, as if her strong and rolling body might contain whole towns and cities, countries and continents, of characters: her own and others that she learned about. Memories as well: the child she had dreamed of still inside her, and a tiny figure of the teacher. Certain smells lingered. Her time to herself was in the very early morning, before Barney came rolling up, in a small truck now instead of behind the horse, and in the evenings. In the early morning, she was busy getting ready for the day. At nights she read, and soaked in the bathtub with a book and perhaps a rye, now that Herb had introduced her to that pleasure. She no longer felt especially uneasy at such a relatively calm and comforting life. Barney seemed to have made that difference, rounding it out. The trick, however, was not to fall into mere habit; to keep alert to possibilities, and the continuing need to weigh them.

If her life bore some resemblance to a cocoon, well, it was an extremely busy one; and did she not deserve a certain amount of pampering? Anyway, who knew what might emerge at some point, a new creature struggling free.

The new creature turned out to be Frances; struggling so hard to be free that June, for whom, Aggie sighed, nothing went smoothly, had to be opened with a knife.

And Aggie discovered love, an abrupt and puzzling emotion.

She tried to describe it to Barney. "I had tears in my eyes, real tears, when I saw her at the hospital. I can't think when anything like that has happened before."

"I know. I felt something like that when the boys were born."

"Did you make promises? It sounds ridiculous, but I stood there thinking about making sure she'd never come to grief, that I'd love her so much she'd never be hurt. Is that silly?"

"Not silly. But not very likely, either."

He was right, of course. There is no such thing as perfect protection, and no one could have kept Frances behind glass.

Aggie's love came unexpectedly only to her, took only her breath away. Frances, never knowing any different, took it entirely for granted. And June was understandably a little bitter. Was this not what Aggie should have felt, looking down at her own daughter at her breast? She might claim to have loved June then, but she couldn't deny it was nothing like this. And, further back, when she had thought she might love the strange and knowing teacher, it had only been a shadow, something hunched in the dark. This love, now, was in full light, a clear, distinct, distinguishable form, piercing, sharp, and occasionally painful.

She happily sacrificed some of her hours of quiet solitude to baby-sit when Herb was out of town and June wanted to go to church. In June's absence, she whispered pledges of love, wise advice, an unjudging ear, to Frances. She imagined this as something like an addiction, to something even stronger than food: a powerful, illicit craving. She trembled at the thought of never having enough. She bored, and knew she bored, her customers and even patient Barney, showing pictures of Frances, but couldn't help it. She was amazed at something she couldn't help.

She thought she could now discern the difference between individual days filled with small but significant pleasures, and being able to make out a future. She looked at Frances and saw someone who would, with luck, see this century turn into the next. She herself, born not so long after this century began, would be gone by then. June linked the centre. Aggie saw them stretching on and on. It put things in a different light, a series of lights.

She wanted not only different circumstances for Frances, freer than her own and with a universe of choices, but also that Frances herself should be different: more refined and alert, braver and lighter.

Even the ants and the bees, scurrying in their preparations for
generations that would scurry in their preparations for the same end,
made more sense than they used to. It was, she told Barney, a point
of view that had a certain amount to be said for it, and he laughed.

Worried that she might forget, she was determined to pay attention: to burn pictures into her memory so vividly that they would
never turn brown and fade, like real ones. To see the particular
shade of dusty blue of a small pair of overalls, or the embroidered
flowers across the narrow child-chest. The pleased concentration and
determination as France's arm pumped, up and down, up and down,
faster and faster, the handle of a top, so that the circus figures
painted on the side whirled, blurring. A laughing face, tempting
playful eyes glinting above a mouth ringed with Sunday breakfast
porridge. Warmth and softness in a small body curled into a lap,
light and limp with trust. Sitting on the back step, bent over, earnestly picking rolls of black dirt from between her toes, rubbing at
the skin until it was pink and raw. A plump tummy in the bath,
and an inquisitive finger exploring the belly button and diving into
mysterious places between the legs. Instants of pain: on her tricycle, hair flying, turning to wave back proudly, running smack into
a curb. Frances always looked more startled than hurt when she
fell down, or touched a cake pan that hadn't cooled from the oven.
Pain seemed to surprise her.

These pictures, as handy as a photo album, were also better.
There was motion in them, a leading up to and a falling away from,
with the instant of clear picture, unposed, in the centre. But while
they did not fade or turn brown, time still curled them around the
edges, turning them into more a memory than an event.

"You spoil her," June accused. "You have to say no sometimes."

Let other people say no.

Looking into Frances's eyes, Aggie saw her own. She remembered Frances's dark and curly hair from pictures of herself. She
admired the child's appetite, and her curiosity. Aggie, free to be
foolish, took her out to build a snowman, and found pieces of coal
for the eyes and mouth and a carrot for the nose.

They played. "You count, Grandma, and I'll hide."

Aggie, searching June and Herb's house on a Sunday morning,
following, but not too closely, the little snorts and muffled giggles,
saw with one eye, an adult one, that there wasn't much life showing. June kept the place tidy, but there was a shortage of knick-

knacks, or vases, mementoes of interesting times, or decoration of any sort. There were Frances's toys, but even those were kept neatly in her room. No one who didn't know, she thought, would be able to tell who lived here, or what sort of people they might be, with what sort of life. They might be dead people, except for Frances. Tidiness was understandable—what else did June have to do, after all?—but the aridity was odd.

But searching, looking under beds and inside closets, hoisting her bulk to peer onto shelves, or lowering it to peer under furniture, Aggie also, with her child's eye, played. "Where is that girl, where did she get to? Is she under this pillow? No? Behind the dresser? I guess not. Where did she go?" It was harder when Aggie had to hide; more difficult to find a space to contain her body. She thought how ridiculous she must look, crouching in a closet.

When June came in, things tightened up considerably. She fussed when Frances's clothes got dirty. "Eat up," she ordered. "You won't get dessert until you finish your main course."

"Don't want to."

"No cake then."

"Don't care."

And when it came down to a choice between cake and her own will, Frances really didn't care. Aggie watched with admiration, although she kept it to herself. Poor June, longing for control, must have thought a child would be within her grasp. Her luck to have one who declined.

"I don't know," June sighed. "She's so stubborn. She can't get it through her head that she can't always have her own way."

"Why should she get that through her head?"

"Well, because life isn't like that."

"Then she'll find out in her own time."

"Oh, Mother, you don't understand. You never paid attention to me, how would you know?"

"It seems to have worked, whatever I did or didn't do. You have more rules than I'd have ever dreamed of."

"But I had to find out for myself, didn't I?"

Frances watched them, apparently puzzled. Did June and Herb quarrel? Aggie, trying to remember herself at two, and three, and four, couldn't tell how much Frances might comprehend.

In her reading, she turned her attention to love, but found in the books mainly romance, which wasn't the same thing at all. Pap about melting into arms, flushed cheeks, embraces—all very well at some point, she supposed, but it was a point she had missed. The teacher, unwilling to sweep her into his unbrawny arms, had merely coughed and died. Mother-love as described in the books sounded like mush. She supposed she must have a case of mother-love of sorts, though its fierceness shocked her. Nothing soft about it, nothing melting or wishy-washy or demure or fragile. She even believed she might be willing to die on Frances's behalf.

How remarkable it would have been to have loved a man that way. Two people like that together would be perfectly enormous. Friendship, even with Barney, wasn't the same, although it was a form of love, no doubt.

Frances, she thought, must learn not only June's lessons—that she could be bent and hurt and dented—but also that she could do anything. She must not fall for the first opportunity to come along, through fear of nothing else. The trick was making all this clear to Frances.

Things work out though, even if sometimes somebody has to suffer along the way. If Herb's arrival was one sort of gift—taking care of June, taking her away—his departure, for Aggie at any rate, was another: it gave her Frances.

16

June spent the entire day he left scrubbing and cleaning like fury.

There was so much of him. Upstairs in the bedroom, rumpled sheets were flung back. In the bathroom, the brushes and combs were gone, and there was a splatter of fresh shaving-cream on the mirror above the sink, and a sweet humid smell. A drop of hair oil lay on the white surface of the sink.

With a square of toilet paper she erased the oil from the porcelain. With another, she took care of the dot of shaving-cream on the mirror. Turning, she glimpsed a curling dark hair in the bathtub.

Like a butchered body, it seemed he'd left bits of himself everywhere.

She got rags, soaps, and scrubbers from the kitchen, and began to do the bathroom properly: the toilet bowl, and all around its rim and base, right down to the floor; the mirror, the sink, the walls themselves, and the door and its knob; the tub; everything sanitized and disinfected, getting beyond the dirt to the smallest germs and remnants of him, the invisible remains too small to see.

Stripping the bed, she wrapped the sheets into a bundle, carried them downstairs, took them out to the shed at the back, and dropped them into the trash barrel there. In the living room, she wiped away fingerprints keenly, like a criminal destroying evidence. She dusted and polished, swept vigorously at the rugs, raising lint, dust, stray hairs, into small heaps, collecting it all. There was an ashtray with two cigarettes stubbed out, and glasses into which drinks had been poured, and bottles from the bottom of the china cabinet. All of it went.

She wiped down the stairs and banister. Going through the bureau drawers upstairs, she found a new tie, forgotten in its box, and put it also in the garbage.

Down on her hands and knees, she washed the kitchen floor, scrubbing at where his footprints might have been. Her dress tore beneath the arms as she reached inside the oven, cleaning away lingering smells of the casserole she made last night—just last night?—for his supper.

Looking around, heart pounding, panting, perspiring because anyway it was summer and hot to begin with, she peered and searched. Windows he had looked out of. And the drapes he insisted on flinging open—they would go to the cleaners.

At some point during the past six years, he must have touched each dish. She filled the sink with water as hot as she could bear, and washed them all, and dried them.

The sharp, dry smell of all the cleaning fluids—the soaps and polishes and waxes and disinfectants—was corrosive, but certainly obliterated any traces of sweet aftershave.

But what else, what else? There must be more. Everything hurt. Some of the pain was outside and some inside; mere muscles, but also the heart. Was this a broken heart, or a heart attack? Was it some sort of rheumatism of the spirit, which she could now expect to suffer from forever?

Oh, but if his hands had touched dishes and sinks and drapes, if his fingerprints might have lingered on a table, what about her skin? One way and another, the filthiest thing in the house now was her body.

Dirt clung to her and rolled; she could feel little particles of it on her neck. Her fingernails were broken, and blackness was ground into her knuckles and knees. Her dress was ripped and stained. She could smell herself, but beneath that thought she might still detect the scent of him.

She ran hot water into the bathtub and set out to boil herself. She scrubbed and scrubbed, watching the water darken. Flinching, she reached soapy fingers inside and got clean what she could.

Quite a ring of dirt remained when she got out. That, too, had to be scrubbed. Then a second bath, a guarantee she'd gotten underneath the surface. She came out pink, and wondered if she might have been scalded, but it was hard to distinguish one pain from another.

It was getting dark now, late. That meant she had spent a whole day erasing him; also that she must be twenty-four hours into this pain. She supposed it would be possible to get used to it. Just now it seemed unbearable, but of course it was not, since she appeared to be bearing it anyway. One thing it did was alter time: the moment of the impact was as immediate as if she were still hearing his voice fading to his conclusion, and it also seemed like something in the distant past, as if it had all gone on as long as she could remember.

It was in her mind that the filth lingered, quite out of reach of any scrubbing brush. He'd made her memory dirty, and she couldn't think what to do about that.

She couldn't keep still; paced on through her amazingly clean house that seemed now also amazingly empty. Always she had to keep trying to catch up. Things happened to her and then she had to catch up to them. It wasn't what she did, it was what was done to her, and then she was left to deal somehow with it. Now, when she felt quite violent, might have pounded on his chest, struck out, there was nothing to turn her rage to. She might weep, but tears were too small. A prayer, a word with God? It wasn't fair, she might tell Him that. She might tell Him lots of things, bad words spilling out of control. She was a person who cultivated control; how did things get out of hand? It hurt where she drilled her knuckles into her temples, and when she took her hands away, caught by a dreadful reflection in the hallway mirror, the white spots flushed red as the blood flowed back. Was this her? This wild, pale woman with flying hair? She could not have imagined she could look like this: glittering eyes, and her features seemed askew, as if even her nose had been knocked sideways; like one of those modern paintings, geometric planes instead of portraits.

How could he do this and drive away? She wasn't finished. Where was he when she needed him? He was never here when she might need him: when Frances got sick, or when she was ill herself and had to send the child to Aggie. If she heard a noise outside at night, he wasn't here. Now she had things to say, and where was he?

She must, after all, try not to think about him. Because this was his dirt, not hers.

What could she have said? There must have been a way of stopping it, some words that would change what he was saying, but she hadn't been able think what they might be. She had said some, but not the undoing ones. What would she say now?

She'd seen something different about him the moment he came through the door Saturday morning; not even Friday night, as usual. He was pale, and two weeks ago when he'd been home, he'd seemed to be getting quite a tan. His body seemed wound, lacking its customary looseness. His fingers twisted on the glass of rye he poured himself. He crossed and recrossed his legs, sitting in the living room, and he stared, rather vacantly at times, out the window, and then with a peculiar sharpness at herself and Frances. He held Frances on his lap and tried to read her a story, until she got bored and wriggled away. "Give your dad a kiss," he asked, and then held an arm around her until she ducked from under it. "She likes to be outside, doesn't she?" he said to June. Regret? Sadness in his voice? A little curiosity, or concern?

How could he bring himself to do this to his daughter? Along with all the rest, an unnatural father.

Hindsight. In fact, she hadn't paid much attention at the time; had thought he might be coming down with something. "Are you ill?" she'd asked.

The cruellest thing was that he knew and she was in the dark. She spent the day thinking it was a reasonably normal one, when it was actually the end of the world, and he knew that and she didn't. Hindsight was the only truthful view.

That ringing must be the phone. Funny, having to stop and identify the sound. And then Aggie's voice. "June, it's past Frances's bedtime and I don't know if Herb's coming to pick her up or if she's staying another night. What do you want me to do?"

Do? How should June know? Except, of course, Herb wasn't here to go and pick his daughter up, and she couldn't imagine all the effort that would be involved in fetching Frances and getting her undressed for bed and tucked in and kissed good night, and then, what if Frances asked where he was?

"Could she stay with you?"

"Of course. I just wanted to know what you wanted. You should have called."

"Sorry. Thanks for keeping her. She can come home tomorrow."

Tomorrow. Tomorrow what? What on earth was she going to do? People would know. She must have a face ready for them. Certainly she couldn't show them this one.

At least tonight she was tired. An improvement over last night, when she was so dreadfully alert.

"Do you think," he'd begun, "that your mother would mind taking Frances overnight?"

"Whatever for? She'll be going to bed in an hour anyway."

"Just because I'd prefer it. I have something I want to talk to you about. I'll drive her over, if it's okay with Aggie."

Well, what, she wondered while he was gone. She could only think he had somehow lost his job. What would they do, with no money coming in? What could he have done that would lose him his job?

"Junie," he said. Junie? "Come into the living room and sit down."

So she did; watched him make a drink and wondered irritably why he couldn't get on with it. Why he had to make a production out of things. With the word job on her mind, she didn't think she'd heard quite right when he sat down opposite her, leaning forward, elbows on his knees, hands around his glass, and said, "You know, I don't think we've made a very good job of this. Do you?"

"A good job of what?" Did he mean he wasn't a very good salesman any more?

"Oh," waving a hand vaguely, "all this. Marriage. It hasn't turned out the way we thought. At least not the way I expected. We don't seem to have made much of a go of it."

She frowned, puzzled and impatient.

"Look, June, I can't see that either of us is very happy. I thought we'd have a home and kids and do things together, I thought you liked a bit of fun. But that's not how it's been. You won't go out with me and you don't like the things I like. It's like you changed the rules. You won't even go to a movie with me. You used to, before we got married."

"I haven't changed," she blurted. How could he say these things? "I am what I have always been."

"Maybe. But I didn't know before. Look, I'm not saying it's your fault. I've made mistakes, and maybe I'm not what you thought I was either. I'm just saying it hasn't worked."

She wouldn't hear the last part. "No, you're not what I expected." Her voice, she could hear, had gone high and thin. "You were *nice* before." How could she put it? "I thought you'd be a gentleman." The word was so many things—duty, honor, respect, a sense of proper distance. Anyway, what was the point of this?

"Well, then, maybe it's all my fault, maybe I'm not a gentle-man, whatever that is, and maybe you're just too refined for me."
Now he sounded bitter, on the verge of anger. "It doesn't matter.
Whatever we wanted, neither of us got it. We've given it six years
and I think that's enough. I've thought about it a lot, and I think
once you get used to the idea, you'll see it's the best thing for both
of us."

"What, for goodness' sake? I can't tell what on earth you're
talking about."

"Calling it quits, how much clearer can I say it? While we're
both young enough to start again. I can't see another forty years
of this when we could maybe both be happy instead."

This didn't happen. It wasn't happening. Where was her blood
going, off to her feet, or up to her head? He really wasn't sitting
there staring at her, saying these things.

"So, June? Say something."

All right then, she would. She just wanted to get this straight,
what he was saying. "Do you mean live apart?"

"I mean get a divorce and we both start again."

"Oh no." How could she say how this knocked everything off
its pins, so he'd realize how impossible it was? "But the scandal!
We couldn't possibly."

He looked for a moment as if he might hit her. "I knew that's
what would bother you, what people would think. Jesus Christ, who
cares? Surely to God it's more important to have a life you want
than worry about what people are going to say."

"We made promises," she said. "And there's Frances. What
would become of us? You don't just disregard promises, you don't
just walk out of a marriage."

"Well, you can, you know." In the last few moments he had
gained confidence, seemed larger and determined; courageous in the
way of someone who has gone so far he has nothing to lose any
more. He stood. "Look, there's no easy way of doing this, but at
least it's better if it's quick. I'm going up to pack, and I'll leave
in the morning. I know it's a shock, but you'll see, it's best."

"But Frances."

"I know. I hate leaving her." His eyes suddenly filled with tears,
and that made her hate him. His tears, like everything else about
him, like his promises and his flashy clothes, were cheap. Look at
him standing there with that garish signet ring and the glass of
whiskey and shoes all shined like a fancy man.

"But I thought about her, too. It can't be good for a kid, growing up in a house where her parents aren't happy. She'll be okay with you, you're a good mother."

"And what about me? What am I supposed to do?"

"Don't worry, I'll send money. We can get lawyers and make some kind of settlement. And you know, you can go back to teaching. It's not as if you can't do anything."

The unconcern with which he could dispose of her! Just plop her back in the classroom, send her a few dollars to raise their child.

"I won't give you a divorce. I won't have that."

"Oh, June, be reasonable."

"No, I don't believe in it. And," she went on, not interested right at the moment in dealing with the future, "I won't have your money, either. If you're going, just go. I don't want anything of yours."

"Why not get a divorce then? As long as we're married," and oh, she thought, wasn't this sly, "we're connected."

"You will be, not me. I've kept my promises and done my duty, I have nothing to blame myself for. And I don't want you stopping off to say goodbye to Frances."

"I already did when I took her to your mother's."

"You mean my mother knows?"

"Of course not. I didn't say why, I just said goodbye. You can tell her what you want, it's up to you. I'm going to pack."

She could hear his footsteps up there, drawers opening and closing. It occurred to her that, really, he wouldn't have much to take with him. He didn't seem to have much of his own except clothes here.

What she had forgotten to ask, of course, was what brought this on. Surely something insignificant, or else she would have noticed changes. Something this drastic didn't come all of a sudden. Instead of saying, Leave, I can't stop you, she should have asked, Why? It must be repairable, given the will to repair. Nobody throws out a marriage as if it were an old dishcloth or a notebook that's been filled up.

How could he have possibly decided he wanted a divorce?

Oh. Oh, now she knew, now she saw it.

Because think what divorce meant. It meant going to court and people testifying. About infidelity. Adultery must be proven for divorce. He would know that. So he must have done that.

He spoke of pleasure, of being happy. He must think mere pleasure is happiness. He wanted easy pleasures, and his happiness would be insubstantial. Like him, it would be surface flash. Like some of those women they met on the street.

She shot raging to the bottom of the stairs. "All right then, who is she? You come and tell me who she is."

She could see this was it, across all the distance between them, him at the top of the stairs and her at the bottom. His eyes shifted. "Animal," she spat.

"Now, June, that's not it." But he wasn't coming closer, he wasn't coming down toward her. "It's us, not anybody else."

"Liar. Don't lie to me. You couldn't even suggest a divorce otherwise. Oh, I see it now."

Now he shouted back, as if he still thought he could make her think this was her fault. "Don't be so goddamned righteous! What do you know?"

Now she would not have him back. The contamination, just being in the same house with him. Imagine, she thought, curling herself on the chesterfield, that she had once felt sorry for him, in his lonely hotel rooms. She would have liked to sleep, but how could she close her eyes against all those mean rooms, and all those mean acts?

Early in the morning, she heard him thumping his cases down the stairs, out the door, into the car. She made tea for herself in the kitchen, and admired the steadiness of her hands. She was afraid, though, that she might be sick, right here, sitting at the table.

"June?" He was standing in the kitchen doorway. "I'm going now. I've only taken what's mine. June, I'm sorry, you know. I wish we could have done better, but look, you're still young, and after all it's not as if you've been happy with me. Or even," and a rusty razor-blade of bitterness entered his voice, "as if you needed me for anything."

"And a good thing, too, as it turns out."

"You'll find somebody else, you'll see." Now he was being hopeful on her behalf. "Maybe it'll be different with somebody else."

"It's you that wants to be different. I am who I am."

He sighed, shrugged, said, "Oh, never mind. I just wanted to say it's too bad, that's all."

These seemed poor last words, but apparently that's what they were, because he was gone. She heard the front door close, and just for a moment felt the panic of being left. Just for an instant her body was going to run out after him, and she was going to call to him and drag him back and keep him here because, whatever else, he was her husband and all that meant.

But not hers, after all. Her body, which had half risen, sat back down.

She heard the car door slam, and the motor start, and the tires on the gravel, and that was it. She thought, "But there's so much more I could have said."

Last words: theirs hadn't captured at all what she wanted to express; although she couldn't think just what words might have suited. But last words, surely, should wrap things up, finish them off properly so that a person wasn't left sitting around feeling as if she might be going to have a heart attack.

Because of the tea, she had to go to the bathroom. It was ill-timed, this sort of ordinary demand, when everything else was extraordinary.

However, in the bathroom she saw the dot of shaving cream on the mirror, and the trace of hair oil on the sink, and she cleaned all day like fury. And really she has done pretty well, over the years, at not thinking about it very much at all.

17

It was annoying—actually it hurt a bit—to hear from the women clustering in her bakeshop on a Monday morning that her son-in-law had left her daughter. They regarded Aggie curiously, although not necessarily unkindly, and said, "What a shame. What does June think she'll do?"

"I have no idea." How did they know so soon? Barney hadn't heard when he visited this morning or he would have told her, gently. And only last night she'd spoken with June on the phone to ask about keeping Frances over, and really she might have said something. Certainly her voice had sounded odd, but with June that could mean anything—that Herb was out playing poker again, or that she'd spilled something on her blouse that would leave a stain.

But, after all, poor tight-lipped, tight-souled daughter. Tenderness wouldn't help, though. A bit late, and June had too much pride to appreciate Aggie trundling over to offer—what? Condolences and sympathy? Still, Aggie thought, "My heart goes out to her." And then, "So that's what that expression feels like"—as if her heart had walked its own way over to June's.

"Do you know what happened?" the women asked. As if she would say if she did. But she had a pretty good idea. She'd sized up Herb at first glance, and warned June as best she could. It was all very well for Aggie to like him, but it was June who'd married him. She hadn't considered this precisely, but now she could see clearly enough that a fellow like Herb was unlikely to have gone to all those movies he mentioned on his own, or eaten all those suppers on his own. It should have been obvious he would also not

have slept alone. Also, maybe, that June was geared against pleasure. Poor June. Well, maybe poor Herb as well, but it was her
own daughter who had nothing to fall back on, her own daughter
who was adrift.

Whose fault? Whose fault that a flashy, fleshy man and June had
come together and then come unstuck? Fault everywhere, tracking
right back into this very house like sandy footprints; Aggie's house,
where a little thin, fatherless girl had pretty much had to raise herself.

And now June herself had a child, and no job, and no husband.
Surely Herb, even if he were well-intentioned, and who knew if he
was, could not support a separate household.

Frances was playing in the back yard. Had he and June made
some arrangement for her care between them? Surely nothing so
sophisticated. Aggie could not imagine the sort of weekend they
must have had. June would not have taken this easily.

How amazingly old she looked when she came to pick up
Frances. Bleak eyes in a pale face. She looked, Aggie thought, as
if she had learned too much too suddenly. People get permanently
hurt that way, the shock, their systems can't absorb so much. It
might be better, after all, to learn more slowly, spreading disaster
over a decade or so.

"Oh, June," she said, and impulsively embraced her. She was
sure that briefly there was a struggle between a June who might,
just once, weep on her mother's shoulder, and the June who would
never, in her twenty-eight years, have dreamed of doing such a
thing. The latter, the stiff one with pride, the one, Aggie reflected
sadly, who did not have much reason to believe her mother had the
gift of comfort, straightened and tightened and said, "I just came
to get Frances. I'm sorry I couldn't get her sooner, I hope she
hasn't been in the way."

"Frances is never in the way. You can leave her longer if you
want. Why don't you stay to supper, and then you won't have to
get anything ready?" Something, surely, she could offer—food at
least. A more solid and trustworthy comforter anyway, she'd always found, than arms.

"Thank you, but no. We'll go home."

"Well, if there's anything you want . . ."

"All right. Thanks."

And Aggie did have to admire the way June went out, chin up,
to collect Frances, and came back through the shop, and greeted

two customers quite coolly, and kissed Aggie briefly on the cheek
and said firmly, "I'll be talking to you, Mother," and walked
briskly out the door and down the walk, holding Frances's hand,
making the child run a little to keep up. Aggie was quite irritated
when one of her customers said, "She seems to be taking it well,
doesn't she?" Whose damn business was it, and who the hell did
the woman think she was?

Her love for June might not be on the scale of what she felt for
Frances, but it was certainly ferocious and protective. Right now,
at any rate. Maybe need was the root of love. Maybe helplessness,
or blankness, triggered it. Oh, but surely not; how terrible that
sounded, how bleak and cynical.

But it might be true that if June had ever been more helpless,
she might have drawn more affection. Maybe if she had felt ar-
dently loved by someone other than a father who died and a God
who wasn't exactly on the spot, she would have turned out lovable.

Aggie sighed; back to fault and blame. But she would like to
help. June need not, after all, be entirely alone. A mother was a
mother, and however odd this amputated sort of family was, surely
that essence of being there wiped away the rest, if it came to the
crunch. Would June feel that? This was, after all, her crunch.

Beyond the immediate shock, and looking ten years older than
she really was: what was June going to do? How would she manage? What a terrible spot to be in, abandoned with a small child.

But how stupid; this was the same spot Aggie'd been in herself
once, and she'd managed, had she not, quite on her own? And she
had not had a mother to fall back on. But the only request June
made for some time was help with Frances. "She's so active," she
explained, sounding limp and exhausted.

It was a pleasure, anyway, to keep Frances overnight on occasion. She slept in June's old room, and sat up in bed asking for
stories. Sometimes, sitting back on a hard old wooden chair she'd
brought upstairs, Aggie told stories from her own life. Colors and
smells—trying to describe to the child the smell of a field when the
hay has just been cut, the way rabbits would dart out of the paths
of the stolid old workhorses, whose flanks might twitch with the
surprise, but who never shied or bolted. The cats in the barn, living on mice, and milk directly from the cows. A big grey rat found
dead in the cellar, and her mother picking it up by the tail and
carrying it firmly outside to the barn, setting it down and telling
the boys to bury it, but not to touch it, and then going back to the

house and scrubbing and scrubbing her hands. It occurred to Aggie that there wasn't much that had scared her mother. She tried to tell Frances how it was to have acres to play in, instead of a yard. "We'll go there some time and you'll see." Well, she thought, they should. A child should know her own family; and Aggie might see something new herself, with eyes that could recognize love. Although it would be too bad if she found out it was only sentiment.

Her stories lacked plots, but Frances didn't seem to mind. "Do you think I could ever jump across the creek, Grandma?" she asked, and Aggie eyed her. "Yes, I think you just about could. But if you missed, you'd only get your feet wet. It wouldn't matter."

At some point, the child would be bound to ask about her father. "What do you want said?" Aggie asked June, who shrugged wearily. "I don't know. Just that he's gone, I guess."

At least when Frances did ask, it was Aggie she went to, not June, who was still delicately if bravely balanced, like a child trying on her mother's high heels. Teetering around, hanging on but barely, the effort showing.

"When's my daddy coming home?"

"Well, pudding." Well, pudding, what? "I don't think he is, you know. I think maybe he's gone away."

"Oh no, Grandma, he always goes away. And then he comes home. He brings me presents."

"Yes, I know. What kind of presents?"

"Last time he gave me a chain to put keys on, and he said he'd get me some keys, too. Before, he brought me crayons."

"Well, tomorrow maybe you and I can find you some keys, would you like that?"

"Yes. But what's my daddy going to bring?"

"Oh, pudding, your daddy's moved away. He's not coming home this time."

"But some time." Frances was nodding, so sure.

"No, honey, not some time."

"Not ever?"

"I'm afraid not."

So would she cry? Or turn away, disbelieving and mistrusting? Demand her mother? If she cried, Aggie could hold her. Otherwise, she wasn't quite sure what to do.

Anyway, Frances didn't do any of those things: just stared for a minute and then said only, "Oh." Her eyes unfocussed a little, as if they were interpreting something inside, not seeing out. That was all.

"Do you think that's strange?" Aggie asked Barney the next morning. "Do you think I said the right thing?"

"I doubt there's a right thing to say. It's bound to hurt, isn't it, however you put it? I think you did fine."

She was so grateful to have a friend to reassure her that she did her best.

He also said, in reference to other matters in his own life, "Well, what's done is done. You can't make things happen again so you can do better. You can only go on." She agreed; regrets were a waste of time. Only she would hate to hurt Frances, however inadvertently.

Just what did June feel for Frances? Did she love her, the way Aggie meant the word now, or had she caught somewhere along the line Aggie's own sort of detachment from a child of immediate flesh? Surely that wasn't something just passed on, though, like blue eyes or broad shoulders.

Surely, too, such a feeling was not irrevocable. Did Aggie not, now, looking at her dull-eyed daughter, wish for some offering that would help? Did she not sympathize with so much suffering?

"There's something," June said firmly, arriving one evening after the shop was closed, "I need to talk to you about." Aggie looked at her alertly, ready, she thought, for whatever might be asked. "I've been talking to people at the school board. There's an opening I can have this fall, teaching Grades 4 and 5."

Thank heavens, action finally, some steps toward survival. "Is that what you want to do, then?"

"No, but I don't have much choice." But still that bitterness, instead of healthy rage.

"Is Herb not sending money?"

"Two cheques so far. I ripped them up and mailed the pieces back."

"So you know where he is?"

"No, I just sent them to his company. They'll mail them on. He wants a divorce, too, but he won't get one."

"Why ever not?"

"For one thing, they probably wouldn't give me a job back if I was divorced. Anyway, marriage is marriage. There are promises made."

"But surely they're broken now. What difference would divorce make?"

"Oh, never mind, you wouldn't understand. Anyway, that isn't what I wanted to talk about." Deep breath. Aggie couldn't think what June might be going to ask for that was so difficult.

"If I go back to work, I won't have anybody to look after Frances, for one thing. She'll only be in kindergarten this fall, just half days."

"Well, that's easy enough. She can come here, it's no trouble and I'm glad to have her." And wouldn't it be nice, hours a day with Frances?

"Yes, but that's not it. The house is in Herb's name. I saw a lawyer yesterday, because I thought I'd better get things like that straightened out, and he said if it's in Herb's name, I don't have any rights in it."

"You mean you've nothing to show for all those years? You don't get anything out of it?"

"Apparently." June shrugged. "So I have to start again, and I have a proposition I'd like you to think over."

Again she came to a halt. Aggie wondered impatiently if she was supposed to guess, and then was ashamed of her impatience.

"Can I come back here?"

Could she have heard right? She leaned back in her chair, mouth opening in quick dismay before she could stop herself. June leaned forward, talking earnestly and quickly, now that she'd gone so far.

"You could look after Frances while I'm working, and I'd pay you rent and board; it's not that I want something for nothing. It's just that, I can't stay in the house and I can't afford to do anything else yet. It'd only be till I work out something better, just for a little while."

Well now. She must hate Herb quite a lot, then. She must have weighed them, his cheques against Aggie's charity and their long unhappy history, and decided on Aggie. Was that flattering?

Oh, but think what it meant: so many changes. Just having more things in the house, as well as bodies. Clothes and toys, footsteps and voices, a whole upheaval. No more silence or solitude. Her life would no longer be her own; but then, maybe it would be pleasant to share it. And only for a little while, after all. Until June got on her feet.

How selfish could she get? Hadn't she wondered how she could help? Hadn't she thought that help was what a mother could reasonably be asked for? Just, she hadn't expected anything quite so large.

"You don't need to say right away, Mother. I know it's a lot to ask."

"No, of course you and Frances are both welcome, naturally. Where else? And I wouldn't consider taking money. If you're trying to save to get back on your feet, you might as well save it all."

"No, I'd pay our way. I wouldn't come for nothing, I'd have to think of something else."

"All right, whatever, it's up to you." And then, "I haven't really said it properly, but you know, I'm very sorry." Reaching out a hand to June; could she touch her?

No. June slid away, tightening again. "I don't need your pity, Mother. I'm fine."

Oh dear. "It wasn't pity. I only said I'm sorry, not that I'm sorry for you. When do you want to move back?"

"A week or so? When I get everything together? Is that all right?"

"It's fine. You can have your father's old room and Frances can have yours. What about your house?"

June shrugged. "It's his. It's up to him."

"Oh God, Barney," Aggie confided next morning, "it's awful, but my first thought was that I really don't want this. I love Frances and having her around, but I'm not sure about so *much*."

"But it's only for a little while, isn't it? Look at how much fun you'll have, and a bit of a change, too."

"I know, I thought of that. You're right." She was cheered now, and began looking forward to the move. This, she thought, was the value of a friend: talking things over, having possibilities affirmed. She thought she might recommend friendship to June; although not yet.

June might be deaf, the way she moved around, oblivious. She repainted her father's old room a flat, glaring white and added a small desk and a straight-backed chair. She brought very little with her. Except for Frances, it didn't seem to Aggie there was much to show she'd ever been away. Except, of course, looking at her, Aggie could see tracks of experience. Skin stretched tauter, and lines creasing downward. For some time she was less slender than gaunt.

But Aggie could remember needing a period of recovery herself, and she'd bounced back. After a time, June would pick herself up

and take herself off somewhere, to do something, and Frances
would go with her, which meant Aggie had better pay attention
while it lasted.

Eventually a For Sale sign went up at June and Herb's house.
Aggie assumed he'd requested another route, since he wasn't seen
around town any more. He sent cheques for a while, and June continued to tear them up and mail them back, and after a time he
stopped.

When would June make a move? Nothing was done, and nothing
was done. June wafted around in her old silent way and Aggie,
getting accustomed, continued to work and read and visit with Barney and listen to customers, but Frances was at the centre now.
Aggie remained astounded by love.

Frances was:

A five-year-old coming home at noon from kindergarten, running
into the shop calling, "See the picture I made, Grandma? I made
a picture of you." A crayoned portrait of a tiny head, mounted on
a massive body, bigger than the trees beside it. They taped the
drawing to the door of the refrigerator.

A seven-year-old home with measles, and all the running up and
down stairs involved, having to stick a "Back in 10 minutes" sign
on the shop door every time. A little girl examining her spotted
face in Aggie's small hand-mirror, crying, "Oh, Grandma, make
them go away. They're ugly."

"They'll go away, don't you worry. But don't scratch at them,
you'll just make them worse."

A nine-year-old sitting on a stool by the kitchen window, watching the first snowfall of the year and asking, "Is it really true
snowflakes aren't ever the same as each other?"

"So I understand."

"But how does anybody know that?"

An eleven-year-old face looking up earnestly, sitting in the
kitchen between customers, asking, "Grandma, when we pray for
you in church, can you feel it? Does it make you better?"

"What?" Maybe she spoke too loudly, or sharply, because
Frances looked uneasy. But really! "You pray for me?"

"Mother says to. She says we should pray for all those who
haven't found God. Why haven't you, don't you know where He
is?"

Deep breath. No point in being cross with Frances, it wasn't her
fault. "Tell you what. It's very nice of you to pray for me, and I

appreciate the thought, but you don't have to. Grandma and God have their own arrangement.''

"Do you talk to Him? Mother does.''

"We don't need to. We just try to keep out of each other's way.''

Frances looked puzzled but impressed, apparently accepting the reasonableness of Aggie and God defining their exclusive territories, respect between equals.

"How dare you,'' Aggie began once Frances was in bed, "tell her she ought to pray for me?''

"She prays for everyone who needs it.'' Whatever else she'd permanently lost, June had certainly regained her primness.

"Well, I told her she didn't have to any more. I said I didn't need it. I won't have it. I forbid you to put nonsense like that into that child's head.''

"Really, Mother, even you can hardly stop people's prayers.'' What a wonderfully dry tone June could produce when she wanted to. Aggie was impressed, and then amused. Really, laughter took the zip out of a dispute.

Funny, this idea of June as someone meek, or weak, whatever. Because she always answered back, always stood up for herself. Just like Frances, except that it *felt* different; irritating instead of admirable.

When she thought about it, or for some reason caught a glimpse of June unguarded, trudging pale-faced through her days, Aggie worried. Or at least had twinges of concern. Years were going by here, not mere months, and when, exactly, was June going to take the next step, make some change? Not that Aggie now wanted them to leave, but for June's own salvation?

"What would you know about salvation, Mother?'' June demanded. "Leave me alone.''

"But you know, you can't go on this way. You have to do something. I know about needing time to lick wounds and figure things out, but it's gone on far too long. You have half your life ahead of you. Surely you don't want to waste it.''

"Is that what you think, that I'm wasting it? I'm earning a living and raising a child—what have you done that I'm not doing, anyway?''

Good point. "But friends, June,'' was all Aggie could think to say. "Going out and doing things. Getting interested in something.

Not just going to school and coming home and once a week going to church. What kind of life is that?"

"Mine." Curt and cold. Well, who would want to be told their life had no apparent meaning? Aggie could see she had handled it badly.

On the other hand, June did begin to go out sometimes in the evenings, joined a church group, and occasionally went to someone's home for dinner. Even, very briefly, went out with a man. Something, at least.

How, though, could she go on and on living here when she seemed to dislike it so much? Coming downstairs in the morning into the kitchen, June still regarded Barney with disfavor. She still spent a great deal of time in her own room, or in the dining room working, as her father had, marking and setting lessons. She might accuse Aggie of spoiling Frances, but she was easily worn out by the child, it seemed, and abandoned her own efforts after only short spells. In particular, she couldn't manage Frances's questions about Herb, a subject that came up periodically.

"How come," Frances asked, after she'd made friends at school and visited other homes, "I don't have a father any more? Everybody else does."

"He left," June said in that snippy way she had whenever he was mentioned. "Don't you bother your head about him."

"But where did he go? Didn't he like us?"

"Never mind about him. I told you, it's not important now."

Aggie, overhearing, wondered how June, of all people alert to fathers, could be so stupid. "Your father," she told Frances later, "was very sad when he left. Do you remember when he said goodbye? You were coming to stay over with me, and when he brought you he said goodbye, and he was very sad."

"Why did he go if he didn't want to?"

"Well, he wanted to, I guess, but sometimes grown-ups do things that make them sad because it's better in the long run."

"Didn't he love me?"

"Of course he did, pudding."

"Then he didn't love Mother?"

"At first, I expect, but then maybe later he didn't."

"Is that why he left?"

"Partly, I suppose. I don't really know the reasons, though."

"But when you get married, that means you love somebody, doesn't it?"

"It's supposed to, yes, but sometimes people make mistakes." Young Frances, her face screwed up, trying to make sense out of that.

"Did Mother do something bad so he didn't love her any more?"

"Oh no, I'm sure not. It's just that feelings change, and it's not necessarily anybody's fault."

"So," very seriously, trying to get it quite straight, "if you love somebody, it doesn't mean you always will?"

"Sometimes that's what happens, I'm afraid."

"Does that mean," with a child's inexorable logic, "you might not love me some day?" Unimaginable. She put her arms around Frances—what a gift, a child who responded to embraces—and said, "Oh no, pudding, of course not. That's a different kind of love, it doesn't change."

"What if I did something really bad?"

"For one thing, I don't think you would. Doing something bad is different from mischief, or just making a mistake. Anyway, it wouldn't matter, I'd still love you."

("You wouldn't care, Mother," June has accused, "if Frances murdered somebody, you'd twist it around so it wasn't her fault." Aggie thinks that's likely true.)

"Do you love my mother?" Frances asked.

"Well, she's my daughter. What do you think?"

"Do you love Barney?"

"In a way. He's my friend."

"Did you love my grandpa?"

"I may have thought I did, but I didn't, really."

"How come you got married?"

"I don't really remember. A lapse of judgment, I guess," although that was mainly for the benefit of June, who could hear them from the next room.

"What's a lapse?"

Even then, Frances was a natural interrogator. Sometimes even Aggie grew a little weary of all the questions. "Tell you what," she would suggest, "if you can sit still and not say a word for five whole minutes, I'll give you the first raspberry tart I take out of the oven. Watch the clock now. Ready? Go." But Aggie wasn't often too tired to listen; and was repaid by Frances's gift for spontaneous affection. Even if sometimes an embrace came at an awkward moment, say when Aggie's hands were covered in flour or busy with bread dough, it was irresistible.

"You can do it," Aggie urged, out in the back yard with her on a Saturday, between customers, "it won't hurt, just let yourself roll." That was the day Frances learned to turn somersaults.

"Come and see what I can do," Frances cried, dancing indoors to her mother, pulling at her until she came out to watch, and be horrified. "Frances, stop that, you'll break your neck."

"No I won't. I know how to do it."

"You may think you do, but you could still break your neck."

Thereafter Frances turned somersaults and climbed, quite high sometimes, into the big maple tree at the back, so that even Aggie watched nervously out the window, when June couldn't see.

Poor June, who only dared small and timorous movements—how could they expect her to take pleasure in her daughter's capacity for risk? She reminded Aggie of Neil: courage for taking big steps worn out too soon. He, of course, had died then. June didn't even seem to have the energy for that.

18

What June should have done, of course, was what she'd intended in the first place: live with Aggie just long enough to pull herself together, save a little money, get used to her new and dreadful circumstances. Really, she'd had no intention of staying on.

It exhausted her, just asking; she never would have asked, if there had been some other choice. Who would have thought the house belonged to Herb alone? Before Frances, her own salary had helped to make the payments. She had nothing, it appeared, except a child.

She felt as if this abrupt disintegration might leave her permanently wide-eyed with shock, although she had to suppose that she could get used to it; she had gotten accustomed to other blows, after all. So just for a little while she would live with her mother, and pull herself together.

When she and Frances moved in, she undertook to paint her new room, formerly her father's. A flat, stark white was what she wanted; clean blankness that wouldn't jar.

Just moving her limbs was an effort, never mind uprooting her life. Walking down the street, she felt people staring and talking. She would be poor June Benson, who couldn't hold onto her husband. Going back to school, where she was kindly, perhaps pityingly, offered her job back, was worse: little boys snickering, and teachers discussing her behind her back.

It was extremely difficult to maintain a faith that all this was God's will. "Why me?" she would have liked to ask. It was barely comforting that it might be some sort of test, setting her up for a greater reward. Still, there was nothing to do but believe. It was all she could hang onto of what once had been herself.

She did have to be grateful to Aggie, though, for taking her in without question (except for a sort of flinch that was spontaneous and unmistakable), and for taking care of Frances, although Aggie certainly didn't seem to mind that. Also for letting June be, so that she could spend hours in her freshly painted white room. Just sitting. She had a feeling that if she could sink into that whiteness, enter right into it, she might finally be clean again.

There were also times when she leaned her face into her hands and wept; not specifically for Herb, whose memory made her skin leap, but for loss. She wondered if other people had what they seemed to have: normal lives. Were there people who simply went on with things, in an ordinary sort of way, without disruption?

It hardly helped when Frances asked about her father. "When's Daddy coming home?" she inquired in the early days. Aggie must have managed to set her straight on that, but later she asked, "Why did Daddy leave?" Oh, June would have liked to shake her, take her by the shoulders and shake her until all those memories fell right out of her little head. "He's not coming home," she answered curtly.

The money he sent was undeniably tempting; would have made it easier. There were things, after all, that Frances needed, like any growing child: clothes and shoes and school supplies. But mainly she needed an ordinary home with two ordinary parents. Apparently he thought money could replace him. That was some view of his own importance, or his responsibility.

It was the gold signet ring that kept rearing up, and the flashy linings of his suits. The hair on his knuckles as he gripped a glass, and the smell of the oil he used on his hair. Sometimes, out on the street or in a store, someone passed by her trailing the same sweetish, sickish scent, and she thought she might faint.

From her room, she could often hear voices downstairs: Barney's rumbling early in the mornings to start the day. She no longer had the energy to dislike him. In the beginning, when he started coming around years ago, she'd been terrified: he and Aggie were so obviously becoming important to each other. When June learned he was already married, her first reaction was relief. When she'd had time to consider it, however, she was disgusted. What sort of woman was her mother, encouraging a married man? And never mind any nonsense about friendship. Also, what sort of married man gave part of his day for years to another woman? (She had the answer to that now: a man like Herb.) Although she never supposed Aggie and Barney got up to anything really wrong. How would they, in a kitchen? Just that it was inevitable that the intention, or desire, must be lurking.

Her own daughter's voice also floated upstairs, shouts and questions and occasional sobs. Customers, too. A high-pitched babble, heard from this distance. Laughter even, sometimes. Was it not cruel of people to laugh when she was suffering? This was the real abandonment: that other lives went on, with routine chores and laughter.

She watched herself carry on. Her feet on the stairs seemed fay away and not hers at all, so that she had to watch them very carefully to make sure they did what they were supposed to, and didn't let her down. She washed her face and hands, and bathed her body, but it didn't seem that the water ever touched her skin. In the classroom, her own voice came to her from a distance.

She turned thirty with her life a shambles. She lived with her mother, and her child was stubborn and unruly. Aggie baked a cake, and Frances sang happy birthday to her. June considered vaguely that the thought, at least, was kind.

It was a good thing Aggie took over so much of the care of Frances. June had no idea how she would have managed otherwise. Sometimes, though, Aggie's supervision left a good deal to be desired. She seemed to encourage dangerous pursuits and, like Herb, did not appear to care that the child might be injured. June pictured Frances lying broken at the bottom of a tree she'd tried to climb, brain-damaged, perhaps, or paralysed. It seemed to June there was quite enough danger in the world, without going out looking for it.

What did Aggie and Frances talk about? There were times, coming home, when it seemed that the two of them had secrets from her. Their conversations might halt, and sometimes she thought she caught conspiratorial glances between them; or felt them speaking to her with a sort of benign protectiveness, as if she were too frail to hear what they'd been up to, or would disapprove. Or that it wasn't worth the trouble of telling her.

When June was young, Aggie hadn't given her anything like the amount of attention Frances got. And now June couldn't even complain, or worry out loud about Frances, without Aggie springing to her defence. "Never mind," Aggie said, "she'll be fine." As if a child could tell what was safe or unsafe, what was right or wrong, what was important and what was not.

How stubborn and wilful Frances was: refusing food, kicking up a fuss at bedtime—where did she learn this? "Really, Mother," June complained. "I wish you wouldn't let her get away with whatever she wants. It makes it very difficult."

"But I don't. I just deal with her differently. I divert her. You know, I bet if you didn't tell her she has to have her carrots, she'd eat them with no problem. She just gets her back up."

"But she should do what she's told." Anyway, it seemed a terribly energetic undertaking, trying to seduce a child into obedience.

"If you wonder where her stubbornness comes from," Aggie grinned, "just look in the mirror."

"I was never like this."

"Well, you were, but it came out differently. Let me tell you, carrots are easy compared with how you were stubborn."

June thought Aggie must have her memories confused. Probably she made them up to suit herself.

At least she could try to balance Aggie's influence, tilt one way as Aggie tilted the other. Maybe Frances would come down in the middle, then. It was hard, though, to outweigh her mother's devotion. Love, like many other things now, was simply exhausting.

She did insist, however, on taking Frances to church with her, and she seemed to enjoy it, heading happily downstairs to the Sunday school, emerging later to retell, as they walked home, the Bible stories she had learned, or show a drawing she had made. There was a bit of an uproar one time when Aggie found out that Frances prayed for her, but otherwise she didn't seem to care one way or the other. Another time she roared with laughter at a picture Frances did in Sunday school of Jonah. It showed a man's thin legs dangling feebly from between the sharp white teeth of an enormous black whale, and Aggie said, "I'm sorry I laughed, honey, it's just that it reminded me of your grandfather. Those poor little legs like toothpicks," and roared again.

Frances's drawings were pinned up all over the kitchen, wherever there was space on the walls, or the refrigerator. This too was different from when June was young, although she couldn't precisely recall any drawings she had made that might have been pinned up.

There were, in fact, a great many things she couldn't quite seem to recall. Looking at Frances, face alight with some discovery in a book, or panting and pink as she skipped rope, she couldn't imagine having ever felt anything like such a whole-hearted joy. But it was hard to tell; everything was changed and in a different light now.

Well, she supposed it must be like any break: a leg knitting itself through time. A question only of whether it mended properly or left a person a little crippled, with a little limp.

The great thing was never to be injured again.

Aggie said, "You know, if there are things you want to do, don't worry about Frances. I'm here anyway. You don't have to feel you should be home every night."

Go out? Where? It was all she could do to get through a day, much less a night out. "I'm all right, Mother, leave me alone."

"You can't be all right. Look, I know it takes time, getting over something like what happened (how would Aggie know what had happened? How could she imagine?), but at some point you have to pull yourself together and make a new life. You've got thirty, forty years ahead, maybe. You should be making something of them."

Forty years! She could barely get up in the morning, never mind imagining forty years of mornings.

"June, honestly, I'm not trying to nag. It's just that I worry about you."

Really? That would be a change. She might have worried and warned some years ago, when it might have done some good.

"What do you think I should be doing, then?"

"*I* don't know," throwing up her hands. "Something that interests you. Join a club, go out with friends. You know," assessingly, "you might meet someone. But you certainly won't, sitting here."

Oh no. Go through all that again? The one good thing about her life now was the freedom from hands. Anyway, she lacked trust, had no faith any more.

"I know how you feel, June. Remember, I had to start again too."

But that wasn't the same at all. It had never been in June's mind to make Herb vanish, the way Aggie had let her husband disappear.

"Look," Aggie said firmly, "you're the one who used to say life was a gift from God. Think of the trouble you'll have, explaining why you didn't do much with it."

Oh, really, talk about laughing behind her hand, Aggie of all people trying to use an argument like that. Except June could recall saying that, and she could imagine Him telling her, on judgment day, "It's not that you did anything wrong, heaven knows. But then, you didn't do much of anything at all. Really, I'd have thought you'd have done better, considering the gifts I gave you to work with: faith and health. What more did you want?"

"Anyway," Aggie went on, "do think about it. I may not have put it very well, but I mean it for the best."

She sounded almost forlorn; June was almost touched. "All right, I'll think about it. I'm sorry you've been worried." She reached out to pat her mother's hand, and found hers trapped between Aggie's pudgy palms.

Nothing was more unbearable than tenderness. Tenderness could shred her will, which was all that kept her sitting upright in the chair. She was sorry, though, about the flicker of hurt, and then anger, that flashed in Aggie's eyes when she pulled away. It didn't seem possible to save yourself and not cause pain elsewhere.

Maybe that was what Herb had thought? Not likely, though. He acted on pleasure and sensation, never thought. He would at least have considered his daughter and his duties, if he'd been a thinking man.

But what might God be expecting of her, having tested her so far? At least she might join a church group, something appropriate that would also get her out of the house and out from under Aggie's eye.

The couples club, of course, was out of the question, as was the young people's group. She no longer qualified for either. The women's group didn't appeal, since its members seemed largely concerned with catering weddings and other church events, and June had no intention of getting involved in cooking and baking and similar sorts of drudgery. The only possibility she could make out, scrutinizing the church calendar, was a group that met twice a month to discuss various scriptures.

"Oh, well, if that's what you want," said Aggie. "At least it's something."

The group was led by the minister, the same one who had replaced the white-haired, piercing-blue-eyed man of June's adolescence. There were no particular complaints about this one, who was soft-spoken, not riveting, but probably kind and certainly dutiful. He picked out a passage for the group to read, which would be discussed at the next meeting. The discipline of such assignments pleased June. She did not, however, speak out at the meetings, was content to leave words to the others. Anyway, there wasn't a great deal to be said. It was not as if there were radically different interpretations. Mainly she stared down at the Bible in her lap.

So she was startled, pulling on her coat at the end of a meeting, to hear a voice at her shoulder, a hesitant low one; a man's voice. "Mrs. Benson? I don't believe we've ever been formally introduced, but you probably know my name's Bill Baker." A small man, not much taller than she, with receding grey hair combed directly back from his forehead, no apologies or camouflage there. "I was wondering if you might be interested at all in having dinner with me? Perhaps this weekend, on Saturday?"

He'd rehearsed, she could tell. Had perhaps sat through this meeting with his eyes on her downcast head, speculating and worrying and hoping to be brave. "I don't know," she hesitated. After all, what did she know about him? Anyone could join a church group: although he looked harmless enough, and he'd been a member for a long time; she'd certainly seen him at meetings without especially noticing him. His size was reassuring, too.

"Just dinner," he was saying. "I assure you, nothing more."

Well, why not? She smiled and said, "That would be very nice, yes, thank you."

"I'll be going out Saturday," she told Aggie with satisfaction.

"Are you going to marry him?" asked Frances, who was twelve and at an irritatingly blunt and insensitive stage.

"Don't be ridiculous," June snapped. "I've barely met him. In any case, I am married."

He worked, he told her over dinner in one of the town's fancier restaurants, which had licences to sell liquor (a change from the sort of place she used to go during the war—where she'd met Herb), in one of the new plants in town. It manufactured boxes. He'd used to work for the same company in its former plant, in another, similar town, and had moved on here when the firm expanded and built this new factory. "These days," he said, "it's more automated than it used to be. All new equipment. So I was lucky to have a job when they offered me the one here."

He thought the town pretty. He said he had never married, but hinted at a previous involvement. He asked her what she did and how she lived. "Then you're a widow?" he asked. "For very long?"

She could hardly lie. "No. I'm married. My husband and I no longer live together." She simply couldn't say those words in any other than a forbidding way, couldn't bear it if he inquired further. The result was that he flushed, embarrassed, and she felt clumsy.

She was very surprised when, as he left her in front of Aggie's house, he asked, "Could we do this again next Saturday? Or perhaps take in a movie?"

"Certainly, that would be fine."

She wondered later, though, why she had agreed. Not because he appealed to her, because she doubted that anyone would. Nor was he likely to become a friend, like Aggie's Barney. She didn't even think he was especially interesting. She thought perhaps she might have agreed mainly to show Aggie, to be able to say, "I'm going out Saturday," as if it were a triumph.

But surely it was also flattering to think of him watching her at those meetings, becoming interested. It seemed she could still be wanted, if not, she hoped, desired. She hoped there would not be that sort of awkward moment to deal with.

"I'm sorry about the movie," he said. "I should have checked before I suggested that." There only was one theatre, although there were reports another was in the works as the town expanded. "I'm afraid it's one of those Elvis Presley ones. Perhaps we should think of something else."

Oh dear. There wasn't much else to do, and she'd rather counted on the movie to fill a couple of hours without the need for conversation. "Do you bowl?" he asked.

"No, I'm afraid I never have."

"Would you like to learn? It's a good game."

She wasn't a bit interested in learning to bowl. On the other hand, she had no other suggestions. The only alternative seemed to be going for a walk, which would require a terrifying degree of conversation.

He said he was a patient teacher, and it was a good thing because she couldn't get the hang of it at all. Most of her balls rolled aimlessly and hopelessly into the gutter, or she managed to hit a single pin, but the wrong one. What was really worrying her was

the shoes: having to rent them. Who knew who'd worn them before, the condition of their feet?

"We could maybe," he suggested eventually, "go some place a
little quieter and have a beer."

"I'm afraid I don't drink."

"Coffee then, and a bite to eat after all this exercise."

She thought, "I want to go home," but it was too early. What
a stupid situation, though, a daughter having to stay out late to keep
a mother from fussing.

"So," he said, nervously making conversation in the restaurant,
"how did you come to join the group at the church?"

"Oh, I'm interested in Bible study, and then, it's an outing, too.
Everyone needs interests outside of work and home," stealing Aggie's argument.

He brightened. "Me too. I mean, that's sort of why I go. That
and the bowling keep me busy. I'm on the bowling team at work,
and then I sometimes go on my own. Good bunch of people at the
church, too."

Probably they were. She hadn't especially noticed.

"You have a daughter?"

"Yes, she's twelve."

"It must be nice, having a family," he said wistfully. She heard
an echo of Herb in there, although that wasn't fair, and she was
sure Bill did not resemble him in the slightest.

"My mother looks after her a good deal. I had to go back to
teaching, just when Frances started school."

"That was when, ah, your marriage ended?"

"Yes."

"So it's been some time."

"Seven years."

Seven years was longer than her marriage had been. A daughter
who had been just starting school then would soon be off to high
school, and she herself was middle-aged. She felt pale. While other
people might feel themselves flushing, blood rushing to the face,
she could feel the opposite, blood seeping away.

"You look tired," he said. "You must have a busy life. Perhaps
we should go."

At least it was something, going out, and he seemed safe enough.
She had a sense of time having been wasted this evening, but what
would she have done with it otherwise? Read, marked papers,
watched television with Aggie. Frances was out with a friend.

Probably at the Presley movie (what a good thing she and Bill did not go there after all). He had filled a certain amount of time, and might do so again in the future. That seemed all right, not too strenuous or demanding.

They stopped, walking her home, for a red light. When it turned green and they stepped off the sidewalk, he cupped a hand beneath her elbow. It was like being shot. She whipped her arm away in a reflex movement that took her off balance, so that she stumbled and almost fell. Herb courting her, guiding and protective and aiming for more; so there was no difference, they were all the same, not to be trusted.

He was bewildered. "Did I do something wrong? I'm terribly sorry, what did I do?"

"Nothing at all." Oh, she was cool now, cold. She knew where she stood. "But I can see my own way home from here, there's no need for you to come with me." She marched briskly away, but he followed like a stray puppy, she thought, hoping for a good meal. "Please, tell me what's wrong? I've made you angry, but I don't know why."

She turned and faced him. "I'm not angry. But I am perfectly capable of getting myself home. So I'll say good night right now, and thank you for the evening."

"But will I see you again? How about next Saturday? There'll be another movie on by then, maybe something good."

"No, thank you for asking, but I think not. Good night."

Now that she'd discerned his hidden intentions, she was a little frightened, and walked more swiftly in case he tried to follow. But he didn't.

The trouble, she realized later, was that now she couldn't go to any more church group meetings; would not be able to sit in the same room with him, as if nothing had happened. She wondered just what had happened; perhaps she had over-reacted? Certainly she had behaved without grace. But no, she'd been right. And the important thing was having learned that a Herb could be anywhere, beneath any harmless face.

"You're not going to those meetings any more?" Aggie asked.

"No, I've quit." Aggie looked as if she would like to ask why, but for once did not.

"What happened to your boyfriend, Mother?" Frances asked, grinning.

"He was not my boyfriend," June snapped. "And it's not your business."

"Oh, Mother, I was joking. Can't you take a joke?"

What did Aggie and Frances think was so funny all the time? Their jokes, June thought, were often just camouflage for cruelty.

And Frances, who had stretched up and slimmed down and was turning into a teenager (how did that happen so fast? Here was someone quite different from the child June remembered), this young girl was asking June's permission to go out on a date.

"Certainly not, you're far too young," June ruled.

"But Mother, it's not like a real date, there'll be a whole bunch of us."

"No, I told you, you're too young." She could at least try to protect her daughter from all those clutching, cupping, treacherous hands.

"Then," Frances said, hands on hips, chilly eyes on her mother, "when will I be old enough?"

When? Never, please God. "Sixteen," June blurted, with a feeling that surely that was sufficiently in the future that something might happen in the meantime to keep Frances permanently safe.

"Sixteen." Frances nodded. "All right, I hope you realize you're ruining my life, but you don't likely care. But I'll remember. I'm going to have a date on my sixteenth birthday, so don't bother having a cake or anything. I'll be out."

"*What* a child," June sighed later.

"Not a child, you know," Aggie answered, glancing up from her book.

Aggie's fault, all this, June was sure: opening up so many dangerous possibilities to Frances. And how would Aggie know what she was talking about? Only from books, and whose life was so neat?

What a storm, a tempest, a nightmare of emotions Frances's adolescence was. How cold she could be, and how hot. She also had a long memory and, as promised, announced on her sixteenth birthday that she would not be home for dinner because she had a date. June's mouth, opened to protest, closed again in the face of Frances's defiant glare.

Thereafter she was often out, an airy, "I'm off to the movie, see you guys later" as she ran down the stairs and out the door.

"Don't worry about her," Aggie advised. "She's got a good head on her shoulders, she won't do anything foolish."

Going out at all was foolish, as far as June could see. And boys were even worse than grown-up men, who at least had developed a veneer of control.

Sometimes she wondered, looking at her daughter, where she could have come from. She was like a changeling: switched at birth with some narrower, meeker child in the hospital nursery.

Aggie seemed to have a point about the influence of simply living in different times. Except she said, "Take advantage," while June had to warn, "Take care."

How was it to be Frances, young, with boys coming, shyly or arrogantly, to the door to take her places, buying her movies and soda pop and french fries? How was it to walk along a street holding hands right out in public, and a week later to be doing the same with someone else? How was it to sit on the phone for hours, laughing and gossiping and whispering with friends? Some nights Frances flung herself upstairs to her room and slammed the door, and even from downstairs, June and Aggie would hear noisy sobbing. She seemed to have no sense of *withholding*, which surely made her dangerously vulnerable to those treacherous things, emotions.

"It's a good thing, really," Aggie advised. "She'll know what she's doing better than we did."

Without Frances as a buffer, June and Aggie spent more time alone together, and June supposed it was no wonder they got on each other's nerves. Not that they talked much, but when they did they could hardly agree. Aggie, looking up from one of her news magazines, said, "Isn't it extraordinary, all this civil rights business in the States? Can you imagine people beating other people and threatening them, even little kids, to keep them from going to school together? You'd think I'd know better by now. I keep forgetting how wicked people can be."

She was horrified, too, at American assassinations, shaking her head in front of the television set, saying over and over, "My God."

Well of course June was horrified too, no question about it. She was also terrified by the violence. What if it spread, what if people took up the idea from what they saw on their television screens and brought it here, onto her sidewalks and into her home? But she also felt, although she could never seem to explain it so that Aggie understood, that she could see people driven to certain actions by the terror of change. The desperation of having a foothold and seeing someone trying to slip it away from underneath.

"Of course they're frightened," Aggie said sharply. "So what? That hardly makes them right. Fear can make you crazy, June, it can make you do crazy things."

June's own aim was to do only small things. She thought of Chinese women with their feet bound, taking tiny, careful steps, moving lightly to avert pain.

One of her small steps, taking her out occasionally from an evening that would otherwise be spent again with Aggie, was to have supper at Brenda Ferguson's house. Brenda, who taught Grades 5 and 6, had started at the school a few years after June went back to teaching, and had originally gone to June for information on pupils June was passing into her classes. They had lunch together in the staffroom sometimes, if they had the same periods free, mainly to talk about pupils. One of the things June liked was that Brenda's questions were specific—had one child shown signs in June's classes of a vision problem, did another act up and what discipline methods had June tried? She did not speak of theories or fulfillment. She had taught elsewhere before moving here with her husband, which made her different from the younger, eager teachers.

It was kind of her to ask June home for suppers on occasion. She was a generous person, in her brisk way, and no doubt intended to cheer June up, or draw her out, or give her a lift. "Gosh," she sometimes said, shaking her head, "I don't know how you've done it, raising a child and working, keeping it all up by yourself."

"Well, there's my mother."

"Yes, but it's not the same, is it? Bringing up a child, I mean, that's your own. Not the same for a grandmother."

True enough.

Brenda, of course, would have no idea that it was hard for June to sit at the table with three lively teenagers who laughed and argued through the meal. Worse, though, was before supper, when June was helping Brenda make the salad and Brenda's husband Mac came bounding home from work and into the kitchen and kissed his wife on the cheek and gave her a hug, right in front of June. It wasn't just once, a single outburst of affection, but apparently a custom. Here were ordinary lives! Here precisely was what June had hoped for once (except that Brenda kept on teaching). It wasn't fair. As she walked home, grudges ran through her head like a tune.

"Some days," Brenda was known to complain, "I'm so tired when I get home I can hardly pull a meal together. The kids help now sometimes, they can at least do their own laundries and they get their own breakfasts, but it's still so much! But then, I'd go crazy if I were home all the time. I'd miss teaching, wouldn't you?"

Once when Brenda said that, June had blurted fiercely, "I've always hated teaching," and Brenda looked so startled, even frightened, that June had clamped her mouth closed against anything else she might have said. And Brenda had apparently decided it was wiser not to pursue it.

It was best to keep things to herself anyway. If no one knew where she was most vulnerable, it would be that much harder for her to get hurt.

She thought that small events, like going to Brenda's for supper, might be like being inoculated against some illness: a small effort that resulted in a small pain, perhaps warding off large events with their huge pains. If she could wrap enough of these minor but sturdy incidents around her, they might armor her against further cataclysmic ones.

It seemed to work, in a way. That really terrible pain, the one like a heart attack, went away finally, for the most part, except sometimes when she could still be stabbed by the smell of after-shave or hair cream. The disappearance of that pain, however, had nothing, it seemed, to do with being healed; more like being anaesthetized, as at the dentist's. At least when she'd had it, she'd known she was alive. "Oh, God," she prayed, but then what? Not, of course, "Oh, God, restore the pain," that would be ridiculous. But restore something: sensation, maybe; vision, hearing. The basic senses.

She woke up in the mornings sometimes, staring around her white room, and wondered what on earth she was still doing here.

Once, she'd assumed there would be a day when she would wake up and look around and find herself ready to go. Something firm would have been born and there she'd be, with plans and a future, packing up her belongings and Frances. It was a transformation that would just happen to her overnight, without deliberation or effort. Well, maybe tomorrow, she'd thought for a long time.

But now she no longer hoped for that, and didn't even bother to pray for it. Frances was nearly grown, and years were gone; not only gone, but more or less blank. What of importance had ever happened to her, after all? Only a few things, and they had hurt.

She might wake up some mornings wondering what on earth she was doing here, and sometimes she might, she thought, even verge on despair. But despair was better than terror, if that was her choice. Terror lay in change; despair in keeping still.

It did seem to her very strange, though, that considering her greatest longing was for safety, a guarantee against pain, she seemed to have suffered inordinately. A puzzle, that.

19

Barney wept on Aggie's shoulder the Monday after his son lost his leg; put his head down and let the tears run. "Thank God," he said finally. "I couldn't do that at home. Everybody's so upset, and I sort of feel I have to be strong. Thanks, Aggie."

Not since Frances was a child had she felt the helplessness of someone seeking comfort from her. She patted his shoulder and stroked his hair, to tell him she was glad at least that he felt free to weep with her.

Over the weekend, Barney had aged. So many years of friendship, recounting their days and exchanging their questions in that single hour nearly every morning—simply the routine of smiles, a break, that breather in their days—and suddenly, in just a matter of a weekend's absence, he was abruptly aged. Even his hair seemed more white than grey, and the lines of his face dragged it downward. Some internal sagging had left him shrivelled and small, like a child leaning on her shoulder.

So many hours they'd spent talking about, wondering about, wars and murders, assassinations and atrocities, all those events that consumed the newspapers and television, but always at a distance, trying to imagine, peering at incidents through lines of print and pictures. It was hard, impossible, to grasp deliberate infliction of pain. There was so much pain anyway, they agreed, without going out creating it.

But now this accidental, random sort of tragedy had happened to Barney. His middle son, John, himself by then a father of two young children, worked in the warehouse of the box factory. A transport truck had backed up to the loading dock and John, mis-stepping his usual vault from the ground to the dock, from which he would supervise the loading of the truck, had been an instant too late pulling a trailing leg to safety, and it was crushed against the wall. "They tried to save it, the doctors worked all night Friday," Barney said, "but there was too much damage." On Saturday they had amputated.

And everything was altered. Not only for John, but for a widening collection of people that now included Aggie. The ripple effect of disaster; that shock, she thought, of being reminded that anything can change in an instant, everything can be overturned.

For Barney there was not only the terrible mutilation of his child, his son, but there also would be specific, concrete changes. John would have to undergo long therapy, and then might never work again. He would have a disability pension of sorts, but he also had two children and a wife who did not have a job. They had decided over the weekend that they would have to move in, for some time at least, with Barney and his wife. It would be crowded, but that was hardly the point. "It's tough, two families, and John's going to take a lot of care, and not just physically. He's always been so active—hunting and fishing and building things, all that outdoor stuff—it's going to be hard on him." Also there was Barney's wife, who had grown frail. "She cried all weekend. Nobody could get her to stop, and she wouldn't take the pills the doctor gave her." Barney looked so weary and lost; well, the shock of course, and that awful impotence to prevent or even control the pain of people he loved.

Aggie too felt some of that, able to comfort but not cure. She tried to imagine his home, where she had never been, and this seizure of horror striking it breathless. This friendship of hers and Barney's, it occurred to her, almost seemed to float in the air; it couldn't be set down firmly in any location but her kitchen.

She loaded him up with loaves of bread and a cake to take home with him and watched, worried, as he dragged his way out, off on his rounds again. His own feet stumbled, as if his capacity to walk had been, like his son's, diminished.

"Oh, poor Barney," Frances cried. Unlike June, she was fond of him, even used to give him a kiss on the cheek in the morning when she was a child coming downstairs for breakfast. But then, for her he was a fixture in the routine of the house, not an intruder, as he apparently was to June.

June herself, hearing the news, just shivered.

Aggie looked at Frances and thought, "Oh, God, what if she lost a leg? Or an arm, or a life?" It really was a struggle not to be terrified like June. It really was hard to advise Frances to be daring but alert, brave but comprehending consequences. But fear was as paralysing as a broken back. Look at June, afraid to move. As crippled, apparently, as if she'd actually been in one of those accidents she worried about all the time.

Frances, lacking many fears of her own, was restricted by June's. "But what is she afraid I'll do?" she had demanded when June forbade her to go out with boys, at least until she was sixteen. "Doesn't she trust me? Couldn't you talk to her for me?"

"I could, but it wouldn't make her change her mind."

Well, Aggie thought, Frances had hit on the word. All one could give was blind trust. Whereas June, with all her blind faith, was still afraid.

Later, Aggie heard Frances telling June, impatiently and bitterly, "I can't wait to grow up. Then I'll get to do what I want." And June answering, "Is that what you think happens when you're grown up? You've got a lot to learn, my girl."

If Frances was a somewhat grumpy teenager, it wasn't entirely without reason. Then, too, it was surely strange for her, being raised by two such different women. Bound to be confusing, and perhaps bound to lead to a few years in which she frowned a good deal more than she smiled.

June kept on trying to *do* something about her. She'd say, "Goodness, Frances, do you know how unattractive you are when you pout like that?" or, attempting a more light-hearted rebuke, "Careful, now, your face doesn't freeze that way."

What an exclusive world Frances lived in, though, outside of June and Aggie. Once she was finally old enough to go out on dates she was rarely home, and when she was, she spent much of her time in muffled conversations on the telephone. Aggie, catching only odd words and laughter, thought how natural and easily accepted Frances had turned out to be, despite her moods. So unlike the isolation of her own growing up, or the withdrawn quality of June's. Of course, June came of age in wartime, quite as queer a circumstance as Aggie's, in a different way. Times were freer now, there were more possibilities, more things known, and also more opportunities for pleasure.

Aggie did wonder, though, if June sometimes watched Frances slam into the house and out again, off to parties and movies and dates, and thought this was something she had missed. Did she regret a lack of choice, the result of the war or her own rigidity? Did she envy Frances? Because sometimes when Aggie was lying awake on a Saturday night, listening for car doors closing, footsteps coming up the walk, low voices, and sometimes a long quiet before the front door opened and then clicked shut—sometimes despite herself Aggie felt a stab of envy, or worse, resentment. Not nice, that. Not generous, or loving.

She was reminded, regarding this sturdy young woman, that Frances would soon be leaving home. It would be a triumph of reason and generosity and courage, Aggie felt, over sentiment and greed and cowardice, to help Frances go off to university, instead of flailing about like June, who wanted Frances to stay home, go on to teachers' college, and repeat, as far as Aggie could tell, all their mistakes. "There'll be a job right here for you then," June insisted.

"But I don't want to be a teacher."

"Why ever not? It's secure, you get all those holidays, and if you're that set on going to university, you could do it in the summer. It only takes a little longer."

"But I don't want to be a teacher, and I don't want to stay here. I want to get out and do different things. Anyway, you hate teaching. Why do you want me to do something you hate?"

"Because, as I'm trying to explain to you, it's a good job and something you can always fall back on. It's something for you to do at least until you get married."

"Married! There you go again, wanting me to do something you didn't like."

June's face went white. "Oh, Mum, I'm sorry." Frances really has never been deliberately cruel, just inadvertently, sometimes. "I didn't mean that the way it sounded. It's just, I don't want to settle down here."

"What *do* you want, then?"

"I don't know exactly. That's what I want to go away for, to find out. Do you see?"

"No. Nor do I see how you think we can afford it."

Which was where Aggie stepped in, unnecessarily, she thought later. "I'm sure we could afford it, June, if that's what she really wants. I have money saved, and she can work in the summers, and

there are loans. You might," turning to Frances, "even get a
scholarship."

"Not likely," said June. "Not with her marks."

"Oh, Grandma, thank you," Frances cried, and flung her arms
around Aggie's neck.

So Barney's son lost his leg; and Aggie's granddaughter went
away. These were not comparable sacrifices, of course, but she was
also bereft and sad. To be truthful, lonely. Frances's departure was
trivial in comparison with Barney's loss, and Aggie was ashamed
to tell him how she felt; so when she wept, she did so on her own.
And yet in its way, this *was* an amputation. She even thought of
it that way. Sound had been cut off: no music rocking from
Frances's room, or quick footsteps pounding up and down the
stairs, no slamming doors, or raised voices, or, for that matter,
whispers. The phone hardly ever rang. Absence was in the air. She
missed confidences, secrets: the quarrels Frances had with friends,
and how her first kiss felt. Even the small sins, like the time she
shoplifted lipsticks and a powder compact from the five-and-dime.

Periodically, Frances returned from university and later on spare
weekends from her work. From the world in which, as she told
them, people called her "Fran" and "Frannie", never Frances, as
if she were someone else entirely.

"You'd love it, Grandma," she said, shining with her own pleasure. She talked about men and making love, and books and lessons and friends, protests and discussions. She brought home
dispatches from a world outside that Aggie had never been able to
see for herself. She also brought home petitions against the war in
Vietnam, and wept over pictures of napalmed babies. "My God,
Grandma, how can people do things like that?"

She developed, Aggie thought, a finer sense of rage and a more
intelligent sort of compassion. June said, "Well, at least she doesn't
sulk any more."

Of course, June disapproved of Frances's choice of a career. "So
unsettled," she said. She wondered how Frances could take such
risks as flying frequently in airplanes, or meeting people she didn't
know, with who knew what results. "You simply never know,"
she warned, but Frances said, "Exactly."

As her father had once done, Frances brought home tales of life
out there. Except that hers were more interesting. His had been
about people in furniture stores, and movies he'd seen, whereas his
daughter could fill in unknown, unprinted details about stories they

might already have read in newspapers: an unsolved murder, for instance, in which she knew that the police were quietly waiting, collecting evidence, perfectly aware who had done it. A politician who had taken his mistress on a junket with him, and introduced her to foreign dignitaries as his wife. Aggie loved this inside knowledge, confirming her view of there being so much underneath the surface.

Of course, it was a jolt to have Frances confirm it, too, to learn that this young woman whom Aggie assumed had kept so little from her had had a secret, something almost like a secret life, for years. Only when it was gone, apparently, was it possible for Frances to talk about it.

She was home for a visit and June was out shopping. Aggie was in the front room in her big chair, reading, when Frances came wandering in and curled up in the corner of the sofa. "I did something really stupid a couple of weeks ago," she began.

Aggie's mind leaped to a man who was wrong, or another pregnancy; but maybe nothing quite so serious. "What?"

"I tracked down my father."

"Good God." That brought her upright. "Herb? How on earth did you do that?" She might have meant why.

"Oh," almost airily, "I've been hunting around for years. Whenever I go someplace, I check the phone book. Do you have any idea how many H. Bensons there are in this world? I wrote his old company, too, but he left there years ago and all they knew was that somebody thought he'd gone out west. I remember you said he had a sister on the prairies somewhere, so I thought maybe that's where he'd gone, but it turns out he went all the way to the coast. I found him in Victoria."

"I had no idea." That was what was astounding: that she hadn't known any of this.

"You know, Grandma," Frances said wistfully, as if she were looking so far back at something it was really some other person she was speaking of, "when I was little, I used to pretend sometimes that he was looking for me and someday he'd find me and take me with him, maybe on the road, and everything'd be different."

Different? "Was it so bad here then?" Aggie asked sharply, but Frances didn't seem to notice the tone.

"Well no, I don't suppose it was bad really, most of the time. I mean," catching herself a bit belatedly, "not with you, but sometimes with Mother I used to feel I wanted to get away. And it is weird when you don't have a father. Other kids' fathers were so neat. They'd take us places and make tree forts and all that stuff; I guess I missed that. And I guess I made up something better, so it wouldn't bother me so much.

"So if Mother was yelling about something, or you two weren't getting along, or if something happened at school, or I just got pissed off, I'd think about him looking for me and getting closer and then bingo, here he'd be. I'd lie in bed and wait for the knock on the door and imagine going out to the top of the stairs and he'd be standing in the hall down there saying, 'Give me my daughter, I've come for Frances,' and Mother would say, 'No, you can't have her.' And I'd speak up and say, 'Here I am, Father,' and we'd meet on the stairs running toward each other and he'd scoop me up and we'd drive away like fury. We wouldn't even stop to pack my clothes. I think," and she grinned, "I pictured him in a convertible. We'd go really fast, and there'd be a big wind in my hair. I mean, it was like having another life, kind of an escape."

"But you never said. All these years, you never mentioned it."

"Oh, well, even when I was a kid I must have known that if he'd wanted to find me, he could have. It wouldn't have been exactly hard. I guess I didn't want to know that, and if I'd said anything, I would have had to see."

"But you still wanted to find him?"

"Of course. Because he could have found me if he'd wanted to, and I wanted to know why he didn't." She spoke as if that should be evident to Aggie; and it did seem an obvious enough desire, now that she'd mentioned it.

"Boy, am I dumb!"

"Why?"

"Oh, because by now I should know better. I mean, I made up all this stuff about a reunion, long-lost father-daughter, hugs and tears, all that, and I should know by now that things never turn out the way you imagine." There was a peculiar hard tone there that spoke of other disappointments, perhaps, that Aggie didn't know of.

"I tell you, Grandma," and she laughed, "it scared the shit out of him when I called and told him who I was."

"Why, what did he say?"

"None of the things I'd made up for him, for sure; he just gulped and sputtered and said stuff like, 'My my, little Frances,

who'd have thought, after all these years.' When I said could we
get together because I wanted to meet him, he said sure, but I could
practically hear him thinking how to handle it. I guess it was partly
my fault. I never thought of him having a real life. I only ever
thought of him as my father, not somebody who'd have other things
going on. I can see why he was upset." When she paused, Aggie
just waited silently.

"Anyway, we arranged to get together in the bar at my hotel,
but then he said, 'But how will I know you?' and that shook me
up too. I really am so stupid. Somehow I'd been thinking that of
course we'd know each other, that there must be some kind of instinct about things like that. So I laughed and said I'd be wearing
a carnation in my lapel, and he didn't get it, he didn't understand
I was kidding. So I had to go down to the flower shop and get a
damn carnation for my damn lapel.

"But he was right. We could have passed on the street a million
times, and I would never have dreamed he was my father."

"He's not what you pictured, then?"

"You could say that," Frances said wryly. "You know, when
Mother wouldn't talk about him, I thought he must be kind of sin-
ister or decadent or something, and then you used to say he was
attractive and sort of charming. So I imagined somebody fairly
good-looking, maybe with a moustache, a bit devilish but debonair,
you know? Something like David Niven in those movies in the six-
ties maybe. But here's this old shrimpy, nervous-looking guy saying, 'Excuse me, would you be Frances Benson?' and it wasn't
exactly a moment to stand up and throw my arms around him."

"But wasn't he glad to see you?"

"Not so's you'd notice. What he was, was nervous. Kept on
with that 'Well well so you're little Frances' until I couldn't stand
it, so I started asking him what was new, what he'd been doing
with his life. You know, being the interviewer."

"And?"

"And he runs his own furniture store, which he talked about for
a while, but there's only so much you can say about furniture, so
I started asking if he lived alone, or how he lived, and then he
really got rattled. Grandma, did you know he and Mother are divorced?"

"Divorced! Of course not. She flat refused."

"Well they are. Apparently he got one when the laws changed and all you had to do was be separated for a few years. Why on earth didn't she ever say anything?"

Spilled secrets piling up here. Aggie felt a bit short of breath. But "She probably just went to her room for a while. She has a way of licking her wounds in private."

"Oh, but that's so sad!"

"I don't know. You seem to have managed to keep some things to yourself, too." If Aggie sounded sharp, she didn't much mind. "Anyway, what else did you find out about him?"

"That he's married again, mainly. To a widow who had kids. He's a grandfather now. He showed me their pictures. His wife's kind of dumpy and blonde, and there are two girls and a boy from her first marriage and then this one grandson. He's got a little white frame house with lots of flowers and vines. He said he likes gardening when he gets home from work. He's not a bit what I expected from the way you and Mother talked about him. I mean, gardening!"

"He certainly seems to have settled down, at any rate."

"Maybe," Frances laughed, "it was the love of a good woman. Or maybe it was the good woman he couldn't stand."

"Did you ask him why he left?"

"Oh yes, and he was about as helpful as Mother. Said they weren't suited, and it was nobody's fault and he was sure she was a good woman and obviously a good mother, but he'd thought it best to split while they were still young enough to start again.

"So I said, but what about me, I'd been just a little kid, and I could see somebody walking out on a marriage, but not leaving their own kid." She looked as she might have when she was speaking those words to her father, as if she might cry.

"He just said he was sorry, of course, and he'd missed me and it was all very sad, but he didn't think it was good for a child to grow up in a house where the parents weren't happy."

"What did you say?"

"I said bullshit, and that made him jump. I told him people just say that sort of thing when they're copping out, and he obviously hadn't wanted to be bothered with me because if he had he would have made some effort to see me in a quarter of a century. Old hypocrite."

"Still, you know," Aggie reflected, "he might be right, in a way."

"Oh, Grandma," Frances said impatiently, "I'm not saying he should have stayed, just that he was still my father. You don't get divorced from that. He could have written me letters or even come to see me, but I think he almost forgot I was alive. You know, it was weird looking at those pictures of his family. Even if they aren't really his kids, they're his family and I'm not. I was just some dangerous person from the past he had to deal with so I wouldn't bugger up his present.

"I was going to tell him about dreaming about him coming along and rescuing me, and how we were going to live together and I'd look after him, all that stuff. But he wasn't that father at all. He wasn't that real. The real one turned out to be the one I made up. Isn't that strange?"

Less strange than it might have seemed a half-hour ago. And think of June, divorced and never saying.

"I don't even know if his family knows I exist. He certainly didn't invite me to meet them. By the way, he said to say hello to you. He said he always liked you. He said I probably look like you, except—"

"Except for me being big as a barn. He used to tease me about it. Are you going to tell your mother you saw him?"

"Hell no, why upset her? She's had enough trouble without me bringing him up, don't you think?"

This unexpected sympathy with her mother was a late bloom in Frances's life. Too bad it didn't extend to keeping June's secrets. Aggie wondered how Frances had failed to realize that telling was a sort of betrayal.

"Well, now you know, anyway," Aggie said.

"That I do. Except maybe I should have left well enough alone."

"But surely not. Surely it's better to know."

She was startled that Frances turned on her. "Why do you always say things like that? Don't you ever think that maybe it's better not to know? Just sometimes that it's better to have something that's comforting instead of true?"

She sounded strikingly like June. Aggie said sharply, "No, I don't think that. I had enough fancies when I was young to last a lifetime and, I might add, they did me nothing but harm. They get you in the end, Frances, they really do, and it's worse, the longer they go on. They take root, and it's an awful shock when there's no living with them any more.''

Sometimes with Frances it's possible to see her mind taking over, events clicking into place. It's an odd process to watch: involves a lifting of the head, a squaring of the shoulders, a clearing of the eyes, and a kind of hardening around the mouth that has made Aggie wonder on occasion how her appearance will be affected as she gets older.

"Well, my curiosity's satisfied, anyway. And in a funny sort of way, he was a pretty good father, probably better than if he'd actually been around. The one I made up got me through some hard times.''

They heard June's footsteps on the walk. Frances uncoiled herself and stood. "Don't tell Mother, okay?''

"Of course not.''

Aggie thought later how strange it was that she was old, and Herb and June were aging, and even Frances was no longer quite young. That sense of lost time, making her long again for a comforting hand to drop on her shoulder, some familiar arm to wrap itself around her body. Some man's arm, perhaps; not even a lover's, just Barney's would be fine. It might finally be her turn to weep on his shoulder.

But oh Barney—where was he when she needed him? Gone, vanished, out of reach, the bad timing of events, just when they both might have had more than an hour a day to spare. His disappearance was more gradual, however, than an abruptly lost leg or a granddaughter who moved away; not a shock, just a matter of getting accustomed to absence. And sharp moments, frequent in the beginning, of thinking, "Wait till Barney hears this, I wonder what he'll think?''

First his job was retired from under him, when stores and dairies and other businesses stopped making deliveries. "I guess it's just as well," he said. "It gets harder and harder, lugging cases of milk around.''

His family's income now would consist of his pension, John's disability pension, and the part-time jobs his young grandchildren were able to pick up. "I guess we'll manage. We'll get along.''

He began to do odd jobs himself around town, partly for the money, but also for something to do. Mowed people's lawns, sometimes shovelled out driveways in winter, weeded gardens, mended eavestroughs, and fixed small appliances like toasters and kettles. "You'd be amazed, some of the things I see," he told Aggie. "People you'd think, just from the outside of their houses or their kitchens, that they live pretty well, you get right inside and rooms are dirty or musty, or they're crammed up with fifty years of furniture—I was in one old lady's house yesterday and every square inch of her living-room walls was covered with pictures of people. I didn't think I'd ever get away. She wanted to tell me all about everybody in every photograph."

Sometimes he didn't charge for the work he did. "Well, you figure somebody who has to get a toaster fixed instead of just getting a new one isn't exactly flush. A lot of them are old, like me."

"You're not old."

"Sure I am, Aggie. I'm old and I'm starting to creak and some days I can barely get started at all. But you know, those mornings I can't hardly get out of bed, I lie there and figure, well, Aggie's up working by now, I'd better get on my horse too. Some days I think I only get up because I'd be ashamed not to."

He helped her, too, fixing small things around the house, mowing the lawn. His morning visits, though, weren't quite as early as they used to be when he was delivering for the dairy, and sometimes the shop was already open and she didn't have much time to chat. Then he might only stay a few minutes, just time for a biscuit and a greeting.

What did they talk about? Nothing so much, any more, she supposed. Now it was existence, presence, the connection that counted. They'd gotten, she thought, pretty much down to the roots of the thing.

Of course, whenever Frances had been home for a visit, there was plenty to tell him: stories Frances brought. He'd shake his head and say, "Imagine that. Who'd have thought it," or "I always thought there was something funny about that fellow. So that's why."

He talked about his children and grandchildren, particularly John and his struggles. "You should see him get around," Barney said proudly when John was given one of the new improved plastic legs. "Prosthetic devices, they call them," he laughed. "Sound like birth control, don't they? But he can swing around like nobody's business, almost as good as he could with his own." John still couldn't find work; not only was he handicapped, but he was no longer young himself. And he had no particular skills. "His kids are good," Barney said, "real hard workers. It's a shame, though, they've had to grow up so fast. They've missed a lot of the fun of being young."

Aggie thought not about the fun of being young, but the pleasures of getting on. They were like an old married couple now, she and Barney, sitting briefly together for their chats. Familiarity and fondness. Sometimes she thought, "Whatever would I have done without him?" She would reach out then, perhaps, and pat his hand. She might have burst long ago from too many things kept inside, without his listening ear. Where she might once have taken him for granted, someone fortunate who appeared in her days, she now considered him something of a miracle. The loneliness, bleakness, and narrowness of all these years without him. Or someone like him. If not a sister, or a mother, then a friend.

Poor June, then, she thought: no one to talk to. Might she not burst, with who knew what inside? This was an old concern she could remember vaguely from years ago. Had nothing really changed?

She ought to pay more attention, be kinder. Just, oh, that was all very well in June's absence, but when she was actually in the same room, all righteous and smug, Aggie really couldn't help it. It might be sad from a distance, but up close her desire was to stick pins in and see if anything might puncture that smooth surface.

One Wednesday, Barney didn't show up and didn't show up. By noon, after a morning of anxious glances out the door, and the uneasiness of a disruption in her routine, Aggie knew he wouldn't be coming today. But maybe he'd had something special on, a particular all-morning chore. Or, worse, maybe there was another crisis in his family, another injury or an illness.

On Thursday morning he didn't come. She was worried now, and absent-minded about her work. She gave the wrong change to one customer, and bagged a loaf of raisin bread for another, instead of the cheese bread that was ordered. "I'm sorry," she apologized, "I don't know where my head's at today." Her head was off with Barney, imagining things. The trouble could not be just one of his jobs.

On Friday he didn't come and she was almost, not quite, frantic. There would obviously be an explanation, but it was the not knowing that was upsetting. If anything happened to her, or June or Frances, he'd know right away, because he'd show up here and find out. She couldn't do that, go wandering over to his home.

"You may think this is awful," he'd told her long ago, "but I've never mentioned it at home that I come here every day."

"But why on earth not?" She didn't think it was awful, exactly, but was certainly surprised.

"I'm not sure. It's not that there's anything wrong about it—well, you know that as well as I do—but maybe it's the idea of having to explain. Or that maybe Alice's feelings would be hurt, in a way. She might not understand that we're friends. And of course now it's far too late; I'd not only have to explain you, and coming here all the time, but why I've never mentioned it."

He thought for a moment. "Anyway, I think it's partly just wanting to keep something to myself. Having something that's private, just to me. I don't mean a secret exactly, not something to hide. Just private. We live," he sighed, "so much on top of each other."

So no, she could not now go traipsing over to his house, inquiring about him.

But there was nothing to stop her from phoning. Why hadn't she thought of that before? People must call Barney all the time, wanting him to do this and that. She couldn't come right out and ask, "Is something wrong? What's going on?" but she might find out anyway.

A woman answered: Alice, no doubt. Interesting, to hear the voice and know so much about the person, but not to be able to fit a face to it precisely. "Could I speak with Mr. Holtom please?"

"Oh dear, no, I'm sorry, that's not possible."

"Can you tell me when it will be possible?" Leaping into a lie. "I have some jobs around the house I thought he might do before winter."

There was a little silence before the voice said, "I'm terribly sorry, but I'm afraid you'll have to find someone else. My husband's in hospital. He fell and broke his hip this week, trying to patch someone's roof."

"You mean he fell off a roof?"

"Off a ladder. It slipped."

"Is he going to be all right? Do you know how long he'll be in hospital?"

"I suppose he'll be all right. But he won't be able to work any more, so I'm afraid you'll have to find someone else."

Aggie knew she must have sounded like some stupid woman who couldn't get it through her head that Mr. Holtom was no longer available for home maintenance chores. "I'm sorry to have bothered you," she said, hanging up.

A broken hip. What did she know about broken hips? Only, really, that they were terribly dangerous and terribly common among the elderly. Barney was right, he was old. She was old, too. She pictured him tumbling, rolling, falling through the air, arms flung out to protect himself, landing on that fragile boniness. Did he cry out as he fell? Was he wondering if she knew, or how to let her know? More likely he was lying in a hospital bed, in pain, worrying about how he and his family were going to get along now. What could she do for him? What would she do without him?

She took a taxi to the hospital that evening, but didn't go into his room. Barely caught a glimpse of him through the open door. He was surrounded by people, members of his family, she supposed. She left the package of books she'd brought with a nurse, to be passed on to him later.

She did see him, finally, the next week. He was barely a lump under the blanket. "I'm sorry I couldn't let you know, Aggie," he said in a new, frail, and tiny voice. "There wasn't a chance. But I can use the phone now—I couldn't even move before. And I'll be getting out soon, I hope. Another week or so. They've put in a pin. It hurts like the devil." All of a sudden he was asleep, so she left.

Sometimes she could almost agree with June that changes tended to be fearful things. Maybe just that from now on, possibilities were narrowed and more perilous.

After Barney left the hospital, there was still a long convalescence, and when he did begin to get out, it was a terrible effort. He remained stiff, and the pin still pained him. His face was grey with effort, and he was short of breath. It seemed to wear him out, just hobbling over to the bakeshop. He couldn't manage it more than once a week or so, and she tried to decide, regarding his exhaustion, if it was more difficult to miss him, longing for his presence when she wanted to talk to him, or to have him here, so worn out he was barely present anyway. She hated it, that he was beaten this way; that all his energy now seemed to go into his next step and how to survive it.

"I guess," he said finally one morning, "I've had it. I'm giving up, Aggie, I'm sorry. We've decided to sell the house, and John and his family are going to take an apartment and Alice and I are

going to move out to Winnipeg to Ben's. He and his wife just
bought a duplex, and we're going to take one side of it."

Oh no, lose him entirely?

"But we can write, Aggie."

She didn't think they likely would; not very often. It wouldn't
be anything like this.

"Is it what you want to do?"

"No, it's just apparently what I have to do. Jesus, Aggie," with
a flash of his old self, "I hate it. I hate having to get used to a
new place, and being a burden. I hate hurting all the goddamned
time. Jesus, you know," and he looked at her bleakly, and with
anger, "I think I hate being alive. It isn't fair."

They did write a few times, for a little while, but of course it
wasn't the same.

For all she knows, he's dead now. If he died, no one would let
her know. She would have liked to think that all those years would
mean he could not vanish without some corresponding shiver in her
life, but that's not likely the case. Did he not break his hip while
she was doing something like rolling out biscuit dough without a
twinge?

Maybe Frances, if she's so goddamned clever at finding people,
could find Barney, too, and let her know what's happened to him.

What on earth is this ferocious clutch on life about, when more
and more it requires letting go of one thing and another? It comes
down, it seems, more and more to a slow vanishing of the irreplaceable. One of these times, the irreplaceable vanishing object
will be herself.

Once she saw a series of lights, flashing on and on, lighting up
time into the future, into the next century, with Frances. Now she
sees lights going out, like a city bedding down for the night.

part

THREE

20

It's become terribly familiar, this moment when Aggie's bedroom door opens and she looks up in distress and June looks down with distaste, almost routine. "Up you get, Mother," June says matter-of-factly, deftly hauling and swinging until Aggie is on her feet. June has become adept at stripping the bed and wiping the plastic sheet that no longer crackles, and wrapping the sheets in her arms and carrying them down to the washer.

This morning, as she pulls Aggie's nightgown over her head and stoops so that Aggie, resting a hand on her shoulder, can step into her panties, she says, "Frances called last night, after you'd gone to bed."

Aggie feels her breath catch and her heart set out on that more violent pounding. "Oh?"

"She has this weekend free. She'll catch the train Friday night."

Two days. "What else did she have to say?" Aggie asks cautiously.

"Nothing much. Just that she's coming."

"Did you mention—anything?"

"No."

They seem to have developed a way of speaking that avoids crucial nouns. Like "accident" and "nursing home" or "plans" or "future" or anything terrifying.

Aggie searches June's face for intentions, but finds only that look of studied blankness she has perfected. Oh God, Frances is coming, and what will that mean?

227

Aggie imagines Frances's face, not glowing with life and delight
and stories and energy and love, but drawn with—oh well, what?
Pain, Aggie supposes. Pity. A concealed disgust.

Imagine her coming into this room on Saturday morning and
finding her like this.

Exactly what does it take before love is outweighed? What tips
it over?

21

June could simply kick herself. She's done it again. Or is still doing it. Or, precisely, has not been doing anything at all. Now Frances is coming, and what can she tell her? What arrangements have been made? The biggest actions she's taken since all this started have been buying a plastic sheet and putting Aggie's name on a waiting list. Nor has she pressed George for help, or a decision, or more tests, or just a nudge in the right direction. For all she knows, Aggie's name may still be at the bottom of the waiting list. Or it may be near the top, with a call to come any time, who knows? What happened to that urgent sense of future?

What a coward she must be.

And now Frances is coming. This must surely be a sort of deadline for finishing something that can't go on. So what is she going to say? It's not the sort of thing that drops easily into a conversation. When Frances asks, "So what's new with you guys?" she can't just blurt, "Your grandmother's having accidents and I think she'll have to go to a nursing home."

Or Frances might find out for herself, wandering into Aggie's room on Saturday morning. June imagines Frances coming to her in the kitchen and saying, "Oh, Mother, why didn't you tell me? You can't go on like this, it isn't fair to you, we'll have to do something."

How unnerving Frances is, the difference she makes, the decisiveness she imposes, just by coming.

Aggie sees that, too, June knows from the apprehension that leaps to her face when June tells her. That's never happened be-

fore. Usually Aggie is overjoyed by word of Frances, and immediately sits down with her cookbooks and starts planning treats, like
a child getting ready for Christmas. "Shall I get out your recipes?"
June asks, setting breakfast on the table.

"No, don't bother."

"Aren't you going to bake for Frances?"

"Not this time, I think. She's usually watching her weight.
Probably if you get in lots of lettuce it'll be enough." How dry
her tone is—or is it defeated?

June ought surely to have a sense of victory, then. If one loses,
the other wins, isn't that simply logical, clear-cut? It is necessary
only to make a move. *Do* something, she scolds. Just, what?

For one thing, aim for Frances's support, her sympathy. Not
easy. If she does it wrong, Frances will look at her with horror and
say, "Oh no, you couldn't, it'd kill her, she'd hate it."

Really, this time she must make an extra effort to get along.
Every time Frances comes to visit, June makes promises. This time,
she regularly pledges, there'll be no nagging, no old and new re-
sentments bubbling up. This time she won't tell Frances to sit up
straight and cross her legs properly; she won't ask if any of the
men Frances knows is serious; she won't say, "Surely you have
time to come to church with me, you never do, and people would
like to see you." She'll also try not to sit in church wondering what
Frances and Aggie may be talking about while she's out: what secrets may be spilling, or what judgments being made.

Every time she makes these promises, and every time they break
down. Friday night is usually all right: Frances comes in on a roll
of city energy; enthusiasm gets them through. Saturday morning
when they get up, things are a little saggy. Frances is usually
grumpy, withdrawn, just wanting her coffee and a cigarette. By
afternoon she is really getting on June's nerves, because, after all,
how hard can it be for her to make the effort to sit straight and
cross her legs at the ankles, even at the knees if she must, but not
fling them around, sticking them up on tables or over the arms of
chairs or tucking them underneath herself. How hard could it be to
get through a weekend without swearing or smoking or taking a
drink?

June always winds up aggrieved, Frances impatient and sometimes angry. "For God's sake, Mother," she cries, "can't you let
me alone for just one weekend? Do you know how old I am? Can't
you let me be?"

Sometimes when she leaves she looks sullen, sometimes only
tired. Any animation will have come from the tales she tells of her
life away. Whatever possessed her to take up such an occupation,
going out of her way to find out things it's better not to know? Just
knowing certain information must be corrupting, June thinks.

And it didn't have to be that way; might not have been, if Aggie
hadn't stuck her oar in on June's and Frances's argument over university or teachers' college. Still, she must admit it might not have
been comfortable, having Frances teaching here. June would have
felt responsible, and even back then Frances had a way of going
off on tangents. First thing June knew, Frances would probably
have been out organizing demonstrations—against war, for women,
all this and that she's been involved in. What a mystery it is: a
daughter so righteous about her causes, and so unrighteous in her
lack of faith.

She supposes it's not entirely Aggie's fault. She must herself
have lacked her father's story-telling gifts, so that she never could
grip Frances with his stories or his lessons. She never was able to
impress on Frances the importance of sacrifice or duty.

"Your grandfather, my father, was a lovely man," she tried to
tell her. "It's a shame you couldn't have known him."

"What did he look like?"

"Like me, I guess. Or I look like him. He was gentle and quiet.
He used to tell me about growing up in England and how his parents saved up and did without so he could have an education. He
was so brave, coming here all on his own."

"I don't think he was very nice to Grandma," Frances ventured.

Nice to Grandma! "Let me tell you, young lady, Grandma
wasn't exactly nice to him."

"How come?"

"Well, she had no education. She had no idea what it meant,
being a teacher's wife. And then she always thought she knew better. She brought him down in the world."

"You guys," Frances said, "you guys," shaking her head,
"sure tell things differently."

June knows that Frances has, in fact, finished any number of
projects: university, stories, buying a house and decorating it. But
nevertheless she has a picture in her mind of a Frances who gets
tired of things, disinterested in the middle of them, putting them
down uncompleted and going on to the next.

This is not someone to depend on.

Even Aggie now apparently realizes that.

But how would June feel if she were the one having accidents in her bed, and Frances was coming to find out? She would rather die.

Settling Aggie in the front-room chair for the day before she leaves for school, June glances at her with startled pity. This will be the worst thing Frances could find out about her grandmother.

What would be the worst thing she could find out about June?

Oh, how could she have been so stupid? Startled, she almost trips on the uneven piece of sidewalk. What if she died? What if Frances came home and, as she would have to in those circumstances, began sorting through June's possessions? All those things collected over the years, all of them inoffensive and innocent, except for one.

That brown envelope, with the letters and documents from Herb's lawyer. And the final divorce decree—where on earth did she put it? Surely she didn't stick it in the attic, did she, with all the other accumulated this and that she and Aggie have tucked away over the years? Whatever they didn't want to throw out, but had no particular use for any more?

She imagines Frances coming across that envelope, and idly opening it, without any particular interest, and finding out. "Oh God," she prays, "don't let anything happen to me until I can find that and get rid of it. Let me get through this day and I'll take care of it tonight." She must destroy it, because it's impossible now to tell Aggie and Frances about it. "Why on earth didn't you say?" they'd ask.

Well, why didn't she? It ought to have been reasonably simple, the day the first warning of Herb's intentions came in the mail, oh, years ago, to mention it over supper: to say, "Guess what I got today? Herb's getting a divorce. Apparently there's nothing I can do about it." Something like that, dealt with briskly, as if it didn't matter.

But it did matter. She wouldn't have guessed how those papers would bring it back: the terrible failure of purpose, those desires she neither understood nor felt; and there was Herb out there making appointments with a lawyer, still drawing up her life on paper, no doubt still indulging his desires.

And there was the law, on his side: like some heathen Moslem man, able merely to say "I divorce thee" three times and it was so.

She didn't get a lawyer. There was, she undersood, no way to oppose him, now that it was merely a matter of not being together for a certain period of time. He was neither offering money nor asking for anything to do with Frances, who in any case was almost grown up then, getting ready to leave. If he'd been interested in his daughter, he'd have shown it long before.

At least June was the one who picked up the mail, so no one else had an inkling.

When the final divorce decree came, she sat in her room reading it. Chilly words, legal talk and Latin—how to connect them with endurance and distance? How did they contain bearing a husband's body or a child? What did they have to do with hopes, or even walking down the street with an arm around the shoulder? Or planning a wedding, and a mother who sat up embroidering a secret nightgown? These stiff and foreign words had nothing to do with lying awake listening to silence or a husband snoring, or with washing floors and dishes and making meals, or being tapped on the bottom and told to make more sandwiches. They failed to mention liquor on the breath or hair cream on a pillowcase or a steamed-up bathroom heavy with the humid scent of aftershave. Certainly they did not refer to the dizzy pain of ending, or the humiliation of starting again. If she'd said to Aggie or Frances then, "Herb's gotten a divorce," she would have been afraid of not stopping there, of all these words and secrets bubbling out. So she said nothing and then, of course, it became impossible, since they would have said, "Oh? When did he do that?" and "Why didn't you say so at the time?"

None of this will matter in the long view: in heaven, where earthly remembrances will be cast aside (although surely there will be a recognition and reunion with her father: maybe only briefly, in some hazy period between world and heaven, when the boundaries are unclear). She recalls Aggie joking once about heaven, when they all would come together. "Even Herb eventually, and you and your father and I, and Frances and whoever she may take up with—can you imagine how awkward it's going to be? All the introductions?" Adding, however, "But perhaps you don't think we'll all get to heaven. It'll just be you good folk up there."

All the good folk, June thinks, who, like her, have had to trail around behind events, cleaning up the messes.

There are still a few messes waiting to be cleaned up.

The first thing is to find that envelope, which will require going through those things in the attic. This could have, she realizes, a secondary effect: a sorting out, clearing away, a step toward shifting Aggie as well. She will go home tonight and say, "I'm going to get down all that stuff in the attic so we can go through it and get rid of a lot of it. Who knows what's up there, and most of it must be useless." Starting small, with things, she will work up to something large, to Aggie. Who will see immediately what's going on, in case she's been under the impression June's forgotten her intentions.

The decisiveness of this cheers her and restores the briskness of her walk.

"We can keep out whatever Frances may want, and she can check it when she gets here," June will say. "Then she can take anything she wants with her when she goes."

June doubts that will include Aggie. Even on her visits, Frances just kisses them good night and skips off to her own bed. No help from her, getting Aggie's clothes off and her nightgown on. She said once, "I know Grandma needs help, but it feels wrong." Does she think it feels right to June? If something has to be done, does it matter how it feels? These refinements, these little niceties, are all very well, but when things need doing, you put them aside.

Aggie praises Frances's independence, which is all very well, except that it has another side to it: that she turns her back too readily.

So what has she done to earn devotion?

It's not Frances, after all, who knows every ripple and curve and roll and hair and mole and freckle on Aggie's body. It's not Frances who knows all the places where it folds, or the way the nipples droop to touch those folds, or how the hair below has gotten grey and sparse. It's June who knows the flatness of Aggie's feet, from standing so many years in the bakery, and how the flesh of her arms and legs dimples like hammered silver. It's June who feels the warmth and surprising softness of Aggie's skin. It's June's shoulder on which she leans when she's stepping into her panties, and it's June who slips her dresses over her head. There are freckles on Aggie's thighs, and a mole above her right elbow. Frances has probably never even noticed.

June also knows the routes of the big purple, dangerous-looking veins in Aggie's legs, could trace them from memory, from thigh to calf. She knows that when Aggie is going upstairs, she has to rest on every second step to catch her breath; and that when she stands, the skin on her knees doubles over just like her stomach.

It's June who's seen the bleak terror on Aggie's face when she's had an accident. No one else, not a soul anywhere, knows so much. Certainly not Frances.

Also, no one knows as much about June as Aggie does. Without Aggie, who would know her at all?

Oh, but that's silly, like one of those questions Aggie used to ask about something she'd been reading: what exists if no one sees the existence?

What would June be, if someone weren't there to watch?

But God sees, how stupid to forget. God is always watching. That's a comfort, of course, but also sometimes a little irritating. She might wish occasionally that God would go and watch somebody else for just a little while. It might make all this easier.

Anyway, she never wanted to know all the things she knows about her mother. She never asked to see Aggie naked in the bath. She didn't force her to lust after food so much that she finally can't manage her own body. The perfect mate for Aggie, food: something she could roll around and stir and beat and cook and then consume.

It's Aggie's own fault, what she's become. If she prattles about people being responsible for themselves, well then, let her take the consequences.

Keep going, that minister said years ago when June was still a child: one step and then the next. Well, she's done that. The difficulty has been with the rest of it: doing it with joy and courage. The shininess gets blurred, with all the wearing details of getting through the day. Maintaining joy appears to require some kind of nourishment not provided by teaching small, scary children and raising a wilful daughter and living with a woman whose ideas of nourishment are contrary.

Sometimes, though, she has the feeling that her memories are incomplete, or may have gotten twisted somehow; that words have been spoken and events have occurred that have been turned around in her head, or tucked away. Like putting things for which there's no immediate use away in the attic.

She is irritated by confusion. A few weeks ago she wasn't especially confused. She knew her duty and was doing it. And not only that: there was considerable comfort in having days the same.

It was Aggie's accident that stirred things up. Once, as June struggled to cut a turnip, the knife slipped and caused quite a bad gash in her hand. She wrapped it in a tea towel and called a taxi and took herself to the hospital, where they gave her a shot and bandaged her up and said it wasn't serious. But she couldn't use the hand properly for some time. It was surprising how much she needed it. Until it healed, she was almost constantly aware of what it couldn't do, and she had thought what a poor cripple she would be, how badly she reacted to a minor deprivation.

Now this other sort of accident has happened, and although it isn't even hers—how much worse is it for Aggie?—everything has been disrupted. She has had those wild moments of hope, imagining a different future, the luxury of coming home to an empty house; of being free. To what? It came as too much of a surprise. She still hasn't prepared herself for freedom. She can only think so far ahead.

At the moment, her job is to enter the schoolyard, filled with racing, shrieking, tumbling children who are nevertheless careful not to accidentally bounce into her, and get to her classroom, and, when they file in, to subdue and teach them. Her job is to take one brave step at a time, until it all comes out somewhere.

She watches out the window at recess. The children play tag, throw balls, skip rope. From where she is on the second floor, she can discern the patterns and alliances, the friendships and small rages, all the energy, altering and shifting. She thinks this must be something like what God sees, looking down. Even, perhaps, thinking benevolently that they will pretty much turn out all right, once they settle down.

22

There have been various rumblings and shiftings going on upstairs all evening. "What on earth are you doing up there?" Aggie asks when June finally appears, dusty and straggle-haired.

"Getting things down from the attic. I thought we might as well sort through them and clear them out a bit. Anything worth saving, maybe Frances would like to have. We can ask when she comes if there's anything she'd like."

"Why now?" As if she didn't know.

"For one thing, one of these days I'm not going to be able to do it. I can't believe all the junk we must have put up there."

"So what are you going to do with it now?"

"Bring it on down. I've got it as far as the landing. Boxes and boxes of stuff. I can't imagine what it all is, can you?"

No, not really. Things from away back, Aggie supposes. Even a few things she brought from her parents' house, after they died and their pathetically few possessions were divided up. She remembers how small and insignificant those things seemed, with the people who had used them gone. A cushion, she remembers, with a Scottie dog embroidered on it.

"There's a trunk up there that must be yours, too. I'm going to have trouble getting it down. I'm just taking a tea break. Do you want some?"

Hardly. Is this some none-too-subtle sabotage? Aggie has not forgotten, and has followed, George's advice against having anything to drink after eight o'clock at night. Not that it has made a great deal of difference. Nor did his other advice. She has thought

and thought, going off to sleep at night, concentrating on control,
and has still wakened a number of times to find her body has once
again betrayed her.

Oh God, what is Frances going to say? If she finds out.

Is there any hope she might not? At this point, if Aggie gets
safely through the weekend, it'll be as accidental as any accident.

Her dress is damp. That scares her for a moment, until she realizes it's only perspiration, she hasn't done anything so dreadful
as wet herself sitting up awake.

Imagine being frightened of Frances. Or not of Frances, exactly,
but of having Frances look at her, knowing she is seeing not her
beloved, understanding, helpful, hopeful grandmother, but an appalling fat old woman who has taken to wetting the bed.

She could, of course, be blunt about it: speak right up and say
something, preferably make a joke of it, as best she can. "I'm on
the skids," she might say. "I'm going downhill. Your poor mother,
she wants me to go to a nursing home, and of course I can sympathize with her, but I won't do it, naturally."

Just fine, as long as she doesn't actually wet the bed. Even
Frances might then fail to respond as Aggie could wish.

But what sort of face does Frances have? Not cruel, after all.
Not one that would deliberately inflict pain.

She is fairly tall, taller than June anyway, and slender, although
not thin, and the last time they saw her, a couple of months back,
was wearing her dark hair cut short and tight around her face. The
style made her eyes seem large, giving her a curious and vulnerable look, a bit startling, like a waif.

She is now of an age when bones are becoming important, the
ridges around which her middle age will form. With good cheekbones and a strong jaw, she is unlikely to become one of those
women whose faces, in late thirties and forties, disintegrate, losing
character instead of gaining it. Aggie touches her own face, seeking the bones. Frances is how she might have looked if she hadn't
gone in for flesh. If she peeled herself down to the essentials, she
might find a Frances.

Aggie was struck, the last time, by the webs of lines around
Frances's eyes when she arrived. She hadn't recalled them being
so pronounced before. But most of them vanished after a good
night's sleep. When Frances tilted her head, the light from the lamp
behind her caught her hair, and picked up the little streaks and
slivers of grey in it.

The *pride* with which Aggie regards her. The last time she was here, she stretched out on the sofa and said, "You know, Grandma, Mother keeps saying I get away with anything, as if that's so awful. It's true, I can pretty much. But it's because I can get away *from* anything. The trick is, if something happens that really hurts, to be able to pick up and walk out and survive."

Aggie thought right then that if Frances had done nothing else—had not learned, or gone to school, or made a career out of an inquiring mind—if she had not accomplished any of that, Aggie would still have been proud of her for understanding that most important piece of information.

Although she wonders now if such an intense interest in survival, like her own, will not leave Frances unprepared and bewildered at the end, when it is precisely survival that will be lost.

But how does a person let go and decide it's been enough?

Aggie has let go so often: of her family on the farm, of the teacher and of June, of Frances and Barney and the bakery. But she has never let go of herself.

Wouldn't it be simple? To put her head back and close her eyes, go limp and die? Can a person just die that way, willing the heart to stop beating and the lungs to stop pumping? The mind to stop thinking? Would she dare?

She puts her head back, closes her eyes, and tries to go limp, relaxing her body little by little, a limb at a time. The next trick is the heart. But it rears in terror and goes off racing and thumping, causing her eyes to flash open and her head to leap from the back of the chair in panic. Certainly not. What a stupid, not to say dangerous, experiment. Damned if she's done.

It's not so much pain. There may well be a certain amount of that, but she's had pain before: she's cut her hands with knives and burned her fingers and tripped on steps and gone flying. She's been bruised and sliced and had teeth pulled, and some of it has been quick and some prolonged, but never has it been unbearable.

What a coward, though: telling June for years, and Frances too, "You must be responsible for yourself, and your own actions." With varying results, between the two of them. And then even to think of dying, taking that huge dark step into space, simply to avoid the look on a young woman's face when she sees that her grandmother has peed the bed.

Oh, really, love is one thing, but that would be ridiculous.

She won't die for Frances, and this time she doesn't intend to bake, either. Frances isn't the eater she used to be. "I have to watch my weight," she says, refusing desserts, and Aggie, even thinking how lovely she is, is still a little hurt. The food she plans and prepares for Frances's visits is intended to speak love, and while she knows it isn't true, and isn't fair, it feels, when Frances turns it down, as if she has said, "I know, but there are more important things."

It occurs to Aggie that June may not be the only one who makes untenable demands. That between the two of them, they push and pull in ways that may be hard for Frances to bear.

Only, food is what Aggie has done, and at some point it turned into a way of saying things. Well, though, maybe she can't expect other people, even Frances, to see that.

Just the way they fail to see the art in ordinary things: in her cheese cakes and banana bread, bran muffins, white and dark bread, chocolate chip and oatmeal cookies, rhubarb and apple and cherry pies. What is it if not art, to take ingredients not necessarily useful or desirable on their own and combine them into works of a certain symmetry and grace and usefulness? And not only that: because while painters might look at their work, and sculptors touch theirs, she could do that and consume hers also, containing her own art.

The difference is that with luck, other sorts of artists might never have to quit, whereas she did, although she hung on grimly until five years ago. By then, new types of bakeries had come to town, chains of them like fast food outlets, churning out breads and muffins and tarts, and not bad, either. They were convenient, and people didn't have to go out of their way, as they did to get to Aggie's. Her own old customers, the ones she'd built up through familiarity and loyalty, died, or couldn't get around much any more. So there was that.

But also it was too hard. Getting up in the mornings so early, all that kneading and stirring and bending and reaching took it out of her. The day June came home and found her sitting on the kitchen chair, leaning her head on the counter, grey in the face, all the pans and pie plates piled up still waiting to be washed, and the tins of flour and sugar and bran still out because she hadn't seen how she could ever reach those shelves again to put them away, or how she could stand in the steam over the sink and do the washing up—that day June came home and looked at her and said, "Oh

Mother, that's it, you really have to close this up, you look absolutely dreadful," that was when it ended.

June saw to putting the kitchen back the way it used to be. There are plants in the window now, and curtains on the back door, and a kitchen table. The sign disappeared from the front. What happened to the sign? Maybe they put it in the attic. Aggie hopes it didn't go out in the trash.

How odd it was, to lie in bed in the morning (and finally to have to, waiting for June to come in and help), and having only her own baking to do, and being able to sit down for hours to read or look out the window or think, having nothing that she absolutely had to do. June fussed a bit. "I hope you're not going to be too bored, Mother," but in a way it was something of a relief.

How nice June was about it, how gentle. How kind June often is, really, in her way.

Sometimes first thing in the morning Aggie can still be startled to go into the kitchen and find it has a table and chairs and only one oven and no cash register; that it is missing counters and drawers where counters and drawers were for so many years. Sometimes just for a moment she disbelieves what she is seeing.

June has been staggering in and out of the front room, loaded with boxes, piling them up. "I had no idea we kept so much," she says.

"I didn't even know the attic was big enough."

Now there's a great thudding and scratching on the stairs, and a heavy dragging across the hall and into this room. June is perspiring. "Good God, June, what are you doing?"

"Your trunk," she pants.

"For heaven's sake, that's far too big for you to manage alone. You might at least have waited for Frances to help you."

"Well, it's not too big or I couldn't have done it." Under the weariness there's pride.

This blue hump-backed trunk, with its leather straps and handles and brass catches—Aggie remembers it being lifted into the back of the buggy as she and Neil left her home, and turning around in her seat waving over it. This trunk is what caused the scratches on the floor of the hallway inside the front door when he dragged it in. She doesn't remember who could have put it in the attic, or when. And now here it is, making another appearance, looking a bit daunting and making more scratches on the floor.

"Oh my," she says, "that really takes me back."

"Mmhmm. I'm going to have a bath now, Mother, unless you want to go to bed first."

For the moment, however, it might be unwise to move. She shakes her head. "No, you go ahead."

All of this, all this past—it crowds a whole life, an entire eighty years, into this room, making it feel cramped, like her heart struggling to pound out a space for itself against the pressing flesh.

Funny, that old trunk sitting right beside the big color television set, the one they bought when the bakery was shut down. She hopes she isn't one of those old people who seize on things like that, to point out how much times have changed. But still, how times have changed, her times, between that trunk and that television.

"It'll be nice for you during the day," June said when they got the color set, replacing the old black-and-white they'd bought when Frances was eight or nine because all her other friends' homes had TV and if she didn't have an ordinary family, she might at least have that. A retreat into television, at least in daylight, however, is Aggie's idea of sin: uneventful, passive, dry, and passionless. Even in the evenings it's not turned on very often. What she sees now, looking at the screen, is her own self looking back, a furry grey reflection.

Between the day the trunk and she arrived here and the day the television was delivered came the bookshelves. There are more, added over the years, than the teacher started with, and they're loaded now with her own books. Aggie remembers thinking she'd maybe read some of her favorites again some day, perhaps when she was eighty. Now she wonders why she had ever thought she would manage that when there are still so many stories she hasn't read, so many facts she doesn't know. It makes her feel a little frantic.

Maybe when she's ninety the time will come for rereading.

Ninety? What's she thinking of? It's a miracle this body has held up this long; she can hardly expect another decade out of it. If she were a car, she'd be a collector's item, worth a fortune; although she would also have to be restored with some care, and probably with a fair number of spare parts. "I'm just going to drive her into the ground," people say about their cars. Well, here she is, an old model driving herself into the ground.

Poor old lumbering, graceless, unwieldy, wrinkled, crumpled body, with its aches here and unexpected frailties there and the bits inside that are breaking down, and its terrible anchoring bulk. It's one thing to cling on, trying to fend off death, but consider the alternative. Who would want to be Methuselah? Or how dreadful, to find out suddenly that she's really only at, say, a halfway point. Imagine another eighty years. What on earth would she do with them?

At least death tightens up events, gives them the context of a cut-off point.

What a peculiar thought for someone terrified of putting her head back and letting go. What the hell does she want, anyway: life or death? What a choice. Another joke, she supposes, although at the moment she's not inclined to laugh.

Oddly, considering that Frances lived here the least length of time, there are more signs of her in this room than of either Aggie or June. There's the framed oil painting on the far wall over the sofa, done by Frances when she was about thirteen. June gave her a paint-by-number set for Christmas, and Frances painstakingly did this single landscape, with its little purple flowers blooming beside a stream, and big grey tree limbs hanging down. Aggie had it framed. Instead of doing any more paint-by-numbers, Frances used up the left-over oils by mixing the colors. Eventually they got overmixed, so that what started out as brilliant slashes of color in her little canvasses just turned muddy. Frances said, "I always go too far," and threw them out.

On the same wall, over a bit, is a gallery of photographs of Frances. Well, not exactly a gallery: just three. Formal, so they have a posed, self-conscious look. Even the baby one, with Frances's pudgy arms propped on a cushion, her hands cupping her chin, looks like someone masquerading as a baby. Then she's graduating from public school, in a stiff pink dress that hints of breasts beginning. That was when she had her first nylon stockings, and her first shoes with modest heels. To the right of that one is her leaving university, in gown and cap, the latter perched precariously on sleek long, straight hair that was then in fashion. Under the gown, as Aggie recalls, was a skirt that was a daring five inches above the knee. June complained, but she hadn't seen anything yet. A few months later, Frances's skirts were so short she couldn't bend over and some of her outfits had matching panties, just in case.

Another, much younger Frances gave Aggie that little green ceramic deer on the windowsill. It's actually a vase, although there aren't any flowers in it. That deer's been on that sill since Frances was nine. It has a long, arched neck and thin, frail-looking legs, but somehow they've managed not to break it in all these years. It came to Aggie for her birthday, filled with violets from the garden, picked by Frances. "Isn't he beautiful, Grandma?" she'd asked.

What did a child's eye see? Frances loved that green deer. "It's for you, but do you think," and she was hesitant, picking her words, "that I could have it? Some day?"

By "some day" Frances obviously meant when Aggie died. What a tactful little girl. "Of course you can, pudding. It'll be all yours."

She must remind Frances of that this weekend. Probably they'll laugh. Frances's tastes have changed, and the deer is a poor old thing.

Is there anything else Aggie promised her? What else is there, and in all these boxes, too? Which parts of her grandmother's and her mother's past might Frances care to take away with her?

Or, what parts might surprise her?

Aggie suspects, actually, that Frances dislikes any idea of things in this house that are unknown. Mysteries. She must have an image of them that she carries off with her and comes back to, but Aggie would bet it's an image of them frozen. Like one of those old science-fiction movies, in which the inhabitants of a town are locked by evil-doers from space into a single moment, so that they're caught licking an ice-cream cone that cannot melt, or raising a foot to kick a perpetually cowering dog, or holding someone in an embrace that can't be felt, and there they are, ridiculous and helpless, while the invaders carry on their crimes. There is always a hero who retains the power of movement, sees the truth, and is out there fighting. That, Aggie supposes, would be Frances: the one allowed to move.

Well, maybe that's not so untrue, or so unfair. Sometimes Aggie's events seem, even to her, to have been terribly abstract. Given another eighty years, then, she might go out instead of in. She might pare down her body and take it in different directions. She might hunt around for pleasure and experience.

She does not have another eighty years. She has only a little time, and even less before Frances comes through the front door like the wind, pushing their silences back into corners, brightening rooms as if the light bulbs have been changed. The light she will bring this time now seems ominously surgical, however.

It is quite a new experience, to be afraid of Frances. And even more afraid of the ways she may betray herself.

What's she doing, being afraid? Damned if she will be. Let them take their best shots. She's stood up to worse than this in her time.

But that's a lie. There's nothing worse than this sort of creeping decay, leaving her so vulnerable inside this monument of flesh she's built.

Nevertheless, she finds herself patting her belly, as if it's an upset child she can still find ways to comfort.

23

June's arms, legs, and back hurt. What an enormous job, getting all that out of the attic and downstairs, especially the trunk, which almost got away from her. She might have been crushed beneath it, or pulled off her feet by it, struggling with its weight; she is now amazed by her courage, or her obliviousness to the danger at the time. Several of the boxes, perhaps containing books, were heavy too, and others, while light enough, were oversized and rattly.

Two things, however, were accomplished; the drive to get the job done, and the difficulty of doing it, have kept her mind focussed, so she hasn't had spare energy for feeling badly, going into the front room and seeing Aggie sagging, looking vague. Also, in a box marked clearly "June: papers" she found the crucial envelope. Sorting through, she also found such things as insurance policies and old bank-books. The insurance policies shouldn't have been up there anyway, and the rest could go in the trash. She felt, however, a peculiar stab tearing up the manila envelope, which she didn't bother to open. No point in looking at it all again, but still, it seems like another ending, when there are already so many endings going on. A bit overwhelming.

How much can really be thrown out? It begins to look ominous, all piled up in the front room: so much past. Perhaps too much.

But not her own past, necessarily. The few things of hers she has stored have been clearly, efficiently marked. So most of this must be Aggie's, and perhaps a few of Frances's things as well.

But then, Aggie is eighty years old. A lengthy past adds up, in boxes.

Not much of a future, though.

June feels her will faltering, but that's probably only weariness. She slips to her knees beside her bed to pray. The thing is, what to ask for? But then, mustn't ask. Thy will be done. If only that meant she could stay in bed for the weekend, letting God work His will downstairs with Frances and Aggie so that when she went down on Sunday night, everything would have been settled in her absence. Fine for God to have His will done, but it takes so much participation; He requires speech and action. All the hard parts she has to do herself. Like being a construction worker, digging foundations and building up bricks for some architect who just sits back in an air-conditioned office, drawing lines on paper.

But who's she so angry at? It sounds like God, but surely not. On the other hand, it's not Aggie, either. Aggie brings on irritation, impatience, sadness; a dull sort of hurt, perhaps, but not a sharp rage like this. So who else is there? Well, Frances. June does have a sense of an enemy in the air, a hostility seeping about. But Frances isn't even here. Maybe it's what she is capable of doing when she does arrive, the effects she may have. Her visit is being depended on for something, a decision of some kind. June herself is counting on it, and Aggie is unnerved.

But who gives Frances control over final words? Who says matters of such importance are up to her?

This is all unreasonable, of course, and June does not feel it is like herself to be unreasonable. She's only tired, and is sure things will look different in the morning.

She doesn't often remember dreams, and those she does are generally the bad ones. Tonight she has an awful one. Aggie is dead; and June is at the funeral home, except it's the funeral home grown huge: a cavernous golden room, bigger even than a church, cool and empty, except for Aggie in her casket and June standing beside it. The two of them, even Aggie, are tiny in the enormous space.

Aggie is dead, and June can't move to turn away. Even her blood and her breath seem to have stopped.

Aggie's face is smaller than it was when she was alive, and uncreased. Not young, not as if years have been stripped off, because there's the white hair, except it's long again, and wound around her head. There are people outside the room, waiting, and Frances is calling out and hammering on the door, but first there is some interpretation June has to make of those fixed features of her mother. Death, however, seems to be difficult to decipher.

The bones are surprising. It's years since they've been notice-able, but now the flesh has fallen back, leaving the nose distinct and almost pointed, and the jaw firm. Something about the jaw? Set with determination, but, without the padding, looking exposed and vulnerable and maybe even brave. It is possible that she is about to sit up and tell June just what she thinks of things, in a clear voice carrying once and for all the answer to some vital ques-tion; although June can't think just what that question is. There is also a slight lift at the edges of the mouth, as if Aggie might be on the verge of an embrace, anticipating tenderness.

Time is gone. It seems June might have been here for days, star-ing, trying to discern the message in the dead face of her mother.

But it's not fair. Aggie is dead, so what can there be for June to wait for? It's a cruel tease, she thinks. Too late.

Is that it, then? Because suddenly she can move, and it feels ter-rible that it's too late. She hears her own voice crying out.

That was in the dream, but startled awake, she thinks she can hear the echo of a sound in the air. Could she have called out loud?

Like the sound, the image of the dream lingers: Aggie's face, and her own loss. Something she couldn't find out, because it was too late.

She feels like a child left behind.

And now, more alertly awake, she is reminded of stories of women in wartime, waking violently in the middle of the night, hearing their soldier husbands calling out to them, and learning later that that was the very moment of their death.

It only takes an instant to flick on the lamp, pull on her robe, and notice the time: four in the morning. She slips down the hall to Aggie's room and cautiously opens the door.

It seems Aggie has falled asleep reading. The light is still on, and a book has fallen on her chest. Her head is drooping and her eyes are closed. Her face is big and jowly and frowning a little, not like the one in the dream. June sees the book rising and falling with her mother's breathing. A false alarm, then.

In the dream, this face contained a secret. Aggie merely asleep may look more helpless, but there's nothing mysteriously knowing about her.

June sees that Aggie will have a stiff neck in the morning, lying that way, but hesitates to disturb her. Shutting the door softly, she pads back to her own room, where she falls asleep again a little uneasy that the awful dream may come back.

It doesn't, as far as she knows, but in the morning she has a tiny headache. Aggie's sheets are dry. Frances will be here late tonight. Things of one kind and another are piling up.

June rubs her arms, and Aggie says, "You look tired."

"I am. All that lifting and lugging last night, and then I didn't sleep very well."

"I didn't, either. At least, I don't feel rested."

Actually, when Aggie woke up she had the impression she had overslept. The room was so bright, it might be midday. There was a strange weight on her chest, her neck was stiff, and her back hurt.

She also had an extraordinary sense of dread.

Oh God, that would be Frances coming tonight. Or not Frances herself, but what she signifies: something drastic and irrevocable. Whatever it turns out to be won't be up to Aggie. Will it be up to June either?

Aggie regards her daughter more closely. She has noticed Frances's grey hairs, but has not paid particular attention to June's. She has seen that Frances's body is not quite what it was in the days when she lay in the back yard in her bathing suit, getting a tan; that there are pinchings and drawings, small saggings beginning, little puckerings above the breasts. But how long ago did that start happening to June as well, without Aggie noticing? How drawn June looks this morning; how hollow.

It isn't fair, it really isn't.

What, though, does fairness have to do with self-protection? And, anyway, what would June do with freedom, which in any case she could have had at any time along the line. What might make either of them think that this time she might grasp it properly?

"What would you do without me?" Aggie asks abruptly. "Have you thought about it?" She has a feeling she's asked this same question before, in another context.

"Of course I've thought about it." June turns from the stove, pan of scrambled eggs still in her hand—angry?

"Well then?"

She turns away again. "I'm not sure. But something. Just," in a rising voice, "to be on my *own*."

"Do you feel I've stopped you? I've thought and thought, you know, and I can't see really that I have."

"I suppose not, no." Tone flattened, June spoons the scrambled eggs onto their two plates. "It's just, it's always something. You, or Frances, or having to go to school or do the shopping or clean the house or go to the bank. Something's always in the way. I can't ever see my way *clear.*"

Well, who ever can? Anyway, is June's wish to be clear, or just blank? Still, Aggie nods, thinking she might almost understand what June seems to have in mind: peace, and no demands.

June might even like that for a day or two. Not likely longer, though. Aggie smiles.

June sighs. "Do you want to start sorting through that stuff today while I'm at school?"

"Probably not. I might as well wait for you."

How will Aggie spend the day then? It's not like her, June thinks, to sound so listless; and not even bothering to bake for Frances.

"Then," June says briskly, "we'll tackle it as soon as I get home and try to be done by the time Frances gets here."

"Fine." But isn't she staring at June in a peculiar way?

Peering down, June pats herself. "What's the matter, is my dress ripped?"

"No, sorry. I was just thinking."

What exactly, Aggie wonders, settled in her chair, is it she holds against June? Frances once sighed and said, "Isn't it strange that Mother only sees two sides of things? Everything's either good or bad; it must make life so simple for her." But Aggie, however irritating she finds June's righteousness, still can't quite believe in it. After all, she's bright enough, she's a teacher and no fool.

What does she think June still owes her? To be the daughter she wanted? If so, that's both atrocious and absurd.

Does she still owe anything to June? Surely not: she's provided her with a home all these years, after all, when she certainly didn't have to. That's something a mother could do; something only a mother could be asked to do.

The other obligation of a mother, though, is surely love. Now there is an unpaid debt.

What would have become of her in the last few years without June, who has cared for her in the same unhappy slapdash fashion as the unhappy slapdash way Aggie cared for her when she was just a child. A poor, unloving bargain.

But how difficult does Aggie intend to make it? Where's her pride? "Where's your pride, Mother?" June has demanded, in regard to Aggie's weight. Now, how much pride will she sacrifice to punish June?

Is that all this is, a punishment? How feeble that is. Also terribly simple, which makes it suspect.

It may only, after all, be her body, letting her down at last.

Dear old treacherous body.

Which is getting hungry again. Butter tarts, she thinks, would be the thing. And maybe lemon pie, Frances's favorite, at least in the old days. If there are raisins in the house, and lemons. Supplies have been allowed to run down.

But there are. June will be surprised to find that, after all, Aggie has stirred herself in the kitchen. Frances, when she gets here, will take the food for granted.

Anyway, it's for her own hunger that Aggie is bending over this hot oven once again. Not even for any ulterior motive like proving capabilities, in a weekend when such proof may be required.

She shrugs. There is absolutely nothing she can deliberately do to alter whatever happens. Either Frances will find out, or she won't. Either Aggie will have an accident, or she won't. Either June will tell Frances, or she won't. Is it possible she won't? That's asking a lot.

June, behind the lessons she is teaching automatically, is trying to prepare. Rehearsing lines for Frances. The difficult part will be finding the right moment when they're alone; that and finding the words. "Have you noticed, Frances," she might begin, "any changes in your grandmother since the last time you were here?" She might say, "I thought you'd have picked it up. Sometimes changes are clearer when you don't see somebody very often." Killing two birds with one stone, that would be: letting Frances know she isn't home enough to understand.

"Because," she might continue, "she's been going downhill rather quickly. It's sad." Pointing out that June, too, might pity Aggie, that compassion is not necessarily a quality only Frances has.

"And," finally, "I can't manage her on my own much longer. She's started having accidents in her bed, and I simply can't cope."

Then she will have to manage those words: nursing home.

Beyond that, it depends on Frances. Surely the two of them combined could outweigh even Aggie.

But why can't June do it on her own?

Well, she hasn't, has she?

What, though, if her inaction extends even to words?

Once, when she was a child, she was at a public swimming pool, watching a group of girls diving. From beside the pool it didn't look so difficult or dangerous, and she thought if they could do it, perhaps she also could. Still brave, she had climbed to the diving board, which after all was not very high, just three or four steps up from the edge of the pool, and gone to the end and looked down. And could not move. Could neither go back nor jump. She told herself it couldn't possibly hurt, and wasn't far, and certainly wasn't dangerous, but simply she could not do it. The action was right there, at the tip of her toes, at the edge of her mind, but refused to go further. Less a fear of hitting the water than terror of the space between the board and the water: the falling through air. Something terrible would happen, she could feel it, in that space.

Then suddenly she was underwater, choking and grabbing frantically for the surface, and came up screaming. She heard children laughing. Impatient to get by, one of them had simply pushed her off. She couldn't remember falling, or that instant in the air, or even hitting the water. Just being under it, swallowing and breathing it in, terrified and certain she would die.

Now is there a possibility that words will freeze in her throat, that something will only happen if she's pushed? If, for instance, Frances finds out for herself?

The terror, maybe, is of what cannot be undone. Any irrevocable occurrence. The moment Frances knows, everything is altered, certain things are put in motion, and if they turn out to be a mistake, June can't call them back, undo them, or begin again some different way.

24

"Where do you want to start?" June asks, right after an early supper. They have, she estimates, just over three hours before Frances arrives.

"Wherever. It doesn't matter." Aggie still sounds listless, but on the other hand she did bake today. The mixture of inertia and energy is puzzling to June; attracts pity, an emotion which for different reasons neither of them would welcome. She hauls over the first of the boxes.

Aggie leans a little forward in her chair. Oh yes, those old school readers of Neil's, which she put away to make more room for her owns books on the shelves. June holds up one of the shabby, battered, faded little volumes. The Third Golden Rule Book. Inside the front cover are the spidery lines of his signature, so finely drawn with a nibbed pen. Aggie remembers the scratching of those nibs and the pauses while he dipped them into the black bottled ink. "Let me see, June."

The pages are yellowed and feel fragile. Aggie tries to recall the days when she was so painstakingly teaching herself the rudimentary lessons here. Imagine, just learning to read! "Oh, listen to this," she says, struck by a once-familiar verse.

> "I am glad a task to me is given,
> To labor at day by day;
> For it brings me health and strength and hope
> And I cheerfully learn to say:
> 'Head, you may think; Heart, you may feel;
> But hand, you shall work alway.' "

"Good grief, that's a grim thing to teach kids, isn't it?"

"What's grim about teaching children to work hard? You always have, and I have. It's something people ought to learn, that that's what they have to do."

"Well, yes, to a point, but a little more might have been nice, don't you think? More than just working? To have time to travel, maybe, see different things? The whole world there, and all we've ever seen of it is pictures and words." Aggie has continued to flip through the book. "Listen to this one: 'Attempt the end and never stand in doubt; nothing's so hard but search will find it out.' Imagine never standing in doubt."

"I don't know, I think it sounds nice. That if you try hard enough, you can have anything." This sounds so unlike June that they are both startled.

"So what should we do with all these? Throw them out, or are they worth something, do you think?"

June has reached for the book, is stroking its cover, turning it over, leafing to the page inside where her father's name is written. The signature is faded now, and faint. Almost half a century ago. He would have been nearly ninety now, if he'd lived.

What an odd thought: imagining him still alive. What would he be like now? Stern is the word that leaps to mind. Aged and frail, perhaps, but stern. June has a vision of a shrunken, angry old man; strange, surely, when her recollections are of tenderness? "No, I don't want to throw them out or sell them. There aren't so many of his things left."

Almost, Aggie thinks, as if June is intent on turning these old books of his into his body, here in the front room. How morbid.

"Not a very effective beginning, then, is it?" she suggests. "By way of getting things cleared out?"

June doesn't answer; she has repacked the box, pushed it to one side, and hauled over another. "Oh, look, old pictures." She unfolds the grey and brown paper frame of the top one. "It's Father, when he was little. With his mother."

Aggie leans over to see. "You know, I could never connect him with those pictures of him as a little boy. Like he'd borrowed some other family photographs to bring with him."

"He looked happy, didn't he?"

"Yes, he did. I used to wonder about his mother, what she was like. She seemed to be the only woman he ever admired."

Maybe it's just June's hearing, but she detects sadness, rather
than bitterness, in Aggie's tone. "I used to wonder about her, too.
I used to imagine I knew her. Sometimes that I lived with her."
Now, why did she reveal that? She looks at Aggie anxiously,
flinching from the anticipated crack.

"You did?" No crack at all; just surprise.

"In a way. When I was little, if I was unhappy."

"Were you so unhappy then?" Aggie remembers saying almost
the same words, in another conversation, that one with Frances.

June shrugs. "Sometimes." She folds up that photograph and
takes out another. "This one's your family," handing it over.

The family portrait. There she is at eighteen, all their lives ago.
The stern, mysterious faces of her childhood, and her own the most
mysterious to her now. She would reach back and warn that hopeful young woman. The way she feels sometimes watching a sus-
pense movie on television, where the dangers are clear to any fool
except the hero, so that she wants to call out, "You idiot, don't
go up those stairs, can't you tell there's danger up there?" And to
the small brown young woman in this picture she might say, "Stop
and think. Be careful what you decide to want. Listen to your first
impressions."

Although maybe not. Here she is, sixty-odd years later, her body
crammed with food of her own making, her mind crammed with
stories and with information that sometimes comes in handy, and
she's in her own living room with her daughter and a pile of boxes
from the past, and her granddaughter will be here soon and she
sometimes has accidents in her bed. Some things she might change,
but maybe not so many, on the whole.

There are only a few photographs in this box of Frances, and
none at all of June's childhood. Nor are there any of Herb. They
seem to have left large parts of their lives unrecorded.

The next box is quite large but not very heavy. "The old pots
and pans from the bakery, remember, June? You took what we
didn't need day-to-day and put them away."

Here is a stack of bread pans tucked in each other; and pie plates
and cake tins, with the levers on the bottom that swivelled around,
neatly freeing the finished product. And pots for boiling fruit, and
mixing bowls and measuring spoons and cups and flour sifters—all
the equipment with which Aggie supplied herself as a recent widow
for quite a different life. "Well, these can certainly go. Why on
earth didn't we throw them out at the time, June? Or maybe the

Salvation Army would be interested. They're a bit battered, but they're still usable. Unless Frances might want them."

"I doubt it, she says she doesn't bake and there'd be far too much here for one person anyway. But we can put them aside for the Salvation Army, that's a good idea."

Another box contains piles of large black notebooks. These are the ledgers from the bakery, going right back to the beginning when she didn't quite know how to keep accounts. Looking at them, Aggie can see the clumsiness and uncertainty in the early figures. Like learning to read, that was, a different language, arithmetic, adding up sales in one set of columns, costs in another, the numbers getting regularly larger until the business was a going concern.

Here and in those pots and pans are more than forty years of batters being mixed as the sun rose, her hair slipping loose as she bent over the hot oven; hundreds and thousands of hours of stories, women coming and going with their tales of life being lived out there beyond her door. All her beautiful sweet food. And Barney, her friend. She feels tears stinging.

Gradually things are being separated: what will be kept (the pictures and books), what will be given away (the pans and bowls and pots) and what will go to the garbage (all those ledgers). Aggie supposes it's a good thing to have order emerging; and, really, it would be foolishly sentimental, and she loathes foolish sentiment, to hang onto any of this.

They haven't yet found anything Frances might want, but now they encounter several boxes of clothes: old dresses and sweaters, with rips in the armpits and unravelled elbows, a shabby black cloth coat so ancient the teacher was alive when Aggie bought it. She can't imagine why she would have stored all this away so carefully. Really worn-out clothes she tore up to use as dustcloths. These things are merely damaged, but repairable.

June is holding up a dress, a calf-length print with a ruffled throat and long sleeves flaring out from elastic at the wrists. "Good grief, Mother, was this yours?"

Aggie remembers wearing it to go shopping, in the early days of being married. Its hem is coming down, but aside from that it seems in good enough shape. Why did she keep it, though? With the thought that at some point she would reach some peak of bulk and then begin to go backward until she could fit into such a dress again, once she fixed the hem? As if she had another body entirely, tucked away, waiting for her to come back to it?

It's something, finally, that Frances might like. This sort of thing is back in style.

Aggie isn't sure, however, that she wants to give it to her. Because, she thinks Frances might treat it lightly, as a costume; whereas for her it had been a kind of uniform.

June, feeling the shiny, thin material, is shocked. She has a memory of this dress, but the mother who wore it was young, and slim. All the times and ways she has remembered the Aggie of her childhood, she has forgotten to remember her slim; the way she must have looked when June was very small. She has been putting the wrong figure to some of her recollections, then; a disturbing discovery.

"Do you think we should set the clothes aside for Frances?" she asks. "There's still a lot of use left in most of them."

"I don't think so. She has plenty of clothes. Let's give them away, too." Aggie thinks she would be much less unhappy to see these things worn by a stranger on the street than by Frances.

Lying in the bottom of this box, for no apparent reason, is a small, thick white leather-covered volume. "What's that?" Aggie asks.

"Well, for heaven's sake," June breathes, reaching in, "I'd forgotten that. It was mine, when I was little. Daddy gave it to me."

Daddy? Aggie looks at her fifty-nine-year-old daughter with distaste. "A Bible, is it?"

"He gave it to me for some reason. A reward for something. Learning verses in Sunday school? I can't remember." She stares at the inscription inside the little volume: "To my daughter June, with great expectations".

Not even "To my beloved daughter June", which she might have assumed. And what were those expectations of his that were so great? What did he want from her?

So even he had had grand visions, large demands. She feels suddenly hemmed in and surrounded. Also judged.

What is Aggie smiling about?

"Oh, I was just thinking about you, remembering you going off with your father on Sunday mornings, holding his hand and carrying that Bible in the other. It was sweet, in a way."

Now Aggie laughs. "I remember you coming home one Sunday and telling me you wanted music lessons. Do you remember that?"

"No." June is puzzled. What's Aggie getting at? Something, likely, with a twist.

"Well, I thought you meant singing, because your father always said you liked the hymns." (So they must have talked? They must have had ordinary conversations about their child? This comes as a surprise. She ought, perhaps, to consider this later: what other words she may have forgotten.) "Anyway, I was busy getting lunch and I just said, 'Yes, that's nice, if you like singing so much perhaps you should have lessons, we'll talk to your father.'

"But you said quite firmly, 'Oh no, I want to learn to play the harp,' and I thought for God's sake what next, there can't be a harp teacher within two hundred miles, who teaches harp? But I wanted to take you seriously, that you were interested in music, anyway, so I suggested the piano, because of course every little town is hip-deep in piano teachers. But you said a piano wouldn't do either. You don't remember any of this?"

June shakes her head.

"Well, of course I asked why it had to be the harp, and you know what you said? You said, 'So when I get to heaven, I'll already know how to play, so I can be a better angel right away. They don't play pianos in heaven, you know, Mother,' as if I were stupid not to know that."

June also smiles now. "But I didn't get the lessons."

"No, so I'm afraid you're stuck being just a beginner angel." But this is said lightly, kindly.

How very odd, what's been put aside, and not merely in the attic. And the atmosphere is interesting too: like a Christmas truce in wartime.

June hauls the trunk closer. "This looks like the last of it."

"You know," Aggie says, "whatever's in there will go away back. Things I brought from home. It's queer, all these years piled up like this together in a heap."

"You feel queer?" June looks up, alert.

"No, not that, really. It's just strange, everything."

June struggles with the stiff old trunk straps, pushes the lid open and back.

The trunk is divided with trays, lined with a faded flowered cotton that has disintegrated in places. Here are things Aggie has not seen for years, had forgotten all about. Like the white hat on the top tray, with the veil that went over the eyes and the jaunty little feather that stuck up in the air—her first grown-up woman's hat that she wore to her engagement showers. Of course it's crumpled now, and certainly not as white.

June is lifting out more delicate items: scarves and undies. "What's all this? These don't look as if they were ever used."

"Ah, that's part of my trousseau; hope chest," but Aggie immediately regrets the irony, damaging the atmosphere.

Here is also the vanity set her brothers gave her as their wedding gift: bone-colored comb and brush and hand mirror, a shoe horn and manicure set, all in a case. Pooling their small resources to buy something nice for their big sister who was getting married. Once again her eyes fill—how teary she is tonight. She hardly knew those boys, who were little, and then big, red, rough-handed men, and out of touch. She's the only one left, and she barely knew them at all.

A tiny box also in the top tray contains the heart-shaped locket Edith gave her: not real silver, but silver-looking. Aggie wore it at her wedding, pleasing Edith.

She tells this, in an absent sort of way, to June, who asks, "What did your parents give you?"

Aggie has to think for a minute to remember, visualizes the buggy being loaded up as she and the teacher got ready to leave. "Oh yes, that table over there."

This is a piece of furniture against the far wall that has been there for years, pretty much unnoticed except for having to be dusted. Short-legged and oval, it has no obvious purpose. Mainly they're in the habit of laying things on it temporarily, like unfinished books or mending. "My father made it," Aggie says, and suddenly sees the curves of the legs, and how it is put together without nails. All the shaping and carving and sanding he must have done, out in the barn, to please his daughter. A gift of his own efforts, a speech he couldn't make. And at the time she hadn't heard.

"Oh," she says, dismayed, weighed down, "there is a lot of past here."

"Do you want to stop?"

"No, never mind. Let's keep going."

June lifts out the top tray. On the one below rest all the supplies for a marriage. "Heavens," says June, shaking out a pillowcase, "look at the embroidery on this, look at that work!"

Pink and yellow flowers are twined on green stems, at the edges of what at the time was white cotton, now yellowed. Hundreds and hundreds of tiny stitches. Likewise, hundreds of hours sitting around the kitchen table with embroidery hoops and coils of thread, needles and concentration and talk.

"Even the towels are decorated," June exclaims, removing other items, "and washcloths, sheets, everything. Didn't you ever use any of this?"

"Doesn't look as if I even unpacked it."

"But why?"

Why indeed. "I must have thought they were too nice to use, I guess." Or more precisely that the hope and care that went into them would be unsuitable in that marriage of discord and dislike. June may know that without being told.

June is struck by yet another picture of her mother, this one just a girl, stitching away at all this.

"We liked pretty things, you know," Aggie explains. "People can buy patterned sheets now, but we had to make our own." It's not exactly that these things are frivolous, but they do remind Aggie that not everything back then was grim and geared only to survival. "It was a custom, too, something women did together."

June is now lifting out a quilt, unfolding it, holding it up. "Did you do this, too?"

"No, I believe that was done by the church women. They had quilting bees, and made one for each bride as the wedding came along. The designs were supposed to mean certain things, but I don't remember if I ever did know what this one's about."

It is mainly yellow and blue, in different materials, with different patterns, flowered and plain and striped. It's the intricacy and the care that astonish.

"Frances would like it, I expect," Aggie says finally. "Unless," she remembers too late, "you would."

June might have, if her mother's first thought had been for her and not for Frances. "No, she can have it. She'd probably like the rest of this as well," indicating the towels and pillowcases and sheets. "Not to use them, but to have."

"She might. I can't see giving them away, at any rate." When it comes down to it, Aggie can't feel any real attachment to the things themselves. They're only recollections and reminders, and beyond that only towels and sheets and a quilt, taking up room.

June carefully folds each item and sets it all back in the tray. "There's one more layer, I guess," peering into the trunk. "What's all this, wrapped up in tissue paper?"

At a glance, Aggie remembers. She remembers them stitching it, with more intricacy and care than any pillowcase, and she remembers wearing it. She sees the teacher's pale, strained face waiting at the end of the aisle, as she approached on her father's arm.

"My wedding dress," she says shortly. This is more than a small sting of impending tears. She feels that if she allowed it, she might break right down and bawl her heart out.

The dress looks like a museum piece, as if it could be worn by a mannequin, with a label beneath it bearing a date. The collar is higher than Aggie would have remembered, the shoulders are puffed, and the sleeves are straight and narrow to the wrists. There are tiny fake pearls sewn into the embroidery around the throat and sleeves and waist.

Her mother would have done this, Aggie thinks: taking the dress from her and folding and wrapping it so carefully that after sixty years it has merely yellowed, but not crumpled.

Clear as a bell, June can see Aggie in this dress. Getting married to him, her father, the teacher. Why, she thinks, they must have had hopes. They must have had all kinds of private moments. Maybe even love.

So this is what Aggie has been saying all this time: that June's memories of them are only childish ones. The woman, after all, who put all this into a dress, all those tiny pearls and stitches, evidently had higher hopes than June ever would have dreamed.

All this time, perhaps, Aggie's been saying, in her way, "Look at me, it wasn't only him, I was disappointed too." And maybe hurt. Also, of course, all those times she has said angrily, "But I cared about you too, it wasn't only him," and all June heard was the past tense.

She looks at her mother's great sagging body, the face with its expressions camouflaged by flesh, and sees it young and slender, buttoned into this dress, leaping happily into a new and different life, getting away, eager. Aggie flings herself into things; she must have been flinging herself into this, too.

"I'll put it away again, shall I?" she asks, preparing to refold and rewrap it with preserving care.

Aggie, however, reaches out to touch it, drawing it away from June. She regards it for a moment with an expression June can't interpret. Then she begins folding it again, but roughly, without care.

"Here, Mother, let me do it, it'll get all wrinkled that way." June pulls at it, and the seam of a sleeve, weakened by time, tears. They stare at hanging threads.

"That figures," Aggie says finally. "Just throw the damn thing away, for God's sake." These sudden sinkings of her spirit, these abrupt sadnesses, make her angry.

June doesn't argue, but has no intention of throwing out the dress. She doesn't quite know what to do with it; thinks maybe if she hung it in her room and stared at it for a time, it might reveal something to her she has never understood. The thing to do at the moment is fold it again, ignoring the rip for the time being, and remove it from Aggie's view, since it seems to have upset her.

They are surrounded now by a litter of boxes, things to be saved and things to be thrown out. It looks, Aggie thinks, as if they've been packing up to move.

Well, though, maybe they have.

Oh, but she's tired, so tired. She would like to sleep now for a while; maybe until the weekend's over, whatever is going to happen. "I get frightened, you know," she hears herself saying. Did she actually say that? Must have, June's looking at her so surprised.

"I'm sorry. I didn't mean you to be afraid." This is not quite true, but truth is not necessarily the best thing at the moment. "I don't know. I really don't," June adds, sounding neither angry nor despairing; just speaking a flat fact.

Aggie thinks, "She's tired too." Well, June has every reason to be tired. "We'll think of something, June. I know we'll have to do something."

June stands, "I'll make tea, shall I, while we wait for Frances?"

In the kitchen, putting on water to boil and warming the teapot, setting up the tray with milk and sugar and little spoons to take into the front room, June wonders what came over Aggie, admitting fear, so unlike her. Although she is no longer so sure of precisely what is like Aggie, and what is unlike.

There are all those faces, without much resemblance to one another: the girl sitting in a farmhouse kitchen, stitching pillowcases; the young woman in that family photograph, who made that dress; the mother who apparently danced and sang with her child, although the child cannot remember; the widow who sat staring out of windows after her husband died; the woman who punched holes in walls, and rose before dawn, and sat with her feet up on the kitchen counter in the mornings, laughing with the dairy man; the one kneading dough and hitting cash register keys; the one with her nose buried in a book; the one sipping her first drink, laughing about how it tickled; the one who stitched a nightgown for her daughter, and took that daughter back, along with a grandchild, even though she didn't want to; the one whose eyes were rimmed with redness on a few occasions, although she would not weep in front of June: when her granddaughter finally left home, when her friend finally moved away; the one defying June and God with irritating, blasphemous questions.

The one who sometimes in the mornings looks up despairing from wet sheets. And also the dead one with the secret, from the dream last night.

25

They wait together at the front room window, Aggie watching from her sunken chair, June standing, leaning forward, hands propped on the windowsill, looking out into the darkness. They are watching for the sweep of headlights around the corner down the block, a car with a lighted sign on the top that will say "Bert's Taxi".

Aggie is alert, sharp-eyed, uneasy. June, glancing down at her, thinks, "Look at her, so excited, waiting for that wretched girl." Except of course it's a particular sort of excitement this time: not the pure pleased expectation of an ordinary visit, but tinged with tension and apparently fear.

June herself feels a little of that, too, and it makes her cross and snappish. "Wretched girl," she thinks again.

Aggie thinks how stupid she was to have a cup of that tea June made; what a fool, to drink it down without thinking, until she tipped it up to drain the last of it and realized too late what she'd done. In just a few minutes' heedlessness, she has vastly increased the odds against herself, in the circumstances that may arise tomorrow morning.

The other question is whether June did it on purpose.

But she has never known June to be downright vicious.

Aggie also wishes she'd thought to suggest a bath after the sorting was finished. It would have been better to present Frances, surely, with skin smelling of soap; let her first impression be of cleanness and freshness. She wonders if she may not smell a little musty, like a closed-up room. "I should have had a bath," she says.

"You can have one tomorrow."

Unspoken is, "You may need one tomorrow." Or maybe she reads too much into words. June may not be thinking any such thing. What makes her think she has any idea what goes on in June's head, now pressed against the window, looking out? She sighs.

June, thinking the sigh is impatience or concern, says, "The train may have been a bit late. It often is."

Aggie nods, although June is turned away from her. How thin June is, especially from the back. It's almost possible to make out her shoulder blades and the stepping stones of her spine, not to mention her ribs, beneath her dress. She even seems shorter than she used to be. Aggie is startled once more to realize that June is also getting old. "She's shrivelling," she thinks. "Poor child." It does not seem inconsistent, from Aggie's point of view, to see June as both an aging woman and a child.

Why not reach out for once then and place a hand on her daughter's narrow back and say something tender? Except, what? Anyway, they obviously don't use words well between them. Original meanings tend to disintegrate into awful misunderstandings. So then why not reach out and place a hand on her daughter and not say anything at all? Just that it's such a straight back, formidable and uninviting.

One way and another, bodies block people's views. Aggie has difficulty seeing past her own flesh to the slender hopeful young girl who didn't know words, much less stories, and married a teacher in ignorance. At some point she must have decided to choose between appearances and cravings, and come down on the side of banana cake and bread.

Just that now, things are collapsing in there. She pictures organs like balloons, losing their air, deflating with slow leaks.

Columbus had such trouble with his sailors because they thought the earth was flat, and were sure they would fall over the edge if he insisted they keep going. People laugh at that now, but it seems a perfectly reasonable fear for the time. Aggie is in a similar position now: sailing to the edge and slipping over into nothing. Maybe later, knowing better, she will laugh; that would be a good joke on her.

June can see her mother's reflection in the glass, a pale circle like the moon, featureless and indistinct. She has a sudden painful vision of Aggie in that nursing home, nightgown rucked up around the waist, a stranger's busy hands. Being diapered at nightfall. Diapered! That's what they do, isn't it, with the incontinent? The vision stabs her with pity, a wound in that region she thought had been anaesthetized long ago, below the breasts.

If she were dreaming this up, she would have conjured a sense of triumph: victory over oppression. She leans her forehead once more against the cool glass, so that she can see the darkness outside, and not her mother's moon-face.

Aggie has made a promise of sorts, but only a vague one: that something must be done. The words might have been only an effort to buy time, bribe June beyond this weekend. At the moment June doesn't have the energy to unravel such complexities as her mother's intentions. Things will fall into place. She still has no clear idea how, but it will be soon. This weekend. She feels a clutching in her stomach, and thinks of making more tea, to soothe. It occurs to her to wonder what possessed Aggie to have that cup of tea. June made it and as always offered it, but certainly did not expect Aggie to accept. Self-sabotage is not something her mother has ever gone in for. Self-preservation, always. She closes her eyes but sees again those remote adept hands, busy with pins—do they use pins?—and cloth, dealing briskly with Aggie's warm, soft body.

Aggie has made a promise of sorts and now wonders what on earth she meant by it. Well, then, she thinks, shape up or ship out. Could she shape up, and how could it be done? For one thing, obviously, by remembering not to drink tea so late at night. But maybe also to let June be, test her, if she must be tested, a bit more kindly? What harm does it do if June wants a small, safe existence? Who is Aggie to insist on something else? Well, she is a mother; but then, if she demands that June stop looking at her with a child's-eye view, she must surely stop, herself, looking at June with a mother's eye. Which, it appears, has been after all an insistent, punishing one.

All very well, except it seems to be the habit of a lifetime, just taking occasional new twists, as in recent weeks.

So, then, she could ship out. But there's only one way of doing that, and she's not about to take it, voluntarily.

If they had more time. If Frances weren't coming so soon.

If they had more time what? She might say to June, "Sit down, let's talk this over without our grudges." By "this", she would not mean only the future.

June thinks, "I'm not ready," and wishes for more time. She feels unprepared for Frances. Inaction, after all, has a comforting sort of rhythm. It's the process of indecision that has kept her going these past few weeks, or maybe even a good deal longer. It might be another case of hopes and expectations failing to live up to reality.

How far might she go to maintain hopes and expectations?

"I think she's here," Aggie says, and June's eyes flare open. She has missed the headlights rounding the corner, but here indeed is the car with the yellow lighted roof light, slowing and stopping.

"Help me up," Aggie requests, reaching out. Ordinarily she can get out of a chair, at least, on her own. June feels the trembling in the grip, but can't tell which of them is causing it.

A rear door opens in the taxi, the interior light flashes on, and they can make out a woman's figure turning and lifting and stepping out.

Aggie, her arm still linked with June's, begins, "You know . . ." but then can't think what. An appeal of some sort? Maybe just that: You know.

"What?"

"Never mind."

The figure on the sidewalk leans to the window of the taxi and hands the driver money. She picks up her suitcase and briefcase from the sidewalk, turns toward the house, and pauses—looking at what? She straightens her shoulders, tightening her grip on her cases, and strides briskly up the walk, toward the porch and the front door.

Aggie and June move toward the hall to meet her. As Aggie lets go of June's arm so that she can walk ahead, June drops back a step. They do this automatically, so that if Aggie wavers or trips, June will be right there behind her, ready to steady her, or catch her.

By the year 2000, 2 out of 3 Americans could be illiterate.

It's true.

Today, 75 million adults...about one American in three, can't read adequately. And by the year 2000, U.S. News & World Report envisions an America with a literacy rate of only 30%.

Before that America comes to be, you can stop it...by joining the fight against illiteracy today.

Call the Coalition for Literacy at toll-free **1-800-228-8813** and volunteer.

**Volunteer
Against Illiteracy.
The only degree you need
is a degree of caring.**

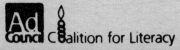

Ad Council   Coalition for Literacy